Anne Goring was [...]
until she married. [...] travelled with her husband to
Singapore where they lived for six years before returning
to the UK to live in South Devon. She has previously
had published a number of articles, short stories and
novels including, most recently, a West Country saga,
A TURNING SHADOW, which is available from
Headline.

Also by Anne Goring

A Turning Shadow

A Song Once Heard

Anne Goring

HEADLINE

First published in 1994 by
HEADLINE BOOK PUBLISHING

First published in paperback in 1995 by
HEADLINE BOOK PUBLISHING

10 9 8 7 6 5 4 3 2 1

ISBN 0 7472 4629 7

Typeset by Avon Dataset Ltd., Bidford-on-Avon, B50 4JH

Printed and bound in Great Britain by
Cox & Wyman Ltd, Reading, Berks

HEADLINE BOOK PUBLISHING
A division of Hodder Headline PLC
338 Euston Road,
London NW1 3BH

For Loris, with love

I wish I were a little bird
That out of sight doth soar;
I wish I were a song once heard
But often pondered o'er,
Or shadow of a lily stirred
By wind upon the floor,
Or echo of a loving word
Worth all that went before,
Or memory of a hope deferred
That springs again no more.

From: 'A Wish', by Christina Rossetti

Chapter One

On a fine spring morning in the year 1830 I stood at the altar of the old chapel on Highgate Hill and promised to love, honour and obey Mr Daniel Penhale. At that moment I was supremely content. I had at last achieved, it seemed, those desirable attributes which had eluded me all my twenty-four years; security and respectability.

As I made my vows my heart was light. Daniel was a fine man. I intended to be a devoted and caring wife. I was so impatient for my new life to begin that I could scarcely bear to contemplate the delay we must suffer before we could shake the dust of London from our feet and leave for the West Country. But a lavish wedding breakfast awaited us at the house my mother – or, more exactly, her lover Sir Richard Merton, Baronet – had leased for her nearby and which had been my home also for the past few weeks. I must contain myself for a few more hours yet before I could bid, thankfully, a final farewell to the uncertain existence I had always known.

'Are you happy, my dear?' Daniel whispered as we walked back up the aisle.

'I think I have never been happier,' I said.

No more long hours spent trying to instil the elements of French and Italian into the heads of wilful young ladies who would sooner be choosing silks for a new gown or learning the art of flirtation. No more urgent, imperious demands from Mama. *'You must return instantly, Sophy . . . I cannot bear it – I am ruined . . .'* Or ill and like to go into a decline. Or wracked with despair. Or so lonely that only my presence could possibly bring her comfort.

My hand in its cream doeskin glove rested lightly on Daniel's sleeve. He laid his own gloved hand protectively over it. We smiled at each other in complete understanding.

We were still smiling as we stepped across the threshold of the chapel into the sunshine, from the close and concealing dimness of sanctified brick and timber to the hard, sharp light of an April morning.

And, though I did not know it then, that moment of abrupt and startling change was prophetic. A forewarning, perhaps, that the change for me, and for others close to me, was to be as intense and dramatic as the sudden passage from darkness to light.

But in my innocence – my ignorance – I could not know that. It was Daniel who had the first presentiment. His confident step suddenly faltered. His gentle grip on my hand tightened.

I looked in alarm at his pallor.

'Daniel? Are you unwell?'

He seemed scarcely to hear me. His gaze was fixed upon the little knot of idlers gathered to watch the wedding party leave. A few gossiping women, a scatter of children. And beyond them someone else standing motionless in the shadow of the burial-ground wall. A tall man, hatless, dressed in a ragged jacket and breeches, his rough hair a startling white in the velvety shade. An old tramp perhaps. Or some beggar drawn by the prospect of good pickings from the guests.

Daniel frowned, shook his head, seemed to collect himself.

'I thought for a moment . . . but no, it is nothing, Sophy. A trifling dizziness. The sun is dazzling, is it not?'

I was greatly relieved to see the colour surge back into his cheeks and his smile and his attention return to me. Daniel did not look back, though some odd compulsion made me glance over my shoulder before we left the chapel grounds.

But no one now stood in the shadow of the wall. The tattered man had gone.

My mother awaited us at the house in Elm View. She had refused to attend the ceremony and, in view of our argument last evening, I had half-expected she would not put in an appearance at all. But though she was dressed in a sombre grey taffeta more suitable for a funeral than a wedding, she moved among the guests smiling, accepting compliments – on the arrangements of spring flowers that made a bower of the hall and drawing room, on the delightful weather, on the suitability of the match – as though she had personally organised everything. I would not spoil this happy day by allowing myself to believe that she had chosen that dour gown to discommode me. I told myself that Mama merely intended to display to best advantage the gold and emerald necklace Sir Richard had given her when he had last proposed marriage. And been rejected, as had happened many times before.

My mother did not approve of marriage, neither for herself nor for me. 'Marriage means bondage for a woman,' she had cried, dramatically, several times over the few weeks since Daniel had formally – but with a firmness and directness that brooked no argument – asked for her blessing. But she was shrewd in her opposition. To Daniel she was all charm and acquiescence.

'But I shall not allow you to call me Mama,' she said,

laughing. 'I am scarcely older than you and I refuse to become that antiquated creature, a mother-in-law! Why, I am more of an age to be a sister to you. I insist you shall call me Hannah.' And Daniel, wholly aware of her dark, devastating beauty – what man could not be? – but hearteningly impervious to it, bowed and said, 'I will, naturally, respect your wishes,' but with such a dry edge to his voice that Mama looked at him sharply, a brief frown bringing into relief a delicate tracery of lines on her forehead and around her eyes. In that instant it was possible to observe that the years she refused to acknowledge – forty-two of them – would not, perhaps, be denied for much longer. Then she laughed again and said lightly, though with a note of reproof, 'Mr Penhale – Daniel – you must understand that I was little more than a child when I bore my daughter and Sophy herself was born, I declare, with an old head on her shoulders – always so grave and sensible when a little youthful exuberance could well have been expected and excused. The informality of our life abroad, without the strictures and regimentation so evident in family life here, has also served to make less distinctive the division that usually separates one generation from the next. We are, indeed, more like sisters than mother and daughter . . .'

She saved all the persuasive scorn of her powerful nature to pour upon me later. Last evening she had made her final assault. 'You are a fool not to comprehend the trap that opens up before you! The moment that you allow yourself into that trap and the door clangs behind you, you are lost. I know! I was once caught and imprisoned. I shudder at the deadly suffocation of mind and spirit that was my lot. It is not yet too late for you to give back word.'

'You were unfortunate, Mama,' I had countered mildly. 'It cannot be the same for every women or marriage as an institution would have foundered long since.'

'How can it benefit any woman of intelligence to chain herself body and soul to one man?'

I paused before I answered. To engage in heated argument with my mother was to give her the upper hand. She revelled in the kind of melodramatic confrontation that as a child I had dreaded and even now found unnerving. Stormy scenes, tears, outpourings of accusation and recrimination were the stuff of life to her, a constant nourishment for her passionate, volatile temperament. Even the merest hint of bridal nerves would be pounced upon in order to support her argument.

But I was no longer a child, to be reduced to guilt-ridden silence because I had ventured a contrary opinion or pricked her well-defended conscience. I remained calm, knowing my best defence was to be cool and rational.

We stood in my mother's studio. Pale, clear light from the north-facing windows flooded over the easel with its half-finished portrait of the stout dowager who had only ten minutes since gone wheezing down the stairs well pleased with the flattering image that was emerging on the canvas. The smell of oil paint mingled with the heavy jasmine fragrance my mother always wore, the very essence that had haunted my childhood and adolescence. Redolent with the promise of love, of belonging. Yet symbolising, ultimately, only rejection and loneliness. I straightened my back.

'I wish you would not use such emotional terms, Mama. I am not chaining myself to Daniel. I am to become his wife, his companion in life. Daniel is not some species of monster, but a kind and considerate man.'

'You do not even mention love!'

'I have a deep affection for Daniel as I believe he has for me. If I do not indulge myself in torrid glances and sighs and other such visible displays of infatuation it is because my nature is more reserved than yours.'

'Infatuation? You do not even know the meaning of the word! As for love – why, your heart is as untouched and virginal as your body.'

I shrugged. 'Can that be so very wrong? Surely in polite society modest behaviour in a bride is to be recommended.'

Mama tore off the paint-smeared linen cuffs she wore to protect her sleeves, screwed them into a ball and hurled them into the mess of pots and brushes ranged on the work stand. A half-full jar of linseed oil crashed to the floor and spread a slow, golden puddle across the polished floorboards.

'Polite society!' she cried. 'I spit on polite society and its mealy-mouthed pretensions!'

I had clung to the hope that for once she might attempt to understand, but it was not to be. I smothered a sigh and said resignedly, 'I should not like us to part in anger and bitterness. Will you not share in my happiness instead of condemning me because my wishes – my deeds – are different from yours?'

There was a small, calculating silence while she watched me from the corner of her eyes. Then, swiftly, she came towards me, hands outstretched in a pleading gesture. She was suddenly all gentle smiles and beseeching words. 'Foolish child! It is your happiness I am thinking of when I beg you not to marry Daniel Penhale and bury yourself among the backward peasants and narrow-minded cliques that compose rural society in that God-forsaken corner of the country.'

'Have you ever been to Plymouth, Mama?'

'No, but . . .'

'Or across the River Tamar to Cornwall where Daniel has his country house? No, I thought not! I should be more

6

inclined to take note of your opinions if you had chosen to pass judgement on the qualities, say, of Paris or Florence or Venice, where you have lived for most of these last twenty-odd years.'

'You know very well that it was from the clutches of such provincial society that I was forced to flee after your father died.' She clasped her hands theatrically to her bosom. 'Turnip-headed peasants, hidebound by convention, with scarcely one cultured or original thought between them! Had I stayed in Bovey Tracey, marooned among such people – your papa's dreary, elderly friends, not mine, never mine – in that empty countryside in the shadow of the moor, I should have sunk to a dark melancholy of the spirit that would have surely led me to a swift decline. You would have been an orphan within months.' She swung round and paced the length of the room, her brilliant skirts swishing against the canvases piled up against the walls, her heels rapping out a loud tattoo on the wide oak boards. 'Instead, I chose freedom. Freedom to live as I pleased, to be true to my own nature. And freedom for you too, Sophy. Never forget that. Think of the travels you have had, the people you have met, the experiences we have shared. Would you have exchanged all these excitements for a routine life in some dull backwater?'

'Excitements? Oh, to be sure there were excitements,' I said dryly. 'So many in fact that throughout my growing years I became satiated with them and I have felt no more need of them since.'

She drew in her breath sharply. For a moment there was an expression I could not read in her green eyes. Could it have been remorse? Compassion? But it was so swiftly gone it was impossible to read and temper swept her up once more.

'If you will not listen, you must go to the devil in your own way.'

'As you yourself have always done, Mama.'

'I had a calling! A true purpose!'

'Why cannot you see that *my* purpose might be just as important?'

'What? You honestly believe that becoming the chattel, the unpaid housekeeper, the bedmate, of a man you do not love and who does not love you is the purpose for which you were put on this earth? All he is interested in is his own comfort and convenience, and that of his child.'

'No!' A little too emphatically. A steadying breath, then, 'You are quite wrong.'

'If you must marry, let it be at least someone whom you love deeply and passionately and who returns that love. Otherwise it is a sham and a pretence!'

'There is no point in further discussion.'

She swept me a scornful glance. 'Then go! And do not expect me to be present to see you throw your life away.' She turned her back and busied herself at the work table.

I left the room quietly. Only when I was up in my bedchamber did I allow the hurt, the resentment, to surface. I was angry to see that my hands trembled as I poured water from the jug into the basin and splashed my hot cheeks. But it was anger with myself rather than her. I should not have expected support or encouragement from Mama. I should not even have tried to believe she would be moved to listen and understand. She was blinkered to everything but her own viewpoint and she had never forgiven me for not being a mirror image, physically and spiritually, of herself.

'You are dull, Sophy, and becoming duller by the day!' she had once flung at me in a tantrum when I was eighteen and she had come across me making a bonfire of my old sketches and paintings in the garden of our lodgings in Nice. 'You cannot help being saddled with the charmless looks of your father, but at least you might have turned yourself into something above the ordinary by fostering your potential as an artist. But no! You refuse! You will not take tuition any more. Now you have destroyed all the work you have ever done and which showed such promise!'

'It is merely clutter,' I said stubbornly, kicking a fragment of unburnt paper into the blaze. 'I have decided not to waste any more time on useless pursuits.'

Mama snatched at the fragment, pinched out the smouldering edge and thrust it in front of me. 'Look! Look! How can you say it is a useless pursuit when you are able to paint like this?'

An old olive tree filled the foreground. In the distance, revealed only in the spaces where the twisting branches parted, was a line of misty blue hills. A black-garbed woman rested her back against the trunk of the tree, her head turned so that only the line on her cheek was visible under the enveloping head cloth. It was part of the large watercolour sketch of an olive grove I had made the year before in Tuscany.

'I see nothing special there,' I said, moving sharply from her to poke the ashes with a stick.

'Fiddlesticks! Even this scrap is full of excitement and interest. The tree has so much life that you might almost imagine the leaves to be moving in the wind. And as for the peasant woman . . . her weariness, her longing to be away from her drudgery is clear in every line of her body.'

I told myself fiercely that it was the smoke that brought the sting of sudden tears to my eyes, not the remembrance of that afternoon when I had laboured in the golden, soporific heat to capture the enduring quality of the olive tree and the exhaustion of the old woman. She had leaned against the tree as if to draw strength from it and it seemed that I also drew some special quality from that place. My brush had moved with a certainty that was almost magical. When the picture was finished I knew that it was the best work I had ever done.

And the last.

For when I rose stiffly to my feet my mind was unexpectedly sharp and lucid. The creative force which had enabled me to capture the spirit of the scene seemed to have stripped away all pretence. I knew exactly what I must do if I was ever to achieve peace of mind and a measure of contentment. I knew in which direction I had to go. And it was not Mama's way.

Until that moment in the olive grove I had clung to the belief that Mama and I might fashion a tolerable life together. I had refused to acknowledge the worry and distress her vagabond mode of existence brought to me. But Mama would never change. She had made her choice long ago. She had chosen to throw in her lot with the artistic and radical element in society whose ideas and mode of living were a constant source of outrage and titillation to conventionally minded persons. It came to me then as clearly as the humming of the bees in the warm, thyme-scented grasses that I was a misfit in her world. And would remain so if I allowed myself to drift along helplessly in her wake.

I made the right decision then, if not the easiest. For, in the end, it had led me to Daniel.

The heavy wedding band felt new and strange on my hand as Daniel and I led the guests to the table with its lavish spread provided by kindly Sir Richard. (He had insisted on it, just as he had insisted on escorting me to the chapel, saying, 'Had your mama ever consented to marry me – though I still have not given up hope – I should now be your stepfather and that is a role I should have assumed wholeheartedly.') This was the time that I quite dreaded. The Vaiseys, Daniel's business connections and my late employers, had sent their apologies, pleading a prior engagement, so the guests were all friends of Sir Richard and Mama. Unlike my mother, I hated to be the centre of attention, particularly among virtual strangers. I knew myself to be plain and ordinary, and there was a reserve in my nature that denied me the ability to converse about nothing at all in the sparkling, witty way that was thought to be such an agreeable asset for any female. Despite, or perhaps because of, the quality of the cream silk dress with its weight of stylish frills and tucks, I felt stiff and awkward. And I must sit here, trapped, the focus of all eyes, while I nibbled food I was too unnerved to have any appetite for and listened to speeches that would bring me only embarrassment.

But when we were seated Daniel, whom I was beginning to realise noticed a good deal more than the somewhat abstracted air he habitually wore would allow, leaned close and whispered, 'Bear up a little longer, Sophy. The formalities will soon be over.' And he laid his hand warmly over mine so that I felt again that surge of comfort and relief that I had found someone so kind and understanding to share my life with. How fortunate we had been that chance had brought us together.

Mrs Vaisey stood plump and composed in the blue and gold drawing room of her Portsmouth house.

'Miss Beardmore, we have the pleasure of Mr Penhale's company for a few days while he discusses shipping arrangements with Mr Vaisey.' A tall man, soberly dressed, bowing courteously. 'He has expressed a wish to see the improvements I have made to the gardens. Pray bring down the girls and join us. We shall all benefit from a turn in the fresh air now that the rain has stopped.'

We walked slowly down newly flagged paths, the rich smell of turned earth hanging heavy and fragrant in the cold air. Minnie and Estella walked either side of me, their mama ahead, pointing out to Mr Penhale this newly planted shrub, that stark, twiggy tree which would be a mass of blossom in the spring.

Daniel, having to stoop to catch Mrs Vaisey's comments, turned from time to time to include us in the conversation. All that I particularly remarked about him then was his good manners, being more watchful of the girls' behaviour which, though improved, still left much to be desired, their former governess before her retirement having been too old to cope with such ebullient, spoiled young misses.

Then, a day or so afterwards, a few moments when I could observe him more closely and feel the first stirrings of – not liking, that was too strong a word – but perhaps of empathy.

We stood on the wide staircase with the girls hurrying ahead to remove their cloaks and warm chilled hands at the schoolroom fire. Daniel, descending, had paused to comment on the sharpness of the frosty morning and, when my charges were out of earshot, to remark that Minnie and Estella were turning into charming girls, whereas his memory of them from a previous visit had been, well, of a rather boisterous pair.

'You seem, Miss Beardmore, to have wrought a remark-able change for the better. When did you take up your post here?'

'In September, Mr Penhale.'

'Really? A mere four months ago?'

He had unusual colouring. His hair was flax-pale, worn long and inclined to curl about his ears, yet he did not have the fair, easily reddened complexion that made the sun such a trial to so many English people. His skin had the kind of smooth golden cast that would turn to a rich brown should he be out of doors much and his eyebrows were dark and straight above eyes that were a deep greenish-blue. That sea-dappled gaze was steady and intent upon my face as I said, 'The credit cannot all be mine, sir. The natural progress of growth towards maturity often has a quietening effect on high-spirited children.'

'To be sure, but I have watched you together and I see a respect for you on their part that was certainly not in evidence with their last governess. They seem happier for it, too.'

That was all, but the brief conversation left an agreeable flavour in my mind. There had been none of the forced heartiness or condescension I associated with people who considered that a mere governess, a creature indisputably above the servants yet of little social standing, should be grateful to be noticed. He had spoken naturally, as one genuinely interested in my charges and my care of them.

Whenever he was in the house after that Mr Penhale made a point of stopping to exchange a few words and even, surprisingly, accompanying Mr Vaisey on his weekly visit to the schoolroom. He stood quietly by while Minnie, whose love of the outdoors I was attempting to channel into more sensible activities than teasing the gardener's boy or gathering spiders to set free in the house and frighten the maids, showed off her nature diary with its pressed flowers and accounts of the animals we saw on our walks, and Estella read a few paragraphs from a ladies' magazine on the new season's fashions which she had translated into tolerable French. Her papa, not understanding a word, smiled proudly, the smile turning to a frown when he learned of the frivolous subject matter as Estella excitedly showed him the magazine and explained that Mama had promised she might have a satin gown with a pleated skirt and puffed gauze sleeves, similar to the one she had spoken about, for the summer, when she would be sixteen and quite of an age to wear something so grown-up. It was Mr Penhale who smoothed over the moment by saying how much more sensible it was for a young lady to have a French vocabulary dealing with fashion rather than having her head filled with all manner of abstruse words which would be of no possible use to her in later life. And cast an approving glance at me over Mr Vaisey's bent head, which unaccountably warmed me. I realised he understood as well as I that pretty Estella would never settle to study unless her fickle attention was caught by some subject dear to her shallow heart.

But none of this could possibly have prepared me for our final encounter in Mr Vaisey's well-stocked though little-used library. It seemed quite accidental that Mr Penhale should be there, leafing through a book. But of course it was not accidental at all.

I halted when I saw him, prepared to retreat, but he snapped the book shut, returned it to the shelf and said coolly, 'Ah, Miss Beardmore, just the person I hoped to see. Forgive me if I beg a few moments of your time on a private matter.'

'It is rather late,' I said, somewhat piqued. Most evenings I slipped into the library after the Vaiseys had retired to bed and before the maids came to damp down the fire and put out the candles. I had come to value this little solitary interlude when I could return a book I had borrowed and take my time to make a further selection. 'Perhaps tomorrow, sir . . .'

'I shall be leaving early. And it is important that I state

14

my case so that you may have time to consider it.'

'What case is this?' I asked, puzzled.

'I rush ahead. Please, will you sit a moment?' He smiled. The smile disarmed me. He was a man whose manner, generally, was grave, sometimes abstracted as though he was lost in thought. But his smile surprised me into realising he was not nearly so middle-aged or staid as Mr Vaisey. For the first time I realised that he was a handsome man with high cheekbones and a firm, shapely mouth, and that some inner excitement sparked a light of boyish eagerness in the sea-blue eyes.

That was the moment when I should have left. We were alone, it was late and a woman in my position must be above any suspicion of irregular behaviour if she values the regard of her employer. Instead, and against all the principals I had resolutely set myself when I first decided to move from my mother's orbit, I hesitated. And having hesitated, it seemed churlish to do other than allow myself to sit for a moment – remaining, of course, straight-backed, composed, head tilted in an attitude of cool formality, so that should a maid come upon us there could be no possible misinterpretation of our circumstances.

Daniel did not sit. He strode about as he talked, as though impelled by an uncontainable nervous energy. 'Miss Beardmore,' he began, 'I ask only one favour: that you do not condemn my proposition out of hand. I should like you to consider it carefully in the coming weeks. I shall make it my business to return to Portsmouth in early March and you may give me your answer then. Do I have your agreement on this?'

Mystified and more then ever curious, I said firmly, 'I cannot promise any such thing, Mr Penhale, not knowing what it is you want of me. However, I am willing to listen to

15

what you say, which must be of some importance or you would not have waylaid me in this fashion.'

'Of course you are right. It was too much to expect. As to waylaying you, yes, I am guilty of it, but I could see no other means. I shall not take longer than is necessary.' He strode about as he talked, long legs in white nankeen trousers scissoring across the Turkey carpet, black coat-tails flying. 'First, it is necessary that I say something of myself. I am a widower with a daughter of nine years old, my wife, Meraud, having drowned in a tragic accident when my daughter, Kensa, was still a babe in arms.'

'Charming names,' I said politely. 'Unusual.'

'Cornish. The language itself is no longer used in common parlance, though some words remain to colour the local dialect. My wife inherited a name which had been in her family for generations.' He waved this digression aside a touch impatiently. 'It is not of my late wife I wish to speak, but of my daughter.' There was an imperceptible softening in his tone. 'She is a delightful child, very pretty, but delicate, and her poor health has been a great source of worry to me over the years. The brewery and maltings that I own in Plymouth oblige me to be a good deal of time there, where I have a modest residence, but Kensa is happiest and most comfortable away from the noise and press of the town. She stays much of the time at Kildower, the house in Cornwall that I inherited from the man who adopted me – and more than likely saved me from transportation or worse – when I was a poor orphan brat thieving to keep myself alive in the stews of Plymouth.'

I had been of a mind to interrupt, to say that if his daughter was in need of a governess, then he must look elsewhere, for I was perfectly satisfied with my present employment. But that last sentence brought me up short.

The blue eyes regarded me gravely. 'I trust your sensibilities are not offended by my frankness, Miss Beardmore. As a gently reared person you will perhaps find it difficult to comprehend my life as it was then, but I feel I should make it quite plain that I have no grand connections, nor indeed any connections at all. I was born in Devonport, a town near to Plymouth, to a servant girl who was cast out of her position and reduced to penury when she formed an unfortunate liaison with a seaman from one of the Scandinavian countries. She was not certain which country, only that he was blond-haired and blue-eyed and could scarce string two words together in English. However, their alliance was soon severed when she told him she was with child. He made haste back to where he came from and she never again saw him.'

Daniel smiled wryly. 'My adoptive father had a history much the same as myself, which I believe created a bond between us despite the unfortunate circumstances of our first meeting. However, by the time I knew Saul Penhale he was made hard from a lifetime at sea in which he had eventually captained his own vessel. He was always reluctant to speak of the manner in which he had gained his wealth – it was very likely some form of privateering during the war with the French from which many legally, or illegally, gained – but a fall down a companionway had left him with a crippled leg and in constant pain so he was forced to turn his back on the seafaring life. It was a kindly fate that threw us together that day . . . a lonely man, uncertain of his direction now he was landfast, and an urchin who attempted to pluck coppers from his pocket.'

He chuckled deep in his throat. 'I shall never forget the terror of the moment when that beefy fist hauled me into the air and a voice that was used to making itself heard

17

above storm and tempest thundered terrible oaths in my ear. I thought my end had come, but when he brought my face up level with his, all he said was, "By God, I thought I'd a fine catch, but 'tis naught but a jack-sharp and a puny one at that. I'd turn you over to the constable to clap in gaol save you're so skinny you'd be like to escape through the keyhole. Reckon you need a dish of tripe and onions to put some meat on your bones before I decide the best punishment." He promptly hauled me into the nearest chop house and ordered me the finest meal I'd had in my life. When I was finished and he had prised from me that since my mother had coughed her lungs away months before I had been scavenging around the docks and alleys, he said he had need of a willing lad to clean his boots and run his errands and that as he'd taken a liking to the cut of my jib he was inclined to offer this fine position to me.'

The pacing stopped. Daniel stared into the dying embers of the fire, caught up in a vision I could not see, but could imagine the more vividly perhaps for its recounting in such a calm tone of voice. Then, seeming to recollect himself, he said, 'The outcome, Miss Beardmore, you see for yourself.' He shrugged in some embarrassment. 'For better or worse he turned me into a gentleman. I was the son he had never had. He became devoted to me and I to him. Once the bond was forged between us all his endeavours were concentrated on ensuring that I should never want. I was clothed, fed and educated. He invested his money shrewdly, his main investment being to buy a small, run-down brewery which he built up to a good business. But he became more and more reclusive after he bought Kildower, which he came across in one of his solitary rides. This man, whose life until then had been bound up by the sea, succumbed instantly and powerfully to the allure of the neglected house and its

18

wild gardens. He thereafter devoted himself to wresting Kildower back from dereliction. I was twenty-one by the time Kildower was restored to beauty and that summer, as though the house had gobbled up all his strength, Saul Penhale succumbed to a brain fever. When he recovered, the doctor advised him that his constitution was so seriously weakened that he would not see the winter out and it would be prudent to set his affairs in order. Old Saul sent for his lawyer and made everything, including Kildower, over to me, requesting only that he might be left to live out what little time he had left in peace and tranquillity in the house he loved.'

'How sad,' I said, feeling some comment on his extraordinary story was called for. 'To have worked so long and then not be able properly to enjoy the fruits of your labours.'

'Do not waste your sympathy, Miss Beardmore.' His tone was amused. 'It is twelve years since the doctor pronounced his verdict, but Saul Penhale was ever contrary. He is now well over eighty and though frail still manages to spend much of the day wandering the countryside alone. The rest of the time he lives solitary in his rooms. Which is perhaps as well, for anyone he meets he is like to shower with insults. He has not mellowed, you see, but grown more crabbed and eccentric with the years.'

Daniel faced me squarely, hands laced at his back, chin tucked into his crisply folded cravat. He regarded me from under his straight brows. 'So there you have it. A brief account of my life, which though satisfactory in many ways – my business is much expanded and, with Mr Vaisey shipping my light ale to the Baltic countries where it is highly prized, looks set to improve even further – is less so in others. You see, a man who must be absent from his household needs the assurance, if he is to be comfortable in his mind, that while he is away all will run smoothly and harmoniously. Of course there are servants at Kildower who are paid to perform the many tasks a house of its size demands, but one can never entirely rely on servants, especially young ones, who are like to up and leave if something does not suit them or to get up to all manner of sly tricks if they are not supervised properly. It is a constant worry to me when I am away that I have no one whom I might totally trust to oversee the welfare of my old father and my daughter, who though admirably cared for by her nurse will need more worldly advice and instruction as she grows older . . .' He broke off, then said carefully, 'Miss Beardmore, to be quite plain, I am in need of a wife. I feel you could fulfil that role admirably.'

Shock rendered me speechless for a moment. I had an odd sense of disorientation, as though this quiet room, with the familiar furniture, the bookshelves, the dying fire, was totally strange and I an alien being trapped within it. 'But that is impossible!' The words burst out. 'You know nothing of me!'

'I know you have many qualities that I find most agreeable. You have a firm but kindly way with children, you are intelligent, diligent, well mannered – though not subservient – and, above all, you are a serene person, quietly confident of her own abilities.'

'The observations of one week's acquaintance!' I said. 'That is nothing at all!' But he was unperturbed.

'I have also gleaned from the Vaiseys a little of your background. How you and your widowed mother have lived abroad for many years and returned to England only when she became ill last summer. That now she lives quietly in the country on a modest annuity and you are obliged to earn a living, as you always have done. You have excellent references from several titled Italian families to whom you gave English lessons while living in Venice and Florence and a glowing recommendation from a family friend, Sir Richard Merton, a person well thought of in scientific circles for his papers on magnetic electricity.'

So many half-truths mingled with the true facts. They stabbed my conscience like sharp slivers of glass. All those regrettable white lies that were necessary if one was to obtain a position with decent, respectable people. For what sensible mama would entrust her young daughters, who must, naturally, be shielded from undesirable influences, to someone whose background was unstable at the best, ramshackle at the worst, and whose mother was a living example of the worst kind of radical immorality. I rose to my feet. 'I see no point in continuing this conversation, sir.'

'No? Then look at the proposition in another way. I have given some intimation of what you could do for me – care for my child and my old father, oversee my household – but think what I might do for you, Miss Beardmore. I am a wealthy man and although I have always lived quite plainly, I would have no objection should you wish to live in a more lively, sociable fashion. You would have a beautiful country home to organise and entertain in as you wish and another in Plymouth itself so as to attend any entertainments or exhibitions in which you may be interested. And I would be happy to settle a generous sum on your mama – indeed, if she is so minded, there is room to spare at Kildower, where she would be welcome to spend her declining years.'

The sudden, tempting, ridiculous picture of myself as mistress of a grand house fled as I saw my mother as Daniel believed her to be. I had to choke back a threatening bubble of laughter at the thought of Mama transformed into a sweet, grey-haired gentlewoman nodding over her crochet in the chimney corner. 'I think not,' I said, gently. I began to move to the door.

He put out a hand as though he would restrain me, then recollected himself and stood motionless once more, saying, 'I asked in the beginning that you should not condemn my proposition out of hand. I beg you now to let the idea lie fallow in your mind until I return and that in the interim we may write to each other in order to further our friendship.' He hesitated, then said slowly, the words dragging painfully as though from a dark and private misery, 'I do not ask or expect that we should fall in love with each other, Miss Beardmore. I have known the agony and the rapture of that relentless passion. I would not wish to know it again.'

I stopped, compelled to do so by the harsh emotion in his voice, sensing the loneliness underlying his words and feeling its shivering echo in my own heart. I felt the delicate tendrils of compassion undermining the stout defences of common sense.

'It is friendship I seek, Miss Beardmore,' he said, 'and companionship. I think we might build a marriage better than many on those two sturdy foundations.'

I could walk from the room. I could close the door behind me and forget this odd incident had ever happened. I could turn my back on Daniel Penhale, a lonely man. And yet . . . and yet . . . I felt myself caught by his story.

With my hand on the door I said, 'I shall not commit myself, but if you wish to write, sir, I shall answer your letters.' Then turning sharply, because I could not let him go away believing that I was this perfect, agreeable, genteel person, I said almost defiantly, 'There is much you should learn about me. But I would warn you, if once you know of it perhaps you will wish to withdraw the offer you have made.'

I slept badly that night, my mind scrabbling over that unbelievable, shocking, *stimulating* conversation. Well before the first maids were up I had lit my candle and, the scratch of my pen loud in the stillness, had begun to write down all that I must honestly confess to Daniel Penhale before we should meet again. Whether I should ever send the account to him remained to be seen. So I told myself. But even when grey daylight took the power from the dancing candle flame and spread its cold clarity into my small room, I knew that an altogether different flame lit my mind and my imagination. Daniel Penhale had ignited it and it would not be easily extinguished.

My mother was born in Bovey Tracey in the county of Devonshire to middle-aged parents and had married young. At nineteen she had run away after a winter ague had carried off her elderly husband. 'A cold, carping man, your papa – my parents' choice, naturally. How cruel and unfeeling they were to their only child! But I was born to them too late. I was an interruption, a nuisance, and far too pretty and talented for their peace of mind. They could scarcely wait to have me off their hands, married and safe from unsuitable admirers. They were impatient, too, because I pleaded with them constantly to allow me to have more drawing materials, more paints, more painting lessons. They saw such an occupation as frivolous and useless, when I should be concerning myself with practical domestic matters. They could not look into my heart and see the passion that burned in my soul with an unrelenting flame to record what I saw around me on paper or canvas.'

I had heard the story many times. How these unknown grandparents of mine had arranged her marriage when she was seventeen years old to a corn merchant in the town, a widower with a middle-aged son and grandchildren older than she was. The week after his death, a scant two years later, Mama had walked out of the house in Bovey and never gone back.

'Such an adventure, my dear! I had nothing with me but a few shillings I had saved from the meagre housekeeping I was allowed by my skinflint husband, the clothes I stood up in, gruesome widow's weeds, and my child.' At this point she would always favour me with a sentimental smile. 'Ah, but you were a pretty little scrap at six months old, with the sunniest of natures.' A regretful sigh. 'It was the greatest pity that as you grew up your hair darkened to that mousey brown and you took on a look of your unlamented papa, who exhibited no refinement or delicacy in his features. Unfortunate, too, that you developed so many of Thomas's less pleasing traits – a prickly stubbornness and a certain dourness of nature tending towards secrecy and severity.'

Here, the strong, thin fingers would make an elegant, dismissive gesture. 'Indeed, since you have grown to womanhood I see so little of myself in you that I am inclined towards serious disappointment. Especially since out of this contrary inclination of yours you have chosen to disregard the more interesting, artistic talents – and you need not frown in that disagreeable manner for you know the truth of it – that you have undoubtedly inherited from your mama . . . but where was I? Ah, yes, fleeing to London with my babe and my few shillings, to seek sanctuary with those I could call true friends . . .'

She had run to find shelter with a man who, three years previously, had spent the summer in Bovey Tracey. William Woodley was a young artist drawn by its grandeur to paint the moorland scenery but not averse to turning his hand to painting a portrait of someone's prize pig or to giving drawing lessons to the daughters and wives of any gentlemen with the means to pay his fees. Grandfather had, grudgingly, been persuaded to allow Mama to join several other young ladies to be tutored by Mr Woodley at the house of a respectable neighbour.

'The other girls were dull, plodding creatures with no more brains in their heads than the sheep who ran on the moorland slopes. It was inevitable that an instant sympathy sprang up between William and myself. It was the meeting of like minds. William saw how it was with me, the daughter of philistine parents, imprisoned by convention. An artistic talent doomed to be suppressed like a flower crushed in the bud before it has a chance to bloom to its full glory. I was eager, unschooled of course, my gifts raw, but that summer – ah, that long, warm summer – I drank in everything that he taught me and demanded more. I had such hopes, such a fever to learn. William was constantly astonished at my progress, at the inspiration I showed. But at summer's end he returned to London. There were no more drawing lessons.'

Here, dramatically, she would pace about in agitation. 'I was fastened once more in the fetters of this little backwater and I felt more trapped than ever because I had tasted a little of what life could be. Worse, Papa, sensing my rebellious mood and beginning to regret his leniency, packed me off to the house of an invalid friend, a reclusive man whose wife, lonely in that bleak place on the moor and without relatives or children of her own, was in need of companionship through the dark winter months. I could readily see that in such a desolate place one might go mad out of loneliness! I swear I almost did. Especially since the old couple followed Papa's edicts to the letter and allowed no spare-time occupation other than plain sewing and mending or the reading of improving books. Never was I so glad when spring came and I was released from this bondage. I could almost have flung my arms about Papa and hugged him when he came to fetch me home, though he would have thrust me off, for he was a man much against any show of affection. I was ecstatic – but for such a short while. For on the journey home, between grumbling at the state of the road and the laggardly pace of the horse, Papa informed me that I was to exchange one form of bondage for another. A marriage had been arranged in my absence.'

At this point my mother's shoulders would sag and her head droop, as though she took upon herself all the cares of the world. As a child I had rushed to comfort her. 'Mama, do not be sad. I am here with you. I will do everything to make you happy.' But her martyred smile would tell me what a poor and insignificant thing my love for her was compared to the agonies – the indignities – she had suffered.

I suffered with her – for her – with each retelling. But as I grew older, traitorous thoughts would make me uncomfortable as the performance, for performance it was, was re-enacted to impress some confidante, I the silent observer.

I wondered about my unknown grandparents, my unknown father. Had they been so unremittingly cruel as Mama insisted? Or was the tale twisted, as I knew she was capable of, to put herself in a sympathetic light and feed her sense of drama? And what of William Woodley's young wife? Mama showed scant regard for a woman who had been kind enough to take her in when she arrived penniless on William's Camden Town doorstep after her flight from Devon, dismissing her, airily, as a placid, cow-like creature with no thought in her head beyond the ordering of the next meal. 'I had it in me to feel sorry for William, tied to this domestic millstone. It was at his family's insistence that he married her. He would have lost his inheritance otherwise, his father being narrow-minded and disapproving of his son's mode of occupation and radical ideas. William's was such a free and intelligent spirit. I fear in later years she held him back, for he never fulfilled his great promise.'

The few works of his that I had seen I thought third-rate and lacklustre, but Mama would not have it. I had given up trying to persuade her otherwise.

'You have little judgement!' She would draw herself up, her nostrils flaring with indignation. 'His work had subtle qualities imperceptible to the untrained eye. And as one who has turned her back on the finer things in life you are scarcely in a position to pass an opinion, Sophy. No, he made a grave mistake when he married. She did him no good at all.'

Except love him, support him, give him sons, attend to his correspondence, turn a blind eye to his *amours* and run his home efficiently so that his artistic mind need never be troubled with domestic problems.

I was too young to have had any true remembrance of her, but occasionally a shaft of yellow sunlight making a particular pattern on a flagged floor or a snatch of song sung in a young, light voice would bring a sudden nostalgic longing. The memory was so formless as to slide away in the blink of an eyelid. Yet I believe it was from that time this feeling came. I think Mrs Woodley must have been very gentle and kind to a child whose mother was all too often preoccupied with her own interests. I heard that after her husband died, she opened a coffee house, made a great success of it and spent her profits feeding and clothing beggar children she gathered from the gutters.

The Woodleys had been married several years when Mama had taken shelter with them. Within a very short time, Mama and William had discovered that their rapport was more than intellectual. Mrs Woodley, breeding her second child and sickly, was confined to the house when, apparently without a qualm, William embarked upon a three-month painting tour of Switzerland, taking with him his talented protégée and her infant daughter.

William's irregular liaison with Mama was to last but a few months longer than their return to Camden Town. Mama's beauty and charm were already making an impression among the artistic and radical circles in which William Woodley moved. She soaked up the flattery and attention, was swept along by the swell of heady new ideas. She snatched eagerly at the tenets of radical thinking most conveniently relevant to her own circumstances: free love, atheism and the principles of feminist rights. She swept out of William Woodley's arms and into the embrace of a rich young man, a would-be poet, intent on squandering his inheritance on fine living and beautiful women. Infatuated, he carried her off to Brussels in order that she might further her painting studies. 'It was eighteen months of bliss. He was so generous. I wanted for nothing. Nor did you, Sophy. But I had my Art to pursue. It had to end. We parted friends and went our separate ways.'

Was it then a false memory I had? Of my own terrified screams rising to match the crash of flung objects, the violence of screeching arguments, of being torn from the arms of my weeping nurse and bundled out into the dark and cold?

'We went to the sun, then. My spirit had begun to crave the hot, rich colours of the south. I had heard so much of Florence. Oh, and I was not disappointed. My senses were dazzled. I was giddy with the abundance of beauty. Churches, galleries, palaces – masterpieces in sculptured stone and marble in themselves and each crammed with paintings and sculptures – it was almost too much. I remember one morning standing before Ghirlandaio's *Birth of the Virgin* in Santa Maria Novella and feeling such a sense of despair at my own insignificant talents that I ran from the church in tears. I was sated, glutted on beauty. So much so, that I had to retire to the tranquillity of the countryside to recover before I could even consider going on to Rome.'

So the pattern of our lives was set; my mother forever restlessly in pursuit of a goal I could not comprehend. Some vision, some key to harmony or contentment or knowledge that might be found in Paris, Venice, Rome then back again, always, to Florence. We became part of the ever-shifting populace of artists . . . painters, musicians, poets, novelists, who crossed from the British Isles to the continent in search of enlightenment and inspiration. Some, like Lord Byron himself, had private means or the prospect of inheritance to borrow against, like his fellow Radical, Shelley. They could afford to flout convention. Respectable society might throw up its collective hands in horror at the latest gossip about their shocking manner of living, but it made little difference to the offenders. For the rest, the ones like Mama without connections or a private income, they must shift as best they could to make a tolerable living.

Mama was doubly burdened because she was a woman alone. And a woman, at that, who was beautiful beyond the ordinary and who challenged the world with her bold, dark eyes.

She worked constantly, concentrating more and more on portraiture. She had a gift for catching an expression, of creating an image that was livelier, more attractive than the reality. She excelled at making a pleasing harmony of flesh tones against embroidered velvet, a fall of lace, a swathe of crisp lawn frills. As the years went by she made a modest, if irregular, living from these portraits.

To me it always seemed incongruous that my strong-minded, intense and passionate mother should have such a flair for turning out pastelly-delicate pictures only a whisker short of sentimentality. But there it was. It made me wonder if somewhere in her heart or spirit there was, locked away, some gentler, more conventional aspect that she would never openly acknowledge.

Whatever money she made never lasted long. We were forever teetering on the verge of insolvency because she scorned frugality. Money was made to be spent on clothes and paints and a round of pleasure, not saved against leaner times. Yet it was the days when we were poorest and alone that were the happiest for me. We might have to quit comfortable lodgings and remove to some bug-ridden hole where we existed on stale bread and bruised fruit, but these were the times when we were closest. If she wept with despair I was the only one left to comfort her. If we were unable to afford candles or wood for the stove we huddled together and she would tell me magical stories about the moors where she had grown up, of enchantments and piskies and giant black hounds. By day we would walk, my hand in hers, and I would learn to look as she looked. At the inky blues and umbers staining a shadow, at the patterns of lichen on a tree trunk, at the way the midday sun sucked colour from the sky. I stored this knowledge away carefully and on the scraps of canvas and paper Mama gave me I would try to create a picture of my own when she was busy at her easel with a new commission.

I was her darling then, her pet, to kiss and hug and spoil with attention. It was the other times that I remember as dark and desolate. When she had money . . . and when she was in love.

With a portrait painted and the fee paid she would

suddenly recollect that she had been lax in her maternal duties. 'Dear God, what a little urchin you have become these last weeks. We shall see about new clothes this very day. Why, you could be mistaken for one of the brats who run wild in the *piazza*! And it is time you had some schooling or you will become ignorant as a beggar's child.'

So I would be packed off. If I was lucky, to somewhere close by, under the tutelage of an indigent spinster from the British community who would treat me with chilly disapproval because of my raffish background, only to be summarily taken away when the money ran out. If I was unlucky – and my luck generally evaporated at moments when Mama's concern for my education coincided with the onset of a distracting and consuming new love in her life – I would be despatched, despite my tears and protests, farther afield to a convent in the Tuscany hills. Despite Mama's professed abhorrence of religion, she found it convenient at these times to set aside her prejudices.

I spent several wretched spells there. Never staying long enough to become part of the cliques and giggling friendships of the other girls that could have made bearable the harsh discipline and austerity of the regimen that the sisters imposed, but long enough to convince me that the purgatory of which the sisters spoke so constantly could be no worse than the fear and misery that was my shadow. Each day that I was there dawned bright with the hope that this was the day Mama would come and rescue me, and die with my homesick tears soaking the pillow. I felt that I was being punished by Mama for some unknown crime for her to have incarcerated me in this hushed, alien world of bells and rules and incomprehensible rituals. I could not even write to tell her of my distress. The fortnightly letter we were allowed was inspected for misspellings, blots and sentiments that might reflect badly on the convent. Mine were frequently torn up by Sister Ignatius, my knuckles soundly rapped with the short cane she always carried, and I was made to rewrite the one page allowed with bland, reassuring phrases. Mama's scrappy notes to me were infrequent and full of exhortations to be a good girl and take full advantage of the excellent tuition. I was bewildered that she could not know the sort of existence to which she had condemned me.

Sooner or later the sentence would be over, the prisoner released. Mama, tiring of her latest passion or once more finding herself in the annoying position of being unable to pay the convent's fees, would sweep me off and smother me with hugs and kisses, crying, 'My precious child. What a fond, foolish mama I have been, to deny myself your company for so long. Oh, how I have missed you! Yet what else could I have done, knowing that your needs must always come first? But I shall be selfish and keep you by me from now on!'

And my chilled heart would grow so warm again, that I was willing to forget all that I had been through, so that I could not spoil the bliss of reunion by complaints, and buried all the hurt deep in my mind. Until the next time.

When I was twelve and growing plainer and gawkier by the day, Mama fell quite desperately in love with a French poet ten years younger than herself. He had repaired to Florence, where one could, if one was delicately placed financially, live very cheaply, though the rooms he had rented, he sighed, were somewhat damp, which was detrimental to his weak chest, and the smells from a noisome midden below his window were *très désagréable* . . .

Mama was enraptured by his languid good looks, by his exquisite manners, by the throaty cadences of his heavily accented English. It seemed ridiculous – he apparently being equally entranced by her – that he should be forced to remain in that squalid quarter when we had an airy apartment. So he moved in and Mama was delirious – ethereal – with a happiness I had never seen in her before. Perhaps it really was the one true love in her life as she ever after declared it to be. Or perhaps, with the first stirrings of womanhood within my own body, I was more sensitive to her emotional state, to the workings of her mind. Whatever it was, I sensed that Jean Pierre presented a threat to me far more lasting and dangerous than any other of Mama's lovers.

I was at this time having some indifferent but agreeable schooling at the house of a Mrs Constantine, the wealthy widow of a Lancashire mill owner who, with her daughters and their governess, repaired for a few months each year in spring and early summer to a large villa on the outskirts of Florence, returning to England before the heat became too oppressive.

Mama had recently painted a portrait of the eight-year-old twins, imbuing their podgy features with a cherubic delicacy they did not possess and refining their plump arms and hands to a perfection of white skin against the rose pink of their much-befrilled dresses. Mrs Constantine expressed herself delighted beyond all expectations with the portrait. She was a florid and talkative woman somewhat despised and largely ignored by the English residents because her money was new and she herself had a roughness about her that spoke of a less than genteel ancestry, but she was shrewd, and intent on giving her daughters all the advantages she had clearly never had. During one of the sittings she had overheard me chattering and laughing to our landlady on the back stairs and begged Mama to allow me to visit her daughters at the villa.

'Your Sophy has a right good command of the language, and of French, too, she tells me,' she said. 'Yon governess came with excellent references and she's a decent enough young woman, but languages are not her strong point. She gets in a right pother if she has to say more than "Good morning" to the servants, so if you could spare Sophy for a few hours each day, just to talk to them and play with them so's they'll pick up a bit of Italian, I'd reckon it a favour, Mrs Beardmore. And Sophy might as well sit in on their proper lessons if you're agreeable and take dinner with them afterwards.'

Mama sprang at the chance and for a few short weeks I made the daily journey on foot to the Villa Rosa. It was a happy house, the governess young and gentle and given to pleasing ideas about fresh air and exercise, so a great deal of time was spent walking in the garden and the olive grove beyond while Miss Armitage pointed to various objects and I repeated the Italian names.

But it could not last, like most things in my short life. The Constantines would soon be leaving. And Mama had met Jean Pierre.

Now I am able to understand how it must have been for her. Then, I only felt the bitter bewilderment of rejection. She was in the grip of so strong a desire that it bred a terrible insecurity. She saw me as an inconvenience. No, more than that, a threat. A constant reminder to herself and to Jean Pierre that she had reached her thirties while he had scarcely turned twenty. Of course, she told herself, these age differences scarcely mattered in one so mature as he, while she herself was still so very young in appearance and outlook. Love, that mysterious alchemy, knew no barriers of age or condition. All the same, perhaps it would be for the best if there were no reminders at all.

'I have the greatest plans for you,' she cried, on a brilliant morning with the sunshine slanting through the shutters like slices of yellow butter. 'I have decided to spare you from the wicked heat of the coming months. Look how you suffered last year when you took that dreadful fever in Venice. I swear it was the effluvia rising from the canals that caused it and I should never forgive myself if you were so ill again when you might be living in a healthier place. I wept for a day and a night when your hair had to be cropped! You looked such a pathetically shorn lamb and it has grown back so wispy and fine that I fear it has quite lost all its lustre. Besides, you are beginning to speak English with an accent as thick as a Tuscan peasant. No, no, do not argue. It is the truth. You are sadly in need of a good schooling in a cooler climate.'

'But you promised I should not go to the convent again! You promised, Mama. And I do not mind the heat. Truly! I am happy here, with you.'

'Silly child! It is not the convent, but somewhere far superior, where you will be blissfully content among girls similarly placed to yourself whose parents live in tropical places. I have made the most extensive enquiries and received excellent testimonials for the establishment, which is very prettily situated on the outskirts of Salisbury in Wiltshire so as to take advantage of the healthy breezes for which the area is noted.'

'Salisbury? Wiltshire? But where is this Salisbury? Oh, I hope it is nearer than the convent.'

'That I should have allowed you to become so ignorant!' she cried, throwing up her hands in pretended horror. 'I see now that I should have sent you home to complete your education long since. Why, Salisbury is in England, you little goose, where you were born.'

'But this is my home,' I wailed. 'With you, Mama. Please don't make me go.'

I was allowed no protest. I was put in charge of Mrs Constantine when she left Florence. Mama smothered me with kisses as I clung to her, weeping. Then she thrust me off briskly. 'I shall write often, my pet. And I shall send for you as soon as maybe. It will be no time at all before we are together again.' But this promise, like too many of Mama's promises, was so much chaff in the wind. It was a full four years before the summons came.

My darling.

I have been through the pains of hell and I can only now bear to write. It is six weeks since my beloved Jean Pierre was set upon, robbed and murdered by villains, and I have been so ill and distraught since the terrible events of that night that my trembling fingers can even now scarcely hold this pen. I am, in my weakness, desperate for a sight once more of my child, my flesh and blood. How I have yearned to have you at my side these past years! But you will realise that it was for your sake – for your health, your education – that I sacrificed all my maternal instincts on the altar of duty. You have been the sole benefactor of this long separation, for I am a woman broken in heart and spirit – indeed I feel I shall never again have the energy to rise from my sickbed. Only you can bring me comfort now. I am desperate to look upon the face of my child before it is too late. I am entrusting you to the care of someone who has proved himself a good friend in the past, Sir Richard Merton, a patron of the arts and sciences who has bought several of my paintings on his regular visits to Italy. He will escort you to Florence. Hurry to me, my darling girl . . .

It was the moment I had yearned for, yet I was anguished beyond words at the tone of the letter. And, had the reason for my leaving been happier, I should not have wished to leave Salisbury in such a rush. Within the plain stone building that housed Miss Smythe's Academy for Young Ladies, which had seemed at first in my distress much like the prison the convent had been, I had benefited from a great deal of kindness. I had grown to appreciate the ordered calm of days devoted to study, evenings to quiet recreation, the regular if monotonous diet. Sunday walks two by two, to morning service at the cathedral and, above all, the lessons with the drawing master, Mr Gardener, who singled me out for special praise and persuaded Miss Smythe that, as I had a feeling for landscape, extra tuition should be considered. Miss Smythe had already tactfully solved the problem of my fees (the draft often arrived late with profuse notes of apology from Mama, or in dribs and drabs with no apology and twice not at all) by engaging me to instruct the little ones in their letters by way of making up the shortfall. With the practical kindness that caused her pupils to bless the day they had been consigned to her care, she arranged for me to pay for the extra tuition by assisting Madamoiselle Hubert, who was becoming rather deaf, in her language classes. Which was scarcely a burden, for I enjoyed the experience greatly. Indeed, I would willingly have scrubbed floors or scoured greasy pans in order to be granted the privilege of the extra lessons that gave me the chance to set up my easel along the banks of the Avon, on some chalky downland height or in a picturesque corner of Salisbury itself, and sketch or paint under Mr Gardener's watchful eye.

But though it was a wrench to leave Salisbury, I was

more than anxious to be gone in case Mama . . . No! I must tear my mind from the terrible possibility that I might be too late, though my sleep was interrupted by the most dreadful nightmares until Sir Richard arrived three days later.

'My dear Miss Sophy,' he boomed after I had shyly made my curtsey and he had taken my hand in his big paw and shaken it vigorously, 'I am delighted to inform you that by the very same mail that I received a missive similar to yours from your mother, I heard from an acquaintance in Florence – the letter was written more than a week later, but the foreign mails, as you will know, are never reliable – that Mrs Beardmore had made a recovery that was perfectly miraculous and had been seen taking the air quite restored to her normal spirits. Is that not good news?' He beamed at me. 'Now, come, my dear, we must make haste if we are to reach Portsmouth in time to catch the Genoa packet. With these good tidings to hearten us, our journey will be a happy one. Indeed, it will be my pleasure to make it as comfortable and interesting for you as I am able.'

I was weak with relief and suddenly impatient to be on my way. And there was, thankfully, no time for long fare-wells. All of a sudden my trunks were on the hired chaise, we were rattling towards Portsmouth and I found myself nervously assessing this man in whose company I must travel.

I was shy and awkward with him at first, for he was overlarge in person and in character and he had a booming voice that seemed extra loud after the genteel female tones I had grown used to. But I soon warmed to him, as I observed most of our fellow passengers did when we embarked on the packet, because he was quite without guile and unfailing-ly cheerful and considerate, even to the three tiresome spinster sisters forever twittering about their ailments and morbidly certain that every thief and murderer in Rome, where they were to visit their brother, would be lying in wait for them.

Sir Richard was a big, shambling, untidy man in his middle years. His hair sprang from his head in a wiry grey frizz as though startled by the energy of the intellect beneath, for his was a mind that had a great openness and a depth of knowledge that made journeying with him a fascinating experience. Any curiosity observed, from a school of dolphins to the workings of the sextant, would bring forth a scholarly and lucid address on the subject. By the time we reached Genoa the three maiden ladies were almost brought to blushing tears when they took their leave, each having fallen a little in love with him. Not that his was a flirtatious nature. On the contrary. It was merely that he would bring the same quality of attention to a dreary account of an attack of neuralgia as he would when he questioned the captain on the manner and method of the rigging. Besides, as I came to understand later, there was only one woman he wanted – my mother. Upon her he bestowed the dogged devotion of a man who, until he met her, had been a contented bachelor, too absorbed in his many diverse interests to be sidetracked by thoughts of marriage. The scientific studies and experiments with electricity and steam power that he pursued in his Hampstead mansion, his trips about the country to attend lectures and demonstrations, his travels abroad in search of paintings and sculptures to add to his collection, had been enough to fill his days. Until he met Hannah Beardmore. And once captivated, was held unshakeably in love and tenaciously devoted.

I came to believe he was as fascinated and amused by the mercurial, self-seeking, venal side of her character as by her beauty, her independence and her bold spirit, and for all his lack of experience with women he had a way of managing her that many another might have envied. With the patience of a man used to setbacks and frustrations in his experiments, he was prepared for a long, steady siege upon her affections. He set out to become the one person in her life who never failed her, and though Mama fell in and out of love, or infatuation, with several men younger and handsomer than he in the years following my return to Italy, it was Sir Richard who would always appear unexpectedly to comfort and restore her spirits when disillusion set in.

It was no miracle that he knew the politic moment to arrive. He had a network of correspondents among the English community, and even the most learned of them was not averse to a little gossip. One of them, for instance, had alerted him when Mama had become ill last summer and she herself had been, for once, too suddenly and desperately sick to write to anyone. I was in Sienna, giving English lessons to the young family of a Contessa, and it was an urgent letter from Sir Richard that had me scurrying to Venice where she lay in a frowsty room suffering from a dreadful jaundice.

On that occasion, once she was a little improved, though still too weak to make any but the feeblest of protests, he had acted swiftly. Within a short time he had organised the packing up of all Mama's worldly goods and had them – and us – on board ship and sailing for England as though it was the most natural thing in the world that he should take charge of us. Then, having installed us in the Highgate house, he repaired back to his own Hampstead property and allowed Mama, when she had made a full recovery, to believe that she herself had sought the change of climate and had quite decided that a spell away from the torrid Mediterranean heat would be beneficial both to her health and to her work, for

Sir Richard's patronage enabled her to find more than one commission among his wide circle of acquaintances.

That was the one time I had known her to be genuinely ill. But in the weeks after Jean Pierre's demise (he had died, I quickly discovered, not at the hands of thieves but in a drunken brawl when he was caught cheating at cards in a low tavern) she was not sick, but lonely and bored and bereft. The years with him had been stormy, his weakness for a pretty face and low pursuits had seen to that, but when he was dead Mama remembered only the moments of pleasure and passion. 'What can my life be without my one true love?' she would cry, flinging herself sobbing onto the sofa. 'I have lost everything! I cannot go on! Life has lost its savour and I shall never again be able to paint.'

I would try to comfort her, feeling her pain as my own, distressed at my inability to relieve her anguish. Yet there was a corner of my mind that watched now in complete detachment, that saw her as a stranger might, as strikingly beautiful, nor merely for the perfection of her creamy skin and her sultry green eyes with their thick black lashes, but for some inner quality of confidence in her own worth that commanded admiration. A woman talented beyond the ordinary, lively and determined. And running below the surface like a flaw in the heart of a superficially superb gemstone, a seam of jealousy and possessiveness and selfishness.

From the first moment of our reunion she refused to allow that anything I had suffered in my exile could be compared to the torments she had gone through. If I admitted that I had grown to be happy at school she shrugged and said that Miss Smythe was well paid to ensure that her pupils were kept contented. When I shyly brought out my drawings and paintings, she grudgingly admitted that they had some technical merit, but insisted that they were totally lacking in originality. 'You have quite forgotten all that I taught you, silly child. You have allowed your drawing master to force you into his mediocre methods of working. The man was a fool. No, no, do not protest. You are not of an age to have any judgement in these matters. And, great God, in matters of dress you have no judgement at all! I suppose it was your beloved Miss Smythe who encouraged you to wear that dreary colour and style. Why, it would be more suitable on some elderly dowager than a young girl. I shall send word to my dressmaker straight away, for I could not bear to be seen about with you looking as you do.'

And so, to please her, which I then still wanted most eagerly to do, I had to abandon the plain dresses in which I felt perfectly comfortable in favour of garments laden with girlish frills and flounces and to have my hair tortured into curls and ringlets that all too soon wilted about my ears. And though Mama thought to keep me a child, even her strong will could not hold back the woman in me. I saw too much now. I knew too much. And two years later, there came a moment in an olive grove when I knew I must free myself of Mama's strong and suffocating grasp and build a different sort of life for myself.

The wedding breakfast was almost at an end and Sir Richard was on his feet. 'Today we are here for the happiest of occasions,' he began.

Involuntarily, I glanced towards Mama. She was watching me, smiling, to all intents and purposes the picture of a woman well pleased. Yet in her narrowed green eyes I caught such a dark, uncompromising glitter that my fingers, lying loosely laced at the table's edge, tightened into a painful grip. Whatever face Mama chose to show to others, she had not reconciled herself to my marriage. Nor forgiven me for disobeying her wishes.

'My acquaintance with Mr Penhale has been a short one,' Sir Richard boomed happily, 'but he has struck me as a man of intelligence and foresight by taking to wife a young lady I have known for many years and have come to hold as dear as a daughter.'

It was Daniel I must think of now, not Mama. Daniel, my husband, who turned his head and with the lift of one eyebrow and a small, wry smile shared with me his amused discomfiture at the obligatory flattery. Such a fleeting, subtle intimacy, yet in an instant there was comfort and reassurance, like a warm tide lapping and smoothing my jangled feelings. Daniel, who when I had plucked up courage and told him about Mama, had written, *'You can no more be responsible for your background than I could help being the natural child of Prudence Yeo. I think we may safely set aside the vagaries of our parentage, for it has no bearing on our friendship and on the mutual happiness we shall, God willing, achieve.'*

I let out my breath in a relieved sigh and moved my arm just enough to allow the puffed and tucked cream silk of my long sleeve to touch the dove-grey broadcloth of Daniel's coat. I drew from that tenuous contact the sense of his quiet, controlled strength and knew it was foolish to brood on what could not be altered.

'And so I ask you to raise your glasses and drink to the health and continuing happiness of Sophy and Daniel Penhale.'

I heard Mama's voice light and clear above the rest, but I did not look at her again. I kept my eyes on Daniel as he responded to the toast. It was nearly over. Soon we could escape. When we rose from the table there must, for politeness sake, be one more circuit of the guests, then I was slipping away to the room that was mine when I stayed in my mother's house and where Clarrie, my mother's maid, was waiting to help me into my travelling dress.

I was thankful when Clarrie had unbuttoned the length of tiny pearl buttons down the back and I could step out of the fussy splendour of my wedding gown. It was my mother's choice. She had ordered it, harangued the dressmaker over it, paid for it. 'If you must marry, then no one shall say that I allowed you to go to the altar looking like a frumpish spinster grasping at her last chance of a man. No, do not argue. I am adamant.'

To keep the peace I let her have her way, though I was disheartened by the peevishness of her attitude and knew the style was wrong for me. All the same I looked at the gown with regret when Clarrie folded it away in my travelling trunk, for it was beautifully made and very expensive. On Mama it would have looked ravishing, but it did nothing for me beyond making me feel uncomfortably weighed down with ornament.

I exchanged smiles with my reflection in the looking-glass when I was dressed once more. This gown and the matching pelisse I should travel in were new also, but they were of my own choosing, and because Daniel had generously insisted that I refurbish my wardrobe with no regard to the cost, the merino was of the best quality in a brown shade that took on a subtle gold cast when the light caught it. The gown, with its plain, fitted bodice and gored skirt, showed off my neat, rounded figure and small waist to advantage, and the simple lines made me appear more than the average height that I was and, perhaps, added a certain dignity. At least that is what I hoped. I had to make the most of the few advantages that nature had bestowed upon me for I was not over-blessed in the matter of looks, as Mama so often reminded me. My face had the same oval shape as Mama's but my features were far from perfect and there was no way I could disguise or enhance them. My nose was too definite, my mouth too full, my eyes an undistinguished hazel and my complexion too healthily rosy rather than the delicate ivory that fashion favoured. I had learned, at last, to manage my fine hair by dispensing altogether with torture by hot tongues and rag curlers and now I dressed it simply, parting it in the centre and looping it back into tidy coils. It looked well enough today, ornamented with a favourite tortoiseshell comb, though a few errant wisps, as usual, had managed to escape. I was carefully smoothing them back into place before I donned my bonnet when with a swish of skirts Mama swept into the room with such suddenness that I jumped and jabbed a hairpin into my neck.

'Leave us,' she said peremptorily to Clarrie and the moment the girl had closed the door she gestured to a chair and said in the same imperious tone, 'Sit down, Sophy.'

'Daniel is waiting,' I said coolly, wondering uneasily if even at this late hour Mama planned some dramatic denouncement of my marriage. 'We have a long drive to . . .'

'This will take but a few moments.' Her eyes still held that strange, unfathomable glitter. 'Surely you would not deny your own mother this one last request before you remove yourself to Devonshire.'

'You make Devonshire sound like Timbuktu or Van Diemen's Land or . . . or some other impossibly remote place,' I said in some exasperation. Then, because this had been an emotional day, a happy one, and I wanted nothing to spoil it, I said quietly, 'Oh, Mama, please do not let us part with angry words.'

'Or perhaps,' she went on, as though I had not spoken, 'you are anxious to leave because you burn for privacy so that your ardent lover may be free with kisses and caresses. Well, that is only natural, I suppose, for two such impassioned young people who long to consummate their love.'

I felt a hot blush suffuse my cheeks as she looked at me with a sly, knowing smile, as though she knew perfectly well of the chaste kisses which were all that Daniel and I had exchanged. Then she turned aside to the mirror and contemplated her reflection. 'Heaven's above, child, I am not angry. Not now.' She shrugged carelessly. 'I have had my say. You will not be dissuaded from the course you have set yourself. Time will prove whether you should have heeded my advice. No, it is not your unfortunate marriage I wish to speak about. It is of something far more important. No, do not move away. Come stand by me.'

Reluctantly, still embarrassed, I did so.

Our two reflected images stared back at us. Mama's emeralds dazzled with a cold, hard glitter in the creamy hollow of her throat. She was not smiling now. I saw that in her hands was a small box. Her fingers moved restlessly over its worn, cracked surface as she spoke.

'You are your father's daughter,' she began slowly. 'I have told you so many times. You have his ordinary looks, his stubborn ways and his plodding nature, though I had hoped that the talent you inherited from me might override these unfortunate characteristics. But you chose to set aside your talent in favour of becoming that creature of low standing and little reward – a governess.'

'I found it satisfying, Mama,' I said quietly. 'I believe I had – have – an aptitude for teaching as much as for painting.'

'Perhaps. It is no matter now. You are as lost to me as . . .'

She hesitated. Her glance was fixed on mine in the mirror, yet her eyes were curiously unfocussed, as though she stared through the glass at a vision beyond. 'There is something I have to tell you, Sophy. And it is not easy for me because I have not spoken of it, ever, to anyone, not even to William, because it was something best forgotten and too painful to be healed by words and tears.'

She spoke in a flat, unnatural voice and there was a sudden tension in the air. Down in the street below a horse plodded past, harness jingling. The clock on the mantel ticked the light seconds away. Familiar, ordinary sounds. I tried to concentrate on them, but they seemed far off, remote. It was Mama's words that crowded into the silence. Words that dropped fat and heavy like thundery rain beating the surface of a pool into frantic disturbance.

'You have an older sister, Sophy. Born to me when I was sixteen. William Woodley's child.'

Her face was expressionless. All her usual vivacity had drained away, taking with it the pretences and posturings with which she normally dramatised any conversation. I knew it was the truth she spoke, without ornamentation. And it was from the heart.

'We became lovers that summer when I was sixteen, though he had left Bovey before I knew I was with child. When my father found out, he was beside himself with rage. He took away my clothes and locked me in my room for a week, giving out to his respectable neighbours that I had a fever. My mother . . .' Her voice faltered. She cleared her throat and began again. 'I had never seen my mother cry before that time. I think . . . I think whatever hopes she had for me were washed away by her disappointed tears. But she was gentler than Papa. Perhaps, had he not been so adamant, so angry, and I not so young and frightened, some

47

other, less harsh course of action might have been taken. Well, no matter. Papa had made the necessary arrangements and he took me away to the house of a couple in the heart of the moor who made their living by looking after girls from respectable families, girls like me, who had disgraced themselves and who had need of someone discreet to guard them until they gave birth and then remove all evidence of the shameful event by finding homes for the bastard children.' She shuddered. 'It was a grim, hard place. We were treated with contempt and made to do the menial work in the house, for there could be no servants who might spread tittle-tattle. When a child was born they allowed it to stay with its mother until it proved healthy and likely to live. Then it was summarily removed – sometimes forcibly – and sent away. We were never told where.'

Her voice sank lower. 'I had two weeks with my daughter. Two weeks. Then they took her from me and bound my breasts and sent word to my parents that I could be fetched. The rest you know. I was married off and I did not care. I thought my life had ended when they tore my daughter from my arms. I could not scream or cry any more. My heart was empty. There is part of it, still, that remains so.'

Silence again. We both stood motionless, staring at the frozen figures in the looking-glass.

'My father died soon after I ran off to London with you. You were a burden, a handicap to me, but I could not bear that I should lose another child, though in the end it was to no avail. It is your father's blood, after all, that runs strongest in your veins and that has taken you along your own path.'

I wanted to speak, to protest, but my lips were too dry and my heart was burdened with the shivering echoes of a frightened girl's desolate tears.

'My father never forgave me, but after my mother died,

some years ago, the lawyer sent this box to me in Florence. It contains his letter and a few mementoes that my mama gathered after my papa died. She had kept in touch with the woman who had disposed of my baby. My mother's grandchild. Through her she learned that the childless couple who took her in lived in Moretonhampstead for a while, then Plympton near to Plymouth. There is a miniature, crude and amateurish to be sure, but clear enough, done when Juliana was three or four.' She drew in her breath and her eyes began to glint again with that dark excitement. 'She is the very image of me.'

'Juliana? That is her name?' I whispered.

'Juliana Sinclair.' Animation flooded once more into my mother's face. 'It is fate, is it not, that you should be removing to Plymouth, so near to where she was last heard of?' She lifted the box, pressed it tight to her heart. 'This is all I have of your sister, Sophy. You are going from me, but it may be that in losing you, I shall gain the daughter I lost twenty-six years ago.' She held out the box. 'Take it! When you are quiet and alone, study what it holds, then, if you have any feeling for the mother who gave you life, find your sister. The one who was cruelly torn from your mother's breast and handed to strangers.' Her smile was brilliant, triumphant. 'Find Juliana, Sophy. Find her for me . . .'

Chapter Two

Daniel had planned our journey to Plymouth with the care and consideration I was coming to expect of him. As I had seen so little of the country west of Salisbury, he had decided that we should travel overland rather than to go to Portsmouth in order to catch the steam packet which he had previously favoured as the most convenient route. But not for us the breakneck, uncomfortable dash by mail coach that would have had us at our destination in little more than twenty-four hours. Ours was to be a slow journey of discovery. Of each other, as much as of the picturesque towns and ever-changing scenery we passed on our way via Bath to Exeter, where we should spend several days before travelling to Plymouth.

'You are, after all, Devon born, Sophy,' he said, as we sat over dinner in a quiet inn by the River Thames that first evening of our marriage. 'It will give me great pleasure to show you the splendours of our county town before we turn for home. Though you must tell me, of course, if there is anywhere else you particularly wish to visit. For instance, we may stay extra days in Bath if you feel the need to linger there and explore its many delights.'

'No, no,' I said quickly. 'I am sure that the itinerary you have planned is very agreeable and interesting. And I would not wish to prolong our journey when Kensa will be waiting for us in Plymouth. I long to meet her. That was a charming little note she sent with you, to welcome me as her new stepmama.'

'And it was entirely her own idea,' he said, his voice softening as it always did when he spoke of his daughter. He smiled. 'She has delightful ways and is quite unspoiled despite all her illnesses, though I am afraid her spelling and handwriting leave much to be desired. But apart from her illness she has been so badly served by unreliable governesses that it is hardly surprising that her education has suffered. I sincerely hope she remains well enough to make the trip to Plymouth and that Jess does not fetch her across the river when the weather is at all inclement. The crossing can be very rough with a gale out of the west or south, and Kensa is easily frightened.'

'The nurse, you say, is a capable woman?'

'Very. Jess has looked after Kensa since my wife died. She is devoted to her. Other servants have come and gone but she remains faithful.'

I toyed with my glass. It was almost empty again. Candlelight sparked and dazzled in the golden dregs. I had already drunk too much and still it was not enough.

I did not refuse when Daniel again filled my glass to the brim. When I had drunk it down my busy mind would perhaps close itself to the chaos of thoughts churned up by Mama's revelations. Compassion for the frightened, distraught girl my mother had been warred with shock, excitement that I had a sister and a growing and painful resentment that all my life this absent, shadowy being had influenced my mother's regard for me. Always, always when I displeased her or did not come up to her expectations she must have yearned for that other daughter, the one whose handsome and artistic parentage was bound to be reflected in a beautiful, vivacious, amenable, *interesting* first-born child.

'Juliana was born of love,' Mama had said with a dreaming sigh, once again reliving the past in her usual dramatic, self-indulgent way. 'Later, William and I, as you know, were reunited though time and events conspired to part us again for ever. But that summer we were caught up in a maelstrom of passion, heightened perhaps because the times when we could be entirely alone were few and forbidden. Then it was that the intensity of our feelings overrode all other considerations. But it was our destiny to be reckless and the results of our union must surely reflect the passion and joy we shared. Indeed a child born of love, I have often noticed, tends to be favoured with the best qualities of both sides.' She cast a sly, measuring glance in my direction. 'With your own papa, of course, it was very different. I had no feelings for him, save distaste for his inadequate fumblings and old man's flabby flesh.'

From the moment she had walked into the room she had meant to humiliate and harass me, to wrest what triumph she could out of the day that was intended to be mine. I would not allow her to see how well she had succeeded.

Calmly, holding my hands steady, I took up the brown pelisse with its simple trimming of cream velvet and slipped it on, then I lifted my new bonnet, arranged it carefully over my hair and tied the strings firmly under my chin. Only then did I feel my voice steady enough to say lightly, 'Well, Mama, whatever foolishness you got up to before I was born is no concern of mine now. You have spoken frankly and I am not unmindful of the honour you do me in confiding this distressing episode, but pray do not believe I shall go on any wild-goose chase in pursuit of this ... this half-sister whom you have chosen to tell me of so belatedly.' Years of practice in dealing with Mama's histrionics stood me in good stead now. I faced her squarely, unemotionally. 'No, Mama,

I shall not search out Juliana Sinclair for you. However cruel it was to part you from your baby all those years ago, the fact remains that for twenty-six years she has not belonged to you. Whatever her life is, neither of us has any part in it, nor should we intrude upon it. We might cause untold mischief.'

'Or great delight,' Mama burst in, 'to know that the woman who bore her has never ceased to love her.'

'If you feel so strongly, why have you not sought her out yourself before this?'

'Oh, believe me, I have thought of it many times. But I knew that it was impossible for me ever to return to a place where I suffered such torments. And the matter was too delicate to place in other hands.' She closed her eyes as though even to think about it brought unbearable agony, then opened them to fix me with her mocking green glance. 'But who better to make these delicate enquiries than my other daughter? Why, it has all fallen out most conveniently, has it not, Sophy?'

'No it has not,' I said brusquely. 'Besides, even if I wished to take on this commission, which I do not, suppose this Juliana has never been told anything of the circumstances of her birth? How would she feel to learn that she was born a bastard?'

'Blood must count for something.'

'Must it? Do you think she will fall upon you with tears of joy and welcome when she discovers the kind of life you have led? The chances are she was raised respectably, in a decent home. And what if she is married, with children? How might her husband feel to be related to someone such as yourself, who has always flouted convention in order to satisfy her own lustful appetite?' I meant to be cruel. To hurt as I had been hurt. 'For once, Mama, try to think of someone other than yourself and your own selfish wishes. Leave Juliana in peace. You have no claim on her. Perhaps you forfeited that right from the first moment you began your affair with William Woodley. A shameful, sordid business which was bound to end disastrously. You deceived your parents and deliberately cheated on William Woodley's wife, then and later. They must all have suffered abominably through your behaviour. Why, then, should you expect to go unpunished?' I stopped, breathed deeply. The words had bubbled up unchecked from deep, long-suppressed bitterness. Other emotions that I could not allow to be released swirled dangerously near the surface. I pushed them away. If she realised that the distressed child, eager to please her, wanting only to be loved and kept secure, hid still in the heart of the grown woman who faced her so coolly, the full weight of her scorn, her mockery, would be unleashed. Or she would use the knowledge, somehow, to her own gain and my disadvantage. I knew her too well to believe anything other.

I saw her flinch as my words struck home, but in a moment she was recovered, drawing around her the comfortable protection of her own convictions.

She smiled. 'Your naivity would be quite disarming, Sophy, if one did not realise such immature reasoning can only lead to frustration and unhappiness. You, like so many women, have not yet learned, poor dear, that human nature and the inner passions refuse to conform to man-made rules. And to live entirely by those rules is to live a shallow half-life.' She moved then, thrusting the box at me, swishing her silk skirts impatiently as she swept to the door. There she paused, turned, and said in the flat, unnaturally composed voice that moved me, had she but known it, far more than any dramatics, 'God help that you never know the loss of a child. Whatever the rights and wrongs of it I had sooner have the heart carved from my breast than suffer such a torment again.'

Then she was gone and downstairs my new husband, my new life, awaited me.

The bottle was empty, my glass drained and Daniel said quietly, 'I think I shall take a turn in the fresh air before we retire.'

The door behind him, the door to the bedchamber which led off from this small private parlour, stood ajar. Through it I could glimpse the blue and white hangings of the bed, the crisp white coverlet already turned back to await its occupants. Blessedly, the wine had done its work. All the memories of the day, the good and the bad, were softening, receding. I was able to smile easily at Daniel, thinking myself lucky indeed that there was a man so discreet as to make easy these moments which might have been awkward, and say, 'I shall ring for our landlady to remove the dishes while you are gone. It has been a tiring day and I am more than delighted that you have found us such clean and pleasant lodgings for the night.'

I was apprehensive about what must take place, but not afraid. After all, I had reasoned, every married woman went through this same initiation and I did not go to my marriage bed in total ignorance as so many women did. I had been used, since childhood, to view impersonally the naked male and female body cast in bronze or sculpted in marble or painted on canvas. Mama, in our closer moments when she set me to copying some great work of art, had spoken frankly of human anatomy, the differences between the sexes and the reasons for them. I appreciated her honesty at this moment, though there were less happy memories I associated with the act of love itself, that still lingered uncomfortably.

Of a time, once, when I was very small and had wakened in the night to such a groaning and moaning from Mama's room that I had run from my bed, believing she was being murdered. When I burst shrieking into her bedchamber, the frightening noises had instantly changed to curses. Half-blinded by sleep, I had groped frantically towards the bed in the darkness, but Mama had leapt on me like a tigress, boxed my ears, hauled me back to my own narrow cot and threatened me with further punishment if I should stir an inch. It was not long afterwards that I was despatched to the convent for the first time and, for all her kisses and re-assurances that she loved me, I took with me the raw hurt of knowing that Mama preferred the company of the half-dressed stranger I had found laughing and whispering with her over the breakfast table the next morning to being with me.

I tried not to think too closely of those noises in the night as I hastily undressed, donned the nightgown I had spent many hours decorating with minute tucks and drawn-thread work and slid beneath the sheets. If the act was so painful, there must be some recompense or Mama, who never suffered so much as a scratched finger without donning the air of one who had been dealt a mortal wound, would not have taken even one man to her bed let alone the string of lovers I knew of. But I grew more nervous as the minutes ticked by. Less convinced that I should find this consum-mation of our wedding vows pleasurable. More certain that this was the price to be paid for the achievement of respec-tability and security. I knew I should have to take care to endure everything stoically in order not to offend or upset the man who was otherwise giving me so much. All the same, I was hopeful that perhaps I should find the satisfaction in this intimacy that Mama had always seemed to do.

A tap at the door and Daniel was in the room, filling it
with his tall, masculine presence and the scent of cool night
air as the draught billowed the curtains at the open window.
I turned my head modestly away from him, but, tense as I
was, every sound translated itself into a mental picture. Now
he was removing his coat and laying it carefully aside. Now
he drew off his cravat . . . unbuttoned his shirt . . . poured
water from the ewer into the basin . . . Then, 'There is a
fine new moon out tonight, Sophy,' he said, his voice so
calm and ordinary that I automatically shifted my head on
the starched pillow to glance at him. And was instantly,
breathtakingly rivetted. 'Our landlord has just informed me
that all the signs point to a spell of settled weather until the
moon wanes. We should have a splendid journey of it back
to Devon.'

I had left one candle burning on the washstand. By its
unsteady light my husband stood with his back to me,
drying himself with a linen towel. He was naked, and
here was no inanimate statue to be admired solely because
some great sculptor had caught in cold marble the exact
likeness of a perfect human figure. Daniel moved, lived,
breathed. Was healthy flesh over supple muscle and
hard bone. Was beautiful. More beautiful than any statue
I had ever seen. For there was something extraordinarily
tender and haunting in the play of amber light and umber
shadow over his pale skin as he moved. No sculptor or
painter, however great, could ever catch that particular
quality in inanimate stone or on paper or canvas. Though
in one brief burning instant, I longed to try. All the
long-buried enthusiasm and eagerness to capture what I
saw on paper shot through me. And, as suddenly, was
gone as Daniel pulled his nightshirt over his head, picked
up the candle and carried it towards me. The spell, for spell

it had been, holding me entranced and still, was broken.

Daniel set the candle on the table by the bed, climbed in beside me and extinguished the light. Then he turned to me and, promising to be as gentle as he could, briefly and methodically took possession of my body.

Afterwards, when he slept, I lay awake for a long while watching the thin silver arc of the new moon cross the gap where the curtains did not quite meet. I was truly married now. No longer a virgin, but a wife. All the more strange, then, that lying there beside my husband, listening to the steady rhythm of his breathing, I felt as cold and lonely as the moon suspended in the dark and limitless sky.

The weather did, as the landlord had prophesied, stay clear and sunny as we journeyed westward, then south, and with every passing day I became more confident in my role as Mrs Daniel Penhale. It was very agreeable, I discovered, to be accompanied by someone who was accustomed to ease the rigours of travel by staying at the best inns and lodgings. Daniel expected good service and there was a quality of command about him that ensured that he received it. My experiences of travelling alone both in England and on the Continent were less pleasant. It was rarely that I could afford more than the cheapest rooms, which all too often meant frowsty beds, grudging service and liberal quantities of fleas or bugs or both. Nothing so unseemly as a flea dared to hop into the pristine rooms we inhabited at the various inns Daniel had chosen along the road to Bath and I was grateful, indeed, to be so pampered. Grateful in other ways, too.

I suppose at the back of my mind I had wondered if Daniel, once we were married, might show a less considerate side to his character or I might quickly discover some dreadful fault in him that he had chosen to keep hidden from me. But it was quite the opposite. The more we talked and the more I learned of him, the more I appreciated my good fortune. Our discussions were lively and free-ranging and whether we were discussing the recent emancipation of the Catholics, his novel venture into purchasing small inns round and about Plymouth in order to provide outlets for his ales or merely the quality of the beef we had for dinner, Daniel did not pander to my opinions or put me down in a patronising way as so many men did with their wives, but spoke and listened to me always as though I were a person of intelligence whose words merited his whole attention. I discovered he had a rather dry sense of humour too. As we grew more comfortable together, this often expressed itself in gentle teasing. And he was incredibly, wholehcartedly generous. By the time we reached Exeter I had a box full of gifts he had pressed upon me. I had only to admire a shawl, a pair of gloves, some pretty knick-knack in a shop window and he would sweep me inside and order the shopkeeper to show us the finest of his goods so that I could make my choice from them. 'What is money for if it is not to be enjoyed?' he would say when I protested at the extravagance. Then one day, with that wry, somewhat cynical smile I was coming to know so well he said, 'My dear Sophy, I am doing this for purely selfish reasons. It gives me pleasure to see you happy. Bear with me in this small weakness of mine, I beg you. And while we are on the subject, I have always felt that it must be uncomfortable, if not degrading, for a wife to have to account to her husband for every penny she spends. I intend that once we are settled you shall have an allowance to do with as you please, and it is so long since I had to consider . . .' He hesitated. He had meant to say 'a wife' I am sure, but smoothly went on, 'well, let us say I am unacquainted with the cost of the necessities and fripperies a woman needs to keep her comfortable and happy, so you must be sure to tell me if you need more.'

It was the first time he had come close to any mention of his first wife since the evening in the Vaiseys' library. It could have been out of respect for my sensibilities that he did not speak of her, but I knew it was more likely that her loss was still too painful to contemplate. I felt sad for him and more than ever determined to make him a good and useful wife.

'Daniel, you are in a fair way to spoiling me dreadfully,' I said. 'And as I am perfectly used to practising what Miss Smythe at school called "useful economy" you may be sure I shall feel myself in paradise if I have more than two shillings to myself at the month's end.'

'Oh, I think you may rely on a little more than two shillings,' he said, gravely. 'Maybe even so much as two and sixpence three farthings. So take care such a vast amount does not go to your head.'

'I will try not to let it,' I answered equally soberly, 'though the very thought of those extra three farthings makes me quite giddy.'

We enjoyed many such teasing exchanges, though the full extent of Daniel's generosity was only brought home to me when we arrived in Exeter. He scarcely gave me time to settle into the lodgings he had bespoken in Cathedral Yard before he whisked me off on a mysterious journey down a maze of nearby alleys. In a narrow street of venerable houses he led me into an ancient, timber-framed building and up a narrow, dusty staircase. There in the workshop that occupied the whole of the first storey I was bowed by Mr Watkins, the jeweller, to a seat in the window while one of his apprentices spread out on the table before my dazzled eyes the adornments that Daniel had ordered for me as a wedding gift.

'Though if there is anything here, Sophy, that you do not like,' Daniel put in quickly, 'please feel at liberty to say so, and we shall order something different.'

'No, please!' I found my voice at last, though it was a little husky. 'I . . . I am overwhelmed. Everything is so . . . so beautiful. Oh, Daniel, can all this really be for me? I have never owned anything so fine.'

'It is all for you, my dear,' he said warmly. 'And if you should care to try on the different pieces we may see if any adjustments are necessary.'

There was a necklace of pearls and a silver brooch, delicately chased. If Daniel had chosen but one of these items for me I would have thought myself lucky indeed. But my eyes were drawn in wonder to the finest pieces of all, a set of necklace, ring and earrings. Square-cut topaz and intricately fashioned gold glowed against the black velvet cloth on which they were placed like splinters and whorls of captured sunlight.

I hardly dared touch them. It was Daniel who lifted the necklace and fastened it about my neck, slid the ring on my finger and held one of the earbobs against the lobe of my ear so that I might see the effect in the mirror that the apprentice held.

The light slanting in from the window glimmered against the golden translucence of the topaz, throwing a faint warm reflection from the stone in the earring into the hollow beneath my cheek. The ring on my hand fitted snug and heavy against my wedding band. The necklace lay over the modestly high neck of my brown dress, but I could imagine exactly how it would look and feel lying warm and perfect against my skin.

'Perfection!' Mr Watkins exclaimed, echoing my own thoughts. 'I see now why Mr Penhale insisted upon stones of that particular shade. Why, Mrs Penhale, the colour complements your complexion in a way that is both subtle and agreeable whereas anything more showy would not have suited at all. I do congratulate you on your good taste, Mr Penhale for – and this is in confidence, mind – I do admit that some gentlemen I have the pleasure of dealing with have tendencies towards ostentation rather than quality and suitability for the lady's style.'

Such salesman's flattery would have made me smile had he not touched exactly upon the truth.

'I hardly know what to say,' I said when eventually I found my voice. 'Nobody ever gave me a present of such magnificence.'

'You are satisfied?'

'Satisfied! How could I not be?' An errant impulse, totally contrary to my nature, and born of the surprise and pleasure in his generosity, made me want to leap recklessly to my feet, fling my arms around his neck and spill out my thanks, laughing and crying together. I suppressed it instantly, shocked that I could even contemplate such a flamboyant and embarrassing action as embracing my husband in public when the whole tenor of our marriage was against even a private display of that nature. I was, too, uneasily aware that I had seen Mama more than once acting in that unbridled, childish way when some trinket she had been given momentarily pleased her. And, like a child, she would carelessly dispose of the gift when she had tired of its donor, selling it without a second thought when she was low in funds. I had no doubt that Sir Richard's emeralds would go the same way if she grew bored and restless under his patronage and she had a mind to be on her travels again. So my thanks to Daniel were restrained, yet I felt I must make some gesture to show him how deep was my delight in his gift. That evening, even though it had been an exhausting day and we intended merely a light, leisurely supper before retiring early, I dressed as carefully as if we were going to some fashionable soiree.

Daniel was in our private parlour, long legs stretched before the fire that had been lit against the evening chill, absorbed in the copy of the *Flying Post* he had purchased that afternoon. Our bedchamber lay across a small landing and, as I fastened the tiny buttons down the bodice of my dress, I heard the scurry of footsteps and the clink of china as the maid came upstairs to set the supper table, then the sound of her hasty steps back down the stairs. Almost time to make my grand entrance. I lifted the topaz necklace from its velvet-lined casket and put it on, then the earrings, and turned this way and that to see the full effect in the mirror.

After so many years living in countries where spring was blissfully warm and summers long and hot, I felt the cold and was inclined to keep the less agreeable temperatures of an English spring at bay with warm gowns and shawls. Tonight I had made the sacrifice of putting on one of the new summer dresses I had ordered for my trousseau and, though my arms and neck felt uncomfortably exposed, it allowed me to display Daniel's gift to full advantage. The silk gauze of the gown was of a tawny yellow with a fine self-stripe which I had at first rejected as being too light in colour, the material too delicate. But the dressmaker, tactfully, had persuaded me that it suited me very well and styled in the simple way I preferred would be most appropriate for summer days in the country. I saw now that she was right and, being more worldly in these matters, had understood better than I, though I was learning fast, that it was no longer necessary to consider everything for its serviceability and hard-wearing qualities.

I crossed the landing a little nervously and went into the parlour, opening the door softly. For a moment Daniel did not notice I was there. Then, shaking out the newspaper in order to turn the page, he glanced up and saw me.

I dropped a deep curtsey. I had wanted to be very solemn and dignified in order to show him that I was worthy of the honour he did me in giving me such a valuable gift. But try as I might, I could not hold back my smile. I felt it spread across my face in an unbecomingly fatuous beam.

'Sophy!' he said, rising to his feet and casting the paper on one side. 'Sophy, why you look charming. What a pretty gown. How well that colour suits you.'

His eyes were warm with genuine appreciation. I was suddenly shy under that sea-blue gaze and when he came forward, raised my hand and bowed over it, I felt hot colour flood my cheeks as his lips brushed against my fingers in the lightest of kisses. I scarcely knew how to respond, I was so unused to compliments on my appearance. And never before had Daniel made such an impulsively affectionate gesture towards me. But then he stepped back, considering me with one dark eyebrow raised and said, coolly teasing, 'Are you sure you are not the seventh child of a seventh child? For I cannot believe it is sheer coincidence that you have a dress that so beautifully matches the topaz stones.'

'Sheer coincidence it is, Daniel, for I am the most earth-bound of women,' I assured him, relieved to be able to take refuge in light banter. 'Though perhaps the dressmaker might have been a creature secretly given to crystal-gazing or prophesy by the stars, for it was she who persuaded me to choose this shade.'

'Ah, that will explain it. She was, no doubt, some exotic gypsy creature, a-swirl with gaudy skirts and jangling bracelets and with a good trade in lucky charms and clothes pegs.'

'To be sure, though she was disguised well enough in black bombazine and her apprentices were well trained to hide all evidence of the clothes-peg trade whenever a respectable customer came near.'

He nodded with pretended solemnity. 'A wily race, the Romanies.' A tap at the door and the maid staggered in with yet another laden tray and a waft of tempting, savoury smells. And Daniel said, so softly he might have been speaking his thoughts aloud, 'But I am reassured by your declaration that you are earthbound. Take care not to change, Sophy. I have no liking for fanciful indulgence in prognostication and phantasms born of too vivid an imagination, for confusion and distress are the natural companions of these foolish activities.' Some unidentifiable emotion flickered in the depths of his eyes, and for all the quietness of his voice there was an underlying note of steel in it. 'Do not ever be tempted by outside influences to become something other than the practical, level-headed woman you are. That would not do at all. No indeed.' An instant of stillness when not even the rustle of the maid's skirts penetrated the silence, then he was smiling, bowing me to the table, concerned that I should take the chair closest to the fire, though I assured him that I was perfectly warm and comfortable and it was merely a stray draught that had made me shiver as I did.

Of course, without my shawl and in such a summery gown, I was bound to feel every draught. What else should it be? Yet the chill lingered for a while after the door was tightly closed and the fire stoked up by the maid before she left us to our supper of lamb cutlets and roasted parsnips. Daniel was his usual courteous, kind self, urging me to another helping and insisting on heaping yellow scalded cream, a most delectable confection, on to the excellent junket which followed.

'It is wickedly rich and filling,' I said, laughing a protest. 'If Devonshire food is all as good as this, I shall have need of new gowns every week for I shall soon outgrow the old ones.'

'I have to say,' he said gravely, 'that unfortunately Mrs Venables, my housekeeper in Plymouth, keeps a good table, which has suited me well enough in the past. And Mrs Dagget at Kildower is turning out to be in much the same generous mould. You are at liberty, of course, as the new mistress, to take either of them to task for feeding me too well, or to make other alterations as you think necessary, given the need to conserve your wardrobe.'

'Wardrobe or no wardrobe, I would not presume to make any changes without consultation with the ladies concerned,' I said, serious now because it was a matter that had given me much thought in the past. 'I have been a silent observer too often in houses where the mistress was high-handed with the servants and ignorant of their sensibilities. It makes for nothing but trouble below stairs and above. For neither the youngest kitchen maid nor the grandest butler will give willing service if they are treated as though they have no more feelings than pieces of furniture.'

He looked pleased. 'The Daggets – Dagget is my coach-man – have not been with me any length of time, but Mrs Venables is a widow without relatives and has been with me since I bought the Plymouth house in order to be close to my business. The house in Nutmeg Street is as much her home as it is mine, even though she has tended to fuss over me like a mother hen. In particular I should not like to have her upset.'

'Then I shall tread lightly.'

'Good, though I think you will find her amenable. Her nature is generous and her inclination is to be helpful. She looks forward, I know, to welcoming you.' He turned his head towards the window. The blinds were not yet drawn and the great black bulk of the cathedral could be made out against the darkening sky beyond. His face was expressionless in profile, the high cheekbones, the long straight nose, the sweep of his flaxen hair seeming to be carved from stone. Then he said in a level voice, 'At Kildower I have not been so fortunate. Apart from old Zack Bligh, whom only death will part from the gardens he has brought back to a singular beauty, only Kensa's nurse, Jess Southcote, has remained faithful over the years. It is her love for the child, of course, that keeps her loyal. Others have not been so stalwart. Cooks, maids and governesses have come and gone, disliking the isolation of the house, falling to petty squabbles and feuds and rumours, I know not what. Up till now the Daggets have proved reliable, though as I say, they have only been with me since last summer. I took something of a chance with them, because they lost their last post due to Dagget suffering a bad kicking from a horse. He was many months recovering and still has weakness in the arm and leg that were broken. However, his duties are light, with only one horse, and a good lad from the village to help him. The three maids are very young. They manage adequately, under Mrs Dagget's supervision. But with all the unfortunate experiences I have had with servants at Kildower I have learned to place no great stakes on any of them staying loyal for long.'

I said firmly, 'I would not like to make any judgements before I have lived in the house and seen for myself how things stand.'

He remained staring beyond the window and said slowly, 'I have not spoken to you of my first wife, Sophy, and I should not wish you to think me disloyal to her memory if I say that she was lax with the servants. It is merely that I state a fact. She was very young when we married and her family, though once influential in the district, had fallen on hard times. Well, that is no matter, except that she was unused to servants and they took advantage of her youth and sweet nature, becoming lazy and insolent. And she had the same fragility of body and spirit that my daughter has inherited. She ailed a great deal both before and after Kensa's birth, which naturally made her prey to those who had no conscience about abusing her trust.' He sighed. 'I had hoped that she would learn by experience to cope. Perhaps she might have done in time. But it was not to be and I suppose, because I must be away so much and because I worry about the welfare of my daughter and my old father, I have tended to be impatient with any inefficiency or misdemeanour that has come to my notice.' He turned his gaze back to me. 'So you see, Sophy, one way or another Kildower, though very beautiful, has always had a certain lack of tranquillity within its sturdy walls. Never truly been the comfortable, restful house I have wished it to be.'

I was moved by the sadness that now seemed to have fallen on him. 'I give you my promise, Daniel,' I said softly, 'that I shall do everything in my power to make Kildower a happy place.'

'I have every confidence that you will,' he answered. 'I have felt that from the first.' But his sober mood did not lift. He remained quiet, and when we retired to bed he quickly turned to his side and slept without troubling me.

My body was becoming accustomed to the act of intimacy and no longer tended to the pain and soreness that had accompanied the loss of my maidenhead, though I was still embarrassed with the indignity of the process. Yet tonight, contrarily, Daniel's failure even to press the usual brief good-night kiss on my forehead left me feeling restless and distressed because I was unable to comfort him and drive away the unhappy shadows raised by the thoughts of his first wife. He slept restlessly too and though I dozed for a while I was awakened by the sound of his voice muttering in some dream. Sleepily I raised myself against the pillows.

The moon was full and despite the drawn blinds there was enough light in the room to see Daniel clearly as he lay on his back amid the dishevelled sheets. He was sound asleep but caught still in his dream, murmuring disjointed phrases and moving his head from side to side on the pillow. I leaned over him and touched his face, smoothing back the tangled hair that lay damp against his cheek, meaning to soothe him as I would have done any child in my care. The result was unexpected and frightening.

He moved quick as lightning. One hand caught itself in my hair, bringing my face down to his. The other wrapped itself tight around my shoulders so that I could not escape.

And he was kissing me. Such kisses as I had never before experienced. His mouth moved with infinite tenderness across my throat like the soft caress of butterfly wings, then up over the line of my jaw to my mouth. 'I have waited so long, my darling,' he murmured against my lips. 'I thought you were forever lost.' His kiss, then, was not tender at all, but fierce and desperate, and there was an almost fevered intensity in the way his fingers tore at the neat plait with which I bound my wayward tresses each night and tugged and loosed my hair, then slid down my neck and wrenched at the buttons that kept my nightgown modestly fastened to seek the heavy curve of my breast.

He was a stranger. All courtesy, all control, all gentleness abandoned. I wrenched my head away and cried, 'Daniel! No! You are dreaming!'

My voice must have penetrated his consciousness. He released me so suddenly that I tumbled back from him on to the bed. But still the dream – the nightmare – claimed him. Her name was an anguished sigh escaping his lips. 'Meraud ... Meraud ...' Then, blindly, he half-raised himself, turned to where I lay rigid and breathless and sank his head onto my shoulder, as though seeking comfort.

I could do no other than wrap my arms about him and hold him safe until, at last, his breathing became calm and steady. Only then did I allow myself to sleep. But when I awoke in the cool dawn light the memory of those abandoned kisses was so strong and disturbing that I could not lie still. So I rose, made a hasty toilette, dressed in a plain dark gown before Daniel stirred and was sitting quietly by the window when he at last roused from sleep. He smiled, yawned, stretched his arms and said, 'Good morning, Sophy. Have I overslept? You should have woken me.'

Everything was normal again. And everything was changed. Not for Daniel, who apparently had no recollection of what had happened in his dreaming state, but for me, because the change was in myself. I felt as though a barrier had been breached in my emotions, a threshold crossed, leaving me strangely exposed and vulnerable. I disliked the sensation greatly, but, used as I was to putting a front on my emotions, I hid my discomposure so well that Daniel saw nothing in my appearance or demeanour to suggest that I was at all upset. By the time we had eaten a leisurely breakfast and emerged into the mild sunshine, the events of the night were for me also beginning to fade to the quality of a dream.

* * *

Daniel had no more sombre moments or bad dreams and during the rest of our stay in Exeter my spirits were raised to a level of contentment that I had seldom before experienced. The spring weather continued breezy and mild and all Exeter seemed to be afoot as Daniel took me on walking excursions about the narrow streets overhung with ancient timbered houses and the rosy-red brick of smart new dwellings laid out in crescents and pleasant terraces. We strolled the airy heights of the Northernhay Gardens in the shadow of Rougemont Castle, and viewed the rich meadows and market gardens stretching away to the distant, encircling hills. There was an air of bustle and prosperity within the ancient red stone walls that girded the city even though, as Daniel told me, the serge trade on which Exeter's wealth was founded was now seriously declined. 'But it is becoming quite the thing for colonels and admirals and gentlemen retiring from long service in the colonies to take up residence here. The mildness of the climate and the wealth of genteel amusements available to those with money to indulge in them recommend themselves to persons wishing an agreeable and pleasant place in which to end their days.'

'I had no idea that Exeter would be so beautiful and with such an interesting history,' I said one day as we paused in passing, as we so often did, to admire the carvings on the west front of the cathedral. I thought it more tactful not to mention that until we had actually crossed the border into Devonshire I had worried that Mama's description would prove to be right and that I should discover the whole county to be dreary, dull and backward, as she had insisted. I scolded myself for not knowing better than to be half-convinced by her exaggerated opinions when I had long understood that she had difficulty in separating fact from the highly coloured fictions with which she preferred to decorate her recollections. 'I find the cathedral quite as impressive as Salisbury. This west front is magnificent, and I get such a sense of history standing here before it, knowing that Roman centurions must have tramped across the spot, as well as the Celtic Dumnonii before them. They perhaps worshipped at some pagan temple here, for I understand that our oldest churches and cathedrals are often built in the vicinity of an ancient holy shrine or sacred spring.'

'Indeed.' He smiled down at me. 'And have you thought that, with your Devonshire roots, one of your twelfth-century ancestors might have stood where you stand now, and looked in awe at the masons working on Bishop Grandisson's paeon of praise in stone?'

My imagination was caught by the idea. I turned away from the tiered ranks of saints and angels motionless in their niches and narrowed my eyes as though my vision might pierce the crowded brick and timber and tile of the buildings that crowded the fringes of the cathedral ground. 'And long before that,' I said, softly, 'perhaps some native forebear, come to worship at the shrine on this green hill, might have paused in surprise to see sunlight glittering distantly on lance and shield as the Roman legions advanced.'

I saw it clearly in my mind. A day, perhaps like today, of bursts of sun and racing cloud shadows, and a woman shielding her eyes against the light to look down to the river coiling round the foot of the hill, and feeling the first apprehensive tingle of fear at the steady approach of the alien invaders.

I would have lingered, intrigued by this novel idea, but Daniel was impatient to be on time for the lecture we were attending and we walked on briskly towards Southernhay.

In recent years I had given little thought to my ancestry, beyond a faint regret, left over from childhood envy of Italian playmates who belonged to large, comforting, loving tribes of relations, that because Mama had severed herself so completely from her family and was so adamant in her dislike I had never been allowed any contact with my grandparents when they were still alive. Now it came to me strongly that there was no harm in allowing myself the extravagance of becoming warmed by the thought of my forebears. I should never now know anything of them, but there was something comfortable in the thought that by blood ties alone I was connected to this lush and pleasant countryside and that I truly belonged here in a way that I had never belonged anywhere else in my nomadic life.

I settled to listen to the lecture, entitled 'Steam and its Particular Application to the Railway Locomotive', though my mind tended to stray from what I was sure was a most instructive and educational talk into realms of fanciful imaginings about my forebears. I jumped as a minor explosion from the apparatus on the dais brought me back to earth. Several ladies similarly affected emitted squeaks of alarm and there were even a few gasps from the many gentlemen present. I set myself after that to concentrate on understanding the role of valves and regulators and boilers, though I confess I could not bring myself to the rapt attention that Daniel displayed. When the talk ended, Daniel was keen to examine the apparatus more closely. 'And I should like to take the opportunity of asking the speaker if he is able to visit Plymouth. I have told you, my dear, of the group of forward-looking friends who meet from time to time to debate all manner of modern scientific and philosophical matters. I am sure they would welcome a chance to engage Mr Turner to repeat his exccllent discourse. Should you mind waiting a few moments longer?'

'Not at all. We have no need to hurry.'

'It has all been so stimulating, has it not?'

'It is certainly remarkable to think that one day it may be possible to travel on a permanent way to even the most remote corners of the country,' I said, hoping that I should not be obliged to comment too particularly on the precise workings of the steam engine, which were a little unclear in my mind. But Daniel was too carried away by enthusiasm to notice any vagueness on my part.

'Think of it! The comfort and convenience of a mode of haulage that does not become exhausted after a few miles, or cast its shoes or bog down in a muddy road, but achieves a steady rate of twenty miles an hour or more whatever the weather.'

'Forgive my interruption, sir, but I must inject a note of caution.' A stout gentleman who had been seated next to Daniel during the lecture and had hovered at his elbow when we moved from our seats now thrust himself forward, quivering with indignation. 'I am a medical man and I find this obsession with speed exceedingly disturbing. The human body is not designed to cope with such unnatural forces!'

'I respect your greater knowledge in these matters,' Daniel said, the light of battle in his eye, 'but I would have thought that the only danger lay in accidental injury such as the unfortunate business at the inauguration of the Liverpool and Manchester Railway.'

'Mr Huskisson's death should be taken as a warning. One cannot interfere with the forces of nature without the risk of incurring severe penalties.'

'Come, come, sir. One man accidentally falling under the wheels of a locomotive, though to be regretted, must surely not be construed as a condemnation of progress.'

'Progress? What price progress if people are submitted to forces that can only wreak suffering on the human body? Many of my colleagues agree that at continuous speeds of more than fifteen miles an hour the bony skeleton of a man will become unnaturally bent by the forces placed upon it and the consequence will be disastrous injury to the internal organs.'

'Mr Stephenson seems not to have suffered any harmful effects and it is some months since he won his purse of five hundred pounds for attaining a maximum speed of twenty-five miles an hour in his Rocket engine.'

'*Continuous* speed, I would emphasise, has never been tested upon the human frame. I shall make that point clearly to our lecturer before I leave.' Heads bent in animated argument, they moved towards the knot of people gathered round the apparatus. The room was emptying and alone for the moment I wandered to the window.

The lecture room was on the upper floor and I looked down idly on to the street. Late afternoon sun slanted on to be-plumed bonnets and sober beaver hats as people left from the door below to hurry away over the cobbles or climb into one of the line of carriages. A cumbersome antique coach lumbered away bearing off its elderly occupants, and as it did so I noticed a man cross the road and dodge under the noses of the horses pulling the next carriage into position before the doorway. He earned the curses of the driver, who raised his whip and with a flick of the wrist caught the brim of the man's battered hat and whisked it down into a nearby heap of fresh, still steaming horse manure. The coachman guffawed but the man ignored him, bent to retrieve his hat, examined it, shook it free of dung and set it back on his head. Only then did he slowly pace towards the carriage and speak to the coachman. There was no way of knowing what he said. It was quietly spoken, a few words only, but it had a remarkable effect on the coachman. The jeering bluster seemed to die on his lips and he shrank down in his fancy, gold-braided coat as though the stuffing had been knocked out of him.

Then the man stepped aside onto the pavement below, slowly raised his head and looked straight at me.

Recognition was instant. And mutual. He knew me. His smile told me that. It held no warmth but merely twisted his mouth to a grotesque parody of humour in his gaunt, weather-beaten face. He was not an old man as I had supposed from the whiteness of his shaggy mane of hair, yet there was nothing youthful about him. He was a man hardened by experience, embittered by adversity, worn down by hardship. But strong. And purposeful. And full of a hatred so intense that it was almost palpable.

It was perhaps for only seconds that we stared at each other through the smeary glass, yet so strong and clear was the impression I had of him that when I stepped hurriedly back from the window I had the strangest feeling that he could see me still and knew the way my heart beat as though I had suffered some sudden shock.

I told myself not to be so silly. Perhaps it was not the person I thought. Perhaps I was mistaken.

It was no mistake. My heartbeat slowed. I was able to review the incident more calmly. I knew quite definitely that it was the man I had first seen standing outside the church in Highgate. Now he was here. Well, that was not so unusual a coincidence. I could almost bring myself to believe that some quirk of fate, not unknown among people who travelled a great deal, had caused our paths to cross in Highgate and again in Exeter. What was less easy to explain away was the impression that he knew me and that it had come as no surprise to him to see me standing at the window.

And for the sensation of hatred for me that had seemed to flow from him I had no explanation at all. How could I

have endowed a man I had never met and whom, so far as I
knew, I had never wronged, with such feelings? I looked
across at Daniel, still absorbed in conversation with the
lecturer. Kind, practical, generous Daniel. Who had told me
himself that he had no time for foolish fancies. There was
nothing to be gained by telling him of the incident or he
would begin to believe that I had tendencies towards the
kind of vapourish, hysterical behaviour that silly women
employed in order to display the delicacy of their feminine
sensibilities. No, indeed. Why, if I had myself listened to
some similar story I should have dismissed the teller of it as
ninepence short of a shilling.

There was no sign of the stranger when we eventually
emerged into the street. There was no possibility – no reason
to believe – I should ever see him again.

But in both particulars I could not have been more wrong.

Daniel hired a post chaise for the last stage of our journey
to Plymouth. 'I am glad you see south Devonshire at its
best,' he said as we bowled away from Exeter under a breezy
blue sky, with cloud shadows chasing across the green hills
and valleys. 'Everything is so fresh and colourful at this
time of the year, and see how clearly the Dartmoor heights
are etched against the horizon. They look benign today, do
they not? But it is harsh country up there. When the clouds
mass over the moor and the rain sweeps down it is a bleak
place for the traveller to be. Worse still in the ice and snow
of winter.' He shook his head. 'There are many who appreciate
Dartmoor for its wild beauty, but I should not care to stay for
long among those bare tors. I was born within sight of the sea
and I have always had an inclination to live where the salt air is
strongest and the climate less formidable.'

I gazed up at the purple-brown silhouette of the moor

rising behind the gentler landscape of fields and wooded slopes. Somewhere under its southerly edge was Bovey Tracey, Mama's birthplace. My father's, too. Where I, my mother's second daughter, had first seen the light of day and briefly lived before Mama had carried me off when she decided to pursue her own adventures. And somewhere on that same moor my mother had lain with William Woodley and conceived her first child, my sister Juliana, whose fate it was to be born in disgrace and to be disposed of in a way most convenient to those who wished no reminders of her or the reason for her existence.

The resentment and hurt I had experienced at my mother's announcement had faded to a faint, aching sadness. It stirred now as we rattled along the winding road, with the moor a constant brooding skyline to our right and, to the left, that particular lucidity of light in the sky that betokens the sea. But the ache now was not so much for myself but for my abandoned sister. There was anger there, too, and a growing pity for the poor, helpless mite that she had been. I found myself praying, not for the first time, that she had been taken in by kindly people and raised as their own with love and understanding.

I had determined at first, for my own peace of mind, to put all thoughts of Juliana from my head, but she had come more and more into my consciousness. There was no form to her, no features, for I had not opened the box Mama had pressed upon me. I had buried it away at the bottom of my travelling trunk scarcely bearing to touch it leave alone examine whatever likeness of my sister it contained. But the fact of her existence could not be denied and her shadow, however amorphous, persisted in intruding into my thoughts. Particularly today, perhaps because I was at last returned to territory we both might honestly consider home.

I had no conscious memory of this Devonshire landscape, but I had the odd sense that something in my blood and my bones responded to the particular quality of light, recognised the generous contours of the rich pastures, the deep, primrose-starred hedgebanks, the woods and copses springing fresh with the soft pinks and mauves and acid greens of newly bursting leaves. I felt curiously familiar with everything I saw, from the cob and thatch of the cottages we passed to the cattle, sturdy and red as the earth itself, grazing in the meadows. It was as though the land was claiming me back as its own. Common sense told me that it was merely that Daniel had vividly described it beforehand, but the fancy would not leave me that I was linked to this land and it to me, as Juliana was. A fragile, will-o'-the-wisp bond with the half-sister whom I had never known and likely never would know.

There was comfort in that sense of kinship for, despite the freshness of the day and the variety of the scenery, I grew increasingly nervous with every passing mile. The pleasant limbo in which Daniel and I had drifted for the last two weeks was coming to an end. Easy weeks, devoted to the pleasing of each other without the concerns and distractions of everyday life. Today we must both step back into the real world with all its responsibilities. For Daniel it was merely to take up the threads of the life he was used to, but I had to learn to accommodate myself to a completely new way of living and, with the prospect almost upon me, I could not help but quail a little.

I was distracted from these uncomfortable thoughts when we stopped at Ashburton, a prosperous-looking little town on the fringe of the moor, to partake of a light luncheon, but they returned in full measure when we climbed back into the chaise for the final stage of our journey.

Daniel's expectations of me were high and as we clattered the last few miles into Plymouth I felt them for the first time as a burden. Suppose I failed him? Oh, I knew in the practical matters of housekeeping or attending to the physical well-being and education of his daughter I should manage well enough and I was too self-reliant, too conscious of my good fortune, to become clingy and demanding, and ultimately tiresome, as a more sheltered young woman unused to standing on her own two feet might understandably do if married life turned out less satisfactorily than her rosy expectations had suggested. It was to our advantage that Daniel and I had a calm, thoroughly commonsensical understanding on which to build our marriage. There were certainly no romantic illusions to cloud my vision. All the same, I wondered if I had been unduly optimistic in thinking myself capable of encompassing his family within the same web of affectionate understanding that bound me to Daniel. I was not naive. I did not expect that his beloved daughter and his old father would offer me their trust and respect straight off, leave alone their affection. All that must be earned. But suppose – and it did not seem so outrageous a supposition, unnerved as I was at the imminent prospect of my first meeting with my stepdaughter – as time went on I was unable to strike up any sort of pleasant relationship with either of them? How would that then reflect on Daniel's view of me and our marriage?

Then we were in Plymouth and I tried to concentrate on what Daniel was saying. He was leaning forward in his seat, keen to point out various points of interest as we plunged in among streets brisk with traffic and people.

'That is the road that links Plymouth to Devonport, which is still known as Dock by many people, with contempt, alas, for Plymouthians consider themselves superior to the inhabitants of Devonport and Stonehouse. You will have a glimpse of the citadel in a moment . . . there! The fortress lies on a headland above Sutton Pool and the Barbican. And here is St Andrew's Church . . . the Theatre Royal . . . the Athenaeum . . .'

I nodded as though it were not all passing me in a blur. Then we were turning into a short street of modest terraced houses on the hill sloping down behind the Hoe, the houses lifted above ordinariness by the pleasing proportions of their windows and porticoes. The horses clattered to a halt, and Daniel was opening the door, leaping out before the carriage had stopped juddering on its springs.

'Journey's end, Sophy!'

He held out his hand to help me down, and there was a sudden impatience in the set of his shoulders, the turn of his head towards the house with the open door and the dark-clad woman waiting quietly within.

'This is Mrs Venables, my dear.'

The woman, stick-thin, with iron-grey hair taut under the frill of her cap, smiled warmly, bobbing a curtsey. 'Welcome to Plymouth, Mrs Penhale. And Mr Penhale, sir, 'tis good to have you back.'

'My daughter, Mrs Venables? Where is Kensa?' And that eager, impatient glance beyond her down the narrow hallway.

'Oh, sir, the dear little soul was took poorly again a few days' since, though her's recovered and you'm not to go fretting for she's well on the mend. But Jess Southcote thought it best not to take a chance bringing her over the water. There's letters from her and Miss Kensa herself that'll no doubt ease your mind. I've put them in the parlour, where I've refreshments ready and waiting, for you'll be parched after all that journeying.'

I saw disappointment leach the eagerness from his face.
I had an urge to take his hand and pat it comfortingly and
though, later, I could see that perhaps the impulse was born
out of my own relief that I had been given a little more
breathing space before I should have to face my stepdaughter,
it might have been better if I had obeyed my instincts and
showed him by one simple, silent gesture that I sympathised
with his disappointment, even if it had taken him by surprise
and possibly embarrassed him. Instead I spoke too briskly,
the practised teacher in me automatically responding as it
would to a child suffering a minor mishap who must not be
allowed to mope lest moping bred mischief. 'No matter,
Daniel,' I said. 'I am truly sorry, of course, that Kensa has
been ill, but we shall meet soon enough, I dare say.'

He narrowed his eyes as he looked at me, straight brows
drawn down in a puzzled frown. 'No matter?' he queried
softly. And it was clear, in his voice, in his face, that what
he felt was more, much more, than simple disappointment.
He cared most desperately and deeply that his beloved
daughter was not here. Then he turned from me sharply and
said in an overly polite voice, 'Mrs Venables, kindly show
Mrs Penhale to the bedchamber so she may remove the dust
of travel before we take our refreshment.'

He immediately strode outside to supervise the unloading
of our baggage and I followed Mrs Venables upstairs, feeling
rebuked and chastened. I berated myself for underestimating
Daniel's sensitivity about his daughter when it was only
natural that he should be upset that she was not waiting here
for us. He must have been yearning to see her again, this
child who was the living reminder of his first marriage and
his adored first wife.

In the bedchamber, I removed my bonnet and pelisse,
rinsed the grime of the journey from my face and hands and

vowed, in future, to tread more circumspectly with Daniel where Kensa was concerned. Which resolution brought all my earlier apprehensions back in full measure. For if I could so easily and unwittingly upset him when I had not even met Kensa, what would be the case when I properly assumed the role of stepmama?

We rested but two nights in Plymouth before we travelled on to Cornwall. 'I shall not be able to stay at Kildower, Sophy,' Daniel said somewhat grimly when he returned from a visit to the brewery. 'A host of problems has occurred in my absence.'

'I am used to travelling alone, Daniel,' I reminded him. 'I should not mind going on to Kildower by myself if you feel obliged to remain here.'

'Out of the question,' he said curtly, then gave me a rueful smile. 'Forgive me. I should not take out my frustration on you. It is just that I so hate my plans being upset. It seems that ever since we set foot in Plymouth everything has gone awry. No, no. It would not be right for you to go to Kildower unescorted this first time. I should wish to introduce you properly to your new home.'

And to see for yourself if Kensa is making such good progress as the communications from Kildower insist, I thought but did not say. Since that little *contretemps* on our arrival I had carefully avoided upsetting him with any remark which might have given offence. Thankfully, his displeasure with me had not lasted long. He had remained stiffly polite for a while but as the tea and the excellent sandwiches Mrs Venables had prepared revived our spirits we became easy with each other again. Perhaps it was merely tiredness that had made him react so sternly. Perhaps not. Either way. I wanted nothing more to spoil this homecoming.

For I quickly discovered that I liked this little house very well indeed and if it had been our final destination I should have happily settled down here feeling well pleased at the convenience of the location between the open spaces of the Hoe and the main attractions and thoroughfares of the town, all of which begged exploration.

It was a double-fronted house faced with silvery-grey stone like the rest of Nutmeg Street. On the attic floor Mrs Venables had her room. In the basement were the kitchen, scullery and washhouse, which opened out onto a flagged yard where the linen could blow on fine days and where Mrs Venables' marmalade cat, reputed to be a fine mouser, defended his territory by patrolling the top of the high stone walls against all incursions by neighbouring toms. There was nothing dauntingly grand about the principal rooms on the two middle floors. A parlour to the left of the narrow hall ran the full depth of the house so that morning and evening it would catch the sun through its sash windows. A dining parlour lay to the right with a smaller room behind it that Daniel used as his study, and upstairs were three bedchambers, as sparsely furnished as all the other rooms.

This sparseness pleased me. It was evident that Daniel had never given much attention to the house beyond ensuring it was kept in good repair and furnishing it with basic necessities. It was, after all, his secondary residence, a *pied-à-terre*, entirely suitable for a gentleman living alone who spent much of the time at his place of business. Consequently, it still seemed to hold the raw air of the new house it had been when Daniel had bought it eight years since, as though it waited for someone to impose a character upon its clean bare walls and polished floors and sparkling windows.

Nothing would have pleased me more than to stay here

Anne Goring

and set about turning the house into a proper home. I believe
Mrs Venables felt much the same for, apart from the weekly
visit from a woman who came to do the laundry, she spent a
great deal of time on her own. She was eager to show me
everything when we were together on that first morning,
from the row of geraniums that brightened the kitchen
window to the orderly contents of the linen cupboard on the
upper landing, delivering a commentary on everything we
saw and begging my opinion on various domestic matters.

'I could wish, ma'am, you was to stay a little longer,'
she said wistfully as we descended the stairs once more after
our leisurely tour of the house. 'Master, he'm a splendid
gentleman and generous to a fault, but no gentleman can be
expected to bother his head with such things as methods of
removing stains from crape or the scandalous price of best
butter, which a lady naturally has an understanding of.'

'Perhaps it will not be too long before we return,' I said.
'The little I have seen of Plymouth has only whetted my
appetite to see more. Such views from the Hoe when we
walked there last evening! And so much activity on the
water! It was a grand spectacle, with naval vessels moving
out on the tide and such a host of little boats bustling about
their affairs. I could have stood there an age, quite
fascinated.'

''Tes a view you never tire of,' Mrs Venables agreed,
nodding vigorously. 'Leastways, I never has and I've lived
in Plymouth all my life. There's always something to be
seen out on the Sound.'

I wandered back into the parlour, Mrs Venables at my
heels, and stared through the rain-washed window at a
passer-by being buffeted down the pavement by the wind.
'What a pity the weather has turned. I should have so much
enjoyed a good walk. Yesterday the air felt wonderfully fresh

86

after all those hours closed up in a stuffy carriage, so deliciously salty and invigorating that it was a pleasure to be out of doors.'

Mrs Venables dropped her voice confidentially. ''Tes what I've said to Master more than once. There's many an invalid brought here to take advantage of the sea breezes and goes away restored to good health, so I can see no good reason why Miss Kensa should come to any harm through spending a bit more time in the town. Perhaps you can persuade him, ma'am, to bring the dear little maid for a good long stay. Oh, I know Kildower is a fine house and the countryside is reckoned handsome, but 'tes my belief that all they trees roundabout trap in the miasmas and mists that rise up from the water. 'Tes a place, you see, full of streams and ponds, with the creek close by . . . and the house being set in a hollow means there's bound to be dampness, which is known to breed all manner of agues.'

'You have visited Kildower, then, Mrs Venables?' I said, alert to garner any scraps of information about my future home.

'Only the once, ma'am, in my early days here, back in 'twenty-four after a terrible November storm. Fair terrifying the gale o' wind and the rain and oh, my dear life, great ships broken up to matchwood on the shore as though they was toy boats smashed by a naughty lad. 'Twas a sorrowful sight to see. We was lucky up here to suffer no damage for the lower town was flooded two and three feet deep. Howsomever, a lot of trees was uprooted and a great old elm come down over to Kildower, smashing some of the roof and near killing the cook – it fell on the attics, see, where the servants was sleeping. They maids was a silly, addle-headed lot o' local girls who was that frighted they ran out all hysterical and wouldn't go back indoors for believing . . .' she hesitated, sending me a sharp, measuring look from under the crisp frill of her cap, '. . . well, for believing there was ill luck in the house and if they stayed they'd come to harm.'

'Ill luck?'

'The only bad luck,' she said briskly, 'was that the tree was an old elm that looked sound enough but had a heart that was rotted through. 'Tes a wonder it stood as long as it did! Anyways, with they maids afearing to go back inside, and master that beside himself with the damage an' all, he sacked the lot of 'em on the spot. Trouble was, no one else local could be persuaded to set foot in the house either.' She gave a disparaging sniff and said with all the smug confidence of the town dweller, and one born and bred on the superior side of the Tamar at that, 'The Cornish are backward bumpkins in they country parts. Proper close and suspicious, man, woman and child. Can't nothing shake 'em if they gets wrong ideas in their heads. So Master fetched me and with the help of Jess Southcote we soon got the mess cleaned up and the place straight once the carpenters and tilers had mended the roof.'

'Miss Kensa's nurse is not a local woman, then?'

'Her's Devonshire born and bred. Barnstaple. Her's got some relatives living on a farm somewhere near Kildower, but her's a sensible woman and don't believe any of they daft tales. Bless you, ma'am, you're not to go dwelling on what I said about ill luck for neither of us suffered the smallest trouble from sleeping under Kildower's roof. Just the opposite, to be sure. For Master was that pleased when we'd got the house all ship-shape again that he give us extra on our wages!' She chuckled at the thought, then went on in her garrulous, friendly way, 'I don't doubt you'll be very comfortable at Kildower, but I do hopes, ma'am, as how you won't forget Nutmeg Street.'

'Of course not,' I said, realising with some amusement
that within the first hours of becoming mistress of my own
establishment I was already transgressing Miss Smythe's
precepts on domestic management. ('Deal with servants
fairly, but firmly, so that they will come to respect your
wise and superior authority as an arbiter in all domestic
matters. And never, *never* sink to gossiping with them. It
will have the most unfortunate consequences, leading as it
will to unnecessary familarity, as well as laxness and jealousy
below stairs.') I consoled myself with the thought that even
Miss Smythe would have had some trouble stopping Mrs
Venables' busy tongue, and to be honest I did not wish to.
There was such a cheerful innocence about her chatter that
I felt myself warming to her evident good nature. Besides
which, I dearly wanted to learn as much as I could of
Kildower and my new family from this willing source. So,
with a suitably casual air, I said, 'It is some time, I
understand, since Miss Kensa was in Plymouth.'

She sighed. 'It must be a good twelvemonth, poor little
moppet. Even then her hadn't been here above a day and a
night and her was took badly with a rash as itched and
tormented her something cruel to see. Master brought in
Doctor Smollet, who said 'twasn't naught contagious but
an overheating humour that had taken hold in her system
due to the excitement of the visit and 'twould all be cured
in a few days. Well, we did our best, me and Jess, dosing
her with senna and manna tea as the doctor had said would
clear her blood, and putting on the sulphur ointment he'd
left, but nothing seemed to touch it. In the end her was so
fretful wi' the itching and stinging and the sleepless nights
as Master took her back to Kildower. Sad 'twas, for he had
such plans for what they should do in Plymouth. An 'er, the

dear soul, had seemed so lively when 'er first come and that pleased to see her pa.'

'Poor child. But she improved when she returned to Kildower?'

'Within a week or two she was much better, though 'twas some time before the rash properly left her. So far as I know it never returned. But Master, he'm that anxious about her that 'till now – this being a special time to meet you, ma'am – he wouldn't take no chances. He seems to think 'twas the strength of the salt air as well as the excitement that set her off, for the worst of the rash was on her face and hands where they'd been exposed when they'd gone out walking together. But I believe like the good doctor that 'tes a general delicacy of the nerves that besets the maid and makes her liable to these upsets.' She chewed her lip a moment. 'P'raps I shouldn't say this, ma'am,' she said, 'but I feel that 'ad we persevered and kept her here in Nutmeg Street the ailment would have taken its course and she would have recovered her health just as fast as she did at Kildower. Oh, I know nerves is peculiar things and Miss Kensa takes after 'er ma, who was similarly afflicted wi' delicacy of this nature, but 'tes my belief that nerves is sometimes best not given in to or they never gets any tutorin' in becoming sensible, if you takes my meaning.'

'Quite.' I cleared my throat to prevent a laugh escaping at the vivid picture that my imagination supplied of Miss Smythe instructing a row or unruly nerves in decorum and good behaviour.

''Course, Miss Kensa's not had the advantage of brothers nor sisters, which makes a deal of difference, for the rough and tumble in families is like to toughen young 'uns.' She shook her head sadly, her thoughts leading her into other, more personal recollections. 'Ah, but, there's naught to compare wi' the sound of children's voices at play. 'Tes what I miss above all things since my own two lads growed and left. And I fear I'll never see my own grandchildren, which is a great sorrow. My youngest lad, he took the king's shilling and went out to India where a fever carried him off. The eldest went to seek his fortune in Americky, married a farmer's daughter in a place called Maryland and now has two babes and a little farm of his very own. I tries not to fret, for I'm a lucky woman in having such a good place here and my lad Jamie had he stayed would still be ploughing someone else's fields and living hand to mouth instead of being his own master. Still, when I visit my sister over to Stonehouse and sees her brood of grandchildren – for three of her five daughters live nearby – I can't help but wish that before Samuel, my dear young husband, was lost in the service of Lord Nelson at the great victory at Trafalgar, I might have been blessed with a daughter as well as my two infant boys. For it seems to me that girls are like to stay close at hand to become a comfort to their parents whereas boys must be off in search of adventure. 'Tes true enough what they say that a son's a son 'till he takes a wife, but a daughter's a daughter all of her life.'

Which was a precept, I thought dryly, that Mama would have liked me to take heed of, having entirely disregarded it herself. To distract Mrs Venables from these nostalgic thoughts that cast a shadow over her normally cheerful expression, I said, 'All that disturbance at Kildower when the tree fell must have greatly upset old Captain Penhale. I understand he spent many years in restoration of the house.'

'Oh, indeed, ma'am. Though I has to say I never saw much of the old gentleman, for he do live quietly in his own part of the house and Zack Bligh took up all his meals like he always do, for the old gentleman don't like being fussed over by women.'

'Zack Bligh? Is he not the gardener?'

'His main duties, to be sure, ma'am, are in the garden, but he's the Cap'n's man as well when the need arises. Not as the Cap'n needs much waiting on, for being a sailor he'm used to looking out for himself and likes to be solitary.' She chuckled. 'Zack and the Cap'n do argufy something terrible, but he's been at Kildower since the Cap'n first come there and he and the old gentleman understands each other's ways and 'abits.'

A gust of wind rattled the windows and sent a puff of smoke from the fire into the room. Mrs Venables hurried to poke the coals into a brighter flame. 'We'm had trouble lately with this chimney in a southerly blow. I reckon we shall have to get the sweep in, ma'am, with your permission. Oh, and if I might ask whether you think 'tes advisable to order new blinds for the front windows in here and the dining parlour. They'm getting fearful thin and I don't see as they'll last beyond this summer. And would 'ee, ma'am, take a look at the tablecloths. Master, he don't take much notice o' they sort of things so long as he has good food put before 'en, and not being in the way of inviting folk in up until now it hadn't mattered too much . . .'

So the conversation swung back to matters domestic and once I had set about sorting through a very poor and mismatched assortment of table linen, most of which seemed only fit for the ragbag, Mrs Venables had whisked away about her other duties, leaving me to make what I would of all that she had told me.

The rain did not ease, though the wind dropped in the night. The Tamar when we reached it the following morning was an uninviting stretch of sullen grey water under heavy skies and, because there was no breeze to lift the sails, the oarsmen on the ferry were forced to labour hard against the tide as we crossed to Torpoint on the Cornish side of the river. There were no fine, sparkling views to admire today. Clouds crouched low on the hills, obscuring all landmarks. The unremitting rain flapped against exposed skin like clammy wet muslin and hung in shifting veils over the wooden walls and jutting masts of the great warships moored along the river banks.

Daniel was very quiet, his face set, chin tucked down into the high green collar of his caped coat, beaver hat tilted well down over his eyes, as though the gloom of the day had penetrated into his soul and darkened his thoughts. Even when we achieved the shelter of the Kildower carriage which awaited us at Torpoint he remained abstracted, staring out of the window with half-closed eyes, his profile etched pale and sharp against the black leather with which the carriage was lined. It brought to my mind the thought that his features, the straight nose, the firmly shaped mouth, the high cheekbones, would not have been out of place depicted on some heroic classical statue of Greek mythology and involuntarily I remembered that first night of our marriage when I had first seen his body naked and beautiful in the golden candlelight.

For a moment there was an odd confusion in my thoughts, as though something of importance, some emotion, swirled up and then receded before I had chance to catch it. No doubt, I thought with a flash of irritation, it was to do with the misguided artistic ambitions that I had once harboured and which I had firmly put behind me. However much I tried not to do it I still tended to see everything in terms of light and shade, tone and colour and line, as Mama had taught me, to make of whatever I saw into a composition that was pleasing. That way of seeing was ingrained, as much a part of me, and as incurable, apparently, as the colour of my eyes or the unfortunate fineness of my hair. It grieved and annoyed me that I had so little control over it that I could not even look at my own husband without calculating how I should set about portraying him. And Daniel did not help at all by sitting so still and withdrawn like someone requested to hold a flattering pose and making no attempt at conversation or commenting on the passing scenery as he usually did.

I wrenched my gaze from his unheeding profile and looked out of the window. And instantly I felt indignation dissolve into a rather shamefaced amusement. Poor Daniel could scarcely find much to comment on when there was hardly anything to be seen. In the gaps between trees or where a field gate broke the line of hedgebanks all distance was blanketed by mist. How could he extol the virtues of the scenery when all was miserably drowned in mist and water? We had climbed steadily upwards into a bank of fog and almost as soon as I realised this we left the turnpike road and turned into the narrowest of lanes where the steady motion of our progress over the good surface of the turnpike changed to the jolting and swaying that betokened ruts under the wheels.

As though this sudden discomfort broke him out of his introspection and reminded him of my presence, Daniel said, 'This stretch is the worst we shall encounter, but it does not last long. Beyond St Bridellan the road improves considerably.' He shook his head and, revealing that I had not been far wrong about the drift of his thoughts, added, 'It is unfortunate that here, of all the places I should have wished you to see in a good light, the weather is against it.'

'That is no bad thing, surely,' I said. 'To see a place at its worst is to appreciate it the better when the weather is fair. I learned that lesson early when I travelled with Mama to Spezia – which is where, you will remember, the poet Shelley drowned – in the most fearful storm. I thought it the most dreary place imaginable in the half-dark and the rain, with the sea a raging, frightening monster gnawing at the shore. I could not understand why Mama had dragged me there. Yet the following day, the sun sparkled on a scene that was pure enchantment – the sea a limpid blue, the people smiling and friendly, the air awash with the scent of the orange and lemon trees . . . I was quite heartbroken when the time came to leave.'

He seemed to relax a little at my words. He smiled. 'I forget you are such a seasoned traveller, Sophy, though you must not depend on the sun beaming down on Kildower tomorrow. The climate is milder here in this south-west corner, I understand, than anywhere else in England, but sometimes it seems we must pay for that privilege by suffering an undue amount of rain.'

The carriage, beginning to descend down a winding incline, gave an alarming lurch into the hedge. A bramble bush scraped noisily along the window. I clutched the strap and braced myself against a further jolt. 'Is this the only road?' I asked.

'The shorter and better one,' he said gravely, but there was a teasing spark in his eye as though, at last, the dark mood that had possessed him had begun to lighten. 'The road along the creek, though undeniably picturesque, especially at high water, becomes a mire in this sort of weather, and winds about through the woods as though it had no intention of going anywhere in a hurry. In any weather it is best tackled only on foot or on horseback when there is no urgency to the journey.'

The hedgebanks suddenly fell back and the road widened among a straggle of cottages that marked the outskirts of the village. We were out of the fog and the horse, as horses will when their noses are pointed to their stable, began to pick up pace.

I was glad there was to be no lingering in St Bridellan. For all my brave words, I fear my spirits really might have suffered a terminal decline had I been forced to loiter there. It looked singularly uninviting. I could not imagine it would look much better in sunshine. Huddled rough grey houses, a squat-towered church set among dismal, dripping yews, a seedy-looking alehouse . . . I might have believed it entirely abandoned save that a few chimneys threw up a thread of smoke and a scraggy dog paddled disconsolately among the puddles at the foot of a rough stone cross that marked where several muddy lanes met. We were thankfully through it in a few moments and clipping between fields bordered with low walls of flat stone laid in the zig-zag pattern that seemed to characterise the district.

A few ragged, bedraggled children without so much as a sack about their shoulders to protect them from the rain looked up from pulling weeds in a field of young corn to watch us pass, pinched faces expressionless under torn bonnets or patched caps. The misery of their situation seemed entirely in keeping with the day and the grimness of the village. Such little ones to be forced out to work in the fields in this foul weather. What must their thoughts be to see us rich and snug and dry in our comfortable equipage? I had not much expectation that at the end of the day there would be a warm fire and good hot food and comfortable beds to reward them for their labour. The very poverty that bred the necessity for them to slave for a pittance in the fields made that prospect unlikely. I knew I should not forget their faces easily.

Another bend in the road and the children were hidden from view. I felt guiltily relieved. I could do nothing about the injustice of their situation, just as I could do nothing about the many instances of suffering that one observed in every country. But I had rubbed shoulders with poverty too frequently in my childhood ever to accept its presence with the equilibrium of those born to riches and a sense of their own rightful and superior station in life. Too often I had to steel myself not to be over-sensitive but there were occasions when some pitiable sight struck through my guard and lingered for days to haunt me. A stick-thin child, painted lips parted in a grotesque parody of invitation to the well-dressed gentleman dawdling under a street lamp; a filthy infant crouching silently at the side of its mother who, abandoned to illness or drink, lay like an abandoned rag doll in the gutter; an old, skeletal horse, laden beyond endurance, falling to the cobbles under a hail of blows from its brutal master. It was the patience of these sufferers that tore at me, the element of enduring hope that I saw in their eyes. *If I'm real nice to this gentleman he might carry me off and set me up like a lady . . . Ma'll be better in a minute and when she wakes everything'll be all right again . . . The beating will not last for ever and then I shall find the energy to go on . . .* It was the sadness, the bleakness, the impossibility of that hope that was almost unendurable and against which the coin pressed into the grubby palm, the moment taken to remonstrate with the uncaring bully, were acts almost of hypocrisy because they merely, and momentarily, salved one's conscience and, in the end, were of so little account.

Such gloomy and unsuitable thoughts hovered in my mind

as the carriage swung between Kildower's stone gateposts. Even Daniel's cheerful cry of, 'Journey's end at last, Sophy,' did not quite dispel them. Indeed, in some odd way the sombre mood that had left Daniel now seemed to have transferred itself to me.

I did not wish to smile and nod, though I believe I did, as Daniel told me how the neat shrubbery that we passed through had been a wilderness of weeds and briars when Captain Penhale had first bought the property. I did not wish to take any pleasure, though I heard my voice light and full of admiration, in the sight of lawns threaded by a watercourse that slid artistically over boulders and into a succession of small pools, all wrested from a sour marsh.

I did not wish to peer out eagerly for the first glimpse of the house, lovingly restored from dereliction, though I did so to please Daniel.

And kept on looking because I could not draw my eyes away from grey slate and stone against grey sky, looming up in a jumble of roofs and clustered chimneys and uneven walls.

So old . . . so formidable . . .

Then we were out of the carriage briefly into the drizzle filled with the song of a storm throstle calling from a mulberry tree and up three deep, worn steps into the house. Across the threshold and into a wide, flagged hall with an angled stairway rising to a gallery. Dark panelling, the musty smell of ancient wood and ancient stone. Of wood fires and beeswax and burnt candles. Starched aprons rustling as the servants waiting to welcome Master's new bride bobbed their curtseys.

And scarcely time to take a few tremulous, steadying breaths before, like a dart of light in the dimness, the child comes dancing down the stairs. A moonbeam wraith, so light, so delicate, that white slippers make hardly a whisper of sound, white skirts barely seem to stir the air.

'Careful, now, Miss Kensa, lest 'ee falls.' The voice of caution echoing from the gallery unheeded.

'Papa! Papa!' Slender arms outstretched, elfin face alight with joy, she runs forward and flings herself into her father's arms.

And as he catches her up and swings her round, laughing, I feel the billow of chill draught at my back, the sudden cessation of the storm-cock's song, as the heavy oak door is quietly closed behind me.

Chapter Three

My stepdaughter smiled up at me. 'I am pleased to meet you, Mama,' she said, executing a graceful curtsey. 'I hope you will be happy with us here at Kildower.'

I bent to kiss her. 'Thank you, Kensa. I have every hope that I shall.' Her skin was cool and petal-smooth, a fleeting, breathy touch. Then she stepped back and curtseyed again. There was something careful about her actions, as though she had practised the little speech, the curtsey, the welcoming smile, and was anxious for all to go correctly. Her earnestness added extra charm to the performance.

She was an extraordinarily pretty child. Not in a cherubic, pink-and-dimpled fashion, but with a face that was all delicately sharp bones and milk-white skin. Like her mother, Daniel had said, yet her eyes were his, in their colour, that brilliant sea-blue, though with an unexpected tilt at the corners that was almost oriental, her brows brushed in with the lightest of strokes and her hair – her father's hair in its flaxen colouring and texture – lying pale and silky down her back.

The nurse was moving forward now to whisk a soft white shawl about her shoulders. 'Miss Kensa, you're only just out of your sickbed. You must keep the shawl on while you're moving about the house or you'll catch another chill.' A voice schooled to be low and pleasant, with little trace of the local dialect. She was younger than I expected. Different. I had imagined someone comfortable and elderly, in the mould of Mrs Venables, not this tall, statuesque women, close to forty perhaps, who walked gracefully, as though her skirts were of the finest silk taffeta instead of cotton print. Whose strong, rather coarse features were by no means attractive but for a moment, born of some mysterious alchemy of poise, of carriage, of confidence, deceived the onlooker into believing her handsome. 'Begging your pardon Mrs Penhale, Mr Penhale, that we were not down waiting to meet you. I thought it best for Miss Kensa to stay upstairs in the warm as long as possible.'

'Very sensible, Jess.' Daniel reached out and tugged gently at a strand of Kensa's pale hair. 'You must promise me not to worry Jess or your new mama by being careless about wearing your shawl or I shall have to quite forbid the opening of certain packages.'

'I promise! I promise!' She clutched his hand, her silk slippers dancing impatiently on the flagstones. 'Oh, Papa, you've brought me presents! I knew it. Show me! Show me!'

'You must be patient until Mama and I have had time to recover our breath from the journey and the baggage is all unloaded. But you shall have them before dinner, I promise. And before you ask, yes, you may dine with us today. You will arrange that, will you, Jess?' Then, to me, 'I keep country hours, here, my dear, and dine at two. If that is not agreeable you may in future make whatever changes you wish.'

The nursemaid cleared her throat, a worried frown creasing her forehead. 'Excuse me, sir, madam, but Miss Kensa's dinner is already prepared. You see, I've kept her to a low diet, thinking it best after her upset not to indulge her with rich food.'

Kensa screwed up her nose. 'Ugh. Steamed fish and rice pudding. I had much sooner have roast beef with you, Papa, and you can see that I am quite, quite better now. Oh, please, Papa, I don't want to stay by myself in the nursery and eat horrible cod.'

Daniel laughed. 'A compromise, then. Go now with Jess and eat your fish, then you may rest quietly until you join us at dinner. If you still wish to nibble a little beef, then I cannot think you will come to much harm, otherwise you may entertain us with an account of all you have done since I last saw you. What say you, Jess?'

She smiled gravely. 'That would seem fair, sir. Come now, Miss Kensa. Do as your papa bids.'

Kensa, mollified, danced away up the stairs, her nurse in dignified pursuit. We followed them, Daniel waving the other servants away save for one maid who came, heavy-footed, after us. 'Kitty will attend you, my dear, for the moment,' he said aloud, then murmured quietly into my ear, 'the best of a sorry bunch, I am afraid, and she soon to leave us to marry a Truro man. But you may engage someone more suitable as soon as you are settled.'

Kensa and Jess Southcote had disappeared along the gallery. We turned the opposite way into a short, gloomy corridor, one solitary window with insets of stained glass at the far end being the only source of light.

'Save that the window is very ancient and bears the arms of the Trewithen family who owned the house from Elizabethan times I would have had it knocked through and a larger modern one installed,' Daniel said. 'Perhaps I shall some day, but to spare my father's feelings I leave it be. He has some sentiment for these old accoutrements. Fortunately we do not lack light in our bedchamber.'

He flung open the door with a flourish.

I stepped inside and stared round. 'How very . . . pleasant.'

Pleasant? It sounded weak upon my lips even as I said it. And a lie, to boot. Whatever else the room was, pleasant it surely was not. It was a large, low-ceilinged room, a masculine room, immaculately tidy, with three tall, stone-mullioned windows piercing its longer wall, so that the aqueous light that drowned the lawns and trees outside spilled lavishly between curtains of heavy, indigo velvet. And was curiously muted by the room itself, so that we might still have been in the gloomy corridor. It was something to do with the weighty furniture of highly polished black wood, ornately carved but devoid of any inlay or ornamental veneer, and the choice of that same purple-blue as the curtains for the brocade bed hangings and as the predominant colour on the heavily patterned flock wallpaper.

'Striking, is it not?' Daniel said, striding to the window. 'And there is a splendid view to the woods and the creek, though you cannot catch even a glimpse of the water today.'

'Most . . . unusual. The furniture, it is Oriental?'

'The Captain brought it from China on one of his last voyages there. The room was refurbished for him to occupy, but he found the stairs too much and decided to remove himself to quarters on the ground floor in the south wing.'

'The plasterwork of the ceiling is very elaborate.' Even there, the background had been picked out in indigo, so that the sculpted beasts and flowers seemed to stand out as though against threatening storm clouds.

'That was created – save for the recent colouring – when the Trewithens rebuilt the house two hundred years since, having demolished most of the old property that previously stood on the site. There is very little left of that original building save for some small rooms at the back which I shall point out to you when we tour the house later.' He did not quite meet my eye and his tone was perhaps a trifle too hearty as he added, 'This is quite the finest room in the house, I do assure you.' I found some small comfort in the thought that he too might be less enthusiastic than he would have me believe, for I found the room sombre and depressing in the extreme.

'And see, my dear,' he said, ushering me forward, 'this door leads to your dressing room. I have a similar one at the other side.'

Here at least there was no effort to impress. The room contained merely a range of white-painted cupboards, a comfortable chair, a washstand and a hip bath drawn up before the small grate where a brisk fire scented the air with the spicy tang of apple wood. 'And my latest purchase – the Bramah Patent Water Closet,' Daniel announced proudly, drawing back a screen in one corner and flinging up the mahogany lid of a large box. He pumped vigorously at a handle within. 'The water flows into it from a reservoir in the casing and flushes the contents into the hidden pail beneath. We may be remote at Kildower but I see no necessity why we should not take advantage of the most modern sanitary artifacts.'

At least I could comment with genuine approval on this room with its admirable water closet. It gave me a glimmer of hope that elsewhere in the house there might be other corners where I might not feel too intimidated.

Intimidated? Was that the correct word? I decided it was best not to dwell too closely on that but concentrated instead on the practical matter of instructing the eager but undoubtedly stupid Kitty in the unpacking of our bags. Every instruction had to be repeated slowly and at least twice before it penetrated her mind. But she could be forgiven a great deal for her cheerful gap-toothed grin, which did much to restore my flagging spirits. She did not have the wit to be overawed or nervous so when she was not giggling over her mistakes she kept up a constant flow of chatter in her loud, rough voice. Daniel did not stand it for long. Casting a half-anguished, half-amused glance at me he said, 'I must pay my respects to the Captain. Kitty will show you down to the dining parlour when you are ready,' and fled.

So until the trunks and bags were empty Kitty entertained me with all manner of inconsequential information about her luck in finding such a good place at Kildower after her mother, her only relative, had died last year, and of her forthcoming wedding to Jem, the carrier's lad. 'And, could I please ask, Mrs Penhale, ma'am, what do 'ee think the best way to rid a place o' the stink o' pigs? For I can't abide 'en and we'm to live wi' Jem's old granfer an' he'm mortal attached to they beasts and lets 'em roam in and out o' the cottage like they was pet cats.' My experience with pigs being sadly lacking, I could not help her, but I was so grateful to her for diverting my thoughts that I gravely promised to bear the matter in mind should I come across any suitable receipt.

By which time it was close to the dinner hour and some-what bemused – she had now embarked on a graphic account of her mother's last gruelling illness and death from a purging of the bowels – we descended the staircase and crossed the hall, where Kitty showed me into the dining parlour. Making sure that Daniel and Kensa were already waiting she then clumped off in her misshapen shoes about her other duties.

I had fetched down the gifts we had brought. Daniel had purchased from the Exeter jeweller's a slender necklace of pink coral and, learning from Daniel that being so often sadly housebound Kensa took great pleasure from quiet pursuits and enjoyed reading, I had made a selection of

books. Daniel had told me that Kensa was particularly fond
of the works of Mrs Eudora Phipps and though I had thought
them a little babyish for someone of Kensa's age I had found
a new one which seemed to be directed at an older age group.
I had also bought her some breadths of summer materials
that might be used for dressmaking and embroidery.

She squealed with delight as she tore off the wrappings.
'Oh, Papa, you knew exactly what I wanted. A new book by
Mrs Phipps. And is all this for dresses? Jess was only
grumbling yesterday that I have grown out of all my clothes
– and this one with pink daisies just matches the pretty
necklace. May I wear the necklace now, Papa?'

'Of course,' he said indulgently. 'And you must thank
Mama for the other things, for she was at great pains to
choose them for you.'

A quick glance at me – no, beyond me – from under
long, gold tipped lashes. A moment of hesitation. 'Thank
you, Mama,' she said, her tone losing its excited edge and
becoming carefully polite. 'I am very pleased with everything.'

'What a lucky girl you are, Miss Kensa.'

I turned sharply. I had not realised Jess Southcote was in
the room, but she must have been waiting in the shadow of
the open door. Daniel, Kensa and I were standing by the
tall, mullioned window at the far end of the long, polished
table. Now Jess advanced towards us in her steady, dignified
way, hands gracefully clasped in front of her against the
starched whiteness of her apron. 'If there is nothing else,
sir, I'll return upstairs to tidy the nursery.

'By all means, Jess,' he said.

'And shall I take up Miss Kensa's presents out of harm's
way ma'am?' Her dark gaze, eyes the colour of rain-wet
damsons, transferred itself to me. 'I shouldn't like to think

of anything getting marked or spoiled. The maids are young and might be a touch careless when they are serving.' And as she spoke, as though already taking it for granted that her perfectly sensible suggestion would be immediately accepted, her hands unclasped themselves and began to reach out towards the books and materials Kensa in her haste to examine her treasures had scattered over the end of the table.

Beautiful hands. Long, narrow and pale. The fingers fleshy and supple, curiously so, as though some substance more pliable than hard bone lay beneath the smooth, cared-for skin. Exceptional hands for a nursemaid, with not a trace of roughness and the nails shaped to unchipped ovals. Hands that might never have done a day's work ... or of which the owner was so proud that they were creamed and oiled and nurtured to eradicate any trace of the menial tasks they were called upon to perform.

And hands that aroused such a sudden and inexplicable feeling of distaste in me as they moved like blind and groping white worms among the objects scattered on the polished mahogany of the table that it almost choked me to hold back from crying out in disgust and brought sharply to my mind a recollection of other times when I had experienced that same shuddery shrinking of the nerves, of the skin ... lying sleepless in the dark in some new lodgings, where rustles and flutterings might herald all manner of unknown creatures in the room from scurrying beetles or rats to moths and bats. And of a time, years ago, when I had been painting in a field near Salisbury and the rag with which I wiped my brushes had fallen to the ground. When I picked it up from the grass something soft and giving squirmed within it. It was not that I was afraid of the huge brown slug that I hurriedly shook out, it was the unexpectedness of the repulsive contact that had unnerved me. Like the rustlings in the night, it was that instant of not knowing what manner of creature was lurking to bite or sting.

So it was with Jess Southcote. I looked at her and I saw as I had seen when I had first entered Kildower a tall, dignified woman, dressed in a nursemaid's print gown and apron. A helpful servant doing her best to please her new mistress.

But her hands . . . her hands were so shockingly at odds with the image she wished to convey that it was as though they belonged to a different, infinitely less pleasant person.

I took refuge in action, turning to the child and saying crisply, 'I believe it is Kensa who shall decide.' She blinked up at me and I added with an encouraging smile, 'Perhaps you will like to look at the books again when we have finished our meal and we could take a few moments to decide which styles you would prefer for your new dresses. I do not suppose anything will come to too much harm if we put it all tidily on the window-ledge here until we have eaten.'

Again that flicker of gold-tipped lashes as her glance wavered past me to Jess. Her hand crept upwards to the coral necklace lying round the collar of her dress. She gave a careless little shrug. 'If I may wear Papa's necklace,' she said, 'then Jess may take the rest upstairs.'

So we sat down to eat a splendid dinner of roast sirloin and all manner of other delicacies which might have been stale bread for all that I enjoyed any of it.

For I could not rid myself of the image of Jess Southcote gathering books, folding swathes of pastel-tinted lawn and muslin and finest linen with those long, pliable, *acquisitive* white fingers, and wondering why I should feel such an instinctive and unreasonable aversion towards a woman for whom everyone else had such a high regard.

* * *

If I was quiet during the early part of dinner neither Daniel nor Kensa noticed. They were too busy talking and teasing each other. It occurred to me that this was the first time I had seen Daniel so completely at ease. Though we had become perfectly comfortable together even in our most relaxed moments there was still a reserve about him that kept me at a distance. To be honest, I suppose that was a reflection in part of my own natural inclination towards reticence and a wish to respect the privacy of others, as I should wish them to respect mine. But as I watched them both and heard the unfamiliar tenderness, the laughter, in my husband's voice, I could not help feeling a little tremor of wistfulness at being excluded from this shared happiness. They seemed quite to have forgotten that I was there.

As a governess I had grown to appreciate being ignored by my employers and their servants alike. If I was quiet and conscientious in my duties I could live a satisfactorily independent life within the busiest of households, coming and going as I pleased in such free time as I was allotted. And even as a child I had shied away from being drawn into close friendships. I knew it was best not to become too attached to any one particular person, for it made the inevitable parting, when Mama and I moved on, that much more painful. By the time I went to school in England the habit of being solitary was so ingrained that I found it difficult to respond to kindly overtures from the other girls and quickly gained a reputation for being cold and aloof. I believe I grew to be respected – certainly by the mistresses – for working hard at my studies, and there were many times when I was glad not to be involved in the petty jealousies and arguments that flared up among the girls. But though they grew fewer, there were also occasions when I was tired, or particularly missing Mama, when I was hard put not to feel regret that I was not one of some cosily whispering group of friends, or that there was no one sympathetic special person with whom to share my worries and hopes.

It had been a long time since that feeling of being an outsider had been so acute as it was during that seemingly endless dinner. Which was perfectly foolish and due entirely, I told myself sternly, to the undermining effects of the – to me – unnatural cossetting I had experienced since my marriage. It was a timely reminder that I must take care not to sink in future into silly vapourings or discontent and self-pity would be the result. It was, after all, perfectly natural that a man so devoted to his daughter as Daniel had to make the most of the short time they could be together. Besides, as I knew very well, it was far better for me to remain a little detached. One learned a great deal by being quiet and observant. That applied to my situation here as Daniel's wife and mistress of Kildower as much as to any position I had previously taken as a governess.

I sat up a little straighter and helped myself from the bowl of lemon cream that had been dropped somewhat roughly on the table, along with a dish of shortbread biscuits, a platter of jam tartlets and a Cheddar cheese, by a tiny young maid whose thin arms scarcely seemed strong enough to support the tray laden with dirty dishes with which she staggered off. There was no evidence of an upper housemaid. Both of the serving maids were equally gauche and entirely unsupervised as they rushed in and out of the dining parlour, to the great danger of the fine china, which they handled as though it were so much tin plate.

If the service left much to be desired, the quality of the food could not be faulted. The cook was a person of talent, which was something, at least, to be thankful for. I made a mental note to convey my appreciation to her when Daniel showed me over the house after dinner, and to put into effect as soon as possible some form of training for the maids.

One other fact impossible to ignore during that first meal was Kensa's shameful lack of table manners. I was astonished that Daniel, so correct and particular in other ways, was apparently not the slightest bit affronted by his daughter's behaviour. She insisted on helping herself generously from every dish, mashing all up to a horrid mush with her fork or spoon, then leaving most of it. She talked with her mouth full, she dripped gravy on the pristine damask tablecloth, she licked the jam out of the tartlets and left the pastry. I felt a spark of grim satisfaction that Jess Southcote, that sensible, well-regarded person, had evidently failed in this particular. And what about the various governesses who had come and gone? They must have been singularly ineffective. I should have expected better from a four-year-old, leave alone a great girl of nine, however prettily she chattered, however charmingly she smiled. And Kensa was pretty and charming. Precociously so. There was artifice in the turn of her head, in the self-conscious way she toyed with a strand of her pale, silky hair, in the widening of those brilliant blue, tilted eyes. I found it all a trifle disconcerting, perhaps even a little sad. Daniel had said she was unspoiled, but I regarded her with clearer eyes and already I saw imperfections in the child whose glowing portrait he had painted.

After dinner we adjourned to the parlour, where we all took coffee and Daniel poured himself a glass of port. The parlour was as formal and gloomy as the dining parlour across the hall, with a great quantity of linenfold panelling round the walls and heavy crimson drapes at the windows. It seemed an interminable time before Daniel suggested we embark on our tour of the house, culminating with a visit to

Captain Penhale's quarters whence we had been summoned, Daniel said, before the first dog watch. I looked at him blankly. 'Before four in the afternoon,' he said gravely. 'If we arrive any later we shall find the door bolted and the Captain gone for his walk.'

'On a day like this?'

'Whatever the weather. I have seen him struggling through deep snow and nearly knocked off his legs by the force of a gale, but he has a choice vocabulary of oaths for anyone who would try to persuade him to a more prudent course. Now, Kensa, sweetheart, do you feel well enough to accompany us to visit Grandpapa?'

'I am a bit tired,' she said in a suddenly frail little voice, though a minute since she had been chattering fifteen-to-the-dozen. She favoured her father with a sweet, sad smile. 'Oh, Papa, I should truly like to visit Grandpapa, but the last time Jess took me to see him nasty old Pirate nearly knocked me over. He's a horrid, bad dog and he frightens me.'

'He will not be there, I promise,' Daniel assured her. 'When I saw Grandpapa earlier he agreed to banish him for the entire afternoon. He is a gentle enough hound,' he added quietly to me as we began our progress around Kildower, Kensa skipping ahead, as though it had slipped her mind that a few minutes since she had complained of tiredness, 'but he is overlarge and over-friendly and quite terrifies poor little Kensa.' He shook his head. 'It is the delicacy of her nature, I am afraid, that makes her subject to so many fears. Even the kitten I gave her once had to be despatched to the stables after it scratched her in play. She screamed every time it came near her after that. And she has nightmares over the smallest upset that a more robust child would take in its stride.'

'Children often grow out of such fears,' I said soothingly,

though my thoughts were somewhat less charitable. I was beginning to wonder if the artifice that I sensed in Miss Kensa Penhale turned her into something of a play actress when it suited her book. That was something that warranted closer observation.

Then I was too caught up in what I was seeing – experiencing – of my new home to take much note of my stepdaughter.

Kildower. Too big, I thought, for the few people who lived under its roof. Too many unused rooms, a few with furniture hidden beneath dust sheets, carpets protected by strips of drugget. Still life. Some rooms empty. As though the house were frozen, like a picture forever posed at the particular moment when Captain Penhale had finished his refurbishment. Kept clean and ready . . . and for what? For guests who had never been invited? For Daniel, the adopted son, who would marry and raise a rumbustious brood of children to fill the lifeless rooms with all the clutter and noise of family life? Instead of which his wife had died untimely and left him with a daughter whose delicate presence was rendered even more insignificant by the weight of emptiness about her. A cold, cold house. Even the kitchen managed not to be cosy, for it was a vast, echoing cavern which dwarfed the thin, unsmiling cook, Mrs Dagget. She took my compliments in lip-pursed silence and I had no way of knowing if I had pleased her with my appreciation of her cooking. More likely, I thought glumly, she was resentful because my presence in the house would cause her more work.

As I followed Daniel and Kensa out of the kitchen I allowed the bright, interested expression I had so far managed to maintain to slip. Mrs Dagget's taciturn manner was the last straw. I could pretend no longer. Try as I might to hope otherwise, I disliked this house. From that first glimpse across the gardens I had been struggling with my conscience, for I knew it was unreasonable and unfair to make such a swift and damning judgement. But every reluctant step I took round these gloomy passages and rooms only served to reinforce that first impression. There was no welcome here for me. Worse, the chill in the air was not merely a physical thing of unlit fires and damp walls, but something more intangible that deadened and oppressed the spirit, as though the very atmosphere bred a chill of its own, a chill born of too great a weight of age and misery and distrust.

I could not help the shiver that had me pulling my Kashmir shawl more tightly round my shoulders and glancing warily at Daniel's back. Thank heavens he was occupied with Kensa and could not see the dismay I was sure was written on my face. I could not bear the weight of his disappointment and displeasure on top of everything else. For displeased he would most surely be if he guessed anything of my thoughts when he had such expectations of me.

We walked from the kitchen down a low-ceilinged passage towards the Captain's quarters. I had collected myself by the time Daniel turned to say that we were now in the oldest part of the house. He lifted the latch on a door set in a low arch. 'This short stair leads to a room left from the original building. But it really is of little interest as it is only used as a storeroom.' He made to close the door again but I heard myself say – and I did not know why, for I was depressed enough already without burdening myself with more gloom – 'No, it is important that I see everything, Daniel.' Whereupon he ducked his head through the arch, Kensa at his heels, and I trailed after them. Three worn stone steps, another three at an angle, a door of battered, wormy oak which creaked on dry hinges and opened . . . to light, space and a sense of airiness that came as such a relief after the sombreness of the rest of Kildower that I stood gape-mouthed for a moment.

'Oh, Papa,' Kensa whined, pulling her skirts tight around her legs, 'it is all dusty and horrid. I shall get my dress dirty . . . and there'll be spiders.'

'Away with you, then,' Daniel said easily. 'And mind how you go on the stairs, sweetheart.' Then, to me, as Kensa began to pick her way daintily back down the steps, 'You see, Sophy. Just a storeroom. And it would seem no maid has been here in years. Perhaps when you are settled you might arrange for a thorough turn-out.'

I did not see what he and Kensa saw – a jumble of chests and boxes piled haphazardly against cobwebbed walls, the abandoned clutter of years heaped up almost to obscure the massive granite chimney piece and the floorboards furred so thick with dust that our footsteps were clearly imprinted – I saw the room clean and empty and full of sunlight. A peaceful, comfortable retreat.

'Certainly, Daniel,' I said calmly. 'I shall make it one of my first tasks.'

But not for his sake, nor Kildower's. For mine.

This poor abandoned chamber, inconvenient for the rest of the house and unworthy of attention . . . so strange that I had instantly felt its appeal. Felt as though it had been waiting patiently here for me to rediscover its charm.

And following close on that another surprise. Already heartened by the discovery of at least one small corner of Kildower that was pleasing, I was even more gratified to find when I stepped into Captain Penhale's quarters that I had no need at all to pretend to be charmed.

I stared around, my smile widening in delight. We had

stepped aboard a ship! More particularly the great aft cabin of some splendid merchantman. Save for the fireplace with its massive granite overmantel, very like the one in the chamber I already thought of as mine, the walls were transformed by great swoops of golden polished planking to the resemblance of curving bulkheads, pierced by a window at which stood a spy-glass on a tripod and a compass in its brass binnacle. And through the window the outline of a woman's head poised stiffly against the misty greens of the foliage outside, her sculpted yellow hair rippling backwards, profile lifted towards the grey clouds. I could almost believe that the floor beneath our feet, and the brass lanterns suspended from a beam that ran the length of the ceiling, dipped and swung to the movement of waves.

To complete the illusion the lanterns above the centre table were lit against the gloom of the afternoon, and the figure who looked up tetchily from the charts spread under the lantern glow might have been interrupted at some matter of plotting a course that required his urgent attention.

'Father, may I present my wife, Sophy. Sophy, Captain Saul Penhale.'

I curtsied politely and stared up into a pair of fierce, pale blue eyes buried in a mass of wrinkles and overhung with eyebrows as thick and white as sheep's fleece. A frothing white beard obscured the lower half of the Captain's face and bushed out over a turquoise silk coat of a curious cut with frogged fastenings and a high collar, such as I had once seen a Chinaman wearing.

'Sophy, eh?' he growled. 'So you're the one that's been chose to warm Daniel's bed of a night.' He looked me up and down. 'Well, you've more flesh on your bones than the other, I'll grant that in your favour, though what else you have to commend you remains to be seen.'

117

'Captain,' Daniel said warningly. 'You promised.'

'Aye, I promised to be polite. This once.' He drew himself erect and, despite being hampered by a stiffly awkward leg, made an old-fashioned bow, sweeping off the embroidered silk cap he wore to reveal a bald pink pate, the surrounding fringe of hair scraped back and tied into a scanty queue. 'Your servant, ma'am,' he said. 'Welcome aboard, though 'tis a ship that's foundered and not likely to be carried off the rocks at the next high tide.' He bared crooked yellow fangs in a grin. 'And I see you've persuaded the wench to visit her old grandad. Will I be favoured with a kiss, this time, I wonder, Miss Will-o'-the-Wisp? After all, there's no hellhound on watch to set you into a pother. He's chained in the brig, poor brute, condemned to weevilly biscuit and bilge water by way of penance for sins he don't know he's committed.'

He bent down and thrust his cheek towards Kensa. She stepped forward warily and at the same time, as though on cue, a blood-curdling banshee howl came loudly from somewhere close by. Kensa squealed and shot back to her father's side, to bury her face in his sleeve. 'It's Pirate! Oh, Papa, don't let him bite me.'

'Rattle me bones, child, the poor critter wouldn't harm a soul save in defence of his master, and you know that well for I've told you so many a time,' the Captain growled. His voice was stern but I fancied there had been a glint of hurt in his eyes, quickly masked, as the child turned away from him.

'Kensa is too young to be rational about her fears,' Daniel said, frowning.

The Captain scowled. 'Fears is better faced than run away from, in my opinion.'

'I was not aware I had asked your opinion.'

118

'More's the pity.'

'And what possible relevance can the opinions of a washed-up old reprobate like you have, eh?'

'Washed-up I may be, but I've more common sense in my little finger than many a one has in their over-bred brainboxes. And a deal more experience than a jumped-up whippersnapper such as yourself, Mr Know-it-all-Penhale. And remember your place, sir! Why, I've known better men than you flogged around the fleet for giving less lip to his elders and betters.'

For all the roughness of their words I sensed there was more affection than malice behind them. This was a well-established ritual, pleasurable to both men. Reassured, I allowed my attention to drift away on a further inspection of the other artifacts scattered about the room, from sections of rope contorted into complicated knots to the gaping jawbones of a sharp-toothed fish mounted above the chimney piece.

'Cat got your tongue?' I jumped. Captain Penhale's walking stick was pointed accusingly in my direction. 'Don't have much to say for yourself, eh?'

I floundered for a moment, still caught in something of a dream cast by the impossible sensation of being on board ship. 'I beg your par—'

'Women!' He thrust his head forward belligerently. 'Never trust a woman who's too quiet, for she's bound to be plotting.'

'But I was not . . .'

'Nor one whose tongue's never still, for she'll gossip away your good name and drive you to drink with her prattle.'

'Sir, I . . .'

'The good Lord should have left Adam with all his ribs intact. It would have saved honest men a deal of trouble and grief. There's never a girl-child born that doesn't imbibe slyness, cunning and vanity with her mother's milk.'

'Saul.' Daniel's voice held a warning. The old man shook his head irritably, his fierce little eyes never leaving my face. 'I'll speak plain as I please in my own quarters. If it don't suit your new wife, there's no need for her to stay and listen.'

I gathered my scattered wits. As I stared back at the old man, all the correct, polite phrases died stillborn on my lips. I realised that what I said next was important. I wished to gain his goodwill or what passed for goodwill in his belligerent, crusty nature, but it was clear that soft talking and appeasement would cut no ice with him. Yet how should I answer?

'Well, madam?' He had a wicked, knowing look in his eye, as though he was testing me and fully expected me to fail. 'Speak up! How do you respond to my pleasantries?'

With directness. That was the only way.

I held his glance without flinching because that too was important. He must not know how uncertain I truly was. And I almost blessed Mama in that instant because of the long practice I had had in disguising nervous feelings.

'I am completely captivated at finding myself unexpectedly on board a ship, sir. I marvel at the thought and effort that have created such a splendid ambience,' I said steadily. 'But I am sorry to hear that your experience with women has been limited to such sorry drabs as you describe. Or do you suppose that the fault lies within yourself? Perhaps any gently reared woman might be rendered silent or over-talkative due to nervousness on encountering such a forceful – not to say rude – gentleman.'

I had taken a chance and was appalled even as I heard myself speak. How could I have been so . . . so outspoken?

The Captain's beard quivered alarmingly. Even the unseen hound bewailed my affrontery with another ghostly moan.

The Captain's beard continued to quiver as though he was struggling to find words. But what came out was a great bellow, like a bull in pain, that was instantly answered by a joyous woof and a scrabble of paws on the door at the far end of the room. 'Blast the hound! Pirate, hush your racket,' the Captain roared. 'As for you, Sophy Penhale, I'll tell you straight, I'll not put up with interference from a woman who thinks she knows it all.' He struck the floor with his cane. 'Do you hear? I'm too set in my ways to make changes. If you've any ambitions in that direction, stay in your own part of the house and be damned.'

I was in so deep now there was no other recourse but to plunge on recklessly.

'Other than to examine this fascinating room further, I cannot think there is much to draw me back here,' I said. 'After all, why should I pay a visit to a crabby old gentleman merely to be subjected to a tirade of insults and untruths?'

'Because you believe it is your duty, madam. And because your husband expects it of you, young fool that he is. You've the look of a hussy who'd not neglect her *duties*.' He sneered the word. 'I don't wish to become one of 'em. Women's fussing turns a man into a milksop.'

'I think there is little chance of that in your case, Captain Penhale,' I said dryly. 'I think you have charted your own course for far too long ever to be influenced by anything I might do or say.'

The stick jabbed out again, this time in the direction of the window and the figurehead beyond. 'That's the only sort of woman who's peaceful to live with.'

'She's a handsome woman,' I said. 'But you'd be hard pressed to have a sensible conversation with her.'

'Exactly. So if you come a-visiting, remember that. I don't want to chitter-chatter about the state of my bowels or whether I'll be catching a chill if I set foot over the doorstep.'

Then he laughed. *Laughed.* A great infectious boom of laughter, that set Daniel chuckling behind me, that made me smile though I was not sure why, except out of relief.

The clock in the corner wheezed, then boomed out the hour. The old man sobered instantly, turned his back and hobbled awkwardly to the far end of the room, where a frantic whining and scrabbling began. 'Daniel, get that child away before I let Pirate out,' he bawled over his shoulder. ''Tis time we were off for our walk. As for you, madam, if you want to see what manner of brute sets Miss Will-o'-the-Wisp all of a-tremble, stand your ground.' A sly challenging grin at me as he put a gnarled hand on the doorknob. 'If you dare, that is.'

'We will wait for you outside, my dear,' Daniel said and added softly. 'Have no fear. The hound is like his master. All noise and bluster outside to protect a nature which is far more tender than he would have you believe – and never any threat to anyone he considers his friend. You have won over the one, you should have no problem with the other.'

Which went some way to reducing my fright as the door closed behind him and from the far end of the room, with a great scrabbling of claws, a vast, bounding animal, the size and colouring of a donkey, flung itself at me.

'I can well understand why Kensa is scared of Pirate,' I said to Daniel that evening. 'I have never seen a dog of such a size.'

'His sire was pure wolfhound, I understand, his dam some other large, hairy breed brought in on some foreign ship out of Newfoundland.'

'A formidable mixture,' I said.

'But you won his favour, as you won old Saul's.' Daniel looked pleased, almost smugly so. 'Well done, Sophy. I shall leave with an easier mind tomorrow, knowing that you and my father have struck up a friendship.'

We lingered over the remains of supper and, despite the good fire and the extravagance of candles in the room, the dining chamber still seemed so heavy with shadows that I felt them to be solid as the furniture. I tried to ignore the niggling edginess that seemed to possess me. Perhaps I was tired after the long day, which inclined me to be prickly, and my moodiness had nothing at all to do with what I imagined to be the oppressive atmosphere. But try as I might, I could not control the querulous note in my voice, nor stop myself from feeling that Daniel had been somewhat cavalier in the matter of preparing me for the encounter with his father.

'A friendship? I think that is overstating the case somewhat.'

He smiled. 'An understanding, then.'

'I wish you had warned me, given me a better idea of what to expect from the Captain.'

'And if I had? If you had rehearsed some polite speech? He is shrewd, you know. He would have pounced on any hint of collusion on our part.'

'I knew the old gentleman was eccentric, but . . .'

'But had you known exactly how much, you might have been more worried than was necessary.'

'It might all have gone badly wrong,' I persisted. 'I quite believed at one point I had antagonised him beyond recovery.'

'Instead of which your straight speaking earned his respect.' He paused, then said gently, 'I felt you would not fail me and you did not. Sophy, you must realise that above everything else I trust your good judgement of a situation and your ability to deal cleverly with people. I saw it first in your handling of the Vaisey girls and later with your mama, and everything since has confirmed my initial impression that you are a person to be relied upon to deal sensibly and creditably with the problems of everyday life. I did not doubt you would gain my father's favour. Nor do I doubt that you will make an excellent mistress of Kildower. You may feel a little discomposed at present whilst everything is new to you, but you have made an excellent start and each day you will become more familiar with, more comfortable in your new role.'

There was an underlying irritation in my mood that struggled against being soothed by his flattering words, that wished the qualities in my nature that he praised did not sound so unbearably dull. That wished, almost, that he would raise his voice in argument, break through the barrier of his control with anger, instead of sitting there so calm and complacent and confident in his masculine authority, the candlelight twisting in a draught to catch shadows under the high cheekbones of his handsome face and streaking his flax-pale hair with umber and gold. And now, believing that I was reassured and placated, turning the conversation aside to other matters before drawing out his pocket watch and saying, 'I think we shall not be late tonight, Sophy. I must make an early start in the morning.'

'Of course. I will go up now, if that is agreeable with you, Daniel, to see if Kitty has managed to follow my instructions in the matter of the warming pan and hot bricks in the bed.' I heard my voice light, normal. It was an effort. 'The poor girl is very willing, but I cannot think that she will be any loss to the household when she marries.'

'Sadly lacking in the top drawer,' Daniel agreed. 'I will finish my glass of claret in the parlour and follow you up in a few moments.'

I shall be restored in the morning, I thought. A good night's sleep and this foolish, contrary mood will be gone. The house will seem different when the sun shines. It has gone cold and clear outside. I should not be surprised to see frost in the morning. My thoughts ran as hastily as my footsteps, as though to prevent me from dwelling on the gloom of the hall, the shadows on the stairs. Shadows that deepened as I moved upwards, for the candle in its glass shade on the bannister at the turn of the gallery had carelessly been allowed to burn out, another item for the growing list of things to attend to tomorrow.

Below, I heard Daniel's steady tread across the stone flags to the parlour, then the counterpoint of lighter, feminine footsteps. Both stopping suddenly, then the murmur of hushed voices. I halted, alerted by the urgency in the woman's whisper, and leaned across the bannister, ready to call down to discover if there was some household emergency.

Directly below stood Jess Southcote and Daniel. They stood very close, she, tall as she was, having to look up at him. She was not in her nursemaid's dress and apron and cap, but wore a gown of some glossy material in a rich violet shade that shimmered in the gloom. Her hair was loosely dressed in black coils. Impossible from here to see the wiry grey threads that ran through it. Or to see the coarseness of her features. From my vantage point she made a striking figure, those supple, graceful white hands moving sinuously in emphasis and, in so doing, brushing softly against Daniel's coat in a gesture that might have been accidental, but had something in it that smacked of a too-ready familiarity. I stepped back, suddenly feeling that I was no longer the innocent witness of some minor household drama, but that I had been caught shamefully spying. At that instant they both turned to look upwards. I stood still, the shadows up here so deep that I knew my dark gown must blend into them. Then they moved out of my angle of vision and I heard Daniel say in a ragged, unfamiliar voice. 'The parlour, Jess. We shall not be disturbed.'

The sound of the parlour door closing broke me out of my breath-held stillness. I flew along the passage to the bedchamber, to be greeted by Kitty, whose gap-toothed grin and cry of, 'See, ma'am, I've done all as you asked. Master 'n' 'ee'll be cosy as two ticks on a hoss's backside in that bed tonight,' was like being folded in a comforting embrace.

Despite the warm bed, there was a chill in my bones that took a long time to disappear. The little scene I had witnessed ran over and over in my head, forcing me to face unpalatable facts that I had carefully avoided thinking too much about.

Daniel had been many years a widower. That was not to say he had lived the life of a celibate monk. However much he had loved and grieved for Meraud, he was young still, and there must have been times when he yearned for a woman's company, a woman's body. That much I had accepted from the first. These faceless nameless women were no concern of mine. They were part of Daniel's past life. But . . .

Jess Southcote?

Oh, please God, let it not be Jess. Her body locked with his in the ultimate intimacy . . . her hands touching, stroking, caressing his golden skin . . . grasping, boneless fingers knowing his body as I knew it . . . holding him close . . . And every time I looked at her from now on to be left wondering if . . .

Any paid slut from the streets ... but not Jess ... Not her ...

Her shiny dark eyes gleamed with triumph in the darkness of the black place where I was trapped. Then it was my mother, her green eyes snapping with laughter, saying 'I warned you, Sophy, but you would not listen. There is no way out for you now, but you are nothing to me for I always loved your sister best.' Jess held the candle closer and closer to my face and I could not move and I knew she meant to burn out my eyes ...

My gritty lids opened reluctantly. The light was already retreating, the bed curtain still swaying as though someone had moved it aside in order to make sure that I was asleep. I had been dozing and waking from frightening dreams for half the night and Daniel was only now coming to bed. Had he been with her all this time? She in her shiny violet dress with her hair all loose and her voice whispering secrets I could not share.

If he had been with her it had given him no ease. I curled rigidly on the edge of the bed while he tossed and turned in wakefulness and groaned in sleep. I made no move to comfort him. I could not bear that he should turn to me as he had that other time with a passion that was not meant for me and which he remembered nothing of in the morning.

I slept from exhaustion eventually. When I awoke the curtains at the window were pulled back and sunshine laced through the mullions. Kitty's face grinned down into mine.

'Master, 'ee said to wake you, ma'am, at nine with hot chocolate.'

I struggled up. 'So late? We have overslept. Oh, and he wished to be away early.'

'Bless you, ma'am, 'e's been gone since afore the clock struck seven.' She plonked the tray down across my knees so that the chocolate spilled from the wide cup into the saucer. 'There now. You don't rush none. Cook'll have breakfast ready soon as you give word. And Master's left 'ee a note.'

I unfolded the paper slowly.

> My Dear Wife,
> You were sleeping so peacefully that I could not bear to disturb you. I am sure the extra hour or two of rest will be of more benefit to you than rising to make the brief farewell which necessity dictates. I hope to be free to return to Kildower on Saturday afternoon, leaving Plymouth by half past five o'clock at the latest.
> Until then, take great care of yourself and that most precious charge, your new daughter, Kensa.
> Your affectionate husband,
> Daniel Penhale.

I carefully refolded the note. Then I drank the hot chocolate and contemplated the long days ahead until he should return.

There was much to be done. First off I must deal with the noise going on in my dressing room. I climbed reluctantly from bed. If I had wished to drift back to sleep it would have been impossible. Buckets clanged, doors opened and slammed shut, water swooshed as though a cataract had opened up and above this Kitty's voice warbled loudly and merrily some ditty about a lovesick swain.

'Oh, that was strong poison, my pretty one!' she sang in a voice that was surprisingly clear and true. 'You'll die, you'll die, Rendal my son.'

I hastened to the dressing-room door, to find her emptying water into the hip bath in a cloud of steam. I looked in astonishment at the number of buckets and jugs, the quantities of towels in neat heaps, and every door and drawer in the press standing wide.

''Tes all nearly ready, ma'am,' she called when she saw me. 'Two more buckets, I reckon.'

'No, no, Kitty,' I protested. 'That is ample, else there will be a great flood over the sides when I get in. Half that amount would have been sufficient! Good heavens, you must have been hauling water up the back stairs this last hour.'

'Oh, it didn't take me and Nan naught but two or three journeys.' Her round face glowed even redder than usual with exertion and enthusiasm.

'All these towels,' I began.

'I knowed 'ee'd want a terrible lot, bein' a lady,' she said, beaming. 'Not as I've knowed any ladies close-to afore but I 'membered Ma sayin' as gentry was raised bountiful and 'twas natural wi' them to need more of everything than ordinary folk. 'Course I had no call for bathing when Ma was livin', it being a fair stride to the pump and 'er reckoning as too much washing weakened a body and let in sickness. Howsomever, Mrs Dagget is mortal set on it and learned me well 'bout keeping clean, it bein' expected in a fine house. Her looks us over every morning to make sure we'm tidy and hasn't skimped washin', and every fortnight reg'lar, winter or summer, me and Nan and Joan has to get in a bath, just like 'ee do, ma'am.' Lest I think this too great an extravagance, she added hastily, 'We uses the same water and shares the towels. 'Twould be wasteful otherwise. An' should you want me to scrub your back, ma'am, or wash your hair, we does each other's so 'twouldn't be but what I'm practised in.'

'Thank you, Kitty,' I said somewhat faintly. 'That will not be necessary,' and scarcely had I formed the intention

not to ask her why all the cupboards stood wide for fear of
setting her off again than she cried, 'Master said as I was to
look after 'ee faithful and true like a proper lady's maid,
which I do be most hopeful to please 'ee in this, ma'am.
Mrs Dagget, 'er couldn't learn me much, though, save as
I'm to lay out your clothes an' look after 'en. But I thought
'twould lessen time and trouble if you could cast your eye
over your gee-gaws straight off and tell me 'zackly what
you'll be needing, so's I can get all ready while you takes
your bath nice and peaceful-like.'

I thoughtfully viewed the idea of bathing with Kitty in
the vicinity. Peaceful was not the adjective that sprang
naturally to mind and observing another burst of information
trembling on her lips I said quickly, 'You have been very
. . . efficient Kitty, though as this is my first morning here I
should like a little time alone to . . . to plan my day. You
will please me best by first closing all the cupboards or else
everything will be dampened by the steam, then going
downstairs and telling Mrs Dagget that all I shall need for
breakfast is a little toast and butter and a pot of her excellent
coffee.'

'No porridge, ma'am? Or eggs? Or a slice off the ham
Farmer Lugg sent over yesterday?'

'Toast, butter, coffee. Can you remember that?'

Her mouth moved as she silently repeated the words. 'Not
even no jam?' She looked so disappointed I agreed that might
be included. 'There's a fine hog's pudding. Fried in a bit of
bacon fat, 'tes powerful tasty.'

'No hog's pudding,' I said firmly. 'And I shall not need
you until after I have breakfasted. Then you may come to
the parlour and we shall have a talk about your duties.'

I shooed her out by the back door and though I planned a
speedy toilette the luxury of the steaming bath proved too

tempting, and the reviewing of my new 'gee-gaws' before deciding on a serviceable grey-green stuff gown made dressing a leisurely and pleasurable business. Greatly refreshed and feeling decidedly more benevolent towards Kitty and the world in general, I went in search of breakfast.

Even on such a sunny morning the house was shadowy, and the draughts seemed to flow everywhere in winding currents like invisible streams of cold water. I could feel them swirling round my ankles as I sat in the gloomy grandeur of the dining parlour. But, fortified by hot coffee and toast that was a perfection of toast – crisply brown outside, tenderly moist within – and which I spread lavishly with rich yellow butter and a raspberry preserve that encapsulated all the summery richness of the fruit, I found I could contemplate my surroundings a little more favourably than I had yesterday. Which was not to say that I liked the house any better, but warm and well fed as I was and with the view of sunlit gardens through the window, it was possible to be less overwhelmed by the depressing atmosphere.

As to the meeting that I had unwittingly observed between Daniel and Jess Southcote last evening, even that seemed now of less significance. I had been tired, I told myself, and my antipathy towards Jess had caused me to read a sinister meaning into what was probably a perfectly innocent incident. Daniel's restless night could have been due to anything from a business worry preying on his mind to a . . . a touch of indigestion.

So I reasoned, for to believe anything other was to invite suspicion and distrust to be constantly at my side, and they would make miserable companions. As the new mistress of Kildower, it was necessary for me to be fair and open for everyone's sake, not least my own. The future was important, not the past. I thanked heaven that it was a more cheerful morning. The kindlier weather and the promise of a busy and useful day ahead was exactly what I needed to distract my mind from further fruitless and unnecessary speculation.

When Kitty stood before me in the parlour, I had to swallow a sigh at the thought of wresting even a trace of refinement from such rough clay.

The ladies' maids I had known in the households where I had been a governess were superior upper servants, discreet women, with receipts for hair pomade or boot polish engraved on their hearts, and all manner of talents from fine sewing to a delicate way with the goffering iron at their fingertips. The prospect of Kitty Parslow achieving even the minor skill of entering a room quietly was remote.

'Kitty, you must not interrupt me,' I said for the umpteenth time. 'You will learn much quicker if you listen properly to what I am saying instead of butting in and letting your tongue run away with you. Now, what have I just told you?'

She frowned. ''Bout not comin' into the parlour wearin' a sacking apron? Oh, an' to walk a bit soft and slow, 'stead of rushing hither and yon. Was that it, ma'am?'

'Well done, Kitty. It is not so difficult to remember when you concentrate, is it?'

'But 'tes daft, beggin' your pardon, ma'am,' she said in bewilderment, 'for I was in the middle of scrubbin' the kitchen floor, and faster I walks, quicker I'll get back to 'ee. Mrs Dagget's particler about 'er floor, see, and 'er reckons Nan and Joan don't have the elbow power to shift the dirt.'

'Then it might be better,' I suggested gently, 'if you continued to do the kitchen work for Mrs Dagget, and I will train up either Joan or Nan to attend me.'

'Oh, no, ma'am!' she wailed, her round face crumpling in distress. 'I'm the eldest and been here the longest – and 'sides, I've told my Jem an' he'm mortal proud. An' don't 'ee fret that I'll not manage. For I'm powerful willin'.'

'But you will leave to be married soon.'

'Not for a whiles yet. An' I give Master my promise I should look after 'ee.'

I looked at her large red chapped hands, her beefy frame, her coarse, untidy appearance. A less likely candidate for the position of lady's maid I had never come across. But then, I thought wryly, who was I to be so choosy, who had never thought to be in the position to employ so much as a maid of all work, leave alone a personal attendant? Besides, this would be a learning process for me as much as for Kitty. When she left I would be able to advertise for someone more suitable and by then I should feel more secure in my own mind and less liable to be intimidated by an experienced servant who might be inclined to look down her nose at an employer who was a touch uncertain herself.

'Very well, Kitty,' I said. 'I am prepared to give you a fair trial, and I shall engage some good strong woman to relieve you of the rougher work. This is a large house and there is far too much to do for three maids who are so young and inexperienced.'

'Oh, thank 'ee, ma'am,' she cried, beaming once more. Then she added loftily. 'I'm seventeen, which is well growed. 'Tes the other two who just be childer. Nan's no more'n thirteen, and Joan's a year younger. A pair o' skinny little rabbits, and they was even skinnier when they come at year end, for they was trying to make a livin' runnin' errands and beggin' and such over to Saltash after their pa was killed by a runaway hoss, their ma havin' died when Joan was born.'

'I did not realise they were sisters. I see now they have a resemblance to each other – that gingery hair and those freckles.'

'Master fetched 'em in one frosty day like two half-froze kittens an' Mr Dagget said 'ee couldn't get the stink of 'en, nor the fleas, out o' the carriage for days, and Mrs Dagget, 'er wasn't too pleased at havin' the learnin' of 'en but Master said 'twas that or the poorhouse and Mrs Dagget bein' at her wits end for help put me to the scrubbin' of 'en under the yard pump.' She guffawed. 'Frost or no frost, they had to go under nekked as the day they was born and their clothes was made a bonfire of. I reckon you could have heard their squealin' over to Antony.'

Fully aware that I was once more breaking Miss Smythe's rules about gossiping with the servants, but tempted to probe deeper into the uneasy relationship that seemed to exist between Kildower and the people living nearby, I said, 'Was it not possible for Mrs Dagget to find help in the village, even as a temporary measure?'

Kitty's misshapen boots shuffled uneasily on the Turkey carpet. 'That's not for me to say, ma'am. Her might've tried, but they'm funny roundabouts. Not like over to Callington where I come from.'

'How did you come to be here?'

'Why, my Jem, ma'am. We bein' sweethearts, see, an' he knowing how I was placed when Ma died, with rent owin' and no work to be got, for I'd 'ad to give up when Ma was ill an' Farmer Jago took on another dairymaid in my place, 'e said, my Jem, he'd heard as they was fair desperate for help at Kildower, for they couldn't get maids to stay. An' I straight off made a bundle of all as I owned and Jem fetched me on 'e's cart and the minute I clapped eyes on Master, I knew 'e to be a good man and not like they makes out hereabouts. And *I* never see'd naught amiss in the house and I 'as a proper little room all to myself and never feels afeard. 'Course Mr and Mrs Dagget goes o' nights to their nice little place near the stables so they sleeps quiet, but Nan and Joan, they'm frightened of their own shadows an' sleeps wi' the sheets over their 'eads an' won't noways go alone upstairs after dark for fear they'll see . . .' Her voice trailed away and she said, awkwardly, 'Daft tales, ma'am, thass all. Don't you listen to none. And I'd best get back to the kitchen.'

'One moment, Kitty.' For an instant I wished with all my heart that I had not ignored Miss Smythe's instructions. Whatever Kitty was to tell me now would do nothing for my peace of mind. Yet how could I continue to live at Kildower without knowing what misery, what oppressive event had written itself so strongly in the atmosphere that the unhappy echoes still troubled the house? I had sensed that unhappiness the instant I had stepped across the threshold, and despite the sunshine that lay in bright patterns across the parlour carpet I knew it lurked in the shadows to creep out again when the sun was gone. My voice was quite calm as I said, 'Tell me what it is that frightens the maids at Kildower.' And, when she hesitated, I went on gently, 'Like you, Kitty, I am not a person to be influenced by silly superstitious talk.'

'Well, ma'am, I dunno. Master might not like me to say to 'ee.' She chewed her lip doubtfully. 'He's been powerful good to me, an' I shouldn't wish to lose this place.'

'I shall find out sooner or later, you know. It is evidently no secret and I should prefer the story to come from someone . . . reliable. Whom I can trust.'

She preened a little at that and the words came out in a breathless rush. ''Tes a poor, sad soul, ma'am, as can get no rest, and 'tes said as 'er wanders about the house all drippin' wet, wi' seaweed trailing about her, and wringing her hands as though 'er's in terrible trouble.'

'And who is this . . . this poor, lost spirit?'

But I knew. I knew with unnerving certainty.

'Why, 'tes 'er who took out a rowing boat on the creek yonder on a wild night and drownded herself out of being unhappy and whose body was carried off by the tides, never to be seen again and – leastways so the tale goes – 'er'll never get no rest until her bones is found and given a decent Christian burial.' Unconsciously, perhaps, her voice lowered dramatically, ''Tes Mrs Penhale, ma'am, the first Mrs Penhale, whose spirit is said to walk at Kildower.'

I had planned to spend the morning indoors. Once I had dealt with Kitty I meant to interview in turn Mrs Dagget, then Nan and Joan. I wished to discuss kitchen matters thoroughly with Mrs Dagget, if I could break through the barrier of her taciturnity, but I was eager to get to know each of the servants better and to set up a climate of understanding in which we might all flourish more happily. The rest of the day I intended to devote to Kensa. An hour or two in the schoolroom, perhaps, so that I might assess how well she did with her studies, then a pleasurable interval sorting through the materials I had brought before I started her off on some embroidery or we both settled to the cutting out and pinning of a dress for her, in which activities we might begin to get used to each other. But after Kitty had left me I cast these plans aside. I was in no mood to make careful observations and considered decisions. I was consumed instead by a great restlessness that would not allow me to sit quietly for a moment longer. I needed fresh air, exercise, brisk activity.

I went quickly upstairs, but before I went in search of my warm cloak and stout boots I crossed the landing to the nursery. In all conscience I could not forget my obligations entirely, though when I tapped at the nursery door and went in I knew that self-same conscience was suffering an unusual and unforgivable lethargy, and that I should snatch at any excuse to leave the child indoors.

After the chill of the passage outside, the warmth of the room blasted against my face. A great fire blazed behind the brass fire guard. In front of it, in an armchair, Kensa was sitting snuggled in a large shawl amid a quantity of dolls. Behind her at the table, Jess Southcote was clearing dishes and setting them on a tray.

For a fraction of a moment before they were aware of my presence there was about them, about the room, an air of careless, lazy indulgence. It was more than the surfeit of toys, the enormous dollhouse, the furnishings that I had noted yesterday to be ridiculously ample and luxurious for a child's nursery and spoke of a rich man's desire to make up to his delicate daughter for the isolation of her life, her lack of a mother's presence. It was the slow, idle movement of Jess's white hands among the crockery, the muffled murmur of Kensa's voice, her pale hair hanging tousled and uncombed about her fine-boned face, her small and narrow bare feet swinging idly to and fro against the deep silk fringes of the overstuffed chair.

Then two faces turned sharply towards me, all movement was suspended, and I said into the sudden hush, 'Good morning. And a glorious one it is, too. I believe it is too fine a day to be wasted indoors. Kensa will benefit from a stroll in the fresh air.'

'Why, Mrs Penhale, you quite gave me a turn.' Jess carefully adjusted the position of a plate on the tray before she slowly raised her head to look at me. 'I didn't hear you knock.'

'Perhaps you were making too much clatter with the dishes,' I said.

'I don't clatter good china, Mrs Penhale.' Her voice was soft, reproachful. 'I'm afraid you find us at sixes and sevens this morning. Miss Kensa had rather a disturbed night. I thought it best to allow her to sleep in this morning and to take a late breakfast, though she's managed to eat very little out of sheer weariness.'

'Poor Kensa. What was the nature of the disturbance?'

'Nightmares, Mrs Penhale. The excitements of yesterday took their toll, as I knew they would. It was far, far too much for her after her recent illness. There's always some upset after her papa has left, but the arrival of her new mama and the resulting disruption produced an attack of nervous agitation. I believe a restful day indoors, keeping warm and quiet, would be in her best interests.' Again that note of reproof as of one addressing a person guilty of thoughtless behaviour. 'Though the sun is pleasant and for a healthy person a walk would be most enjoyable, the air is still far too keen outside for a convalescent child.'

Then she smiled. That smile I was to remember long afterwards, for had she continued to maintain her air of gentle reproach I might have tolerated the annoyance of her attitude for the sake of being able to make my escape and take my walk, and thereby altered in some subtle way the tenor of all subsequent events. But for the better? Probably not. Best not to dwell too deeply on the 'if onlies' that strew life's twisted path and to believe that choices instinctively made are inevitable. Jess Southcote's smile was a challenge that forced choice upon me. Everything that might not be spoken aloud – arrogant confidence in her own superiority, contempt at the feebleness of the importunate newcomer – was contained in that scornful lift of the lips: a certainty that she was able to call the tune and the new mistress must therefore learn to dance to it.

Or it would be the worse for me.

That too. Oh, yes. Behind the contempt, behind the arrogance, which I might have chosen to overlook to prevent a premature clashing of wills while I was still so new here, there was something too dangerous to ignore. The hair on the back of my neck bristled like that of an animal scenting danger.

Retreat . . . or stay and fight?

I glanced at Kensa, who was regarding me sullenly. Her face was flushed. A feverish flush betokening threatening illness? Or the reddening of a sensitive skin in the over-powering heat from the fire? I went to her and touched her forehead. It was damp with healthy warmth, not burning with fever. Her complexion was clear. Her eyes were not heavy or shadowed from this supposed lack of sleep. On the contrary, she looked thoroughly alert although, as I continued to regard her, a sulky scowl drew down the corners of her mouth and she flopped back into the chair, half-closing her eyelids as though overtaken by a sudden weariness. There were other interesting things, too, that I noted about Miss Kensa Penhale. The way her hand slid behind her back to conceal what she had been holding, a certain look to her face . . .

So that was the way it was to be. Both of them united in the belief that I could be easily manipulated and ousted like an unwanted chick from their comfortable nest.

I walked across to the shelf of books, ran my finger along the spines, took one out and flicked through the pages.

'Mrs Penhale?' Jess's voice came soft and querying.

I turned to her, raising my eyebrows in a look of polite enquiry.

'Your walk, ma'am,' she said.

'My walk, Jess? What of it?'

'I thought you were about to take advantage of the fine morning.'

'That was my intention, certainly, before I learned that Kensa was feeling poorly,' I said, pretending surprise that she should think it necessary to question my motives for staying.

'Oh, not *poorly*, Mrs Penhale,' she said quickly. She had left off the pretence of arranging the tray. She stood with hands clasped before her in a stance that indicated, but did not quite manage to achieve, patient humility. 'She is only a little upset after a bad night. As I've already explained, she merely needs to rest quietly indoors. There really is no need for you to be worried.'

To stay, she meant. I understood very well that she did not want me here in her domain. She wished this new mistress off on her walk, out of the way, where she could not meddle and pry and generally interfere with the indolent and comfortable regimen of the nursery, a regimen very much to the benefit of Jess Southcote but perhaps, I was beginning to suspect from what I had already observed of Kensa, a great deal less so to her charge, devoted as the nurse might be to her.

Having made my selection I drew out one of the upright chairs from under the table and placed it next to Kensa's. I sat down and opened the book and only then did I look up at Jess, whose white and supple hands now seemed to be clasped together a little more tensely than before.

'Was there something else, Jess?' I said pleasantly. 'No? Then pray do not let me keep you from your chores. I am perfectly comfortable here. I shall keep Kensa company, for I see that you are more than anxious to remove the remains of your . . . very late . . . breakfast.' I paused to allow the emphasis to go home then said, 'But while you are here, perhaps this is a good moment to tell you that Mr Penhale has spoken warmly to me of your selfless devotion to Miss Kensa and the tender and reliable way you have cared for her since she was small.'

Jess lowered her lids over her shiny dark eyes and inclined her head in acknowledgement, the perfect servant modestly accepting a deserved compliment.

'I can well understand how difficult it must have been at times,' I said. 'The rearing of a delicate child – a motherless child – is a heavy responsibility, especially when the remaining parent is away a great deal. I understand that there have been many occasions when you have refused to take your half day when Kensa has been ailing, or some other domestic problem has arisen.'

'My conscience would not allow it, ma'am,' she said complacently

'Two Sunday afternoons in the calendar month was the original arrangement, I believe.'

'Only when Mr Penhale was in residence at Kildower,' she said. 'I'd never have left Miss Kensa in the care of other servants when he was detained in Plymouth, as he has been quite often over the years.'

'Quite. And your loyalty will not be forgotten. I should like to assure you that such an excellent example of faithful attention to duty will always be taken into account, whatever changes I put in hand.'

'Changes, Mrs Penhale?' Her studiedly low soft voice suddenly had a wary edge.

'Improvements, perhaps, would be a better word. The first one being that from now on I shall, naturally, shoulder all the responsibility for my new daughter's welfare.' My smile was bland but I did not take my eyes off her and I saw her stiffen, the muscles in her heavy jaw twitch as though she gritted her teeth. 'You have given years of selfless service, Jess, so it gives me particular pleasure to know that I shall be the means to make your life easier. For example, I want you to take the full day off next Sunday – no, do not protest – I insist upon it as your due, more than your due. And you shall have much more free time in the future,' I went on in the same kindly tone. 'You see, I do not at all intend to be the kind of remote mama who wishes her child to be brought to visit her twice a day for ten minutes of genteel conversation. I wish to be involved in all aspects of her upbringing. Miss Kensa's education, for example, will be my priority. I shall expect to spend several hours each day with her in the schoolroom. I understand it is some six months since the departure of the last governess and she has had little schooling since, which is a situation, I think you will agree, that cannot be allowed to continue.'

She considered this. There was a hint once more of that unpleasant little smile, as though she saw her way clear to slide from under the obstacle of my unfortunate plans and regain her authority. She said, with exactly the right note of regret, 'You may be sure, ma'am, that I'll help you all I can, but I'd caution you not to be too ambitious in the matter of Miss Kensa's schooling. It's her poor health, you see. In the past we – that is, Mr Penhale and myself, who've been closest to her and therefore more aware of the need for caution – have been reluctant to allow Miss Kensa to overtax her brain, as it seems to have a bad effect on her general well-being.'

'Really? In what way?'

'Listlessness, lack of appetite, stomach upsets . . .'

I shook my head sympathetically. 'This lack of appetite must be particularly worrisome to you. At dinner yesterday I noticed myself how she picked at her food. A good healthy diet is so important to a young child. You said she had eaten hardly any breakfast this morning, she was feeling so enervated?'

'Scarcely a crumb,' she agreed.

I leaned across Kensa's chair, delved behind the dolls and the overstuffed cushion and pulled out the poke of sweets that I had seen her thrust away. 'Is that why you allowed her to fill herself up with toffee, Jess?' I enquired pleasantly. 'Or is this eating of sweetmeats the reason for the loss of appetite in the first place?'

She was startled and annoyance she could not quite conceal flared in her eyes. 'It was just one, a treat,' she said quickly. 'Wasn't it, Miss Kensa? And I made them myself from wholesome ingredients, butter, sugar, cream.'

'All Jess's toffees are lovely,' Kensa blurted out in ill-timed defence of her nurse. 'I like them very well, and she makes them every day specially for me.'

'How very kind of Jess,' I said encouragingly. 'I see the poke is almost empty. Did you particularly enjoy the ones you ate this morning, Kensa? Your mouth is quite sticky from them.'

She began to nod, hesitated, looked from me to Jess's now thunderous face, and subsided to sullen silence.

'So it seems Kensa's appetite is not so bad after all. Merely fickle,' I said crisply. 'That is something of a relief to know. However, I think you may from now dispense with these mistaken attempts to satisfy the child's hunger with unsuitable items. Doubtless you meant well, but there will be no more sweets after today unless it is for a special treat and with my permission. Do you understand me, Jess?'

She was the first to lower her eyes, that smug and contemptuous smile quite gone. The skirmish was over. I had come out best but I did not fool myself that all was yet settled to my advantage. This was just the beginning. If I read Jess Southcote's character aright, under the mask of gracious acceptance which she had quickly assumed once she was recovered from the annoyance of being caught out in her little deception was a grasping, self-seeking woman who would not miss any chance to retaliate. She would now revise her opinion of me as someone easy to manage, and the consequences might reverberate for a long time.

When she had carried her air of martyred innocence out of the room along with the breakfast dishes, I knew I must take care in future to watch my back. For the rest of that first day, though, she was scrupulously polite and helpful, even taking my part when I decided that Kensa was well enough to get dressed and, forgoing the nursery dinner, might perfectly well be able to join me in the dining parlour as I should expect her to do each day from now on. Kensa whined and complained through the lengthy process of being got ready, the charming sprite who had yesterday smiled and danced around her devoted papa quite gone. Her head ached, her legs ached, the washing water was too cold, she felt sick ... which was no wonder at all, I thought grimly, after stuffing herself with toffee and roasting herself for hours in front of an overpowering blaze. I was rapidly coming to the conclusion that liberal doses of fresh air, exercise and disciplined activity would do Miss Penhale a deal more good, mentally and physically, than all Jess Southcote's coddling. Delicate she might be, but she seemed to have every possible encouragement towards becoming lazy and invalidish. Why, the child even seemed incapable of washing her own face and hands, standing there like pampered royalty while Jess soaped and rinsed and patted her dry then moved her about to dress her garment by garment as though it might overtax her strength to put on her own drawers and petticoat.

I kept my thoughts to myself. Direct confrontation would be unwise. Far better to take a slow route to gaining Kensa's trust, remaining unruffled through the inevitable squalls and tantrums. So I stayed calm when we closed the door on the nursery and Kensa immediately set her face to a mutinous glower which did not lift all the time she was with me.

At dinner she spat out the one mouthful she tried of the rosemary-scented mutton stew saying its toughness hurt her teeth, then spurned everything else save the sugary currant pudding with a sickly amount of cream. She spoke only to complain and answered my questions in sulky mono-syllables. The time we spent in the schoolroom afterwards was equally fruitless and frustrating. She sat with her arms folded at her charming little walnut desk and stubbornly refused to co-operate.

The schoolroom was as lavishly furnished as the nursery. Nothing had been omitted that might encourage a child to learn, from a fine set of globes on ebony stands to shelves of text books, copy books, drawing paper, paintboxes, flower presses, dictionaries and embroidery silks. Any hint of the utilitarian was banished by the pretty curtains at the windows, pastel flower prints on the walls that picked up the colours on the French carpet, the quality of the walnut desk which would now be mine and of which Kensa's was an exact miniature replica. It was so remote from the workaday, well-used appearance of every schoolroom I had known as to be quite daunting. For there was an air of such newness about it – the pages of books uncut, the embroidery silks lying in limp, regimented hanks, even the carpet free of the inevitable ink stains – that it was apparent it had been little used and, looking at Kensa's scowling face, I began to have an inkling why so many governesses had proved 'unsuitable' and had speedily taken themselves off, more than likely overjoyed to kick the dust of Kildower from their fleeing heels.

Within a very short time I was simmering with a mixture of irritation and frustration. 'I don't care to' and 'I can't' seemed to be Kensa's favourite phrases and I was forced to subdue a twinge of yearning towards the methods of control and punishment employed by the convent, which I had always deplored as being hateful and unnecessary. By the end of that long hour after dinner I do believe if Sister Ignatius had walked through the door swishing her cane or taken Kensa painfully by the ear and hauled her to the nearest cupboard to lock her in the dark until she repented of her wilfulness, I would have been hard put to make a suitable defence for the child. It was only with the greatest difficulty that I managed not to snap or scold and was just about able to maintain the air of a reasonable and worldly-wise person who was not one whit impressed or upset by her bad behaviour and would be there willing to help when she decided to behave like a civilised young person. Not that it did any good. And in the end I gladly seized upon the opportunity to give up the struggle without a disastrous loss of face when, after a loud banging on the door, Kitty appeared with a more than welcome announcement.

'Beggin' your pardon, ma'am,' she bawled as though I were standing at the other side of a barn, 'but Mrs Dagget sends 'er compliments and says the fish lad's 'ere and 'er wants to know if you'm partial to whiting or there's some fine mullet, if you'd sooner. 'Er not bein' familar with what 'ee likes.'

'Thank you, Kitty,' I said, uncaring of the crudity of the

message. 'Kindly tell Mrs Dagget I shall be down directly to speak to her.'

Kensa was out of her seat with unflattering haste when I told her she might now return to the nursery. But I could not let her go without making one last effort to breach the barrier of her antagonism. She was halfway to the door when I said quietly, 'Kensa, my intention is only to help you. I do understand that my presence here might be upsetting to you at first, but it will be so much pleasanter for us both if we try to be friends.'

She halted, her back to me, then she spun round on her heel.

'Do you know what my name means?'

Surprised by the first voluntary sentence she had addressed to me all afternoon, I shook my head and said gently, 'It is a pretty name. Cornish, is it not? But I do not know.'

'It means "first".' Her tilted blue eyes glittered with fury. 'Papa and Mama – my real mama – gave me that name. Papa says it is because he loves me first and best and he always will. You will never be first at Kildower. You don't belong here. I wish you would go away this minute and never come back. And I don't ever want to be your friend, *Step*mama.'

Then she stuck her nose in the air and stamped away across the passage. The nursery door banged to with a thud that seemed to set thunder reverberating through my head and send my hopes crashing about my ears.

By the time I descended to the kitchen that thunder had become a steady and sickly pounding at my temples and it was hard to raise any enthusiasm for the fish displayed in the wicker basket in the chilly scullery. But as Mrs Dagget suggested dourly that her special anchovy sauce went particularly well with the mullet and would make a tasty supper dish, adding that the whiting was not up to the standard she preferred, I told her I was happy to defer to her greater experience. 'And I would assure you, Mrs Dagget,' I said, 'that I am not difficult to please in the matter of food, for I have a good appetite and am as well satisfied with plain cooking as with more elaborate dishes.' Whether this pleased her or not it was hard to say. Her narrow face stayed purse-lipped and expressionless when I suggested that in future she should come to the parlour after breakfast each day to discuss menus and talk over any particular problems that may have arisen.

'I am anxious that all should run as smoothly as possible for you,' I added, 'so I should be obliged if you would make me a list of whatever you think you might need in the way of extra help or equipment and bring it with you in the morning. I should also like to speak to you about the general running of the kitchen, the marketing, the ordering and the accounting.'

Her nostrils flared. 'Everything's above board, madam. You'll find nothing amiss.'

'Oh, I was not suggesting any impropriety.'

'Mr Penhale never asked for such. He's always been well satisfied.'

'And I am sure I shall be,' I said.

'Neither me nor Dagget's the sort to take advantage.' She was so stiff with affronted dignity that her backbone might have been strapped to a brass poker.

'I am pleased to hear it, but the fact is, Mrs Dagget, I have to acquaint myself thoroughly with every aspect of housekeeping at Kildower.' I smiled to soften the firmness of my words, though it was an effort against the ever increasing throb in my head. 'I shall expect you then tomorrow, after breakfast'

'Very well, madam,' she said grudgingly. I heard her disparaging sniff as I walked away. It did not add any to my self-esteem, which had sunk dispiritingly low. The whole day seemed to have been one long struggle, to no advantage. Jess, Kensa, Mrs Dagget . . . their resentment and suspicion seemed to curdle sourly in my mind. And as I crossed the hall young Nan, carrying a broom and bucket, scuttled across its hollow dimness like a frightened rabbit, seeming to increase her pace when she caught sight of me, as though I might take it into my head to belabour her with the broom handle before she could gain the sanctuary of the kitchen. There was no gainsaying it. Save for rough and simple Kitty, the servants did not want me here any more than Kensa did, than the house did. They regarded me as an interfering outsider they could well do without, let loose in Kildower on purpose to annoy and harass them. It was a discomfitting thought to carry back upstairs to the sanctuary of the bedchamber where I thought I might rest for a while until my headache eased.

But the indigo gloom of the bedchamber seemed more comfortless than ever. I hurried through to my dressing room. The fire had long since died and the air was cold and unwelcoming. I knew, quite definitely, that I could not rest easy in here either. Far better to take the walk I had planned earlier and see if the breeze and the fresh air could charm away the sickly ache in my temples and subdue the painful echoes of Kensa's outburts.

It was as I was wearily hooking up the buttons on my stout boots that the oddness of an earlier thought struck me. I had made a most peculiar association of words. It was clear enough that Mrs Dagget was wary of me, that Kensa resented me. They were flesh and blood and had all the feelings and emotions to which humanity is prey. But the house? *The house* did not want me here? An inanimate object, constructed of other inanimate objects – stone and slate and wood and plaster – how could I have invested a house with feelings?

But even as my mind denied it, something deep within me shivered with a response that was nothing at all to do with sense and reason. *"Tes Mrs Penhale whose spirit is said to walk."* I had sensed unhappiness here from the first, yet I had been inclined after the first unnerving moments not to take too seriously Kitty's melodramatic story of Meraud Penhale drifting about the building in a seaweedy shroud. Such stories were bound to arise nurtured, as was usual after any such unfortunate event, by the ignorant and suspicious. I had come across them constantly in my travels . . . the olive grove where no one would tread after dark for fear of encountering the shades of a pair of fleeing lovers murdered by a wrathful parent; the well from which no water was ever drawn since a girl had gone mad after glimpsing an evil water sprite that lived in its mossy depths; the fissure in the ground that had swallowed a horse and rider without trace and was consequently believed to lead straight to hell. Such tales achieved an awesome credence after repetition, night after winter night, when the wind howled and the darkness pressed like black goblins against the shutters. But I was not an unschooled peasant who saw portents and omens in the flight of a bird or the colour of the dawn, or believed vengeful spirits lurked in every moonshadow. So why should I feel this sorrow, this uncomfortable sense of something *other* soaking the bones of the house. Some ancient, ancient pain hovering closer, too powerful to be forgotten or soothed away, resentful of anyone or anything that might represent an alteration towards happiness.

Not Meraud Penhale, I thought, clearly. Her unfortunate

drowning, already gathering the myth of superstition about it, was too recent. Her passing was but a minor sadness to add to the greater one that possessed Kildower. Too many had suffered here, the echo of their despair lingering down the long centuries.

I found myself staring into the depths of the press, my cloak already around my shoulders, my hand reaching for the bonnet on the shelf. For an instant there was a weird sense of dislocation, as though my mind had awakened sharply from a dreaming sleep. I had no memory of finishing the buttoning of my boots or the donning of my cloak. My hand continued its automatic movement, touched the bonnet's ruched velvet and ribbon, which seemed curiously unreal, as though reality were actually elsewhere.

Such nonsense! It must be the headache distorting my senses, filling my head with strange sounds . . . the distant keening of women's voices, a peculiar crackling as of a fierce-burning fire . . . I pulled the bonnet roughly towards me, dislodging some object that clattered from the shelf where Kitty must have put it. The sounds in my head stopped abruptly, banished by the inrush of normality. I was Sophy Penhale, alive and well as maybe, bending to pick up the fallen object, impatient to be on my way for a wholesome walk in the fresh air and finding that I was holding the box that Mama had given me. I had quite forgotten about it in the press of other, more immediate, matters. I turned it over in my hands. Juliana Sinclair. All that was known of her was in here. Did I wish to open it? I could not be sure that I did. Yet there was not, now, the instant rejection of the idea that I had felt initially. I pondered a moment. If I investigated the contents of the box it did not commit me to any further action. It would merely assuage a curiosity that I had to confess I did feel about her. I still had no wish to search out

151

this unknown sister, as Mama had ordered. Juliana, whatever her life was now, should be left in peace. But there was no harm, surely, in acquainting myself with these few mementoes. But not yet. Not today. I put the box back on the shelf. One day when I was quiet and rested and could put my mind carefully to the task I should look inside and discover what there was to be known about Juliana.

When I stepped outside I was agreeably surprised to find the air considerably warmer than I had supposed. Indeed, it was milder out of doors than within the house. Yesterday's miserably monochrome landscape was now a panorama of bright pastels. What clouds there were blew gently from the south across a fragile blue sky and late-afternoon sunshine drew a wash of hazy gold over the lawns. I stared about me with growing pleasure as I walked, aimlessly at first, content to make a slow circuit of the house with little detours to stroll the gravelled paths through the water gardens or to examine a particularly fine specimen shrub. I found there was a fine walled kitchen garden, where the gardener, Zack Bligh, was earthing up potatoes. He was a gnarled old man, looking as though he might have grown out of the soil himself, but his grin was wide and untainted by the wariness of the other servants – even though it did reveal the unfortunate black remnants of his teeth – and that added to the pleasant feeling of renewed optimism.

But I did not linger and walked on to the higher ground behind the house, where I paused to take in the wider view.

The house lay in a snug hollow protected by the rising land to the west and south and bounded from the nearby farmland on that side by a high wall. In the other direction lawns spread down the gentle slope until they dissolved into the dense woodland that fringed the river and creek which formed the natural boundary of Kildower's northerly and easterly acres. Beyond the river valley the land swooped up again to heights patched with fields and trees.

A tantalising glimpse of water beckoned me down the hill. I would walk down to the creek. It could not be too far. I could not bear to return to the house yet. I could already feel the benefit of being outside, the restorative effects of the sunshine beginning to loosen and soften the hard edges of anxiety.

I followed a grassy track that ran down the edge of the lawn past a heap of freshly sawn logs and through a coppiced thicket where the long grass was patched with puddles of newly opened bluebells and the stiff white globes of wild garlic flowers were beginning to open. A fringe of springing saplings – oak, ash, elm – fighting up through an underbrush of holly and elder and mounded brambles and then the wood proper, trees rising up abruptly in a dense tangle of ivied trunks and interlaced branches which slashed the light into dappled patches.

The path was churned with puddled hoofmarks where a horse had recently been working. I stepped carefully around another pile of logs, probably victims of winter gales and dragged out of the wood for further use as fuel in the house or to be sawn for timber. I paused to listen. There was no sound of human activity now. A jay called harshly and a flock of wood pigeons flew off above my head with a whooshing clatter of wings. Further off still a cow separated from her calf provided a faint mournful bellowing. Nothing more.

I had to pick my way slowly through the morass the horse had made of the path. My boots were soon caked in clinging black mud and the going was made doubly treacherous by the incline and the innumerable threads of small watercourses draining down the hill. Though I managed occasionally to make a short diversion through the trees, the brambly underbrush and tangles of twisted mossy roots were even more hazardous to negotiate. I realised it would take a great deal longer than I had anticipated to reach the creek and I was on the point of turning back when at a bend I saw another path. It was a mere thread of a track leading uphill. But, testing it, I saw that it was firm underfoot and even if it was only used by woodland creatures it was clearly defined. If it led to a badger sett I could easily retrace my steps. I set off more briskly, hopeful that I might find an easier route downhill or at least a viewpoint where I could get my bearings.

There was less light here and it was very still. This part of the woodland seemed older, tree trunks massive in girth, some oaks so ancient they were little more than gnarled and hollowed bark with only a few live branches bearing new leaves. The woodman and his horse had not been at work here. Where trees had fallen they had been left until ivy and bramble and thrusting new saplings had entombed them, the great craters left by their torn-out roots heavy with moss and riddled with the tunnels of small animals.

Then the clear line of the track petered out and became three lesser tracks. I was hesitating, thinking the one to the right seemed the most clearly marked, when I nearly jumped out of my skin. Something bounded past me, zig-zagging wildly in a scurry of frightened paws up the middle track, and disappeared into the trees. It went so fast I scarcely had time to focus on it, but by the time my heartbeat had steadied I found myself following where it had gone, eager to see if it really had been a hare, which I thought it would be unusual to find in deep woodland such as this. More probably it was a rabbit, though its fur had not seemed to be the normal rabbity grey-brown. This animal's pelt had a light, golden sheen and it had flashed past like a stray streak of the sunlight which now only showed itself in frugal glimpses, the canopy of trees was so dense.

I did not see it again. It had found its way out of the wood or hid itself safely away. But farther along the track I passed first one then a second stubby granite post that might well have been markers to indicate I was on some sort of proper path.

But it did not lead down to the creek as I expected. Or if it did I did not bother to follow it, for suddenly the trees drew back, there was blue sky overhead and I was out into a sunshiny glade.

My first reaction was an intense rush of delight. Shafts of sunlight angled down on to the far side of the glade where the hill rose sharply in an outcrop of rocks. A spring bubbled from this miniature cliff face and cascaded into a pool that was bounded in a wide half circle by a low grey wall. It was a sight both charming and unexpected.

My second reaction was far less pleasurable. I was not alone.

Leaning over the wall that surrounded the pool and staring into the water was a man. Perhaps it was the sharp intake of my breath that he heard, for my footsteps had made no sound on the leafmould of the path. He looked up quickly, his body tensing so tightly that I half expected him to go leaping away in alarm like the hare-like animal that I had disturbed.

We stared at each other across the green spaces of the glade. The sound of the water dancing into the pool was all that broke the silence. I seemed unable to move, to speak, as though caught in invisible bonds that refused to release me.

He uncoiled himself, the tension easing out of his body, a small tight smile curving his mouth. He stood up, gave a mocking half bow, sweeping off his battered hat to reveal the tangle of unkempt white hair. 'Mrs Penhale, is it not? Your servant, ma'am.'

I found my voice, though it came out husky. 'You!'

'Ah, you recognise me? I thought you might.'

'You were there in Highgate at my wedding.'

'Indeed I was.' His deep, educated tone was a stark contrast to his ragged appearance. 'I had a mind, you see, to witness the event. When I learned of the imminence of this unfortunate marriage I bethought me that I had more right than most to be there. A charming ceremony. You both made your vows with the greatest sincerity.'

'You were in the church?'

'For a few moments, before some fussy little personage shocked by the contamination of a holy place by such dross as myself swept me out again. And yes, before you ask, I followed your route to Exeter, which was easy enough for an ill-kempt vagabond to discover who is willing to share his bread with an underfed stable lad or cast a flirtatious eye at a bold serving wench.'

He had cold eyes, I thought. The coldest I had ever seen. Bleak as chips of flint in a face so pared of flesh that the sallow skin was stretched drum-tight across the bone save for two deep clefts running from nose to chin and a network of fine lines about the eyes. A face old in experience, but in years, perhaps, not so much older than Daniel.

'But who are you?' I burst out. 'What right have you to spy on me . . . on us.'

'Every right, Mrs Penhale.' A pause while those cold eyes slowly raked me over from the tip of my muddied boots to the top of my bonnet. 'Allow me to introduce myself properly. My name is Conan Trewithen, former gentleman of this parish. You will doubtless recognise the surname but perhaps not the name that I was given at my baptism. That is as I expected. Daniel Penhale believes that I am long since dead and buried and can safely be forgotten. No longer a threat to his peace of mind. Or his new marriage. But as you see, ma'am, I am very much alive.'

'Trewithen?'

'A common enough name hereabouts. But I am of a particular breed of Trewithen. My ancestors built Kildower, which should have been my inheritance had not my great-grandfather frittered away his fortune on beautiful women and magnificent horses and left his male descendants with nothing save a proud name, a misplaced sense of their own importance in the scheme of things and a lust for the land that could no longer be theirs. My sister and I were born the last of our line. I, true to family tradition, furthered the ruin of the Trewithens by espousing myself to a lost cause, for which I was duly rewarded by being removed by the estimable forces of the law to a place as far off as it is possible to be from everything I held most dear. So my young sister was left alone to cope as best she may. A young girl of barely sixteen summers, delicate in health with scarcely a penny to call her own. My sister's name was Meraud. You recognise that name, do you not? She was your predecessor, my dear Mrs Penhale. Daniel's first wife, who drowned herself out of grief and loneliness.' His voice was as icy as his eyes. 'Which makes Daniel Penhale my brother-in-law. And God forgive him for the harm he wreaked on that frail and helpless spirit, for I never shall. I never shall.'

Chapter Four

The pool was known as St Bride's Well and was reputed
among the local women to have healing powers. Conan
Trewithen told me that before he left me there. Once he had
gone I walked across the soft grass and looked down into
the water. Meraud had loved this spot. He had told me that
also. 'My mother fetched her here as a child when she was
desperately sick with a fever and all other remedies had
failed. She retained a fondness for the scene of her
miraculous recovery and often walked here.'

'And this pool is on Kildower land?' I breathed, trying
to gather my scattered wits.

'It is.'

'Then you are trespassing, Mr Trewithen,' I said, my
voice gathering strength, 'and I would be obliged if you
would instantly remove yourself.'

'I have every right.'

'You have no right, sir. None at all. By your own
admission you are some sort of rogue. By your very actions
– spying, luring innocent servants into indiscretions – you
condemn yourself. Now be off . . . or . . .' I faltered.

'Or you will summon the six burly men you have hidden
in the bushes to throw me off Daniel Penhale's land?' His
laughter mocked my helplessness. 'Or will you personally
take me by the coat-tails and fling me back where I belong?'

An unexpected anger possessed me. All the frustrating events of the day seemed to billow up in a hot wave. I had quite enough to contend with without being contaminated by the poison this person claiming kinship to Daniel wished to disgorge. How dare he lurk here, tainting the green and gentle serenity of the glade with his veiled accusations and air of knowing far more than he cared to tell! How dare he stand there as though he owned the place!

I was so fired that I could have flown across the grassy space between us and struck him. Indeed, I clenched my fists and took a step towards him, though the anger erupted into words rather than action. 'If you, sir, are a sample of the Trewithen breed, then it is to be hoped that you truly are the last of the line. A gentleman? Hah! I have known beggars in the streets of Florence behave in a more seemly manner towards a lady! Whatever punishment was meted out to you for your misdemeanours – transportation, was it? – it has evidently taught you no manners. But when it is known how you have trespassed today, in order to harass a defenceless woman on her own property, the magistrates might arrange for you to have a second chance!'

For an instant he was disconcerted. I saw it in the flicker of his eyelids, the tension springing back into his gaunt frame. Whether my words forced him to realise how his chance meeting might be interpreted or whether it was my anger that surprised him into being more cautious, I do not know. But when next he spoke his tone was almost conciliatory.

'Well, well, Mrs Penhale. There is more fire in you than I should have supposed. How very interesting that Daniel should have chosen such a spirited little mouse to be his wife. I wonder if that was wise of him.'

'It is not for you to suppose or wonder, Mr Trewithen, but to be on your way.'

'And you were quite right. It was transportation to Botany Bay that was my punishment,' he said. 'Ten years I had of it, of squalor, cruelty and degradation. And no tuition whatsoever in good manners, unfortunately, so I must regretfully refuse the offer of a second term among the flies and heat. It would be of little benefit.'

'Then go this minute, sir, and I may choose to overlook your trespass.'

'Of course.' Another bow, pressing his battered hat to his heart. '*Au revoir*, then.'

'Goodbye, Mr Trewithen. My husband will be returned to Kildower on Saturday evening. I am sure he would be willing to grant you an interview should you wish to repeat your insinuations to his face.'

He went very still, the mockery dying away, then he said quietly, 'You see before you a poor man, Mrs Penhale, but I do now have one precious luxury at my disposal after the long years of having to guard even my most private thoughts against those who believed they had the privilege to command them. That luxury is freedom. The freedom to speak as I choose, to go or stay as I please. So, no, I will not go creeping to Kildower when it suits Daniel Penhale to grant me a few moments of his precious time. If I wish to speak to him I shall choose the time and the place. And maybe I shall make him wait. There is no hurry, and I shall enjoy the waiting. I fear Daniel may not. But then, I have nothing on my conscience and he has a great deal.'

'What do you mean?' I demanded.

'My sister was an innocent, helpless girl until she took Daniel Penhale's eye. It was his lust that turned her smiles to tears, his ruthless demands that forced her into a marriage she never wanted after I was taken to the living hell of the hulks and the stinking heat of slavery in New South Wales

161

and could no longer protect her.'

'No! that cannot be!'

'You think not?' He gave a short, bitter laugh. 'How little, then, you know your husband, Mrs Penhale. But I know him, make no mistake about that, and I shall extract much pleasure from making him pay for Meraud's suffering – and for mine whenever I thought of how he had destroyed her young life and set mine into torment because I should never see her again.' He lifted his bony shoulders in a careless gesture that went oddly with the cold flint of his gaze. 'You may tell him or not as you please about our meeting. That is your freedom also.'

He turned on his heel and was gone, melting back among the trees, his ragged clothes momentarily blending with the broken shadows like the dappled coat of a deer.

The water was deep and clear below the wall. It eddied gently over pebbles and smoothly waving weed and I could see minute creatures darting in and out of the slanting shafts of sunlight that speared down into the water. My knees were trembling. I was glad to sink to the low wall. God in heaven, such hatred. It emanated from the very pores of Conan Trewithen like a deadly perspiration, as though his whole being was soaked in it to saturation point. And Daniel – my kind, generous Daniel – No! I would not believe that he had been guilty – but guilty of what? Some supposed wrong inflicted on a man whose brain had been turned by years of brooding while he served his punishment . . . *gentleman of this parish* . . . he was lying . . . *lustful hands on my sister* . . .

Down among the pebbles at the bottom of the pool I saw an oyster shell, new and white, the water drifting over the pearly sheen of its inner surface. And there were other things. A copper coin, a fragment of pretty china – and surely that could not be a ring. Even if it were only brass it was a valuable thing for some poor person to have lost. Lost?

I raised my head and looked at the tree that stood nearest to the pool. An old ash tree. Among the new-sprung leaves on its lower branches there was a fluttering of strips of cloth, handkerchiefs, ribbons, some so old and weather-worn that they were reduced to a few grey threads. Of course. Votive offerings. Small tokens left for the saint . . . the spirit . . . of the spring when her powers had been invoked.

Meraud. Meraud had come here often. Had she prayed to the saint then tied a ribbon to the ash tree or dropped some small, precious gift into the water to ensure that St Bride looked kindly on her request? I wondered what she had prayed for. Good health, certainly, if the well had a reputation for healing. But the spirit of a benevolent saint would surely be sympathetic to any trouble that afflicted those who sought her aid. Had Meraud, the lonely and helpless Meraud her brother had portrayed, sought comfort here for her despair in being married to Daniel? And, not finding it, drowned herself?

No! No! No! It had been an accident. Daniel had told me so. To believe anything other was to feel the solid foundations of my trust in him, in his honesty and in our new life together, shiver, as a trembling in the ground presages the beginnings of a great earth tremor that will twist and crumple the land until it is unrecognisable.

I tore off my glove, thrust my hand into the pool and raised it, cupped, so that a tiny puddle of water remained in my palm. I splashed the stinging drops across my burning cheeks and pressed my wet palm to my forehead, where the fading headache had sprung up again to a sickly pounding. I closed my eyes against the smarting dazzle of sun reflecting from the water.

I do not ask or expect that we should fall in love with

each other, Miss Beardmore. I have known the agony and the rapture of that relentless passion. I would not wish to know it again. So much pain in those few spare sentences Daniel had uttered. Daniel. Guilty, surely, only of loving too much, hurt so badly by Meraud's death that he had waited nearly nine years before he felt able to marry again. A considered marriage to a woman he perceived – and I had always striven to be so – as capable and sensible. Not a weak, shaking creature who found herself bent this way and that by confused emotions like the weeds in the water eddies.

I wiped my damp hand against my cloak, drew on my glove and slowly inhaled the scents rising strongly about me. The good, natural scents of rich growth, of warm sun on damp, fecund earth. The gentle trickle of the water into the pool, the faint rustle of the breeze in the tops of the trees, the calling of birds busy with nests to guard, chicks to feed. So sheltered here, so peaceful that even the ugly discords the ragged man had brought into the glade became absorbed into the deep calm, were rendered harmless. The chaos of my thoughts smoothed and settled to lucidity.

My loyalty was to Daniel and his child. Nothing could be allowed to interfere with that. I must put aside all other distracting notions. I had no business with rumour and ill-wishing and muddled, highly coloured interpretations of plain facts. I must hold firm to my promise, my intention, to love, honour and obey my husband. Nothing else would bring either of us contentment.

It was hard to leave this pleasant spot but I had sat longer than I intended and my feet and legs were cold and stiff. I cast a glance backwards before I left, as though to imprint the scene on my mind. The sun had dipped behind the trees. The pool lay in green translucent shadow, tranquil in its leafy bower.

I walked briskly back through the woods to restore my circulation. I was halfway home before I realised that the distant cow was still bellowing dismally for her calf. And that my headache was quite, quite gone.

Kensa, the moment her father appeared on Saturday evening, magically changed back to the sparkling, charming little creature who had been entirely absent these last few days. I was both amused and surprised at the ease with which the transformation took place, for she had been all glowers and complaints as we sat by the parlour fire to wait for Daniel. I patiently attempted to show her some easy embroidery stitches and almost immediately she scratched herself on the needle. I tried not to believe it was deliberate, but the triumphant way she threw down the linen, and her declaration that Papa would be very cross if he knew how cruel I was to insist that she carry on when she felt so very faint and dizzy at the sight of the blood, convinced me otherwise. The minute red speck was scarcely discernible, though she nursed her finger as though it had suffered serious damage.

'Dear me,' I said mildly, 'how very unfortunate that you should feel poorly when Papa is due at any moment.' I returned my needle to its flannel case and laid my own embroidery back in my workbasket. 'Still, he will perfectly understand that it was not possible for you to be waiting here for him.'

'What do you mean?'

'Now please do not be alarmed at the giddiness,' I said, my voice full of concern. 'I will help you to your room, for I should not wish you to stumble on the stairs and hurt yourself.' I shook my head sadly. 'Papa will be disappointed not to see you looking so pretty and wearing your coral beads, but I know he would far rather that you rested quietly in bed than overstrain yourself by pretending you are well when you are not.'

She was clearly disconcerted, the wish to play the martyr warring with her need not to miss her father's arrival. I made to rise, which prompted her to say quickly, 'I think the dizziness is passing.' She drew her hand across her brow in a manner reminiscent of an actress in the melodrama that Daniel and I had seen at the theatre in Exeter. I was hard put to suppress a smile. 'Yes, yes, I feel *much* better now.'

'Well, if you are sure.' I settled back with a show of reluctance. 'All the same, you had best sit very still lest there is a recurrence of the trouble. For if there is the slightest sign that you are at all sickly we must make haste to get you to bed.'

So she sat in sullen silence until there came the sound of the carriage, when the sulky child was instantly transformed into the beguiling sprite her father knew and adored.

Even to me she was careful to be polite and smiling, though I had a feeling this would not continue beyond Daniel's farewell on Monday morning. But it was to be welcomed while it lasted.

'Have you been a good girl for Mama?' Daniel asked when the first greetings were over and we had returned to the parlour. Kensa had clung to her father's hand, drawing him to the sofa, where she snuggled up against him. I took my seat on the opposite side of the hearth and opened the letters he had brought, a scrappy few lines from Mama, the first she had bothered to write since my marriage, and a long, gossipy missive from Sir Richard. I was content to let the child hold centre stage. Best to do so, I thought. She saw me as an interloper, a rival for her father's affections, and I must tread delicately when the three of us were together in order to reassure her that she had nothing to fear.

'Yes, Papa,' she whispered, then gave a world-weary sigh and leaned her cheek on her father's sleeve. 'I do try to learn, Papa, to please you and Mama, but my back aches so when I sit for too long at my desk and I get very tired. Then I have bad dreams because of it and I wake Jess up and she worries dreadfully.'

He stroked her hair. 'Poor little moppet,' he said. He cast an anxious glance at me.

'It will come easier when you are used to it,' I said quietly. 'It is a long time since you did any proper school work, is it not? It is bound to be a little tiring at first.'

Daniel could not see the cross expression that drew down her brows. 'But I'm not clever,' she said in the same frail little voice. 'Girls don't have to be, do they, Papa? You said so. Not like boys.'

'Certainly it is not necessary,' he agreed.

'Well then.'

'Sweetheart, there are still some accomplishments required of a young lady,' he said tenderly. 'You have a kind and clever mama now to help you to grow up wise as well as beautiful. One day you will be glad you paid attention to your lessons, when you are married yourself and have your own house and family to manage.'

'Never!' She clung to his arm. 'Papa, I shall never want to leave Kildower. I love it too well. I shall stay here with you and look after you for ever and ever.'

He smiled. 'Ah, yes, you may believe that now, but in a few years' time some handsome young man will come a-courting and you will fall in love and not give a fig for your poor old papa. Which is how it should be or the world would stop turning and the moon would turn to green cheese from the shock.'

'You're teasing me, Papa.' She pouted prettily, but

perhaps she could see that he was not to be coaxed and let the subject drop. To me, when Jess had fetched her up to bed, Daniel allowed his anxiety to resurface.

'You will take care, my dear, not to overtax Kensa's strength?'

'Of course.'

'In her desire to please you she may set aside any little symptoms which may indicate that she is becoming wearied.'

'You need have no fear on that score.' I hoped he did not catch the dryness in my tone.

'And you find her a satisfactory pupil?' He spoke casually, but I sensed behind the words a desperation to be reassured that all was well. I was glad that I had decided to make no mention of the difficulties I had encountered. I did not wish Daniel to return to Plymouth burdened with unnecessary worries, not least among them that I was unable to cope with his daughter.

'She is an intelligent and imaginative child,' I said, concentrating on the working of a stem-stitch tendril, 'but with all the schooling she has missed I think she has got out of the way of settling down to steady work.' I tied off the thread and snipped it with the scissors. 'There, Daniel, do you think that looks well? It is the first of a set of table napkins for Nutmeg Street. You see I have embroidered the letter "P" for Penhale in the corner entwined with vine leaves.'

'Charming,' he murmured, scarcely casting a glance at the square of linen, 'but this inability to settle to work . . .'

'She will learn in time,' I said comfortably. 'We must take a steady course with her, neither pressing her too hard nor being too indulgent.' I smiled at him. 'What is important in these early days, Daniel, is that Kensa and I should get used to each other. And, above all, that the three of us should make the most of every moment you are at Kildower. I have given Jess the whole day off tomorrow as the poor woman has scarcely had an hour to herself while you were gadding about the country with me, and I am being entirely selfish in this, for I shall so much enjoy having Kensa with me all day. I thought we might all three go to church – you told me you generally go to morning service when you are here – then after dinner take a walk if the weather is fine. Otherwise we can stay indoors and entertain ourselves with cards – could Captain Penhale be cajoled to join us? – perhaps toast some of Mrs Dagget's excellent muffins on the fire . . . in fact, be thoroughly lazy and profligate.'

Roseate pictures blossomed in my head as I spoke; of Daniel and I walking arm-in-arm in the sunlight with Kensa skipping happily ahead; of the church porch full of smiling country folk imbued with kindly interest towards us; of the rigidly formal parlour transformed into a cosy, firelit cave where laughter spilled about as freely as buttery muffin crumbs. If my belief was firm enough, surely some of it might actually be brought to reality.

Daniel looked at me intently. I could not read the expression in his eyes. Then he rose so abruptly that I thought I had offended him by being over-eager with my plans.

He went to the window and stood with his back to me, a bulky silhouette against the evening light, and when he spoke his voice was tight, almost curt. 'I have dreamed of this, Sophy, that we might be united as a family.' He cleared his throat. 'It is gratifying that your intentions are in tune with mine. I shall be happy to co-operate with you tomorrow in whatever you suggest.'

He said nothing more, but that evening I felt that he watched me rather more closely than was usual. Several times I was a trifle disconcerted when I glanced up to find that his attention was not on his book or his newspaper but on me. I was quite relieved when he suggested we retire early and I need no longer search my mind for subjects of conversation to fill what seemed to be a kind of charged silence between us. I eventually decided that I was allowing my imagination too much play. I was very anxious to please him. Too anxious. And the few days apart had made us a little self-conscious with each other. That was all. Daniel's touch upon my body was no different when he turned to me after he had snuffed out the candle. It was my over-active imagination that supplied a hesitancy that had not been there before, a lightness in the play of his fingertips against my skin that made me shiver suddenly and violently. I heard the catch of his breath, then, and his hand lifted to carefully draw the sheets up around my shoulders, though I was not cold at all. After he had made love to me in his usual careful, respectful way and he slept, I lay awake consumed by a restlessness of mind and body which I could only put down, crossly, to a tendency in my character, hitherto unprovoked and most certainly inherited from Mama, which was now beginning to surface as a tendency to exaggerate my feelings until they began to play upon my nerves. I eventually fell asleep vowing to guard against such self-indulgence in the future and by morning I was fully restored to cheerful spirits, greatly helped by the brightness of the day and the knowledge that Daniel, Kensa and I were to spend the whole of it together, free of the reproachful presence of Jess Southcote.

Jess was clever, though, in ensuring that we did not shake her off too easily. When she fetched Kensa down the next morning Dagget was already with the carriage at the door and Daniel was impatiently snapping open his watch as we stood in the hall. Jess, too, was dressed for the outdoors in a cloak the colour of port wine and a straw bonnet heavy with ribbons of the same rich shade. Her bearing and manner seemed to imbue the cheap quality of the materials with a distinction above the ordinary and made a mockery of her humble tone of voice when she said, 'I'm sorry for the delay but Miss Kensa's muff had somehow been mislaid and we had to search for it. When that silly girl Nan brought up the clean bedlinen on Tuesday, she put it in the wrong cupboard and must have pushed a quantity of gloves and the muff to the back of the shelf in order to make room. Oh, dear, I do hope I have not made you late for church, Mrs Penhale.'

'Not if we make haste,' I said. 'Come along, Kensa.'

'Papa,' Kensa cried, 'may Jess drive with us? She is going to church, too, and if she has to walk she will never be there in time.'

'Yes, yes,' Daniel said, frowning at his watch. 'Hurry now or we shall none of us be there until the service has started.' He swept us all into the carriage, Jess sliding herself in next to Kensa, bending over her to smooth back a strand of pale hair, to remove an invisible speck from the fine light blue cloth of Kensa's skirt, to stroke a proprietorial, cotton-gloved hand over the smooth white fur of the pretty muff, and all the time wearing a small complacent smile as though in acknowledgement of some previously planned objective satisfyingly gained.

'It's most kind of you to allow me this privilege, Mr Penhale,' she began as the carriage made brisk progress along the drive. 'I would not have troubled you for the world.' Then with a low, teasing laugh, 'Miss Kensa, you are a naughty girl to have suggested that I ride with you, though I mustn't be too cross when you show so much evidence of care for your poor old nurse, dear little soul that you are.'

These fulsome and patently sycophantic words grated so severely on my ears that I was amazed to see Daniel smile in agreement. But then, his vision of Jess or his daughter was not mine and perhaps I was over-sensitive where Kensa's nurse was concerned. Nevertheless, I said, a touch brusquely, before she spilled out more toadying phrases, 'What plans do you have for the rest of your free day, Jess?'

'I have relatives living nearby, Mrs Penhale. I am to meet them in church and return with them to the farm for Sunday dinner.'

'And which farm is that?' I enquired, hopeful that it was a long way off.

'Trebarth, madam. Mrs Lugg is a distant cousin of mine.'

'Farmer Lugg's land lies alongside Kildower's, my dear,' Daniel explained.

'Ah, yes,' I said. 'It is he who supplies us with dairy produce and excellent bacon and ham.'

'It was through Mrs Lugg that Jess came to Kildower in the first place,' he said. 'You had come on a visit to your cousin had you not, Jess?'

'Indeed, sir, I'd come from Barnstaple to help her look after the children when they were all laid low with scarlet fever. 'Twas while they were convalescing that I heard Miss Kensa was in need of a nurse, and offered to help out.'

'And proved such a tower of strength that I persuaded her to stay on.'

She bowed her head modestly. 'I took little persuasion, sir, for the plight of the dear motherless infant had quite touched my heart.'

And doubtless the fact that there was no mistress to interfere with the comfortable regimen she quickly established had appealed to her too. I crushed down this cynical thought. It was Sunday, I was on my way to church and it was scarcely Christian to be so uncharitable. I turned my face resolutely to the window in an attempt to achieve a more seemly frame of mind and my attention was instantly caught by the sight of Captain Penhale, resplendent in navy broadcloth and much gold braid, coming across a field towards the lane, making brisk progress in the direction of the village despite the awkwardness of his gait. A shaggy grey shadow loped at his heels.

'Is Captain Penhale bound for church also?' I enquired.

'He never misses since the vicar allowed him to bring Pirate in to the service,' Daniel said. My look must have registered my surprise, for he laughed and said, 'My father believes Pirate to encompass all the highest traits of human nature. That is, he is faithful, obedient, trusting and devoted. The previous incumbent would have no truck with the Captain's argument that his hound merited a place in the house of God more than those among the parishioners who paid lip service on a Sunday and spent the rest of the week philandering, cheating and lying. The dog was barred and the Captain out of pique refused to enter the church without him. He would stand outside during the service and bellow the psalms and responses loudly to the yews and gravestones, with Pirate adding his own voice from time to time. The vicar was a choleric old man and his wrath was a sight to behold. I often wonder if the apoplexy that finally forced him to retire to his daughter's home in Truro was in some part due to my father's weekly performance at the church door, though the Captain says that it was God striking the vicar down for his lack of charity.'

'And do not people mind to see such a great dog in church?'

'Some have taken offence, but the new vicar, Mr Miles, is a benevolent man and given to tolerance rather than confrontation. Though I am inclined to think his children may have influenced him,' he added mischievously. 'They are a lively brood and make a great fuss of Pirate each Sunday, bringing him all manner of titbits.'

'I think the vicarage children are very rough and noisy,' said Kensa in a plaintive little voice. 'The last time you brought me to church, they all had colds and I caught it from them and had a terrible cough as well and was very poorly. And the smallest one, Violet, pulled my hair so hard that my head hurt for an hour.'

'That was back in the winter, sweetheart. They will surely be free of colds now, and the little one more sensible. She thought your hair so pretty and she did not understand that she was hurting you.' But he looked uneasy as he spoke and I knew the worries he had voiced earlier were troubling him.

'I have been thinking, Sophy, that the church is still cold and damp at this time of the year, and there are always all manner of infections rife among the village folk,' he had said at breakfast. 'I am not sure that it is wise for Kensa to accompany us this morning. Do you suppose we should leave her with Jess until we return? I am sure Jess would not mind.'

'That would be quite unfair on Jess, when I have promised she should have the day to herself,' I had said quickly.

He frowned. 'I suppose it would.'

'Besides, the day is so fine and mild that it would be a shame to leave Kensa indoors when she would get so much benefit from the walk.'

'If she is to come with us we shall take the carriage,' he said firmly. 'On that I must insist, otherwise she will be wearied before the day has properly begun.'

And with that I had to be content, even though I felt that the child suffered more from a lack of exercise than a surfeit.

I said now, brightly, to distract him, 'I look forward to meeting the vicar and his family. How many children are there? And what of Mrs Miles?'

174

'I have only spoken briefly to her, but she seems a warm and pleasant person. There are five little girls though the eldest is away at school in Exeter. Ah, here is the market cross. We shall not be late, after all, I think.'

We turned right into one of the lanes that met there and followed it round to where it widened to a roughly cobbled triangle before the church. The village looked a deal less dreary than it had in the rain. The sun cast a kindly light even on the poorest of the tumbledown cottages and round about the church there were one or two houses of the better sort, with a well-preserved look to them and tidy front gardens.

The church bell was still pealing when the carriage drew up before the lych gate and we alighted. Jess continued to fuss about Kensa, whose bonnet strings seemed to have come loose. The business of retying them to Jess's satisfaction took some minutes so that Daniel and I were obliged to wait in the church porch for them to catch us up. I could not rid myself of the impression that this was deliberate. I was sure of it when I saw the way her dark eyes narrowed as I said briskly, 'We must not impose on you any longer, Jess.'

'Oh, you are not imposing.'

'Come, Kensa, we must not be selfish, walk alongside Papa now or poor Jess will begin to suspect that we do not intend her to have a day off at all. Why, the morning is half gone already while she waits upon us.'

Jess's smile was a little tight as she released her hold on Kensa. I stood back and indicated she could go ahead, which left her no option but to proceed. Her chin was very high as she swept past. She favoured Daniel with a gracious dip of the head, Kensa with a pained smile and me, who had thwarted her from making the entrance she would have preferred as a valued and necessary component of the

Kildower party, with a view of her high-nosed profile. I could not help feeling a certain guilty satisfaction at being rid of her at last as I watched her stiff back retreating into the dimness of the nave.

Kensa was happy enough to transfer herself to her father's side, especially as it meant that she could occupy this supreme position while we walked down the narrow centre aisle, for there was not room for the three of us to walk comfortably abreast. Our footsteps rang hollowly on the uneven flags and I was aware of sideways glances and, in the sudden cessation of the bell, of a ripple of whispering amongst the sparse congregation. Only two or three pews were full. Jess was squeezing herself into one already occupied by several large, stout persons whom I presumed to be her Lugg cousins. The front pew to the left of the aisle contained, I supposed by the number of bonnets in a descending order of sizes, Mrs Miles and her daughters. On the other side of the aisle was the Kildower pew, well furnished, I was pleased to see, with faded cushions to ease the hard angles of the seat and stout kneelers to protect against the discomfort of the lumpy paving stones.

We had barely time to settle ourselves when the minister, a stoop-shouldered, scholarly-looking gentleman of middle years took up his place, cast a vague glance over his flock and began the service.

Two weeks since, Daniel and I had attended matins at Exeter Cathedral. The memory of the glorious harmonies of the choristers, the fine sermon and the magnificence of the setting was still strong. Such a contrast then this small country church smelling of damp stone and mildew, the singing led by two old men with unsteady voices, a boy and a bass-viol player who, though vigorous in action, was inclined to coax a regrettable number of squeaks and painful discords from his instrument. The occasional protesting moan from the back of the church when a particularly excruciating note was struck signified the delicacy of Pirate's sensibilities and signalled an eruption of giggling and shushing from the Miles' pew. I confess that my own composure was sorely tested at these moments and I was forced to gaze fiercely at a stern angel carved on a memorial tablet on the south wall just beyond the Kildower pew in order to concentrate my mind. Daniel seemed at the same time to have some difficulty with a cough which necessitated that he muffle his mouth in his handkerchief.

The unfortunate discords had no effect on the Reverend Mr Miles, whose expression never wavered. He evidently dwelt on a saintly plane where even execrable harmonies might be construed as pleasing to the Almighty in their intention, however painful their execution. When he climbed into the pulpit, the text for his sermon, 'Comfort ye, comfort ye my people, saith your God,' seemed peculiarly pointed and caused me once again to seek the stern admonition of the marble angel, though presently I settled enough to be able to take in what Mr Miles was saying.

His scholarly air did not incline him to distinction as a preacher for it was a rambling sermon with many learned but abstruse references. I soon lost the thread altogether. I feared I was not the only one to do so for there was a great deal of restlessness and throat clearing among the congregation as the minutes stretched out to ten, to fifteen. Kensa, on her best behaviour, sat very quietly, hands tucked into her white muff. I saw that her eyes were unfocussed and her lips moved as though she was in an engrossing world of her own. I wondered what it was that claimed her imagination and then, a little sadly, if I should ever be able to grow close enough for her to confide in me her thoughts and hopes. Then my own gaze drifted back to the memorial guarded by the marble angel. I could make out some of the Latin inscription endowing this seventeenth-century Petroc Trewithen with a great many wondrous attributes. They were all Trewithen memorial tablets clustered along this stretch of wall. More than two centuries of husbands, wives, parents and children, every one noble, charitable, worthy to a degree, as persons of all ranks were inclined to be represented once they were no longer in the living world and their lesser characteristics could not be observed. I turned my head to read the one nearest to me, a glossy oblong of polished slate, deeply incised. A beloved and affectionate wife, sorely missed by her grieving husband, tragically drowned when the Lynher was in flood.

Meraud Penhale. So close that I might reach out and touch the name. Instinctively I glanced at Daniel. He looked as lost in his thoughts as his daughter, eyes half closed, chin sunk into the snowy folds of his cravat. Was he thinking of her? Did he look at that memorial each time he came into church and reflect on the long, barren years without her? I realised that I had seen no memento of her at Kildower, no portrait, no feminine trinkets or ornaments arranged to lighten the aspect of the heavy furniture. Her brief residence in the house had made no impression upon it. Her personal possessions had been removed, put away perhaps in one of the attics where the clutter of years was stored. But then, there was no necessity for material mementoes at Kildower, when the most powerful reminder lived and breathed. The image of the mother was recreated in the elfin child, a daughter who could be adored, spoiled and treasured as the mother had once been. Daniel would never lose Meraud as long as Kensa lived. And nor should I. That was a thought I found unexpectedly disturbing.

The congregation stirred. The vicar was descending the pulpit steps. Soon enough it was time for the final blessing and Daniel and I were walking out into the mild air as we had walked before from the chapel on Highgate Hill. And I could not help scanning the faces of the people standing about in a sudden nervous apprehension that Meraud's brother might again be watching, waiting, with his flinty eyes and his hatred, to blight the day.

But he was not there and before I could reflect uneasily on the fact that I had not yet mentioned to Daniel my encounter with Conan Trewithen, and indeed whether I wished to put myself in the position of being the bearer of these tidings, Daniel was drawing me forward to where Mr Miles was greeting each member of the congregation.

'Mrs Penhale, how very glad I am that you have chosen to grace our congregation this morning.' Mr Miles bowed stiffly as Daniel made the introductions. 'And if I might present my wife.'

I think we were friends, Edith Miles and I, from that first moment, though I did not realise it then. I merely found her easy to talk to as we exchanged politenesses appropriate to the occasion at the church door. She was a rosy-cheeked woman of about thirty years of age with quantities of slippery fair hair escaping from under her bonnet and thick eye glasses that gave her a look of owlish surprise. I thought the look deceptive for there was intelligence in the gentle brown eyes and a quiet authority in the way she spoke to her young daughters when they hastened back to her side after bestowing hugs and titbits upon Pirate. The hound, I noticed, tolerated this attention with noble dignity before trotting off after his master, who made no pretence at any civilities but was off through the lych gate and on his way before the vicar or anyone else could catch him up.

The girls made shy curtsies to me. Their rosy faces were scrubbed clean, but they were untidily dressed in a mismatched assortment of what appeared to be hand-me-downs. Mrs Miles herself wore an old-fashioned grey wool gown clumsily darned in places with ill-matching thread. Her fingers were visible through several holes in her kid gloves and her bonnet had at some time suffered a serious crushing from which it had been rendered permanently crippled. These church mice, I thought, were decidedly of the poorest sort. Either that or Mrs Miles was so unworldly that she did not even notice or care about outward show. But I liked her gentle manner and was pleased when she said in a smiling way that did not make it sound too much like a duty she was bound to perform as the vicar's wife, 'I had thought to call upon you in the week, Mrs Penhale, if you should be at home.'

'I should like that very much,' I said warmly. 'Perhaps you would take tea with me on Wednesday afternoon. Shall you bring your daughters?'

She laughed. 'I would not presume to inflict the whole brood upon you, Mrs Penhale, but the elder two, Chloe and Rhoda, I could guarantee to behave tolerably.'

'Then of course they must come with you.'

'That is most kind, Mrs Penhale. Good gracious, the girls will think themselves very grand and grown-up being invited to tea at Kildower,' she added with disarming frankness.

'It will be delightful for Kensa to have girls of her own age to talk to. We shall both look forward to your visit, shall we not, Kensa?'

'Of course, Mama,' she said in a shrivelled voice, at the same time looking down her fine nose with the air of someone experiencing an unfortunate smell wafting by her nostrils. I wanted to take her by the shoulders and shake her. Yet for all her rudeness I could not help but feel a twist of laughter, for her manner was that of a middle-aged woman with pretensions to gentility who could scarcely bear to exchange a civil word with a person of inferior status lest she be contaminated by the association. It had been my misfortune to meet one or two such persons in my time but I had not expected to find this trait exhibited so strongly – and comically, had she but known it – in my own nine-year-old stepdaughter.

Fortunately, or perhaps tactfully, Mrs Miles seemed not to notice. Then she turned aside to speak to two elderly ladies and Daniel offered me his arm for the walk back to the carriage.

Knots of people lingered in the churchyard and in the open space beyond the gate. A sprinkling of respectable villagers in their Sunday best slid sideways glances in our direction. Others, rougher and bolder, openly watched our progress. I had expected nothing less, for in a small village the arrival of a newcomer such as myself was an event. Everyone was bound to be curious. What I had not expected was the manner of this curiosity. Hostility was clearly evident on several faces and though one or two of the more prosperous-looking gentlemen acknowledged Daniel with a polite greeting, their wives, to a woman, seemed possessed of a nervousness which caused them to shrink back behind their menfolk, or busy themselves in sudden scoldings of their children or urgent conversations with friends, as though they feared having to make some acknowledgment of us. Mrs Venables, I remembered, had warned me that the people here were backward bumpkins, dismissing them as close and suspicious. I now began to understand why she had been so vehement. Still, I should lose no sleep over being cold-shouldered by these country wives. Their society was probably as boorish and uncouth as their manners.

Daniel seemed unperturbed. But then he must be well used to the ways of these dour Cornish peasants. He replied pleasantly to those who greeted him and ignored the rest, pacing slowly and deliberately down the path and out through the lych gate. In the centre of the open space the women of the Lugg family, a stout matron and two plump girls of perhaps sixteen and seventeen, all three dressed in harshly coloured silks and much be-plumed bonnets, were squeezing into a light cart.

'Such a pity there isn't room for 'ee, cousin Jess,' Mrs Lugg cried jovially. 'But young Harry'll walk along wi' 'ee, an' 'tis a wondrous fine morning for stepping out.' Her tone was considerably less jovial as she addressed a straggle of children who stood mutely at the tail of the cart. 'Be off back to your duties! An' no dawdling on the road, for Master Harry and Miss Southcote'll be behind you to mark any mischief you've a mind to.' Then she turned again to Jess and said, with a hard laugh that belied her jolly expression, ''Prentices is more trouble than they'm worth, I tell 'ee. Cost a fortune to keep and you daresn't take your eyes off 'en for more than a minute or they'm idling or malingerin'. I'd be obliged if you'd not let 'en out of your sight, cousin, on your way to Trebarth. And don't take no lip off 'en. 'Specially off that big girl, Liddy. 'Er's too uppish by far for her station an' needs a firm hand.'

Jess managed a smouldering half smile at Mrs Lugg. 'I'm only too happy to be of help, cousin,' she answered smoothly, her glance pure malevolence. 'And I don't mind in the least that I must walk for I understand how breathless you get now that you are become so . . . so corpulent. And of course the girls will wear such light shoes. They'd be cut to pieces on the stones in minutes. But with dear Harry at my side to give me his arm over the rougher ground, we'll make good progress, never fear.'

Farmer Lugg, his coat straining over his great belly, flicked the reins over the horse's back, tipped his whip to his hat by way of farewell to Daniel, and carried off his womenfolk. Jess, looking thunderous, snatched at the flabby arm of young Master Lugg, a slack-lipped tubby youth of fourteen or so, and marched in the wake of the apprentices.

We passed the little procession a short way along the lane. From the carriage window the apprentice children looked smaller and even more vulnerable than they had before. The biggest, the girl Liddy, was no more than ten, the littlest perhaps half that age. Five altogether. Two boys, three girls, scrawny-limbed as whippets, dressed in a ragbag of shrunken flimsy garments and oversized boots. Five pairs of eyes stared up at us. The littlest one picked at a scab on his lip. Another wiped his sleeve across his nose to remove green candles of thick mucus that hung there. The girl Liddy had pushed back her bonnet so that it hung down her back by its strings to reveal straight brown hair cropped raggedly around her ears and a purpling bruise across her temple. She stared up at me, her jaw set, her eyes guarded. Her elbows jabbed out a warning into the ribs of the smaller girls either side of her. The three girls immediately bobbed a hurried, ragged curtsey and the little boys tugged at their forelocks. They were the same children who had been stone picking in the rain on the day I had arrived. Their misery had struck at me then and now my sympathy welled up in greater measure. They might be dressed in their best go-to-church clothes, but the flimsiness of these garments only seemed to emphasise the undernourished state of the thin bodies underneath.

I felt a spasm of contempt for the Luggs. The evidence

183

of their own gross bodies and showy clothes proclaimed them to be people who thought a great deal of their own comfort. They were evidently not so particular in the care of the little ones who must spend their childhood in hard labour about the farm. I said as much to Daniel.

He shook his head. 'The Luggs are noted for being tight-fisted to all save themselves. They pay the lowest wages they can get away with and I have taken Tom Lugg to task more than once for the state of the cottages his labourers must live in, which are decrepit and insanitary in the extreme. He is always quick to assure me that he has improvements in hand. But that same hand,' he added dryly, 'is remarkably reluctant to dip into his pocket to put forward repairs.'

'But these children . . .'

'I understand your feelings, but most of them, I believe, are from poor families who are only too glad to have a child or two off their hands.' He shook his head. 'There are those who say that Mrs Lugg is a benefactor to take them in order to save them from the poorhouse or the streets, though I have my doubts as to that. But I suppose there is a benefit of sorts in that they are clothed and housed and learn the value of honest labour.' His voice softened. 'Do not look so grieved, my dear. We cannot take on the sufferings of all those we feel to be overworked and undervalued or we should be bowed to the ground under the great burden of it.'

'I suppose so,' I said reluctantly.

'And the Luggs are not entirely bad, you understand. Tom Lugg might be hard on his workers but he is not brutal, as so many are, with his livestock. Of course his reasoning is in pounds, shillings and pence. He wishes to get the best prices for his animals, therefore they must be husbanded with care and consideration. As to Mrs Lugg, well, as midwife and layer-out she reigns supreme in the village, apparently. And most of the women go to her for the potions she brews to alleviate their female complaints, for there are few that could afford to fetch the doctor or visit the druggist. She has even been known to take in those who are sick with no one to care for them and nurse them well again.'

Kensa called his attention then to something she had seen out of the window and the matter was dropped. I tried to readjust my first impression of the Luggs during the rest of the journey but the faces of those little children were constantly between me and the idea of Mrs Lugg as a benefactor. I found difficulty in conciliating one with the other and eventually gave up the task. There were happier matters to concentrate on this sunny day.

After dinner, in the balmy warmth of late afternoon, Daniel, Kensa and I walked down to the creek. This, I realised, was the route I should have taken the other day instead of blundering about among the woodland tracks. A grassy ride led through shrubberies behind the walled kitchen garden and when it reached the woods it became a well-gravelled path that led directly and steeply down to where the high tide lapped at a small tumbledown quay. The creek was a deep jagged indentation into wooded hillside, the green water swirling gently with the push of the tide. A path wound round its ferny edges.

'Follow it to the left and it will take you eventually to St Bridellan,' Daniel said, 'but we shall walk in the opposite direction just so far as the river. I am glad the tide is up. At low water it is not nearly so picturesque, for there is a great deal of mud.'

'It could not be other than interesting at any state of the tide,' I said. 'Look at the colours of the new leaves! So many subtle shades of fresh green and pink and palest yellow and ochres! The water mirrors them, but with a darker tone, like a tinted looking-glass.'

'Why, yes,' Daniel said, sounding surprised. 'I see the colours now you remark them. How strange that I never really noticed the many variations before.'

'Mama's training,' I said, laughing.

'You have an artist's eye.' He regarded me thoughtfully. 'Do you ever regret that you gave up your artistic pursuits?'

'I have found more satisfaction in teaching.'

'Perhaps you may take up sketching again when you are fully settled. There are so many wonderful views round about Kildower. It would make a pleasant hobby for you and we might frame the best to hang about the house.'

I made some light, noncommittal answer. How could I tell him that this pleasant vision of his wife whiling away an idle hour or two with a little genteel sketching and painting, a perfectly ladylike and suitable pursuit, could never be? I only wished it could, I did indeed. But I knew that it was not possible. When I threw away my brushes and paints and burned my pictures I had known it to be the only way to overcome that undesirable part of me which could not be conquered by lesser means. Half measures would have been inadequate against the strength of that particular compulsion. I had made up my mind to it then that I would not become slave to an obsession as Mama had done. Nor should I now. And I did not pretend that I was, in this case, any different from a drunkard who foolishly believes himself so reformed that he might take just a small sip of brandy without harm, then finds the whole bottle irresistible. No, best to be circumspect and resist temptation entirely.

The River Lynher, when we reached it, was a calm lake. Mid-river a boat with crumpled brown sails drifted on the full, slack tide, awaiting the turn of the current to carry it downstream. The first swallows I had seen this year swooped and dived above the placid surface and the air held the cool smell of the water mingled with the rich dank fragrance of the woods.

'The promontory yonder is Erth Castle. Beyond that, higher up the river at the confluence with the Tiddy, lies St Germans, which once boasted a great priory, though there is little left now save a fine church.'

I heard Daniel pointing out the landmarks, but I scarcely took it in for the other thought that burst into my mind. Out of nowhere, it seemed, the words bubbled up and were out, 'Was it here that Meraud drowned?'

He went so still that I thought I must have offended him by the abruptness of the question.

'Forgive me,' I said hastily, 'It . . . it is just that I know so little of how it happened beyond the mere fact of her drowning. And now . . . here . . .' I floundered, unable to voice what was in my heart, that it was not merely idle curiosity that drove me, but a yearning for him to share with me his memories. The feeling had been growing within me since I had looked at Meraud's memorial in the church this morning, try as I might to suppress it. It bewildered me a little. I had been happy until now to accept his reticence. Indeed, I had been grateful that I had been spared continual reference and comparison to his first wife, which might have been my lot had I married a widower of coarser sensibilities. I was at a loss to explain this urge for him to speak of Meraud, but there it was, whole and complete and commanding my attention. And now I had ruined any chance of breaking through his reticence by speaking out.

I was wrong. He was not offended. Startled, certainly, but after a moment's thought and with a glance at Kensa, who had drifted off to stare at her reflection in the still water, he said, pacing out his words as though each one must be chosen with care, 'Even I do not know the exact order of events. One can only surmise. I did not see her go, or I should have forbidden her to step out of doors on such a wild wet day. You see, she had never properly recovered her strength in the months afer Kensa's birth, which had been long and difficult.' He hesitated, took a breath and went on again. 'Even so, she had such spirit, such a determination to make herself well again. She insisted on taking her little terrier for a walk every afternoon. "I shall never recover properly if I am cooped up indoors all day," she would say. "If I walk briskly I shall not catch cold." Whenever I could, it was my pleasure to go with her. But this ... this day, I was occupied with ... Oh, some trivial matter ... the wind having dislodged roof tiles and rainwater leaking into the attics. It seemed important at the time.'

An edge now, to his voice, a muscle tensing on the hard edge of his jaw. Involuntarily, I raised my hand towards him, but let it fall back before it touched his arm. He did not notice as he half-turned from me to stare across the river.

'Guilt is a loyal companion,' he said, and his voice was light, sardonic. 'It remains constant when other friends fall away. Day or night, it never fails in its terrible duty, which is to remind you of the might-have-beens.'

Then in stark, halting phrases, not looking at me but out across the river, he told me of the events of that October day.

The whole of the month had been calamitous for many villagers and farmers along the river valley. Storms followed days of rain until the land could soak up no more and water cascaded down the sodden hillsides, even the tiniest thread of a stream becoming a torrent. The river swelled and overflowed, engulfing crops, carrying off sheep and cattle and chickens in its brown, tumbling race towards the Tamar and the sea. Kildower's was not the only tragedy played out in those stormy days, for more than one household was cast into mourning by the loss of someone to the flood.

It was already dusk, the rain having eased somewhat, before Meraud left the house, her dog yapping and scampering at her heels. A gardener clearing a fallen bough from a path near the house had been the only one to see her disappear into the woods. When she did not return half the men in the village had been roused to join in the search for her through the rainswept night. But it was daylight before the grim evidence was revealed: a rowing boat half a mile down river. It was the boat usually tied up at Kildower's quay and Meraud's dog, shivering and sodden, guarded it, refusing with snaps and snarls to allow anyone close. When Daniel finally managed to soothe it and the boat was righted, nothing was found of Meraud save the broken strands of the gold bracelet she often wore and a scrap of blue silk torn from her dress caught together in a splintered plank. Though no one would ever know the true sequence of events, the assumption was, he said, that the dog had fallen into the flood and Meraud had taken the boat in an attempt to rescue it. But the turmoil of the water had been too much. Either the boat had overturned or she had been tossed out, the bracelet and the scrap of silk from her sleeve tearing from her wrist as she desperately clawed for a handhold.

The river had swallowed Meraud's body without trace and the dog for all its lucky escape pined pitifully for its mistress. It refused to eat. Time and again it escaped the house and returned to the spot where the boat had foundered, to stand howling and whining its distress. Some days later Daniel had found it lying huddled against the tree root, its dead and sightless eyes still fixed on the water in hopeless expectation.

'I buried it there,' he said curtly. 'It seemed appropriate.'

And buried his own hope, his own heart, alongside. Oh, my poor, poor Daniel.

I took a step towards him. I do not know what I might have done or said to offer him comfort. But I was never to find out because Kensa's clear, childish voice cut between us and the moment was lost.

'Are we to walk much farther, Papa?'

I saw his shoulders relax. Though I could not see his face, I knew exactly the fond, gentle expression that now flooded his eyes. 'Are you growing tired, sweetheart?'

'A little. And I don't want to spoil my favourite boots. The path is very muddy here.'

'You should have worn a more suitable pair, as I suggested,' I said, meaning to speak lightly, but somehow the words coming out with an aggrieved tone that I neither intended nor liked.

'But they are so pretty.' Kensa said, ignoring me and looking up at her father. 'I do like pretty things, Papa.'

'Of course you do. That is as it should be. After all, you are the prettiest young lady this side of the Tamar.'

She pouted. 'I don't at all like those heavy clumpy boots that Mama wanted me to wear. They make my legs ache dreadfully.'

He glanced at me over her head, smiling, attempting to draw me into the complicity of his protective love for the child. My answering smile felt a little stiff and I found a sudden need to turn aside and examine a particularly charming clump of bluebells. 'I expect Mama did not quite understand about the absolute perfection of these particular boots,' I heard him say. 'Why, the finest ladies in Plymouth would give up cream cakes for a week and donate all their grand jewels to the deserving poor in order to own such a pair.'

Kensa giggled. 'Papa, you are a tease. But they are very stylish, are they not?'

'The epitome of style,' he said gravely.

'Then may we go back now? Before they become all muddied?'

Of course we might. Daniel was malleable clay in her small hands.

I deliberately dawdled behind them, regarding the boots with a jaundiced eye. They were of pale-grey silky cloth, side-laced, embroidered with curlicues of fancy stitching and completely unsuitable for country walks. Kensa tossed her head when I asked her if she did not have more sensible footwear. 'I will not wear the horrid black boots Miss Clement ordered for me,' she announced disdainfully, her father being out of earshot. 'I hate the ugly, heavy things. Jess said they were only fit for a common ploughboy. But Miss Clement, who was horrid also and had warts on her nose like a witch, made me wear them out of doors even though I told her I could hardly lift my feet from the floor.'

'Miss Clement?'

'My last governess.' Her eyes glinted up at me slyly. 'Papa soon got rid of *her* when he saw how wicked and cruel she was.'

'It would seem to me,' I said mildly, 'that to provide you with stout boots in order to protect your feet from the roughness of the ground was the act of a thoughtful person.'

'Not so! She was always rapping my knuckles with a ruler so hard that they were quite bruised. *And* she once kept me two days on bread and water when I would not eat some nasty cabbage at dinner – and she said I shouldn't

have anything better until I learned to clear my plate. Ugh.'
She gave a theatrical shudder, then giggled. 'She made me
sleep in her room, which smelled horribly of the camphor
oil she rubbed on her chest for her stuffy nose, so that she
could make sure I didn't eat anything but bread and water.
But Jess smuggled me in some cake and milk and as soon as
Papa came home she told him how wicked Miss Clement
had been and Papa sent her packing because I had cried and
cried myself into a fever and had to stay in bed for a week
afterwards. Then it was Miss Clement's turn to cry.' Her
voice was suddenly full of distressed, genteel tones. '"Oh,
pray, Mr Penhale, do not turn me off! Give me a second
chance, I beg you. A month is scarcely time to judge my
abilities."' Then a gruff tone, '"Long enough, Miss Clement.
I will not have my daughter upset like this. You are evidently
more used to dealing with less delicate children and had
best find another position more suited to your experience."'
She tilted her nose in the air, herself again. 'Papa was too
kind. *I* should not have written her a character, as he did.
She did not at all deserve it.'

Miss Clement's methods might not have been my own,
but I felt a deal of sympathy for her. She had not stood a
chance. Jess Southcote and my minx of a stepdaughter had
combined to defeat her almost before she had begun. Well,
they should not find me so easy to dislodge, and I should
lose no time in providing Kensa with more sensible footwear,
whatever her protests, for I had a strong suspicion that the
grey boots pinched her toes, elegant though they appeared.
She was walking with distinct awkwardness – and it was
not a pretence – by the time we reached the house.

Nan hovered nervously in the hall while Kitty took our
outdoor things. Earlier, when I asked why she seemed to be
following us about, she had said in a frightened voice, 'Miss

Southcote, ma'am. She said particler that I was to do whatever Miss Kensa bid me. 'Elp 'er dress, an' fetch things, an' that.'

'Act as nursemaid in her absence?' I said, surprised.

'Thass it, ma'am,' she whispered.

I had smiled reassuringly. 'That will not be necessary, Nan. I shall see to Miss Kensa myself.'

'But Miss Southcote, 'er said . . .'

'She no doubt meant well, but Miss Kensa is perfectly able to manage for one day.'

I had shooed her away, thinking no more of the matter, but there Nan was again, gingery eyelashes a-blink with fright, yet still stubbornly adhering to Jess's orders.

I beckoned her over and said quietly, 'Did you not understand what I told you earlier, Nan? There is no need to wait upon Miss Kensa. Run along now and attend to your other duties.'

She chewed at her bitten lips. 'Ma'am . . . Miss Southcote, 'er said . . .'

'I am your mistress, Nan. It is to me you must look for your orders. Will you take care to remember that in future?'

She gulped. 'Yes, ma'am, but . . . that is, ma'am. Will you . . . Oh, ma'am, will you tell Miss Southcote that 'tes not my choosin' to disobey 'er.' The words came out in a frightened rush.

'It is not a matter of disobedience,' I began a little more sharply, intending to do no such thing, for it was in her own interests to learn here and now that my authority overruled anyone else's. But the look of quivering alarm on the girl's face intensified so painfully that I could not continue. Her feet shuffled on the flags as though she were torn between running or staying. Scared of me. And most assuredly terrified of Jess. 'Very well,' I said gently. 'I shall speak to her.' Nan's bony shoulders, which had been somewhere up around her ears with tension, sagged down with relief.

'Oh, ma'am, thank you ma'am ... I'll be off then, ma'am.'

I let her go. I did not want to question her further with Kensa standing near, but I did not at all like the thought of Jess Southcote holding sway with the other servants as though they were hers to command. That was decidedly something I must put a stop to. And soon.

I was right about the boots.

I went upstairs with Kensa, leaving Daniel to adjourn to the parlour with his newspaper. Once we reached her bedroom adjoining the nursery she flung her muff to the carpet and stood in imperial helplessness waiting to have her cloak and bonnet removed.

I ignored her and walked to the window, cleared aside a quantity of dolls from the window seat and sat down. 'I will help you with your boots when you are ready,' I said. 'Boot laces can be tediously awkward even for a grown-up person if the knots become too tight.' I gazed out of the casement as though absorbed in the view of the water gardens, but I watched her from the corner of my eye. When I judged the moment to be right I turned back to her. The short cloak and bonnet had joined the muff on the carpet and she was glaring at me with defiance sparking from her slanted blue eyes. She marched to a chair, sat down and stuck out her foot.

Again I ignored her, taking my time to pick up the garments and return them to the press, which bulged with such an array of clothing that I wondered if there were enough days in the year to wear it all. 'How sad,' I said, 'that you are so unappreciative of Papa's kindness to you.'

'What do you mean?' she demanded.

'He buys you so many clothes yet you throw them to the floor as though they were so much rubbish.'

'Not so! It is your fault entirely. You have sent Jess away, and Nan, and you pretend that you will look after me and you don't at all! I shall tell Papa!'

I laughed. 'What shall you tell him? That you are too much of a baby to unfasten your own cloak and remove your bonnet when your nurse is not here? Dear me, I should not think he would be too impressed. On the contrary, I believe he would be very sad to learn that you care so little for his kindness that you actually stamped on your cloak out of temper.'

She flushed. 'I tripped.'

'Did you?' I let the pause draw out. She lowered her lashes, letting her shoulders slump. 'My poor legs are tired,' she said in a whispery voice. 'You made me walk too far.'

'Really? Well, let me help you with your boots and then you may have a little rest on the bed before we join Papa for tea. Goodness, me, is that a bloodstain?' I whipped off the white stocking before she had a chance to protest. 'What a nasty broken blister. No wonder you were limping on the way back to Kildower.'

'It is your fault! I told you it was too far.'

'And look at those other red patches. Your toes have been crushed abominably by those silly boots. You cannot possibly wear them again, Kensa.'

'It was not the boots! They are my very favourites! They make my feet look small and pretty and everybody knows that if you get boots too big for children their feet spread out to fit them. *I* want to grow up with the dainty feet of a lady, not of a common person.'

I frowned. I had heard that piece of nonsense before. And not only from ignorant people but from those who should have known better. But how to convince a mutinous and contrary child otherwise? Not by commanding her, that was for sure.

'How sad that you have been so badly misinformed,' I said with a sigh. 'Still, I can see that you are determined to have your own way, though I cannot imagine why you should wish to embark upon a life of pain and inconvenience – not to mention sheer ugliness – by believing such an unfashionable and laughable notion. Now I think I should bathe that blister and pad it so that your stocking does not rub against it.'

'What do you mean?' she interrupted rudely.

'I beg your pardon?'

'What you said about pain and ugliness?'

'Oh, I am sure nothing I can say will persuade you from the idea that misshapen bunions and painful corns are to be desired. If you are set upon having feet so covered with lumps and bumps that you will barely be able to hobble, then so be it.'

'You're telling lies!' she cried. 'You're jealous because I'm pretty and Papa loves me best. You want to make me wear ugly things so that I'll look as . . . as dull as you!'

I shrugged. 'You may believe what you wish. I have put the facts before you. Overtight shoes and boots will crush and deform your feet.' I went to fetch water from the jug on the dressing table and returned with the basin and a linen towel and as I bathed her sore toes, I said, by way of consolation, 'As you like the boots so well, we could have the same style copied, but with room for your toes to grow. Is there a shoemaker in the village?'

'All my things are brought from Plymouth. Papa patronises only the best and most fashionable establishments.' Then she added scornfully. 'Of course, *you* may find the village shoemaker perfectly suitable for your own boots.'

'Perhaps I shall,' I agreed. 'In my travels I have found excellent craftsmen working in remote places. There now, that should be more comfortable. Shall I fetch your white slippers or the blue silk ones?'

She decided, naturally, on the black velvet ones which I had deliberately not mentioned because they looked the softest and most comfortable. I hoped she would choose them out of contrariness, which she did. But I did not take any pleasure in this small victory. I felt too sad about the necessity for such manoeuvring.

'I shall go back to Papa now,' she announced imperiously as I emptied the soiled water into the slop pail and hung the towel back on its rail. She was gone in a flicker of petticoats and pantaletted legs and I stood for a moment willing myself not to be downcast. Given time, she would begin to understand that I wanted only what was best for her. She would realise that I did not intend to usurp her in her father's affections. Then she would begin to co-operate rather than to oppose my every suggestion just because it *was* my suggestion. Patience, firmness, kindness. That was how I had always dealt with my pupils. Even the most difficult ones had responded in time. Kensa would be won round eventually. *Must* be won round. I wanted so much to love the child, yet I could not even like her!

I straightened my shoulders. I could not afford to wallow in self-doubt or I was lost before I had begun.

Yet as I walked briskly downstairs I knew that this situation, this marriage, in which I had willingly and confidently placed myself, was proving more complex than I had expected. But I had entered into the bargain with my eyes wide open. I had known it would not be roses all the way and now that a few thorns had revealed themselves I must not shrink back in dismay. While respecting their sharpness, I must learn the best way of dealing with them so that they would not inflict too much damage either on myself or on those in my new family to whom I now owed allegiance and respect.

Daniel raised the matter of one particular thorn before he left the next morning. It was some relief to me that he did, for I was feeling increasingly guilty that I had not mentioned my meeting with Conan Trewithen and the longer I left it, the more difficult it was to introduce such an unpleasant subject. But I realised very quickly that, although it had been out of cowardice, I had been wise to hold my tongue.

We had breakfasted early in the chilly dining chamber. Neither of us was given to a great deal of chatter at this time of day, but we were unusually silent this morning. Daniel was profoundly lost in thought, as though he was already claimed by the problems of the week ahead, and I was in no mood to coax him into conversation. I felt dismal at his going and cross with myself that I was allowing myself to be so affected by his departure. But I could not help wishing I might go with him to breezy, lively Plymouth and the pleasant house in Nutmeg Street instead of being left behind in this great echoing mausoleum. I poured a second cup of coffee and warmed my fingers around the steaming cup.

'Are you cold, Sophy?'

I had not realised he was observing me.

'I believe this is the draughtiest room in the house,' I said lightly. 'I should have brought down my warmer shawl.'

'I am afraid these big old houses tend towards draughts whatever is done to guard against them. The Captain spent a great deal of money to ensure that windows and doors were sound and well fitting yet cold currents still abound. I suppose it is due to the lofty ceilings and the great fireplaces, which cause the air to circulate too freely.' He smiled. 'I have always reckoned that it was a house meant to impress with its grandeur with little thought given to the comfort and convenience of those living within its walls.'

'It was a rougher age when it was built.'

'True. And the Trewithen men by all accounts had no pretensions to gentility. They were a coarse, cunning tribe who gained their wealth, so it is said, by extortion and theft, seizing their chance to acquire all the land hereabouts at the time when King Henry removed himself from the rule of Rome and sacked the religious houses. They pulled down most of the convent that had stood here and used the stone to rebuild their own grandiose mansion.' His face darkened. 'Trewithen men had a reputation for violence and cruelty which diluted through the generations into the self-seeking recklessness and dissipation which eventually proved their downfall.' He hesitated then slowly added, 'In the last of the breed, Meraud's brother Conan, these characteristics were displayed in the most dissolute and degenerate form.'

Now was the moment to speak if ever there was one. But Daniel gave me no chance because he was leaning across the table, putting his hand, warm and steady, over mine, looking deep into my eyes.

'Sophy, I have to apologise. I omitted to tell you that Meraud had a brother because I believed him to have died long since in Botany Bay, where he was dispatched for his sins and the world well rid of a devious troublemaker. I learned only recently that he survived and has returned to St Bridellan.' His grip tightened and the sea-blue of his eyes seemed to intensify. 'The last thing I wish to do is alarm you, Sophy, but I must warn you that he may try to make some approach while I am away. You must on no account listen or speak to him, least of all invite him into the house if he comes pleading kinship. You are not at home if he has the gall – and I would not put it past him – to call upon you. Do you understand?'

I shall make him pay for my suffering and for Meraud's.

Those flinty eyes, full of hate. And Daniel's now, shockingly, seeming to reflect that same deadly emotion. His voice gravelly with it, his face so grim and severe that it might have been a stranger sitting across the table from me, not the man who was my husband. Two sides, Daniel . . . Conan, of the same terrible coin and too late, far too late to speak of my meeting with Meraud's brother at the pool. My Daniel might have understood. Not this hard-eyed stranger.

'Why?' The one bare syllable was all I could manage for fear my voice would tremble.

'Because of what he did, what he was. A man with evil in his blood and bones does not – cannot – change.'

'But he was your wife's brother.'

'We do not choose our kin. He was a millstone round Meraud's neck. His dissipation, his . . . his lusts.' He broke off, bowing his head, as though struggling to gain control. When he spoke again his voice was calmer, but so icily bitter that it near froze my blood. 'Gossip being what it is you will doubtless be appraised of the reasons for his final disgrace. He was condemned to transportation for theft. He had fallen so low to feed his appetite for brandy and gaming and low women that he became nothing more than a common footpad. But it was the termination of a career of dissipation. Throughout it, his frail young sister, his only dependant, was forced to suffer the severest tribulation. Yet through it all, she never lost her pride and the inborn purity of her nature. She was like a delicate flower that manages to root and grow to untainted beauty despite a wilderness of rank weeds that twine about it.' His hand crushed mine but I hardly felt the pain. His gaze looked through me, beyond me, to a hateful vision that blanched the skin over his broad cheekbones and sculpted haggard shadows beneath them.

'Despite everything he did Meraud continued loyally to forgive him, hoping and believing that one day her brother might reform himself. But he went from bad to worse. Her faith was finally and cruelly shattered when he was recognised as one of a band of villains who for the whole of one winter had terrorised travellers for twenty miles round about. He was lucky not to be hanged. I reckon it was only his glib tongue that saved him from the gallows.' A pause and then the words ground out as though they were dragged from some dark place in his soul. 'But I will never forgive him for what he did to her, to Meraud . . .' He stopped suddenly, like a man finding himself teetering on the edge of a precipice and, drawing back from what he had been about to say, took a slow breath. His grip slackened and he stared around, his expression a touch bewildered, as though he could not quite comprehend his surroundings. Then, seeming to see me properly, his expression changed. Like a frightening mask removed to reveal the true face beneath, the stranger was gone and the kind Daniel I knew was staring at me.

'Oh, my dear, Sophy,' he said softly. 'I had not meant to alarm you and I see that I have.'

I said carefully, 'A . . . an upsetting story, Daniel.' And not the whole of it, if I was any judge.

'Forgive me. I have burdened you with my anger when I merely intended to caution you to protect yourself and Kensa against the wiles of an unscrupulous rogue. But Con Trewithen has always aroused my worst feelings.' A wry twist of the lips that was scarcely a smile. 'I think you will agree that I have cause.'

I have nothing on my conscience and he has a great deal.

In my mind, Conan Trewithen's words twined with Daniel's. Two men unappeasable in their hatred. Both claiming justification for that hatred. And between them, Meraud's frail, persistent shade. Three links in a sad chain that remained unbroken even though she was long gone to a watery death.

'I will take care,' I promised. There was nothing else I could usefully say.

We made our farewells in the hall, I turning my cheek dutifully for his kiss, Daniel bending to drop a light, husbandly brush of his lips upon it, both of us mindful of Nan, who waited to hand him his hat. We might have been married for years rather than weeks. Then he turned and was gone without a backward glance.

And when the great door closed behind him, the shadowy gloom seemed to creep across the cold flagstones and fasten about me in chilling mockery of the lover's embrace that would never be mine.

As though Daniel's departure was the signal for disruption, within an hour of his leaving my carefully laid plans for the day were in ruins. I had held some hope of settling Kensa into a daily routine which would allow for short intervals of quiet study in the schoolroom interspersed with walks in the fresh air for the benefit of exercise and to gather botanical specimens for further examination. With an eye to mollifying Jess Southcote I had thought to allow Kensa to rest in the nursery for much of the afternoon while I attended to my other domestic duties. I liked neither the woman nor her spoiling influence on my stepdaughter, but I had to consider the child. Jess had been a stable element in her life for so long it would be cruel to part them too forcefully. Better a gentle but steady transition to a new system, rather than a too-abrupt severance from the old, indulgent regimen.

But when I went into the nursery it was to find it deserted. I went through to Kensa's bedchamber, to discover her lying ashen-faced on her bed with Jess wafting a shovel of burning herbs about the room. The sour smell of vomit had not quite been overcome. With the curtains half-drawn and heat bursting out from the blazing log fire, the atmosphere was overpoweringly close.

'Poor Miss Kensa has been taken quite poorly, Mrs Penhale,' Jess said, in a low, anxious voice, returning the shovel to the hearth and returning quickly to the bed. 'She has been sick several times this last half hour.' She placed one white soft hand soothingly on Kensa's forehead. 'There, there, my chick. Lie still and quiet. You will feel easier soon.'

'A little fresh air might make her feel better,' I said, equally anxious, making to move to the window.

'Oh, no, ma'am,' Jess said, stepping smoothly from the bedside so that she blocked my way. 'I wouldn't advise that.'

'But it is far too hot in here.'

'We mustn't chill her any further. The results might be very injurious to one already in a weakened state.' She spoke with the maddeningly patronising assurance of someone blessed with superior knowledge. 'I believe it was the chilling she received yesterday that has caused her to be upset.'

'It was the mildest of days,' I said, taken aback. 'And she was well wrapped up.'

'Of course, I wouldn't suggest anything other.' Her voice took on the false note of humbleness that grated along my nerves like the rasp of sharp nails against splintered wood. 'And for a healthy child the long walk that I believe you took would be quite in order.'

'Scarcely a long walk. Merely to the creek and back.'

She clasped her hands together in a beseeching gesture. 'Not to you, ma'am, but to Miss Kensa . . . Forgive me speaking out, Mrs Penhale, but it's just that I know from long experience that she isn't able to tolerate too much strain on her system, either with bookwork which over-stimulates her brain, or with exercise that fatigues her body. You see, it's when she's overstretched in this manner that she falls prey to all kinds of illnesses. I wish it could be otherwise, indeed I do, but I have nursed her through so many attacks of this nature that I have learned that it's best not to excite them in the first place. Oh, ma'am, I hope you'll not take it unkindly that I should speak so plainly.'

She bowed her head, a kind, humble woman awaiting judgement. If I had not caught the self-congratulatory glint in her black eyes before she lowered her lashes I might have been gulled into being thoroughly guilt-ridden and contrite. As it was I merely felt the stabbing certainty that she was using Kensa's upset to manipulate me to her own advantage and gaining a great deal of satisfaction in paying me back for reminding her that it was not her place to give orders to the other servants. Nevertheless, the child was genuinely ill though I very much doubted if Jess's diagnosis of the cause was accurate. More likely it was due to the amount of clotted cream and jam she had heaped on to her scones when we had taken tea yesterday after our walk. I had tried to encourage her to eat a slice or two of plain bread and butter first, but she had turned a soulful, pleading glance on her papa and he had smiled and said indulgently, 'I think, my dear, we might allow her this little treat.' Little treat! It seemed the child's life consisted of little treats. And, however well meant, few of them were to her advantage.

'Does the doctor live far away?' I asked.

'A few miles, ma'am, but I'm sure there's no need to call out Doctor Stowe. I've nursed Miss Kensa through many an attack like this. In fact, on the occasions when Mr Penhale has sought the doctor's advice he commended me on my care of Miss Kensa. "If all my patients had such skilled and efficient nursing, my professional services would scarcely be called upon." His very words! And he said most definitely that any chill or nervous strain is liable to set off purging and vomiting and fever in girls of Miss Kensa's refined nature and that he could see no need for any other treatment but that which I was already giving her. That is rest, quiet and sips of peppermint water to ease the pangs.'

I looked at Kensa. She still lay limp against the pillows, but a faint tinge of colour had crept back into her cheeks.

'She seems a little easier already,' I admitted.

'Rest and quiet, as I said, Mrs Penhale.'

'You will send for me should there be any worsening?'

'Of course.'

Kensa stirred, whimpered. 'I'm thirsty.'

Instantly Jess was at her side to raise her head and hold the cup to her lips, saying distractedly to me, 'Would you be so kind as to close the door when you leave, ma'am? All the warm air is escaping.'

I was being dismissed, a useless distraction to one who had more important matters to attend to. And with no great desire to remain a moment longer in this close and breathless atmosphere, I said, 'Very well. I shall look in again later this morning.'

For once I was glad of the damp chill of the corridor. Its draughts quickly dispelled the odours of the sickroom and imbued my whole being with a refreshing relief at my own good health. So much so that I walked with extra briskness along the gallery and, seeing the hall empty, ran down the stairs in a most unladylike manner, clutching my skirts high and only shaking them out modestly when I arrived breathlessly at the bottom. A whole day to please myself without a difficult child to cajole and coax into studying! That sly thought was in my head before I could deny it as unworthy. I felt ashamed. How could I feel so released and joyful when I had just left my stepdaughter's sickroom? But there was no pretending that I did not and, if I was honest, Jess and Kensa were probably even more delighted to rid themselves of me.

So justifying my escape, I allowed myself the pleasure of contemplating an assault on the little room I had earmarked for a small parlour of my own. To assuage my conscience I would pay my respects to Captain Penhale *en route*. I knew already from my experience so far that would not detain me for long. A growled greeting, a scowling, 'You see, madam, I've not died in the night!' and a barely concealed impatience until I took my leave were as much as I could expect. And I believe I was only tolerated for this short visit because the great hound welcomed me with overpowering enthusiasm.

'The brute's turned fool,' the Captain would cry as Pirate near bowled me over. 'Get to your place, you son of Satan. I'll not have you besotted by any woman, least off this nosy wench, for naught but trouble ever came of tangling with the interfering breed. Back, I say, or by God you'll feel my boot.' And Pirate would slink away to lie by the Captain's chair, only to inch forward on his belly when he thought himself unobserved, until he could stretch his whiskery head and rest the tip of his jaw on my slipper. Then, by degrees, the rest of his huge frame would ease towards me. By the time I rose to go my feet would be entirely crushed by a contented and doggily-odorous mountain of hair and sharp bones, its head on my knee, its eyes blissfully shut as I absently stroked the floppy ears. 'See! You spoil that creature already!' the Captain would roar, as though suddenly aware of a situation that had been clearly evident for the whole of our interview. 'Come away, damme, Pirate!'

'Thank you, sir,' I would say tartly. 'I was beginning to believe you set that great beast on me deliberately. See how he has shed half his pelt all over my skirt and my feet are quite cramped from his sitting upon them. I must ask you to keep him under better control when I visit in future.'

'Hah! Maybe you'll find the door barred against you when next you come a-knocking. Interfering women! 'Tis a pretty kettle of fish when I'm brought to such torment at my time of life!'

As a method of communication, an exchange of insults left much to be desired, but somehow it seemed as natural as breathing when in the company of Captain Penhale.

I went to the kitchen in search of Mrs Dagget in order to borrow a pinafore to cover my fawn wool dress which, though old, was perfectly serviceable for mornings and had a few seasons of wear left in it. No doubt Daniel would have been amused or surprised at my frugality when I had a whole wardrobe of new garments to choose from, but old habits die hard. Miss Sophy Beardmore, the governess, who of necessity had to eke out every penny of her sixty pounds per annum in the most prudent manner possible, was not entirely banished. And within her lurked more than a trace of the child Sophy who knew that the only certainty in life was uncertainty and today's new gown might be well out-grown before another new gown could be afforded.

'Mrs Dagget, I should wish to borrow . . .' I stopped after two strides into the kitchen, for acrimonious voices were instantly hushed and cook and maids froze in a tableau that might have been labelled, 'Recrimination and Despair'.

Mrs Dagget stood by the white-scrubbed kitchen table, gaunt cheeks flaring pink with rage. In front of her Nan and Joan clung to each other, red-eyed and snivelling. Kitty rushed over when she saw me, her clumsy shoes booming a cannonade across the flags.

'Oh, ma'am,' she bellowed. ''Tis not they maids! They'm honest, I knows it, and too frighted that Master'd put 'em off to do anythin' so addle-pated. 'Tes one o' they gardenin' lads I'll be bound, or that cross-eyed lump of a stable-lad.'

'Thank you, Kitty,' I said, making no sense at all of her outburst, 'I believe Mrs Dagget will explain what the trouble is.' I crossed to the table. 'Well, Mrs Dagget? Is there some problem?'

Her breath quivered in nostrils pinched with indignation. 'I regret . . . well, it's thieving, Mrs Penhale. Something I can't – I *won't* – abide.'

'What has been stolen?' I asked quietly.

'Food from the pantry. I went just now to fetch out a custard tart and an almond cheesecake I'd made ready for your dinner today. I put them there last thing yesterday, and now they've gone! Nary a crumb left! And I know they were still there early on, for I saw them when I fetched out the eggs for Master's breakfast.' She pointed an accusing finger at the two maids. 'It must be these two, for I had to take a stick to 'en when they first come. They were forever sneaking titbits and nibbling and picking at this and that.'

'Only leftovers, Mrs Dagget,' Nan wailed. 'Never nothin' proper. And after you learned us not to do it, we never took nothing save we asked first.'

''Tes a punishment on me for being too easygoing and trusting them to behave when they was left on their own to prepare the vegetables for dinner. Once a thieving street brat, always a thieving street brat!'

'We never stole,' Nan cried as Joan's sobs broke out afresh. 'Even when we was starvin' hungered we stayed honest as we could.'

'You say they were left by themselves, Mrs Dagget?' I asked.

'I'd just slipped out to take Dagget and his lad a couple of pasties I'd made.' She looked at me warily, as though she expected I might reprimand her for leaving her kitchen. 'I was away a bit longer than I'd intended. And I don't make a habit of it, Mrs Penhale,' she added, recovering her composure and her indignation. 'I'm not one to take advantage, you can ask anyone.'

'I am sure you are not, Mrs Dagget' I said easily. 'Joan and Nan were left here alone then. And Kitty?'

'Upstairs turning out your bedchamber.'

'And any lummock could have come in through the kitchen door – an' out again – while they maids were in the scullery!' Kitty cried, unable to contain herself any longer. 'They'd never have spied 'en when they were busy at the sink. Come and see for yourself, ma'am.'

The scullery was a long, narrow room with two sinks at the far end, each with the luxury of its own pump.

'It seems Kitty is right,' I said after a moment's examination. Joan and Nan, no doubt chattering and giggling as they pumped water and scraped potatoes and carrots, their backs to the door into the kitchen, would never have heard anyone intent on making noiseless progress to the pantry.

'I still think it was they two,' Mrs Dagget said, but there was less certainty in her voice.

Joan wiped her sleeve across her eyes, and found courage to say in a frightened whisper, 'We 'as no need to pinch nothin', ma'am, for we 'as such food 'ere as we'm never seed before. An' as much to eat as we like.'

Even if I had not believed her – and I did – they were such rabbitty, scared little things I could not think that either of them was possessed of the will or the boldness to carry out such a blatant theft.

I looked at Mrs Dagget. 'It is a most despicable act and I quite understand how angry and upset you were when you discovered the theft. However, in all justice, I do believe we must give Joan and Nan the benefit of the doubt. Do you not agree?'

Mrs Dagget's lips compressed to a tight line. 'If you say so, ma'am,' she said.

'I do. But I would wish you to be comfortable with my decision, and to be honest in speaking out if you think me mistaken. After all, you know the character of these girls far better than I.'

She looked disconcerted for a moment, then said, as I hoped she would when her sense of fairness was appealed to, 'Well . . . I can see I might have been a bit hasty. How-somever,' she added, glaring at the maids, 'I shall be watching you pair extra close from now on. So don't get the notion that I've turned soft. If you are the sinners you can be sure I'll find 'ee out.'

'But, in case it is someone from outside who is responsible,' I said, 'I think it would be wise to keep the bolt on the back door when the kitchen is unattended.'

Every eye swivelled to regard the stout door.

''Twould be best,' Kitty said, nodding her head so vigorously that her cap came askew. 'For it might not be anyone as we knows but some stranger, a . . . a starvin' tramp . . . or gypsies . . .'

'Thank you, Kitty, but I think that unlikely. The explanation will probably be much closer to home.'

But Kitty, embarked on this interesting line of speculation, was not to be deterred so easily. 'They say Plymouth town's always full o' heathen sailors off they foreign ships,' she said with relish. 'P'raps some of they thievin' brutes crossed the river in search of fine 'ouses to ransack.'

Joan gave a squeak of fright. Nan, closest to the door, immediately edged behind the kitchen table as though she expected hordes of sabre-wielding ruffians to burst in any second. Even Mrs Dagget looked momentarily unnerved.

'Really, Kitty,' I said crossly, 'I scarcely think the loss of a cheesecake and a custard tart constitutes a ransacking. Shame on you for frightening Joan and Nan. Now please, listen carefully, all of you. I shall do my best to discover the culprit. Until I do it is sensible to take precautions against further theft. It is *not* sensible to indulge in wild fancies about intruders.'

Mrs Dagget, recovering, aimed a cuff at Kitty's head. ''Tes my burden to be surrounded by muttonheads. Get back to sweeping the stairs, Kitty Parslow – and you pair into the scullery and finish those vegetables, else we'll all be waiting on dinner.'

I sighed as the maids scuttled off. 'Let us hope Mr Penhale has some success with his advertisement in Plymouth for an experienced housemaid. You are sorely in need of a sensible person to help you.'

'Indeed I am, ma'am,' Mrs Dagget said, adding darkly, 'And one that will stay longer than a week, which was all the last one stayed before she packed her bags.'

'Why was that?'

'*Said* her couldn't settle to country life.'

'You did not believe her?'

Having gone so far as to agree with me over the matter of the housemaid, she would be drawn no further. 'I thought her a decent enough body,' she said with a return to her usual grudging manner. 'But folks has likes and dislikes an' there's no accounting for either. She was town bred after all. Now, ma'am, if you'll excuse me, I shall have to make up for the lack of a pudding. Would a currant dumpling suit? If I make haste I can get it all done and set on the fire to boil in good time.'

I did not find the explanation for the missing puddings that day, nor in the ones that followed. The two youths who helped Zack Bligh in the garden had been scything grass down by the woods. The stable lad had been washing and polishing the carriage after its return from taking Daniel to the ferry, with no possibility he could have escaped Dagget's watchful eye for long enough to dash to the kitchen. I worried for a while that it might have been some passing vagrant who had sneaked into the house unobserved and might still be in the vicinity but there were no other signs of theft. I toyed, then, with the notion that some thieving animal had been the culprit, perhaps a rogue among the stable cats who normally did not wander farther than the yard. Unfortunately, I suggested this in Kitty's hearing, which gave her a wonderful opportunity to embark upon a bloodthirsty tale of rats as big as terrier dogs that were known to snatch babies from their cradle while they slept, and earned her a buffet about the ears from Mrs Dagget when Joan refused to open the pantry door that night to fetch out a jug of milk for fear a similar great beast was waiting inside to pounce upon her and drag her off to its lair.

But the traps Zack Bligh set about the kitchen and scullery stayed empty. No stray starveling cat or dog was seen about the property. For a few days there was rigorous attention by Mrs Dagget to the whereabouts of the maids and an inclination for everyone to be more than usually aware of the streaming draughts and shadows about the house. But presently, when there was no recurrence of the incident, the air of nervous suspicion faded. By the time Daniel returned at the end of the week, bringing with him in the carriage – and somewhat triumphantly, for he had not even had to place an advertisement – one Martha Manning to be our new housemaid, the theft seemed of very little consequence against this stroke of good fortune. For Martha, middle-aged and sober, came not only with a recommendation from Mrs Venables, who had known her from the days when they had been in service together at the house of a clergyman, but with gratitude at finding a good situation so soon after being widowed and losing her tied cottage in consequence of her husband, a farm labourer, having succumbed to a lung fever. It was not many days before her quiet, capable influence began to permeate the shadows and I began to feel that at last some sort of order and comfort might begin to be created in the house that I must now call my home.

Chapter Five

Penns Lane, Bovey Tracey
10th November, 1815
My Dear Daughter Hannah,

I cannot Hope to Express to you the deep Happiness that has been my Constant Companion since I received your letter. Not a Day has passed in these Long Years since you left Bovey without Word or Explanation, when I have not Prayed that some Change of Heart might Lead you to Reconcile yourself to those who never ceased to Love you. Alas, it is too late for your Dear Father, who left the Awful Sufferings of this Mortal World some Two Years since, he never being the Same Man since your Great Trouble which rendered a terrible Despair on his Proud nature. He was a man ruined by Grief for as you know he had bestowed every Indulgence and Benefit upon his only Daughter & had a Loving Father's natural expectation of Devotion & Obedience in Return, not the Disappointment which came as such a fierce blow. His actions upon learning of the Results of your Wayward Behaviour with One whom he presumed to be a Gentleman but turned out False may have seemed Harsh to you, but be assured that he meant only to Protect you from the Judgement of Others as Best he could, for he never ceased to care for you, even in the darkest moments. You will understand the depth of his regard for you & our beloved Grandaughter Sophy, upon whom we both so much Doated, when I tell you that on learning of your Flight from Bovey he was cast down into a Grievous Melancholy of the Spirit from which he never recovered. He had hoped that in the loss of your Husband you would turn once again to those who loved you best, namely your Parents. That you chose to act Otherwise was a blow that reduced all his Vigour & Energy and caused him to shut himself off from the Company of Friends & Acquaintances. So broken in Mind by Tormenting Thoughts & Regrets was he, and so neglectful of his person did he become, that a Dropsical swelling took hold which rendered him Bedfast & eventually Carried him off.

I had read my grandmother's letter many times in the days since I had opened Mama's box. Each time I reached this point, when the crabbed writing became even more wavering, as though the hand that held the pen shook from emotion that could not be suppressed, I was forced to put down the fragile, heavily creased paper.

I stared through a blur of tears at the dust motes moving in the shaft of late morning sunlight spearing down from the high window of the room that I now looked upon as my retreat, clean now and as yet barely furnished, but comfortable to me beyond any other room in the house. It was not at all grand, with its modest size, low ceiling and small arched windows glazed with thick, greenish glass and set deep in the thickness of the wall, but the atmosphere was so different here from the rest of the house that the moment I stepped inside and closed the door I seemed to be in a place quite apart: a place of tranquillity and easeful silence where the discords of the day became less strident and I might sit peacefully and let my mind drift to repose. The presence of the life-sized *trompe l'oeil* figure I had placed beside the hearth – where a fire was set but not lit, for the late May day though breezy was warm, and this part of the house seemed considerably less draughty than the rest – seemed totally in keeping with the harmonious atmosphere. It was of a woman with a jolly baby on her lap. I had seen such figures before, sometimes used to screen an unused fireplace, or to ornament a landing or decorate a drawing room, but never one so fine. It was painted on a canvas-covered cut-out board and was so lifelike that when Nan had spied her smiling face as she helped me move an old washstand from the last uncleared corner, she had jumped and squeaked like a frightened mouse, supposing it to be someone lurking there.

Once the dust was cleaned from the varnished surface all the details sprang to exuberant life – the warm flesh tones, the yellow hair puffing from under the lacy cap, the sinuous softness of velvet and lace. They might have been painted yesterday. Which was clearly not the case, for the woman's dress was of another age entirely, the crisp ruff around her neck, the blue velvet doublet with its embroidered silk panel, the wide farthingale, speaking of a time perhaps two hundred years since. I found her very appealing because of the liveliness of her demeanour. I was sure she must have been drawn from life. Perhaps she was the wife of the one who painted her for there seemed affection in every brush stroke, and her cheerful good nature was so warmly represented.

I looked at her now. Her friendly smile seemed to ease the heartache the letter brought to me. Her eyes, cleverly

217

painted so that they appeared to look straight at me wherever I was in the room, gazed at me with kindly sympathy.

'She deserves a name,' I had said to Nan. 'I think it must be Hilary, which means "cheerful" in Latin. Mistress Hilary and her daughter ... Cara, yes, which is Italian for "dear one". That is appropriate, for she looks as though she would adore her baby exceedingly, do you not think so?'

Nan blinked at me uncertainly, still unnerved by the encounter behind the washstand. 'If you say so, ma'am.'

'I do. There, we shall put her by the hearth, where she may bestow her smile in welcome on all whom I invite to visit me here.'

As yet, there had been few visitors to my little sanctuary. Daniel and Kensa had been, of course, the one to give his benevolent if somewhat mystified approval that I should choose this insignificant corner to make my own, the other to smile sweetly and say, 'A sunny room, Mama,' and to curl her lip in derision when her papa's back was turned. And one day I had heard a scrabbling at the door and opened it to be nearly knocked over by Pirate, who whined and leaped in an ecstasy of delight at having found me. Captain Penhale came puffing and cursing up the worn stone stairs behind him.

'To heel, you damned brute!' he bellowed. Then, growling to me as Pirate reluctantly sidled back to him, 'Takes my eye off him for a minute and he's away up here as though the devil was on his tail.' His beard bristled belligerently. 'No doubt he's had his brains jangled by all the clattering that's been going on. I'll have you know it's been mighty unsettling for me also, madam, leave alone a poor dumb animal. Peace and quiet's what I like and insist on. Not this constant disturbance.'

'I am sorry if you have been troubled,' I said, 'though I

should have thought little sound carried through these thick walls, even though your quarters are so close. As I told you, I have been clearing out this room for my own personal use. I realise it is of little interest to you what I have made of it, but since you are here perhaps you would care to come in and look at it and give me your opinion. And as I have just had a jug of lemonade sent up, should you like to sit and refresh yourself for a few moments?'

'Lemonade? Pah! 'Tis a brew only fit for sickly women.'

'Then I will have something stronger fetched. Whatever you wish. Ale, brandy . . .'

'Don't practise your parlour politeness on me, madam. I only came to retrieve this disobedient brute and drag him back where he belongs.'

All the same, he was staring around as we spoke together, his fierce blue eyes in their nest of weathered wrinkles taking in every aspect of the room.

'At least tell me if you approve, sir.' I said.

'Approve or disapprove, 'tis no concern of mine,' he grunted.

'I had hoped if you found it pleasing that I might persuade you to take tea with me some afternoon when you return from your walk.' I forestalled any derogatory remark about the nature of the hospitality on offer by adding, innocently, 'I understand from Zack Bligh that you take a dish of China tea and a wafer or two at that hour.'

He blew through his whiskers noisily. 'See! Just as I thought. Let a woman within a mile and she's prying and interfering! I gave you no leave to question my servant. I'll not stand for it, I tell you straight, Mrs Penhale. Nor shall I ever wish to pass my time with polite how-de-dos, so think on not to bother asking it of me.'

'I should not dream of it. There was nothing of the sort on my mind.'

'Then what?'

'I – I become daily more curious about this house,' I said. It was all I could invent on the spur of the moment, for my invitation was merely meant as a friendly gesture with no thought to anything else. 'And about the Trewithens who lived here, colourful characters I understand. I have asked Daniel, but he has only the sketchiest interest.' That was true. He tended to brush aside all reference to the earlier inhabitants of Kildower and I forebore to press him for I felt it only reawakened memories of a time he preferred not to speak of. 'I believe you are fully acquainted with the history of the house and neighbourhood.' A wild guess, this, but he did not contradict me so I pressed on. 'If you could spare me an hour sometimes to tell me what you know I should consider it a great favour.'

He scowled. 'I dare say you would. Whether I shall grant you that favour is another matter entirely. To my present way of thinking, madam, I'd not give good odds on it.'

He had called Pirate to heel and stumped off, easing his way awkwardly down the stairs and grumbling all the while into his whiskers.

I brought my errant thoughts back to the letter in my hand. I was composed enough now to read on.

Dear child, if there is Justice in Heaven, your father will know that you have softened towards us enough to write & his Spirit will be eased. About that Other Matter, to ease your own Hart, I have it on the Authority of Mrs Warrener, who Saw you through your Great Trouble, that the child was taken to the Bosom of a Good Family who love her as their own & grows Healthy and Content & wants for nothing. I have been Minded, you see, to Satisfy my own Anxiety on this

Score since your Father died, who was Set against it in his Lifetime, thinking it Best for All to forget that Unhappy time. I would not Disobey his wishes while he Lived, but submitted Myself to this Weakness when he had Gone finding myself without any living Kin in the World, save yourself, & Sophy, who were Cut Off from me. Mrs Warrener promises me some Further Indication that the Child does well, which I shall Relay to you when it is to Hand. She has been most Kindly towards me, being herself now Widowed & Retired from the Trade you Know Of but still taking an Interest in the Results of her Useful and Charitable Actions. I Pray you will Answer this Missive as soon as Maybe. You will gladden a Grandmother's hart if you tell me everything of dearest Sophy. Such an affectionate & sunny little maid she will be now, if she fulfils the Promise of her Babyhood and takes the best from both Sides. You yourself were a delightful imp when you was small and could do no wrong in your papa's eyes, or mine, until that Other Business of which I have Spoke & your late husband Thos. Beardmore, a most amiable, charitable and trustworthy man. He is remembered with affection in the Town for his Kind Actions, many of which were rendered Privately and only heard of since his sad Passing. I have hopes the Child inherited his Calm & Considerate nature which will be a Good Thing for her and a blessing for you. You are so Far off that I cannot bare to think of the Miles that separate us. I only Hope that Land & Ocean will be bridged by many more Letters from now until I go to join my dear Husband in Heavenly Peace & that one day, if God wills it, I might live to once again embrace my dear daughter & granddaughter. I remain,

now and always, your most Loving and Devoted
Mama, Sarah Colyton.

But she had not lived. Until I first read this letter, I had
never understood the depth of my mother's revenge upon
her parents, nor the magnitude of my own loss. The grief
and loneliness of my grandmother surged through every line,
reawakening all the old bitterness I felt towards Mama. I
saw clearer than ever how careless with the truth she had
been when she related the stories of her childhood. Her
picture of a restricted, narrow upbringing with parents who
cared only for their respectability and nothing for her
happiness was in complete contrast to the pictures raised by
my grandmother's words. For Hannah, their only child, had
been loved so dearly that her parents had been inconsolable,
her father fatally so, when she had made her ruthless exit
from Bovey and their lives.

The thought of poor Sarah reduced to searching out pitiful
scraps of information about that other lost granddaughter in
order to ease the burden of loneliness was almost too
wretched to bear thinking of. And what was more desperately
painful than anything else was that her letter had been written
at a time when I myself was miserably unhappy and felt
myself to be entirely lost and abandoned. *Our beloved
granddaughter Sophy. Upon whom we so much doated.*
Given the chance, my grandmother and I might have forged
a link that could have given ease to both of us in our
loneliness. We might never have been allowed to meet, but
just to have been able to write . . .

The letter was dated from the winter when I was nine
years old, a particularly bad one for me. Mama had
despatched me to the convent in the autumn and there I had
languished for the whole of the winter, feeling myself to

have been entirely forgotten, for I think she wrote but once to me during the whole time I was there, and then only to remind me how lucky I was to have the advantage of the benevolent attention and fine education showered upon me by the sisters while she was burdened by a multitude of worldly cares. With my palm swollen and stinging from a caning by Sister Veronique because I had stumbled when reciting a passage from some devout work we had been set and cramps in my stomach from a bout of biliousness which was surely to do with the sour, fatty pork that had been set before us for supper the evening before and which must be consumed in its entirety – for no waste was allowed and those who did not leave a clean plate would be made to remain at the table until every hateful morsel had been swallowed, however long it took – I would have willingly exchanged a gross of worldly cares for the promise of release from incarceration amid such so-called benevolence.

Sarah Colyton. My grandmother. I had not even known her Christian name. And how warmly she had spoken of my papa, for whom Mama had had nothing but contempt. Mama had denied me any chance of knowing her or of allowing me to build any sort of pleasant image of my father. It was intolerable! And still, I guessed, she intended that I should learn nothing, for this letter had slid behind the frayed padded silk lining of the box and I should not have found it myself had my nail not snagged the rotting silk and the corner of the tightly folded paper been revealed. There were no other personal letters in the box. Mama had removed evidence of any others she might have received from her mother, and there must have been others, I was sure. Sarah would have persisted, even had my mother never written another word, as was quite likely. I wondered why she had softened enough to write in the first place. Some whim, I supposed. Some moment of idleness or curiosity. Or like the times when she summoned me back to her side, when a lover was discarded, or had discarded her, and she was bored or had sunk into maudlin self-pity.

I replaced the letter and took out the other items the box contained. A scrap of paper with an address in Plympton written on it in a different hand. Then a short formal note from the lawyer explaining the details of my grandmother's will. There had been very little to dispose of, apparently. She had been forced to live frugally after my grandfather died as his illness had swallowed up most of their savings, and before that he had long neglected his haberdasher's shop which had been sold for a pittance. By the time all was sold and the funeral expenses deducted, my mother's inheritance consisted of a bare twenty guineas. I had known nothing even of that, leave alone these other, more poignant mementoes left to her. Mementoes of Juliana, my half-sister which the lawyer had forwarded as Grandmother's will dictated.

These must have been the 'further indication' of Juliana's well-being that Mrs Warrener had promised. A lock of hair, black and silky, with the same curling life in it that characterised Mama's own tresses; a miniature portrait in a tarnished metal frame, a baby's outgrown satin slipper, with a 'J' worked in pink silk on the toe. Little enough, but how precious they must have been to Sarah.

Juliana's face stared up at me from the miniature. It had been painted with amateurish crudity when she was perhaps five or six but if one made allowances for the poorly judged proportions and garish colouring it was possible to see that she might be very pretty indeed – and very like Mama in her smile and her green eyes.

Loved like their own . . . Wants for nothing . . .

I felt a quiver of envy. I knew it was unworthy, but some-times human nature is not biddable in these matters and it seemed to me, whenever I thought of it, that Juliana had fared better during her childhood than I, being taken in by a kindly, generous family. She had not been required to live in the restless shadow of a woman who, though beautiful and talented, was selfish, feckless and uncaring of any feelings save her own.

Perhaps my face showed my feelings when I had told Daniel the story of my mother's downfall, shown him the contents of the box and explained my mother's command that I should seek out her other daughter.

'And you do not wish to?' he asked gently.

'I am not sure,' I confessed. 'It has taken me all these weeks to look inside the box. I would not have troubled you, Daniel, with such an aggravating matter, especially as it casts such a poor light on Mama's behaviour when she was young, but I am uncertain how to proceed.'

'I believe my own mother was once scarcely older and certainly as foolhardy in that respect,' he said with a dry little smile.

'You have been open with me from the first about your background, which leads me to believe you may be able to give me the best advice.'

'I have never chosen to hide my origins,' he said calmly. 'In trade it makes no odds. Indeed, a man born a bastard who works hard and deals fairly will be better thought of by his peers than someone born in wedlock of noble stock who cheats and lies.' He shrugged. 'Of course, my breeding might have counted had I wished to climb socially, though I rather fancy a deep purse would have counted for more than blue blood among some of the more impoverished gentry, had I wished to marry one of their kind. But such self-seeking has never interested me. Now, what is it you wish me to advise you on?'

We were sitting in the parlour. The evening beyond the window was brilliant with sunset. Restlessly I laid aside my embroidery and walked across the room to stare out at the fiery vermillion and gold and hot pinks of the sky above the hills to the west.

'I think I should not have opened the box at all. It has made me curious and I think one should be wary of mere curiosity in a delicate matter such as this. My first instinct, you see, was to refuse Mama's request, and I believe that is the best course. Juliana probably has a perfectly satisfactory and comfortable life. I should not wish to hurt or upset her by intruding upon it.'

'And if her life has not been such a bed of roses as you suppose?'

I had not heard him move, but he had come to stand quietly behind me.

'From the letter . . .'

'A reassuring letter, true.'

'Do you not think it correct?'

'Your grandmother sounds a good, kind woman. This Mrs Warrener may well have been well-intentioned also, but her view must necessarily be coloured by her occupation, which provided her with a good living. Such people are only charitable for a price. I think you must bear that in mind when you make your judgement.'

'You mean that she would not be likely to admit any fault in the arrangement which would reflect badly on herself? Yes, that had crossed my mind.'

'But you hesitate still.' I felt his hand on my shoulder and, though his touch was gentle, I stiffened. 'What is it, Sophy? What else holds you back?'

'I . . . well, as I said, is mere curiosity a good enough reason for seeking her out?' Not the only reason, but I could not speak of the rest. It was too shameworthy. For how could I confess that the attraction I genuinely felt drawing me into discovering what had happened to my sister was undermined by less reputable instincts. For I was afraid that I should find her as Mama expected her to be, beautiful and graceful and lively and sparkling, all the qualities which I saw in Mama at her best, and which, as she often reminded me, were sadly lacking in my own character. If that were so, if Mama and Juliana were one day reunited, Mama truly would adore her as she had never adored me. My sister, conceived in reckless, romantic passion out on the wild moor. Not the dull outcome of a dreary marriage to a man Mama despised. I could not possibly speak of any of this though Daniel remained, waiting, as though he expected more.

But presently he took his hand from my unyielding shoulder. He moved to stand by my side, only a little way from me though it seemed a great distance, and the loss of his touch leaving a chilly place where his warm hand had rested. He too looked out at the sunset, which was past its best now, the showy colour beginning to shrink and fade.

'I can speak only from my own experience,' he said in a cool, level voice. 'Like you, I never knew my father. Unlike you, I knew that he was alive. The hope was always with me from the moment of understanding that this godlike being would return to rescue us from the squalor of our existence. My mother would speak no ill of him and as death drew ever closer, the memory of him and of a time when she had been happiest became more real to her than the fetid corner of the tumbledown Barbican tenement we called home. To me also. So much so that the hope – the expectation – of meeting my true father lingered for many years. When I was well grown and perfectly content, indeed, deeply grateful for all that Saul Penhale had done for me, whenever I was out of school I never walked Plymouth streets close by the docks without searching the faces of men who passed me by, looking for some feature that I might recognise.' He gave a rueful laugh. 'Even today that old habit sometimes catches me unawares. I see a tall, light-haired seafaring man and I am a boy again, wondering if this stranger might be looking for his long-lost child. Unfortunately,' he added mockingly, 'my perceptions have remained fixed in childish imaginings. I still think of him as young and handsome and dashing, as my mother described him, not the grizzled old man he must be if he still lives.' He was quiet a moment, then said, 'But I think whatever manner of man he was or became, I should have liked – would still like – to have had the chance to know him.' He turned to me, his glance calm and unwavering. 'It is too late and too unlikely that I should ever meet him now, but for your sister . . . Well, we do not know anything of her life, but I suspect her deepest feelings might not be too far removed from my own, however happy she has been with her adoptive parents.'

'Then you think there would be no harm in searching her out?' My voice came out as dispassionate as his.

'You have no need to decide that now. Certainly I think there would be no harm in making a few enquiries.' I saw that he held the scrap of paper with the Plympton address of the Sinclairs. 'All might be done with the greatest discretion. Then, when you have whatever facts that come to light about your sister and her family, you will be in a better position to make a balanced judgement.'

'Yes, I see the sense in that, Daniel. Thank you.' Such relief that the final decision might be put off. 'You are sure that there will be no risk of her learning about these enquiries?'

'I will see to them myself. No other party need be involved. You see, one of the brewery alehouses lies in Plympton and as I may have told you I make it my business to accompany my agent to every inn I own at least once a year. I have a notion to visit the Lamb Inn shortly to investigate the possibility of extending my interests in the town. There is nothing about my visit that will be remarked upon even if I choose to take a solitary walk about the area. It is what I usually do when I am considering purchasing another property in order to make a personal and private evaluation of suitable sites before I am subjected to the blandishments of those who have an eye more to profits than honesty.' He smiled. 'And apart from the tenant's wife at the Lamb keeping a fine table where I always take pleasure in dining, she is the greatest gossip between here and Exeter. Leave it to me, my dear. Whatever there is to know about the Sinclairs I shall discover it and bring you the tidings when I return next.'

Which time grew steadily nearer and I was still not sure whether I was glad or sorry of it.

The clock striking the hour from the great granite slab that formed the mantel above the fireplace of my retreat reminded me that I must make haste. Kensa and I were to call upon the vicarage this afternoon. I had been forced to leave her at home the only other time I had visited Mrs Miles and her daughters. Kensa had been confined indoors at the last moment because she was feeling sick, or said she was. She had drooped so convincingly that I had been thoroughly taken in, and considerably irritated to find she had made a miraculous recovery by the time I returned. But today I should stand no nonsense and there was no one here to abet Kensa in her melodramatics.

I replaced the items in the box and put the box into the

heavy oak chest against the wall. Both chest and clock had been retained from the lumber that had originally cluttered the room. Much of the rest – mouldering rugs, boxes of aged curtains and moth-eaten draperies, pieces of furniture full of worm – had been taken out and burnt. The best of the remainder was dispersed about the house or, like the pair of Turkey rugs and the washstand, which proved to be quite prettily inlaid when it was cleaned, removed upstairs to brighten the cheerless maids' quarters under the eaves.

I turned the heavy ornamental key in the lock on the chest and put the key into my pocket. There was nothing in the chest of value to anyone, but my grandmother's letter alone was treasure to me, and it was comforting to know that it was secure from prying eyes.

The house was extra quiet today. Kitty had begged permission to visit St Germans' fair. ''Tes my Jem, ma'am,' she had explained, blushing. 'Back along, we did settle on it that we should meet there, if 'twas allowed . . . an' me not clappin' eyes on him since New Year, an' he'm bound to be wantin' to set the date for marryin'. Oh, 't'would be a fine thing if you do give me leave. An' I'd be back well before dark, I swear.'

'I see no reason why not,' I said. She had been dropping hints as large as house ends about the fair for some days. 'Mrs Dagget tells me she and her husband would not be averse to a stroll around the fair, it being a great event in the district, so I have decided to allow you all to go.' I would not hurt her feelings by adding that Mrs Dagget had also said, privately, that though she had only seen this wonderful Jem the once, she thought he had a bullying, sly-eyed look, and she'd not have trusted her own daughter alone with such a one. Nevertheless I felt a pang of sympathy to see some of Kitty's excitement die away as I added, 'You shall have the pleasure of telling Joan and Nan that they might go with you to the fair. Mr and Mrs Dagget will accompany you there and back so there will be no danger for any of you on the way and I shall trust you to keep a close eye on the younger girls to make sure they keep out of mischief and do not come to any harm.'

Poor Kitty looked quite downcast, but I could not in conscience allow her to fall unprotected into her lover's clutches if his intentions were as dishonourable as Mrs Dagget supposed. Her guardianship of Joan and Nan would act as efficiently as any chastity belt, for I knew Kitty well enough now to understand that, unlettered and rough as she was, she took every instruction of mine to her simple heart and obeyed it faithfully. She would not leave her charges while she slipped away to some private assignation.

'I shall give you each a shilling to spend at the fair,' I said to soften the blow, at which she grew round-eyed and hurried off importantly, to bestow the exciting news on the younger maids.

St Germans' fair had also indirectly, to my great pleasure, claimed Jess Southcote.

The house might be as gloomy as ever, but I ran up the stairs and to my room to fetch my hat and gloves with a more than usual lightness. When I crossed the gallery to the nursery even the perpetual shadows seemed less dense. Martha was chivvying a reluctant Kensa into her outdoor things and looked up with a pleasant smile. So very different from Jess. I hoped, happily, that *she* was having a thoroughly horrible day up at the farm, having been out-manoeuvred by her cousin, Mrs Lugg, into caring for some sick relative who was in residence while she and her girls made off to the fair.

After church last Sunday Mrs Lugg had waylaid us,

waddling up to ask, after a flurry of apologies and much nodding of the enormous yellow plumes on her green satin bonnet, if we would convey a message to Jess. 'I'd hoped to see 'er today, you see, to ask a favour of her. I do hope little Miss Kensa's not poorly again.'

'Merely keeping indoors out of the cold wind, Mrs Lugg,' Daniel said politely.

'Indeed, 'tes fearful chilly for May, Mr Penhale, Mrs Penhale,' she gushed. Her eyes had the same shiny blackness as her cousin's, though any other family resemblance there might have been was overlaid by billows of fat. 'I'd a mind to keep my own girls indoors, but they'm God-fearin' maids and 't'would have grievous disappointed them not to come to church. But what I did want to ask of her, well, I hopes you don't think it too much of an impertinence, but I wouldn't ask if I wasn't so pushed. And Jess bein' so reliable in cases of sickness . . .'

What the flowery words and apologies boiled down to was a request for Jess to sit with an invalid who was staying at the farm while the Lugg family was absent. ''Tes a pressing matter and Mr Lugg insists I go and I was thinking if Jess had any time due to her . . . well, I know, 'er rarely will take 'er half day, her being conscientious beyond the ordinary and thinking the world of that dear little maid. But if her could be spared, sir, I'd be that grateful. And 't'wouldn't be anything more we'd be asking of her than to sit quiet, for the lady, a young relative of Mr Lugg, is recuperating after a seizure. So sad. 'Er's lost her wits, somewhat, and I daresn't leave her alone for five minutes together in case she goes wandering off not knowing where she is or what she's a-doin'.'

I spoke before Daniel could answer.

'What a worry for you.' I hoped I did not sound too

insincere, for she did not at all seem to me the sort of woman who worried much except on her own behalf. 'I am sure something might be arranged. Pray leave it to me, Mrs Lugg.'

When we returned to Kildower, I thought it politic to tell Jess of her cousin's request in Daniel's presence when she came to the parlour to fetch Kensa to bed. Her face went stony but before she could begin on the reasons why she could not go I said cheerfully. 'Now, Jess, there is no reason why you should refuse your cousin's request, or to turn down outright any other she may make in the future. I shall be happy to grant any reasonable proposition, for blood ties are important and I know you have no other kin. Of course, in the past, with the responsibility for Miss Kensa resting entirely with you in Mr Penhale's absence, it would not have been possible. Now, of course, she will get along perfectly happily with me while you are absent.'

Her glance slid past me to Daniel. 'Sir, I do not think my cousin's business is so pressing as she maintains.' She made a dismissive gesture. 'Why, I guarantee she means only to leave herself free to go to St Germans' fair, which she never likes to miss. I can't think that it would hurt her for once to stay behind.'

Daniel, who had been trying to study documents relating to a new steam boiler he was considering for the brewery, looked up a little irritably. 'Then you must settle it with your cousin, Jess. Mrs Penhale cannot be expected to understand these niceties.'

'Indeed not, sir,' Jess said. 'I'll attend to it straight off.' Now she looked at me and said smoothly, 'I'm grateful for your interest, and sorry that you've been troubled, Mrs Penhale, but I shouldn't dream of putting you to the slightest inconvenience by virtue of my cousin's demands.'

She stood there looking humble, her voice oily and

obsequious, the very picture of a devoted servant. But it was her eyes I watched, those black shiny eyes that held only triumph and pleasure at her own cleverness. And now, so sure of herself and her mastery of my wishes, she moved away, deliberately contemptuous, before I had chance to dismiss her. 'Come, Miss Kensa,' she said silkily. 'It's well past your bedtime. You know Mama will be cross with you tomorrow if you're too tired to learn your lessons and then you'll get yourself all upset when she scolds you.' And, unspoken, but implicit in every word *and we know she doesn't understand you or care for you and we are much better off without her interference.*

'One moment, Jess.' My voice came out with a steely edge to it, jolting her to an involuntary halt. But she found me laughing when she turned back to me, my anger masked with lightness.

'Good gracious,' I said, 'I am sure you did not mean to convey the impression that the household would collapse about our ears if you were not here, Jess, but you must believe that is precisely how it sounded. Did it not Daniel?' Daniel, absorbed in his papers, made a vague murmur of assent. 'You see? Mr Penhale feels quite as I do. You really must take care not to take too much upon yourself. Or—' I paused, gave a little shrug, so that the word took on emphasis and hung threatening in the air. Then I went on with the manner of one prepared to be munificent. 'Well, I shall say no more for the moment. I dare say you will take care not to speak so thoughtlessly in the future. Now, to happier matters. I have deemed Friday a holiday for all the maids save Martha, who professes some dissenting religion that preaches against frivolities of all kinds, so I see no reason why you should be confined here when you might be out enjoying yourself. If you do not wish to accommodate your cousin, then I insist you join the party going to St Germans.'

Daniel bless him, chose that moment to lay his papers aside and say approvingly, 'An excellent idea. I wish I had thought of it myself. I believe Kildower is fortunate to have so benevolent a mistress. What say you, Jess?'

Her nostrils flared and a muscle in the corner of her heavy jaw twitched. After a moment she said woodenly, 'As you say, sir.' How could she have answered otherwise without showing herself in a poor light? And this morning she had gone off to Trebarth, cloaked in martyrdom which barely concealed a glowering temper. 'I feel duty bound, Mrs Penhale, to do as my cousin asks. I've no liking for fairs and besides, how could I enjoy myself, knowing I had denied my cousin her outing?'

'How indeed?' I had said cheerfully and watched her go without a qualm.

'Now, Miss Kensa, don't pull such a face or the wind'll change and you'll be stuck with it.' Martha tugged Kensa's sunbonnet straight with the deftness acquired from the raising of three daughters and standing no nonsense from any of them. 'There, you look a proper picture. I don't know why you were making such a fuss.'

'I wanted the blue velvet dress,' she whined. 'Jess would have let me wear my velvet dress instead of this horrid plain thing.'

'And your mama staying up late last night straining her eyes to finish it? For shame!'

Kensa scowled at me. 'Jess says blue suits me best.'

'Well, her's entitled to her opinion,' Martha said firmly. 'To my mind pink's just right for a maid wi' your fair colouring. 'Sides, 'tes too warm a day for velvet.'

The dress did look well. It was made from one of the

breadths I had bought in Exeter and unlike her other dresses was unadorned save for the wide sash and a trim of braid I had stitched around the hem and collar. It was a style perfectly suited to a young girl, enabling her to move about in play unhampered by a weight of frills and flounces.

'The coral necklace Papa bought matches perfectly,' I said. 'And you must agree that your new shoes are comfortable and do not look at all clumsy.'

She glanced down at them and sighed heavily. 'I suppose anyone who lived in a vicarage might think them very fine. I'm used to the very best, so I think them rustic in the extreme.'

I kept my face straight. Sometimes her tone was so blasé that it was quite comic.

'The cream kid is beautifully supple,' I said mildly. 'And the soles are a sensible thickness. You will find them very comfortable to walk in. We really are very lucky to have such a clever shoemaker in the village.'

She shuddered. 'Ugh! I should never have invited him here to Kildower. Such an ugly, twisted creature. His place is in the yard, not in a fine parlour. I could hardly bear him to touch my feet when he was making his patterns.'

'Kensa!' My tolerant mood vanished instantly. 'Never, *never* let me hear you speak like that again, do you hear? About anyone. Leave alone an unfortunate man like Will Thomas.'

'Why not? Everyone knows he has the evil eye.'

'What?'

'They turned him out of the village years ago. They make him live down by the creek where he can't turn the milk sour or stop the hens laying. Jess says his mother was a witch and it was the wickedness in her blood that caused him to be born a hunchback.'

Shocked, I could almost hear Jess's low voice, insidious, poisonous, speaking through the child. It sent a shiver of despair up my back. For nine years she had been free to shed her pernicious influence over Kensa. A day scarcely passed without evidence of her hold on the child presenting itself and, try as I might, with every skill at my command, I had not managed to loosen her grip. Away from her father's indulgent gaze Kensa still refused to offer the slightest hope of any willing co-operation. She parrotted Jess Southcote's ignorant thoughts and ideas. She still regarded me as an intruder. Nothing I did or said seemed to make any impression on her. I had a momentary vision of the bleak future if I did not succeed with Kensa. It was not pleasant. For her – or for myself.

'For shame, Miss Kensa,' Martha said, straightening up after a last tweak at Kensa's bonnet strings. ''Tes cruel beyond belief to repeat such nasty things. And unkind to speak so. I thought he'd a very gentlemanly manner and a kind face. You just remember poor cripples are the Lord's creatures, same as you and me. 'Sides, fine looks can be deceivin'. I've known many blessed with handsome faces who had Satan in their hearts.'

'I shall say what I please. In any case, it's not your place to tell me what to do.' She produced, with relish, the ultimate threat. 'If you don't take care I shall ask Papa to put you off for impertinence.'

'As you please, Miss Kensa,' Martha said, completely unabashed. 'It was the Lord's will brought me here. If 'tes His wish I should move on elsewhere, I shall go willin'.'

Kensa looked momentarily disconcerted, then collected herself and said airily, 'Well, if you apologise.'

'Be quiet, Kensa! I will have no more of this impudent behaviour.' She took a step forward as if to defy me, but something in my expression held her silent. She made do with her usual sulky scowl and I turned to Martha and said with a smile, 'Thank you for your patience with a very disagreeable little girl who should long ago have learned better manners. And you need have no fear that you will be put off. Mr Penhale and I are very satisfied with your work. You set a good example to the young maids and I know Mrs Dagget thinks highly of you. Now, we shall be out for the whole of the afternoon, so it would please me if you took some recreation like the rest of the household.'

'I'm much obliged, ma'am,' she said. 'There's a dear old soul lives out on the road to Antony I've met at Sunday Meeting who's been pressing me to call on her. If I make haste I'll be up there within the hour.'

When she had gone I turned back to my stepdaughter. She stood there, arms akimbo, the very picture of sulky defiance.

'Come, Kensa,' I said, 'or we shall be late.'

'No! I don't want to go out. I have a headache.'

My patience snapped. I shrugged. 'Very well, you may stay behind and rest. It is of no consequence to me.'

'Call Martha back at once.' She stamped her foot imperiously. 'Tell her to bring me some hot milk with nutmeg.'

'Certainly not,' I said coolly. 'And as there is no one else left to dance attendance on you, you may put yourself to bed if that is what you wish. You will have the whole afternoon to contemplate your many shortcomings in peace and quiet.'

I walked briskly to the door.

'But you can't leave me on my own!'

'That is exactly what I shall do if you do not choose to come with me.'

She let out a great wail. 'I hate you! I want Jess. Jess wouldn't leave me.'

'More's the pity,' I said under my breath. Then, sharply, 'You may screech all you like but there is no one to hear.' I turned in the doorway. 'Well? What is it to be? Do you stay here and sulk on your own? Or do you come with me and have an enjoyable afternoon playing with Chloe and Rhoda? The choice is yours.'

She did not move. I walked out into the gallery and paced steadily along it. I was almost at the head of the stairs when I heard the rush of footsteps behind me. I felt a wash of relief. I had never wanted to confront and threaten her, but it seemed the only expedient. Rude and defiant as she was, I could not have borne to leave her alone in this great, gloomy place, though I was at a loss to think how I would have proceeded had she decided to call my bluff. But it would not be necessary now. I had proved myself the stronger in the battle of wills. I was not particularly proud of it. Indeed, the catch of her sobbing breath, the tapping of her footsteps on the polished boards, seemed unbearably poignant, fuelling remorse and guilt rather than pleasure in my success, weaving a pitiful counterpoint to my own louder footsteps. Neither sound had any significance in the massive emptiness of the house.

I paused. The weight of all those deserted rooms pressed down and round us. I had the odd sensation that the emptiness reached out chilly fingers, intent on subduing the rustle of clothing, the soft cadences of our breathing, the beat of our hearts. Jealous of the human life that disturbed and destroyed its ancient peace, it bore down, smothering all echoes. Such a sad house. Old sadness seeping from ancient stone, reverberating upon fresher, newer pain. No place for a child, with all those grieving voices.

Voices? In the instant I heard them, or thought I did, they were gone, flowing back to the shadows. I listened, my hand seeking the curving solidity of the bannister rail. Nothing.

I looked down at the child. Quicksilver beauty upon bones as fragile as a bird's. So vulnerable. A tear slid miserably down her cheek. Her nose had turned pink and she sniffed up a dewdrop that had formed on the end of it. This was real distress, nothing to do with the pretended weeping she sometimes resorted to. She had believed I really would go.

It was the moment, of course, any sensible governess should have seized to remind her that she had brought whatever misery she was experiencing upon herself and to read her a lecture on the advantages of obedience and the disadvantages of being impertinent and spiteful and defiant. Instead I was washed by such an intense wave of compassion that all the words died unspoken. I found myself crouching to her level and, very gently, drawing her into my arms.

For a second or two her thin, pliant child's body leaned into my shoulder. Then she pulled back, scuffed at her cheek and gave a disdainful sniff.

We did not speak and I did not attempt to take her hand. We walked in silence down the stairs, across the hall. I paced a trifle slower than usual and she hastened her steps just a little. I felt the emptiness slither back as I opened the door and let the summer light flood across the flagstones of the hall. Then, our steps matching, I walked with my stepdaughter out into birdsong and the scent of new-mown grass.

We were buffeted down the lane to the village by a breeze that set all the fresh green leaves dancing and tumbled the clouds across the sky as though they were so many panicky sheep pursued by a snapping dog.

We walked briskly through the village. I supposed that those not at their work had gone to the fair, for the only people about were a pair of bent old women gossiping on a doorstep, the tang of the rough tobacco they were smoking in their clay pipes wafting pungently on the breeze. I told myself it was coincidence that they moved indoors before we could reach them; pure imagination that supplied a picture of two wrinkled faces peering out of a smeary window to watch us pass, toothless mouths whispering, for I kept my eyes ahead and my head erect. It was best to bear their curiosity and suspicion with dignity. I was still a stranger to them. It would take time for them to accept me. All the same, I should have welcomed a pleasant look, a word of greeting, a smile, anything, if only to dispel the image of the villagers as hostile and superstitious, ignorant peasants who would turn a gentle crippled man from their midst for fear of the evil eye, and resented anyone who was not born and bred among them.

The vicarage lay down a narrow passage running alongside the overgrown granite boulders that formed the rough circle of the churchyard wall. It was a four-square house, low and solid, scrambled over by an untamed tangle of climbing roses that were heavy with fat buds and newly opened creamy flowers. The garden was a confusion of rough grass and overgrown shrubs and mossy, leaning apple trees, all bordered with a straggly yew hedge that was in urgent need of a severe pruning. Indoors there was the same careless disregard for neatness and order. The furniture might have had some pretensions to elegance had not surfaces been overlaid with tottering heaps of books and any visible woodwork dull from lack of a good polish. Abandoned toys lay everywhere. I almost tripped over a threadbare woolly lamb as the maid showed us into the small parlour. Miss Smythe, I thought, amused, would have been aghast at the slackness of the housekeeping. But there was smiling welcome here which more than made up for the lack of orderliness.

'Mrs Penhale, I had quite forgotten the time,' Edith Miles cried, rising from a cluttered writing desk. 'And Kensa, too. How splendid! The girls were so disappointed that you could not come the first time your mama visited us.' In one graceful movement she swept a sheaf of papers haphazardly under the lid so that half of them were left protruding, turned the key in the lock, flung down her pen and held out her hands to us, oblivious of the ink stains on her fingers. 'I am delighted to see you.'

'I believe we are a little early after all,' I said. 'We have disturbed you. But we rather hurried, believing ourselves to be late.'

'Not at all. I was merely amusing myself until you arrived.' She chuckled. 'I know a little decorative embroidery is supposedly the only suitable occupation for a lady when she is receiving visitors, but I have so little talent for sewing of any kind that I have not the patience even to pretend.' She pushed back a stray strand of fair hair, one of many that were escaping from the roughly plaited coil at the nape of her neck. Indeed the whole untidy arrangement looked in serious danger of tumbling to the shoulders of a drab blue gown that had seen a great many better days and bore a fresh splash of ink down the bodice. She was cheerfully unconscious of her *déshabillé*. 'Now do come along into the garden. I know it is a boisterous day, but it is perfectly sheltered behind the house, and we shall drink tea out there and admire the view. The girls are already outside playing, Kensa dear, and they have great plans for introducing you

242

to their games and showing you the secret hiding places in the garden.'

Kensa looked less than enchanted at this prospect. I prayed she would not take on the disdainful air she had assumed when Chloe and Rhoda had visited Kildower with their mama. She had patronised them dreadfully. 'You may look at my books if your hands are perfectly clean,' I had winced to hear her say as she led them from the drawing room *en route* to the nursery, 'but pray don't touch my dolls. Papa only buys me the very best and most expensive and I don't wish you to harm such precious things.'

But when we walked out on to a flagged terrace which bore a fine crop of weeds growing between the stones, and the Miles girls, spying us, came charging up the grassy slope towards us, her reaction was different altogether. She unexpectedly took a step nearer to me and her hand reached out to clasp my skirt. She snatched it away almost immediately, her expression readjusting to the look of hauteur she assumed in company she did not approve of. But I had seen the flash of sheer fright that distorted her pretty features, and I found myself forced to regard the exuberant Miles children from a viewpoint different from my own approving one.

As an adult I saw them as exactly the kind of companions I would have wished for my stepdaughter. Exactly as I would have wished Kensa to be, if I were honest, I thought, as they made sketchy curtsies in my direction then crowded round Kensa, all trying to talk at once. For all their flowerlike names there was nothing delicate about them. They were a sturdy, boisterous, lively bunch. Intelligent, too, the eldest girl, Daisy, being so gifted in music that she was studying under masters in Exeter.

'She was very fortunate to gain a scholarship to Mrs

Barton's Academy,' Edith Miles had told me. 'It is an establishment with advanced views on female education, and very highly thought of by those who wish their daughters to have more in their head than the order of precedence at dinner and the art of flirtation.' She had added unselfconsciously, 'We should not have had the means otherwise to further her studies, which would have been a dreadful waste of talent and a sore disappointment to her.'

Bookish Chloe, the ten-year-old, was already studying Latin and Greek under her papa's tutelage. Nine-year-old Rhoda and Tansy, six, were well advanced in their lessons under their mother's supervision. 'Rhoda tries her hand at writing poetry, though it is mostly comic verse, and I feel Tansy will follow her sister Daisy, being drawn towards music.' Even tiny Violet, only just three, could spell out her name on her slate.

But all of this was of no consequence whatsoever to a sheltered nine-year-old used only to the company of adults. At Kildower, Chloe and Rhoda had been overawed and on their best behaviour. Today they were part of a noisy pack of what must seem, to Kensa, like strange and exuberant young animals, their puppyish sociability, *en masse*, as frightening to her as Pirate's lunging attempts to be friendly.

Even as I wondered how I could rescue Kensa from their midst without causing offence, Edith Miles, who missed very little for all her air of gentle vagueness, clapped her hands and cried, 'Come girls. You must earn your playtime. Unhand your guest and show her to her seat. You must try to behave like proper young ladies, or she will begin to think you a set of barbarians. Mrs Penhale, will you take the wicker chair? I think it is the least ricketty. I shall sit beside you on the bench, which is rather less reliable about the legs and has a tendency to sway about, which is alarming if you are not used to it.' She gave me an innocent smile. 'I had thought the girls might entertain us after tea, but I rather think that you might prefer to hear their party pieces first.'

Chloe sang 'Sweet Nightingale', Tansy played a simple country jig on her violin with scarcely a wrong note and Rhoda read us one of her comic rhymes about a canary who could only croak instead of sing. Little Violet, not to be outdone, insisted on reciting a nursery jingle. We clapped all these performances with enthusiasm and they were more than eager to give encores.

'Another time, my dears,' their mama said, her eyes twinkling behind her owlish spectacles, 'or you will get high-flown on all this applause. Now, Chloe and Tansy, you may help Mary to fetch tea while Rhoda shows Mrs Penhale how neatly she has written out her poem. And Violet, perhaps you would take Kensa to Papa's study to see our real canary – and tell Papa he is to put down his work and join us for tea.'

So she diplomatically dispersed her exuberant brood and Violet trustingly put her hand into Kensa's. 'Our canary is called Charlie, like Rhoda's poem. But he doesn't really croak. That's only pretend. P'raps he'll sing for you. He sings for people he likes. Come and see.' She beamed up at Kensa, so engaging and harmless that Kensa gave only a token show of reluctance before allowing herself to be persuaded.

Tea was a plain but substantial affair of thick-cut bread and butter and honey, seed cake and marmalade tart. A rug had been spread on the grass for the children, and the vicar having settled himself in Kensa's chair, Kensa had no option but to join them. She seated herself somewhat aloofly at the extreme edge of the rug. At least in such an informal situation there was no need to worry about her finicky eating habits and lack of table manners. Despite my efforts, neither had improved significantly. I believe it pleased her to defy me on both counts and sometimes my patience was sorely tried. But spilt crumbs and half-chewed leftovers would not be remarked upon here. Indeed, an appreciative flock of small birds was already darting and fluttering around the girls, ready to snatch up food scraps thrown to them.

'The birds have become extraordinarily tame since we arrived here,' Mr Miles said. He smiled fondly at his wife. 'I believe Mrs Miles charms them down from the trees.'

'Dear me, no. It is pure cupboard love. I merely feed them every day and they grow used to it.'

'Mrs Penhale, I tell you, that is only half the story. My children's pleas for a kitten are persistently denied, the garden is allowed to grow so wild that a herd of elephants might shelter there leave alone a few finches and throstles, and the man who comes in to tend the small plot of fruit and vegetables that my wife allows us from this wilderness is forcibly restrained from setting traps for the bullfinches that destroy the fruit buds and the blackbirds that will set upon the raspberries and strawberries and currants as soon as they are ripe.' He sighed unconvincingly. 'I am fond of raspberry preserve, but I fear the inordinate pleasure Mrs Miles derives from her birds counters any hopes I have in that direction.'

'How deprived you all are,' Mrs Miles said cheerfully. 'I think, Augustus, you must preach a sermon on the evils of wives who consider that the loss of a few raspberries to an overfed clergyman is more important than the life of a creature that gives daily pleasure with its song.'

'I shall give it serious thought,' Mr Miles said, sipping his tea and reaching comfortably for a second piece of seed cake.

I had the mischievous notion that had he given himself

to preaching sermons on such an understandable subject it might have done much to keep his congregation from deserting to the ranks of the Wesleyans or others of the Dissenters. The sad case was that his dry-as-dust scholarly sermons, combined with his somewhat detached and formal manner – that covered, I began to suspect, a deep shyness – had already driven many of his parishioners to the arms of more blood-stirring and vigorous sects. Judging from the paucity of the congregation last Sunday, if nothing was done to halt the decline there would soon be no more than a handful left of the congregation he had inherited from the previous incumbent. Yet Augustus Miles, at ease with his wife and family, was more human and approachable than I ever could have suspected from our stilted exchanges at the church door. He looked younger, sprightlier, too, and there was a look in his eye when he exchanged loving glances with his wife that was not in the least sober and clerical. Whatever the restraints that bound him in his public life, his private life was happy and content. That was clearly evident.

He did not stay with us for long. 'I have my sermon for Sunday to finish, if you will excuse me, Mrs Penhale.'

'I should be more inclined to believe you, Augustus, if you had not received another long letter from Mrs Bray of Tavistock today,' Edith Miles said with a teasing smile.

'A sermon does not write itself, you know,' he protested, but looked a touch sheepish as he added, 'Not that I am denying that I shall take pleasure in answering Mrs Bray's comments on the notes I sent her about the Druidic stones I have examined hereabouts. But later. Duty first, my dear. As always.'

He went back into the house and Mrs Miles said, 'My husband is happiest when delving into his antiquarian books or grubbing about the countryside in search of pagan ruins. He is compiling a volume on the subject, you see, and Mr Bray, the late vicar of Tavistock, was something of an authority on the subject. His widow, too, is a clever, lettered woman and passes on what is of interest out of her husband's papers.' She went on more soberly, 'Augustus's father was adamant that he go into the church, there being little money left to allow him to continue his studies at Oxford after the older brothers were put to the army and his sisters given dowries. I sometimes think it was a pity that he was diverted from the path of study that he had preferred. Life in some university cloister, among similarly minded gentlemen, would have suited him admirably.' She cast a gentle look at her daughters, who were gathering up the tea things and carrying them indoors in the wake of the maid. 'I feel that parents have the utmost obligation to consider the talents and inclinations of their children and not force them into a mould that is against their nature.'

'Indeed,' I said quietly, filled with my own disquieting memories.

'Even daughters,' she went on, half to herself. 'I know some would consider it foolish that we have allowed Daisy to continue with her music, or that for Chloe to master dead languages is a dreadful waste of time when in a few years both will be married and such things must be put behind them. But to have one's mind enriched . . . how can that ever be a waste? Besides, they may choose not to marry, and will have a need to fill their days with things other than idle gossip and good works. And if they marry men of scholarship and understanding, how much better to be able to converse with intelligence with one's husband, even at the risk of being considered a blue stocking by those who like to attach derogatory labels to anyone they consider to be stepping out of the conventionally accepted mode.' She broke off, laughing. 'Oh, dear, I am afraid I am on my hobby horse. Do forgive me, Mrs Penhale. You will think me exceedingly tedious. I dare say we should be discussing the price of new bonnets or exchanging receipts for Madiera cake.'

'And be suitably bored in consequence,' I said firmly. I smoothed down the sheet of paper that held Rhoda's poem. It had drawn my eye on and off since she had handed it to me. 'I have every sympathy with your view. Speaking of which, shall you let Rhoda attend the same academy as her sister when she is old enough?'

'If she obtains a scholarship, most certainly, though out of all my daughters I have always felt that she has the least intellectual nature. You think her verse has merit then? I have taught her the rudiments of metre and rhyme.'

'No, no. You misunderstand. Though I am sure her verse is excellent, it is her painting that I find interesting. Unless it is that someone else – yourself perhaps? – executed the border round the poem.'

'No, indeed. I have no aptitude. Nor do the other girls. That is Rhoda's own work.' She leaned across to frown at the birds and flowers interwoven in a flowing pattern round the spare calligraphy that was intriguingly assured for a nine-year-old. 'Perhaps she copied it from somewhere. I think she sometimes does.'

'Ah, yes. It could be that she has traced the pattern. All the same, the colouring itself is accomplished – the shading of the feathers, the petals.' I hesitated, looking across at Rhoda, a plump, giggling, fair-haired child with her mother's gentle brown eyes. She did not seem any more thoughtful or observant than the others, yet her painting told me otherwise, and I was caught and held by the need to delve further. There was a dangerous edge to my curiosity. That I knew, even as I heard myself say casually, 'If Rhoda has any other work she would care to show me, I should be interested to look at it.'

Rhoda brought her paintings and laid them on my lap.

'Come and sit here in my place, then you may tell Mrs Penhale all about your pictures,' her mother said, rising quickly from the bench. 'Violet has managed to scramble up into one of the apple trees. She looks most precarious. I must fetch her down before she tumbles.'

I scarcely heard her go. My attention was only for what I held in my hands. I leafed through them slowly in silence. There was hardly a decent piece of paper among them. Instead, there were torn scraps, pieces of card, unused pages cut from a notebook. Even the backs of some old receipted bills were covered with pencil sketches.

I cleared my throat to ask the questions, but already I knew the answers. 'Do you copy these things, Rhoda? Does anyone else help you?'

She shook her head, then chewed her lip, frowning in thought. 'Once – a long time ago – the lady who gave Daisy her violin lessons, she was clever at drawing as well. She was nice and showed us how to draw an egg shape then turn it into a bird, though nobody could do it but me.' She giggled. 'Chloe's looked like a brick with feathers sticking out. But Mrs Blunt said mine was extra-ordinar-ily good.' She enunciated the word carefully, stretching it out as perhaps the estimable Mrs Blunt had once done in her surprise and pleasure. 'She said if I practised and practised drawing real things – boring things – like chairs and tables and cups and jugs –' she giggled again – 'and my sisters, I should one day be accomplished. Mama told me what accomplished meant. I was only very young then, you see, like Tansy,' she explained with all the wisdom of nine years. 'I decided I should very much like to be accomplished, so I try very hard. And Daisy gave me her watercolours when she went to school because Chloe didn't want them, so now I try hard at colouring, too.'

'Yes,' I said. 'Yes, I see that you do.' With my finger I traced the pen and ink outline of a bowl of apples set upon a table with carved, bulbous legs. Behind the table a cupboard and a wall with a mirror on it. 'And when you practise drawing these boring objects,' I said softly, 'you find they are not boring at all.'

'Oh, no.' She leaned forward, her eyes glinting with excitement. 'They make all sorts of funny shapes – good shapes – one against the other.'

'And the spaces in between make a different sort of shape.'

'Yes! And sometimes you can't see all the shapes properly at first, then when you look hard and start drawing – there they are!'

'Colours, too,' I said softly. 'Sometimes you see one colour and when you look closely there are two, three, or the true colour is not quite what you thought. Then some are so strident they leap forward and others shrink back and . . .' I stopped. No, no, I *must* not . . .

'You understand.' Her voice came in a delighted whisper. 'Mama, Chloe, they pretend to see, but I can tell they don't. They smile at each other over my head and it makes me cross because they're so blind.' She caught her breath, dismayed. 'Oh, please, don't tell them what I said. It sounds too horrid. They can't help it. They're not like me. Like you.'

'I shall say nothing to your mama,' I said in a brisk, dismissive voice. Equally briskly I shuffled the assortment of papers back together. Shuffling her dreams in my adult, sensible hands. Handing them back to her. Standing up and shaking out the creases in my green, summery gown as though there were nothing more important on my mind than making myself tidy. 'Thank you for showing me your pictures, Rhoda. They are very pleasing. Put them away carefully now before you go back to your play.'

Oh, God, how could I do it to the child? Her eager expression fading, and the excitement in her brown eyes turning to bewilderment. But it was the only sensible – the only safe course.

I walked down the steps from the terrace and across the grass to the apple tree where Mrs Penhale had coaxed her youngest daughter down and where Chloe was setting up a battered toy theatre in the shade.

'We shall do my play "The Shipwrecked Mariner",' she announced as she fitted the scenery into position. A fierce sea with white-crested waves was painted on the cardboard backcloth. I recognised, with a pang, the hand of the artist. 'I shall be the hero, of course, the brave sailor, who saves the injured captain.'

'I want to be the Hottentot princess,' Tansy cried, scrabbling among the heap of crude cardboard cut-out figures.

'Certainly not, Tansy,' said Chloe bossily. 'That is the best part next to mine. We have to give that to our guest. Kensa will be the princess. You shall be the Captain and Rhoda the evil cannibal queen who wants to boil us in a pot for supper.'

'Me! me!' cried Violet, jumping up and down. 'Me, the cannibal.'

'You will play the ship's pussy cat, who comes ashore on a door,' said Chloe. 'You are the best at miaowing,' she added firmly, brooking no argument. 'Kensa, this is the Hottentot princess. You move her about the stage with this stick when I tell you and talk in her voice. You'll soon get the hang of it.' She thrust the figure into Kensa's hand. 'Now kneel here, next to Tansy.' She raised her voice to a shout. 'Rhoda! Look sharp! We can't start until you get here.'

'I think we may leave the Thespians to their own devices,' Mrs Miles said, tucking her hand into my arm and drawing me away. 'Mary will keep an eye on them. Come along, we shall take a little stroll.' She smiled. 'Do not worry about Kensa. She is settled now and I think she may even be beginning to enjoy herself.'

Kensa looked bemused but not unwilling to take part in this unexpected event. But it was the sight of Rhoda dawdling down the grassy slope from the house towards us that made me turn away with Mrs Miles. Best to divert oneself with less disturbing matters.

We went through the wicket gate in the straggly hedge. Beyond, there was a stretch of steeply sloping rough common land. A scrawny tethered donkey grazed on the tussocky grass and a small girl tended a flock of geese which honked threateningly when they spied us intruding on their territory. The village straggled along the low ridge to the left, well above the creek shore where a few small fishing boats lay stranded in grey mud. This was the topmost reach of the creek that went down to the Kildower jetty then out into the Lynher. The footpath coming out of the woods in the direction of the river wound around it, bridged a small stream that made a deep channel through the mud, wandered past a cottage or two and disappeared into the woods on the far side.

We idled our way down the path in the opposite direction, slowly drawing away from the village. This was the sheltered side of the creek and the afternoon sun was almost too hot to be comfortable. Instinctively we paused under the only tree growing alongside the path. The bulky oak made a little solitary outcrop of shade. A hundred yards farther on the vast green bulk of the woods began. On the other side of the hill lay the Kildower acres.

'My favourite walk is along this path and through the woods,' Edith Miles said. 'I try to take a stroll here, even if it is only for ten minutes in the evenings, so far as this oak. Is the shade not pleasant?' We looked upwards into the spreading pattern of branches and the dappled light filtering through the leaves. She reached out to touch the seamed roughness of the trunk. 'How long has this stood here, I wonder?'

'A great length of time, I should think. The trunk is enormous and quite hollowed in the centre.'

'It makes one feel insignificant. Do you find that, Mrs Penhale?'

I nodded, perfectly understanding the emotion behind the word. 'Generations of people have lived, died, crumbled to dust and been forgotten while this oak was slowly growing to maturity.'

'Exactly. And remembering that makes our little human lives seem frantic and puny and unimportant.' Her hand still rested on the rough bark. She breathed deeply, her face upturned and rapt, as though she hoped to inhale the essence of the tree. 'It is no wonder that our pagan ancestors had such reverence for the oak and made sacred groves in places where venerable trees grew together. Who knows, perhaps this ancient grandfather grew from an acorn cast from a tree the Druids worshipped.' She laughed and let her hand fall away. 'I do believe that if I did not know better, or different, I might easily slide into worship of trees myself. Which is a terrible confession for a rector's daughter and a vicar's wife to make. Truth to tell, I have always found as much comfort in nature as in church. But then, one might argue that God's handiwork is more evident among natural things than in any man-made edifice. Though I fear those parishioners of St Bride's who trouble themselves to appear on Sunday mornings would take it ill if the vicar's wife deserted her post in order to worship under the oaks.' She gave a little shrug. 'Shall we stroll on farther? And if you are not too tired and could manage an uphill walk I should very much like to show you a most interesting place, one of my favourites.'

Perhaps I should have had more of an inkling where she was heading as we diverted from the path in the woods up a tiny track where we could only walk single file. But I did not, beyond the vague notion that it was some point where we might take a splendid view of the creek and the village. Besides, we had in a companionable way moved on to the subject of the village in general and I was keen to learn what I could.

It became clear as she spoke that Edith Miles was having little success in penetrating the mistrust and suspicion with which the villagers regarded strangers, even their vicar's wife. 'Oh, if they are ill or in need, the poorest will accept what practical help I can offer, invalid food, the loan of a blanket or baby clothes, but the feeling comes strongly to me that they had sooner I sent the things and did not bother them with a visit. As to my grand ideas for a Sunday school . . . well, they might just as well have flung up their hands and cried, "Shame!", for I believe that was what they were thinking when I suggested it.' She sighed. 'We had such a good Sunday school when my husband was curate near Truro. And it was not just boys keen to learn their letters along with the bible stories. Girls, too, were welcome if their parents allowed. And I was even beginning to persuade one or two of the women that it would be no bad thing if they could learn to write out their receipts or a letter to a daughter gone into service.'

'But here no one is interested?'

'Dear me, no. They see no use in it for children who will take up work in the fields or on the quarry face or some other labouring occupation. Even my attempts to persuade Mrs Lugg to release her apprentices for an hour on Sunday morning came to nothing. And she is a regular attender. She said that book-learning led to mischief among the lower orders and she would have no part in it. Ah.' She broke off. 'Here we are.'

When we came out from the trees, panting a little from the climb, into the sunlit glade, I felt the breath go out of me as though I had been punched.

'Delightful, is it not?' Edith Miles said, mistaking my gasp of shock for pleasure.

But it was not pleasure that I felt in that first instant, but fear. Fear that we were not alone. I looked round wildly.

'This is the well of St Bride, for whom the church is named, and the village too, of course. It is reputed locally to have great healing powers for female ailments and for children's diseases.'

Mrs Miles strode ahead, telling me what I already knew. Things that Conan Trewithen had told me the day I had met him here. I felt my face grow hot at the memory that I had suppressed for my own comfort. I had kept that chance meeting secret from Daniel and now the guilt of it rose up to haunt me as sharp and clear as the image of the man himself, which seemed to hang before my eyes, bitter and mocking and vengeful.

I recovered myself and with an effort made my shaky legs move. He was not here, thank heaven. I had seen neither hide nor hair of him since that day. Nor did I wish to clap eyes on him again. Perhaps he had taken himself off, thinking better of his urge to take revenge on Daniel for whatever wrong he imagined Daniel to have done to Meraud, surely the fantasising of a mind warped by his punishment in the harsh penal colony to which he had been condemned for his evil doings. I had told myself that. Now I repeated it again in my mind as I slowly followed Mrs Miles to the rim of the pool.

She settled herself on the low wall. 'Come and sit beside me – the stone is quite warm from the sun – and I shall tell you about our St Bride if you have not already heard the legend.'

I shook my head.

'It is all most romantic. She sailed across the western sea on an oak leaf and a great tempest would have drowned her, save that she carried a splinter from the true Cross which kept her safe. Then she walked the length of Cornwall healing the sick with the aid of the miraculous splinter until one day she dropped it and it was lost. But a spring instantly bubbled out from the rock where it had fallen and St Bride decided to build herself a cell by the spring. And there she lived, healing the sick with the waters of the well and dispensing good advice. After she died, at a great age, a church was built on the spot where they carried her to be buried and a priory was eventually founded in her name on what is now Kildower land, where women might continue her works of healing and prayer. Is that not a charming tale?'

'Delightful,' I said. I looked down into the clear waters of the pool. Pond skaters darted across its surface. Weeds, like fine green hair, undulated in the gentle drift of the current.

Edith Miles sighed. 'The truth is probably much more prosaic. Nobody really knows who she was or how she came here, but it is my guess that she was some practical Irish woman, skilled in herbs and healing, come in the Dark Ages to convert the heathen British to Christianity, for there is scarcely a village in Cornwall that does not bear witness to the flood of missionaries bringing news of the new religion from Brittany, Wales, Ireland. The well, my husband insists, would most certainly have been a holy one long before her arrival, but as Christianity took hold and the old deities who ruled the spring were forgotten it would be conveniently renamed for her.'

I reached down and dabbled my hand in the water. The harsh image of Conan Trewithen was fading. I felt soothed by the gentle trickle of water, the scent of warm grass, the murmur of Edith Miles' light voice. 'I much prefer the first version,' I said. 'How I should have liked to see her braving the tempest on her oak leaf.'

'Then that is how we shall think of her, and sometime I shall show you the carving of her in the church which depicts her with her leaf and her splinter. My husband says it is a relic from the Anglo-Saxon church that must have stood on the site because of course the present one dates mostly from the fourteenth century.'

'The oak leaf and the splinter of the Cross,' I said, my mind idling. 'Do you suppose that has some deeper meaning? You mentioned oak trees and the Druids who worshipped them. If St Bride was the practical woman that we imagine, might she not perhaps have found it politic to draw the best from the old beliefs and to merge them with the new?'

'That could possibly be,' Edith Miles said, surprised.

'How clever of you to think of it. And the original spirit of the spring, a goddess, I feel it in my bones, bound up – confused down the ages – with the spirit of St Bride.'

'Or perhaps St Bride herself merely a convenient disguise for the goddess, who never was dispossessed of her watery home.'

I realised that the walk up the hill had made me thirsty. I cupped a little of the water in my palm and drew it up to drink. It lay icy and reviving on my tongue. Healing waters. Though I was not ill I could imagine the taste of the good sharp water, the soothing *ambience* of the glade, the fortifying knowledge of the countless numbers who had found strength here, would hearten any invalid. Surreptitiously I felt in my pocket. I had a coin or two in there left after I had dispensed my largesse to the servants this morning. No harm, surely, in propitiating the goddess on another's behalf. Good health and strength was a blessing, however it was gained. Perhaps the goddess would hear and understand the silent plea I made for Kensa's well-being.

The coins dropped into the water, a shower of rainbow bubbles marking their passage. Three of them. A shilling, a fourpenny piece, a penny. All there was in my pocket. They settled on the gravelly bottom. I glanced a little shamefacedly at Edith Miles.

But she had not noticed my impromptu superstitious act, though I dare say she would not have condemned me for it. She was staring absently across the glade, locked in thought. Then she gave herself a little shake that was almost a shiver and said, 'Forgive me, I get quite carried away by these imaginings. But it is all so fascinating. And there is something else I should like to show you before we go, Sophy.' She stopped, looking flustered. 'Oh, dear, I meant to say Mrs Penhale. I would not have you think me presumptuous.

It is probably that I feel . . . well, there are so few people with whom one feels true rapport.'

'No, please,' I said quickly, feeling shy and pleased. 'I should like it very much if you could call me Sophy. And you are Edith, I know.' Then, to distract her from her obvious embarrassment, 'But what was it you wished to show me?'

'Here.' She took my hand, pulled me from my seat and took me farther along the wall. There she bent down and tugged back a swathe of sticky goose grass until the lowest slab of granite was revealed. 'Do you see the device carved on it? Augustus discovered it, of course. He tramped about all winter – quite the best season, when the leaves are off the trees and bushes – in search of ancient stones and curios in order to record them for his book.'

At first I could make out nothing but the coarse, lichened contours of the stone itself. I stooped closer and suddenly I could see it, curling and looping in a close woven pattern. I touched the stone, tracing the ridges and hollows with my finger tips. There was an odd sense of familiarity, as though I had somewhere before seen and touched something similar, though the where and when of it for the moment eluded me.

'There is something carved on the next stone, too, though the marking is less clear,' Edith said, gingerly pulling aside a green shoot of vigorously sprouting bramble. 'Augustus chopped back all these blackberries and now they are taking over again. There. Just a few curving lines, but man-made, Augustus is sure. A representation of some animal, he believes, possibly a hare.'

But my attention had returned to the other stone. 'I remember! I remember where I have seen a similar carving,' I said with some excitement.

'It is a pattern quite commonly found where Celtic tribes have lived, I understand.'

'There is something in the house, in Kildower. Oh, not so clear and distinct, and only partial. It is on a great granite slab that forms a lintel, a mantelshelf, across the hearth in a room that I have just cleared to use as my own. I wonder how it came to be there?'

'Our ancestors were never loathe to salvage building materials from any source that lay near at hand,' she said. 'Perhaps when the priory was built there may have been evidence of pagan habitation. Anything that could be re-used would be incorporated in the new building.'

'And I dare say the same thing happened again when Kildower was built. Daniel told me that it was founded upon the ruins of the old priory. Indeed, my room is in the very oldest part, which is all that is left of the former building. The lintel must be part of that original structure.'

We both stood back, gazing down at the symbols on the stones. Then, without thinking, I said, 'There is a different atmosphere in that part of the house to the rest.' I hesitated, embarrassed. 'Oh, dear. That sounds so strange. You will think me very foolish.'

'On the contrary.' Her voice was calm, reflective. Slowly we began to retrace our steps across the glade. 'It is an insensitive person who discards such impressions as mere products of an overactive imagination.'

I managed a smile and said lightly, 'Many a writer of Gothic tales would automatically imbue the oldest part of the house with headless spectres, walled-up nuns and weird groans emanating from the walls, but the truth is that my room seems to me a haven of calm and tranquillity. Now, if I was to hear a clanking of chains and ghostly wails in any part of the rest of the house, I believe I should not think them out of place.' I put the question in as careless and casual a way as I could. 'Did you not find Kildower gloomy beyond the ordinary when you visited me?'

The sun glinted on her eye glasses as she looked at me sharply, blinding me to the expression in her eyes. 'Perhaps. A little.'

My laugh was a touch forced. 'So many shadows. But that is often the case in old houses. No wonder that one imbues them with fancies of dark deeds and unhappiness. In fact I can well understand the servants half-believing silly tales of the first Mrs Penhale, who drowned, dragging her wet and weedy self round the corridors at midnight, though, of course, I naturally scotch such rumours. For what I sense is darker, more powerful.' I broke off, taken unawares by a sudden emotional catch in my throat. We were at the edge of the glade and I turned back to look at the sunlight slanting down across the grass, composing myself, until I could speak calmly once more. 'Well, by daylight, out in the fresh air, fancies take on a different complexion. I shall not bore you any further with them. You will believe me foolish to have spoken of them at all.'

'No, Sophy. Not foolish,' she said softly. Like me she turned again to look at the glade and the tranquil pool. She made an encompassing gesture with her arm. 'This place is blessed. Soaked in goodness. You feel that as I do, I am sure. Whatever the source – pagan goddess, Christian saint or something quite other and unknowable – no harm has come to anyone here.' I heard the quick, light intake of her breath. 'But cruelty and terror and violence, they too leave their mark on places where appalling acts have been committed. It is my belief that they cling to the ether like indelible stains that no amount of soap and water can cleanse.'

'Kildower?'

'It happened long ago. Exactly where Kildower now

stands. Those poor women – the nuns. They were accused on some trumped up charge of turning from the true path and being tempted by demons into sheltering a village woman about to be burned at the stake for heresy, when she sought sanctuary with them. Because the nuns continued to show the compassion and mercy for which their order was noted, and refused to surrender the woman to torture and death, all manner of charges were laid against them by ignorant villagers maddened at being robbed of their victim. They were accused of casting sinister charms along with their healing potions. Of worshipping heathen idols. Of bringing a murrain to their cattle and fetching a blight upon their crops.' A long, long pause, and then her words fell like molten drips, 'So the villagers barred the priory doors and heaped around the building the faggots intended for firing the woman they called a witch. Then the faggots were set ablaze. All the women within were burnt alive.' Her eyes were wide and anguished as I felt mine must be also. 'That is the tragedy that the stones hold, Sophy. That is what you likely hear when you listen to the shadows of Kildower.'

The children's voices came to us as clear as those of birds. We paused at the wicket gate listening, watching. Then we exchanged smiles and Edith slipped the catch off quietly, opened the gate and we walked into the vicarage garden.

The toy theatre had seen its performance and now lay abandoned under the apple tree. The girls were swathed in a motley array of ancient curtains and shawls. Chloe wore a paper crown on her head. Rhoda was stomping about wielding a broomstick as a sword. Kensa, as I had never seen her before, wearing a wreath of straggly daisies in her untidy hair, her cheeks coloured pink from excitement or the fresh air, cowered back against a bush squealing. 'Fie, sir! You may cast me into prison but I refuse to marry that villain! I am too beautiful to marry an old miser.'

'Good heavens, Edith,' I murmured. 'I do not know about miraculous splinters, but it seems your daughters have performed something close to a miracle this afternoon. I have never seen Kensa so animated.'

'It is their favourite game,' she whispered back. 'Princes and princesses. They spend hours imprisoning each other in dungeons, escaping through secret passages, fighting dragons and rescuing noble princesses from the clutches of wicked uncles.' Aloud she cried, 'Girls, you must clear away your dressing-up things now. And your theatre. It is time for Kensa to go home.'

There was a chorus of protests but they began reluctantly to do as they were bid. Kensa, when she saw me approaching, tore the daisies out of her hair and attempted to straighten her rumpled dress, the animated expression that had altered her so instantly disappearing.

'You seem to have enjoyed yourself after all,' I said.

'It was a very rough game,' she said, her mouth turning down into the familiar pout. 'I didn't care for it too well. And Rhoda knocked me very hard with her sword. I mean, that horrid old broomstick.' She belatedly rubbed her arm. The gesture was as unconvincing as her words.

I did not press her further. It was enough that for the few moments I had observed her I had seen her lost in normal, childish play instead of the artificial posturings she usually assumed.

'I think you had best wash your hands before we leave,' I said. From the look of the soil caked on her nails and fingers, the beautiful princess had been digging a secret passage with her bare hands. 'Perhaps Chloe will be so kind as to show where you may wash else you will be wiping smears all over your face.'

Chloe led her off to the garden pump, trailed by Violet on her plump legs and Tansy eager to extract the last morsel of fun from the afternoon. A great deal of splashing and giggling ensued in the distance. I left them to their ablutions and, as I intended, followed Rhoda and her mother into the house to speak to them of what had been burning in my mind all the way back from the saint's well.

I caught up with them at the foot of the front stairs, where Edith was dividing the dressing-up clothes into bundles. 'Take them up to the attic in two lots, Rhoda. That will be easier for you.'

'May I have a word, Edith?' I began. 'About Rhoda.' I smiled at the child and hoped, silently, she would be able to forgive me for my abruptness earlier. 'Your daughter is very gifted, you know. It would be a shame not to give her what help I can.'

'Rhoda?' Edith sounded surprised.

'Her painting and drawing.'

'Really?'

'Beyond the ordinary, I believe,' I said. 'Though she is very young and precocity is no guarantee of future brilliance. However, if you will allow me, I should like perhaps to give her a few lessons, if that would meet with your approval.'

'Sophy, of course it would. But how? Oh, you were a governess for some time, I remember you mentioned it. After you returned from the Continent with your mother.'

I had told her the bare details of my life, selecting as was prudent the happier incidents, just as she had told me of hers in the Shropshire rectory where she had met Mr Miles when he had come to be her father's curate. Now I must be a little more open. For Rhoda's sake.

'I did supervise the girls in my charge in the required amount of sketching,' I said. 'They were all woefully lacking in talent, but it was enough to satisfy their mamas. And if that sounds disparaging, well, my upbringing sharpened my ability to distinguish between what is good and what is mediocre. My mother, you see was – is – a portrait painter of some merit.'

'How exciting. Will I have heard of her?'

'It is unlikely. She is quite retiring.' Even to my new friend I could not yet bring myself to reveal the true circumstances of my mother's existence. 'But that is neither here nor there. I myself studied with her as a child and also under a master when I was at school in Salisbury. I should be more than willing to pass on such knowledge as I have.'

Quell that other voice, the one that cried a warning. It must be defied in the interests of the child, on that I was quite clear. I had been chilled to the bone after Edith had recounted the dreadful tale of the priory. Such evil, born out of a curdling pit of dark emotions – hate, jealousy, fear, blood-lust . . . The horror of it would colour my dreams for nights to come. Worse, I had to face up to a future of long years living in a house shadowed by those events. That prospect might have been dispiriting in the extreme, and might become so yet, except that I did not intend to give in to the forces of melancholy. I would not resign myself to dumb acceptance. I would try everything in my power to counteract those dark influences. And my best defence, I was certain of it, was to battle the ingrained despair of centuries with every opposite quality of light and energy and enthusiasm. I could do nothing for those who had long gone, but for the living . . .

'So, Edith,' I said firmly. 'You would be happy, then, for me to help Rhoda?'

'Of course! Delighted.'

'And Rhoda? How do you feel?'

'Oh, Mrs Penhale!' In a flurried tangle of torn curtains she flung herself at me. 'I knew! I knew you liked my drawings.' Her arms went round my neck in a great hug. 'Oh, thank you, thank you! When can we begin? Tomorrow?'

'Rhoda, Rhoda,' her mother cried, pulling her off, laughing. 'Give Mrs Penhale air. And of course not tomorrow. Mr Penhale will be at home. It will not be at all convenient.'

'But soon,' I promised. 'Very soon. I give you my word.'

If I had not been so full of myself and my intentions I might have been more observant on the way home and made some effort to avoid the unfortunate encounter that occurred on the outskirts of the village. But I was so deep in my own preoccupations that I scarcely even noticed that there were more people about, revellers returning from the fair, judging from the shouts of laughter and joshing voices. More than anything else I was delighted that tomorrow I should have such a positive and interesting account of our afternoon to relate to Daniel.

So often previously I had been at a loss as to how to make something pleasing out of a week that had been dogged by sulks, tantrums, pretended ailments or, worse, one of Kensa's genuine bouts of illness when she would be sick and loose in the bowels or, as she was once, stricken with a sudden inexplicable exhaustion that Jess assured me was caused by growing out of her strength and which a few days resting in bed would cure. She had proved right, and Kensa was recovered by the time Daniel returned for his weekly visit. But anything that disadvantaged Kensa caused him great distress, however I tried to soften the blow when I told him. And it was no help that Jess, given any small chance – and she was adept at manoeuvring accidental encounters with Daniel that were far too frequent for my liking – would pour into his ears her own version of events, disguised as concern for Kensa or even, damn her, pretended concern for me, but somehow twisted to shed a good light on herself.

But Kensa had kept well this week. And if she still stubbornly refused to attend to her school work, at least today she had made strides in a direction that would perhaps, in the long run, do her a great deal of good.

'Papa will be pleased you have made friends with the Miles' girls,' I said cheerfully as we walked past the market cross.

'You are walking too fast,' she complained. 'And I'm not friends with them. I told you, Rhoda is very rough and Tansy and Violet are babyish.'

'Chloe seems very grown-up and capable.'

'Chloe is too bossy.'

'But she was kind enough to lend you Mrs Phipps' newest book.'

'I would not have bothered to borrow it if I had known how heavy it was to carry.'

'And she organised some excellent games.'

'I don't care to be ordered about by someone who thinks herself very superior because she knows a lot of Latin words. It is very rude to confuse other people by repeating foreign words on purpose to show off. She only did it because I showed myself to be much better than any of them with the voices when we played with the theatre.'

'You found it interesting? The theatre?'

'It would have been much better had Chloe been willing

to listen to my ideas,' she said grudgingly.

'Perhaps next time.'

'I don't know that I care to play with any of them ever again.'

'Oh, what a shame,' I said. 'I shall shortly be inviting Rhoda to Kildower in order to give her instruction in drawing and painting. I had fully intended to ask Chloe to come too, as company for you. But still, if you prefer her not to visit . . .'

She sighed heavily. 'It is of no interest to me. You'll do as you please, I suppose, *step*mama.'

'Not at all. I shall respect your wishes, Kensa. If you do not wish Chloe to visit Kildower, then I shall not invite her.'

There was silence for a moment. She frowned down at the puffs of dust rising about our shoes as we walked. Then she said in a surly voice, 'I suppose – just this once – you might ask her.' She glared up at me. 'But only this once.'

'Of course. As you wish.' Then I added, as though at a sudden inspiration, 'If you should think to give Chloe a little of her own medicine . . . But no, perhaps that would not be kind. Just because Chloe behaved in that annoying manner with her Latin, there is no need for you to feel obliged to be equally superior with a different language.'

'How do you mean?'

'The Miles girls do not have any French.'

'So?'

'Would it be fun, do you think, to baffle Chloe with a few words or phrases she does not know?'

She forgot for a moment to hold her sulky expression. Her head came up sharply. Her slanted eyes glinted with excitement. 'But you speak French. Could you – ' Then, bringing herself up short, she said, tossing her head, 'I shall think about it.'

'While you are thinking, I shall say a phrase or two aloud so you may make a judgement of the language. French has quite a musical sound, I always feel. For example, "Good morning, Chloe. Welcome to Kildower," sounds smoother and gentler in the French, which would be "*Bonjour, Chloe, bien—*"'

The words choked in my throat, this first opportune lesson in French cut short before it had begun.

I cursed myself that I had not been more alert, for I had not noticed as we approached that there was a man lounging by the beerhouse at the corner of the market place where the road narrowed. It was too late now to take a detour to avoid him. We were almost upon him.

Conan Trewithen. And a changed Conan Trewithen at that. No wonder I had not recognised him from a distance. The rags, the wild hair, were gone. He was dressed cleanly in respectable grey breeches and black coat, his grey-white hair smoothed back and tied. Though nothing could alter the harshness ingrained into the young-old face. Not even the small sardonic smile he bestowed upon me.

I swung my startled glance away, kept my eyes forward, peremptorily seized Kensa's hand and sharpened my pace. I might have succeeded in ignoring him, except that the jerk I gave Kensa caused her to yowl a protest and drop the book Chloe had lent her.

He stepped forward. 'Allow me,' he said. He picked up the book and blew the dust from the paper wrapping. 'I do not think it has come to any harm.'

Then he paused, still holding on to the book, looking down at Kensa. 'I believe we are well met.' To my horror I realised he intended more than a courtesy. 'You are Miss Kensa Penhale. I should know you anywhere. You are as beautiful and delicate as your mama once was.'

'Return the package at once, sir,' I said sharply. 'We must be on our way.'

'Come, come, Mrs Penhale, would you deny your stepdaughter the chance to . . . ?'

'That is enough!'

'. . . to meet her long-lost uncle, Conan Trewithen,' he continued, soft and smooth. And the damage was done and I could not undo it. 'Well, Kensa? What do you have to say to your Uncle Con?'

'You? My uncle? That is silly. I don't have an uncle.'

'Your mother, Meraud, was my sister. Which makes you my niece.'

She took a nervous step back from him, glancing at me as though for my reassurance that this strange man was merely making up tales to alarm her.

But I could see no point in lying.

'He tells the truth, Kensa,' I said gently.

'But Papa,' she burst out, 'Papa never said I had an uncle! Why should I believe this person. Or you?'

'Papa will explain everything to you in due course,' I said. 'And as for you, Mr Trewithen, you have had your amusement. Kindly return the package and allow us to pass.'

'Of course.' He bowed and proferred the book. I reached for it, meaning to snatch it away, but with the speed of a lash his other hand came out and caught my wrist.

He held my hand captive, his fingers, hard and painful, digging into the soft, pale kid of my glove.

'Mr Trewithen!' I gasped. 'You forget yourself!'

'Do I?' His flinty gaze was fixed on mine, mesmerising in its cold intensity. Then his grip relaxed, though he still held firmly to my wrist. His smile mocked me, mocked my weakness, mocked my inability to free myself unless he chose to release me.

'Leave go of me this instant!'

'I merely wished to offer you the courtesy that I would extend to any lady of my acquaintance when bidding them adieu,' he said softly.

He lifted my hand and gently pressed his lips to it.

I felt a tide of flame rip over my face. I tore my hand from his grasp, turned from him so fiercely that I stumbled, somehow managing to hold on to the book though my fingers felt so weak that I almost dropped it. I propelled Kensa alongside of me at a speed that would normally have set her whining, save that she was too busy twisting in my grasp to look back at the man who called himself her uncle.

Daniel, I thought wildly. Daniel. Why were you not here? Daniel. If only you had been with us, to protect us from that wicked, wicked man. If only I could see you striding towards us and I could fall into your arms and feel safe.

'Mama, he is still standing there watching us.'

'Do not look, Kensa! I forbid you to look!'

'But if he is really my uncle . . .'

'I do not wish to speak to him. Papa will tell you all you need to know tomorrow when he returns.'

But when, at last, we reached Kildower it was to find a note from Daniel awaiting us. There had been a problem at the brewery which demanded that he remain in Plymouth. He regretted deeply that he would not be home with us this Sunday, but his disappointment was tempered by the knowledge that we should doubly enjoy our reunion in a week's time. I read the orderly sentences in disbelief. How could he not come home? I needed him to be here!

We stood, Kensa and I, in the great shadowy hall as I read her the gist of her father's letter.

'I don't like it when Papa doesn't come home,' she scowled.

'I think I shall not like it too well, either,' I said with a sigh. 'But he cannot come and we must make the best of it.'

My heart was slowing its rapid thumping. It was the briskness of the walk home that had made my pulses race so. True, there had been a moment or two of panic induced by the encounter with Con Trewithen, but that was quite dissipated now. He was a blackguard! A man of violence and danger. I detested him! So I told myself as I shooed Kensa off with Martha to tidy herself before supper. But as I slowly peeled off my gloves in the heavy silence of my bedchamber, I found myself looking at the blue veins on the white skin of my inner wrist. And I remembered how his thumb had slid with infinite gentleness under the cuff of my glove and gently, oh, so gently, caressed the tender flesh there.

I closed my eyes. Oh, God help me. It had not been fear that had held me then, but something quite other. But dangerous. Oh, yes. Very dangerous. But what that danger was and how I should defend myself against it, I was helpless to understand.

Chapter Six

It was dusk, the parlour candles already lit and a small fire dispelling the chill of the evening when the servants returned from St Germans. I heard the familiar slipshod clatter of Kitty's footsteps crossing the hall and looked up in expectation of an excited account of the fair and all its wonders. But Kitty was not wreathed in her usual beaming smile. She looked as though she carried a weight of misery on her broad shoulders and her face was woebegone in the extreme. It did not take long to elicit the reason.

''Tes my Jem, ma'am,' she wailed, breaking down in a flood of sobbing.

'What has happened to him? Was he not there? Is he ill? Injured?'

'Oh, 'tes terrible . . . and 'e promised me faithful. Oh, Mrs Penhale, ma'am, he was at the fair, but he 'ad another girl on his arm an' 'e wouldn't 'ave naught to do with me. An' 'er's proper pretty and dainty and they'm to be married three weeks come Sunday.' She flung her apron over her face and bawled loudly into its folds.

I set my sewing aside and went to her, to pat her shoulder and murmur soothing noises until the sobbing abated somewhat.

She sniffed miserably. 'He promised, ma'am. Last time I seed him, he promised. And, and I'd done everything 'e wanted, even though I was afeared that a babe might result.' Her blotchy pink face turned deep scarlet. 'Beggin' your pardon, ma'am. I shouldn't've spoke so. But it was just the few times and naught came of it, thank the Lord.'

'From the sound of things it seems to me to be fortunate that you have escaped Jem's clutches,' I said, thinking wryly of my plans for keeping her chaste when it was already too late.

'Ma'am?' Her watery eyes regarded me blankly. 'But he'm so handsome. All the girls do try to catch his eye.'

'Exactly. And I dare say they will continue to do so after he is wed. He sounds just the sort of rogue to encourage such undesirable attentions. Mark my words, it will not make for a happy marriage.'

'But he loved me,' she wailed, the tears beginning again. 'And I loved him so. An' I was proud he'd chose me out of all the girls 'e could have 'ad.'

Poor gullible Kitty. She had fallen victim to a liar and a cheat whose aim had been to deceive a simple girl in order to take his pleasure of her. But clear though it might be to any observer that he was not worth the candle, it made it no easier for Kitty to suffer the pain of rejected love.

I comforted her as best I could and presently she mopped her eyes and said that she would try her best to think of it as I told her to do, as a lucky escape, and that she was better off without him. She even managed a brave if shaky smile. 'At least, ma'am, I shan't have to leave you now, for you've been good to me and I do dearly like bein' a lady's maid.'

She went off a trifle consoled by that thought and I resumed my sewing feeling perhaps a little less enchanted than Kitty at that particular prospect. But I was given no time to reflect on it, for she was back in a few moments with a note that had just been delivered.

I read the ill-formed words with difficulty.

> Dear Missus Penhale,
>
> I regrets my coz Jess Sowthcot as met with an ackserdent er will need to keep to er bed for a wile pleas be acksepting my deep apologis.
>
> Yr humble servt at all times,
>
> P Lugg

'If there's any message,' Kitty said, 'the girl as brought the note will take it back.'

'Fetch her in, would you, Kitty,' I said, subduing my guilty elation. It was not seemly to rejoice at another's misfortune, though the prospect of a few days without Jess was attractive in the extreme. 'It seems Jess has met with an accident at the farm. I should like to know a little more about it.'

'If you're sure, ma'am,' Kitty said darkly. ''Er reeks o' the farmyard. Mrs Dagget isn't for letting 'er over the kitchen step.'

It was one of the Luggs' apprentice children. The biggest one. She crept in like a thin, scraggy stable cat that knows it has no business in a decent parlour and expects to be fetched a clout in consequence. The aroma of the cow byre wafted in strongly with her.

'I made 'er leave 'er boots in the yard,' Kitty said. 'They was caked in cow muck. Not 'as 'er legs are much better.'

Indeed they were not. Her skinny bare feet and ankles were ingrained with dirt, as was the rest of her, including the patched and outgrown dress that barely kept her decent and the uncombed brown hair hanging in strings round her face. She sent one wild, disbelieving look round the room before she fixed her glance on a spot on the carpet near my feet.

'I believe I have seen you at church on Sundays,' I said gently.

'Yes, missus.' Her voice was scarcely audible.

'And your name is?'

'Liddy Binns, missus.'

'Liddy. Now do not be afraid. I just wanted to ask what you knew of the accident, how Mrs Lugg's relative came to be hurt.'

'Don't know nothing.'

The answer came so quick and pat that I wondered if she had been warned not to speak of it. I tried a different tack.

'You did not go to the fair, Liddy?'

She shook her head.

'Just Farmer Lugg and his family?'

A quick nod.

'So the work of the farm went on just as usual?'

Another nod.

'And Miss Southcote was hurt while the family was at the fair?'

'Yes, missus.'

'So you do know a little about the accident?'

She lifted her thin shoulders.

'Annie said.'

'Annie?'

'Works in the house.'

'So the accident happened indoors. Where was it? Downstairs? Upstairs?'

Her head lifted a fraction and I saw the glint of her eyes under the clotted strands of hair falling across her face. The eyes regarded me stonily.

'So it happened while Miss Southcote was caring for the

sick person. And Annie was there and was able to help Miss Southcote.'

The carpet claimed her attention again. The silence drew out and I saw Kitty's arm move as though she intended to give the girl a good nudge to hasten things along.

'Kitty,' I said hastily, 'would you go to the kitchen and ask Mrs Dagget to cut a slice of bread and cheese for Liddy to take with her when she leaves. And if there is anything left from that plum cake we had yesterday, a slice of that also. I will bring Liddy back to the kitchen myself when we have finished our talk.'

When Kitty had clumped off somewhat reluctantly, being agog as I well knew to learn every detail in order to be first with the tidings to the kitchen, I said, 'We are quite alone, Liddy. Whatever you tell me will not go any further, though I would not wish to press you if you are determined to say nothing more. I shall give you a moment to think about it while I write a note of acknowledgement to Mrs Lugg.'

At the writing desk I scribbled a few lines of commiseration and begged Mrs Lugg, very heartily, to ensure Jess did not try to return before she was properly fit. After the ink was dry and the letter sealed I turned again to Liddy. She quickly resumed her head-hung stance, though when I had glanced up once or twice from my writing I had seen that she was taking the opportunity to give the cold grandeur of the room a slow and thorough assessment.

'Now, Liddy,' I said. 'I understand that you know more than you pretend to. So shall we begin with that? Was it Mrs Lugg who told you not to speak to me of what happened?'

Her head came up slowly. ''Er said . . .'

'Yes, Liddy?'

''Er said,' the words came out in a rush, 'it was nobody's

business save her'n. And 'er told me I'd 'ave a beltin' should I go gossiping about the madwoman an' what 'er done.'

'I see,' I said. I was more and more intrigued by the minute. What on earth had been happening up at Trebarth that it must be kept so secret? 'Mrs Lugg is right, of course. But I am naturally concerned about Miss Southcote being harmed.'

''Er banged 'er head when 'er was set on. And 'er leg twisted bad as 'er fell.' She stared at me, her eyes hostile and calculating. 'The madwoman's allus screechin' an' carryin' on. 'Er's kept locked up, but we hears 'er shouting. Annie says 'er's not properly mad, just got more spirit than t'others. Anyways, 'er got out today. 'Ad a knife hidden and 'eld it to that Miss Southcote's throat. Then 'er run downstairs in her nightshift, but Annie stopped 'er – hit 'er with the poker – and Miss Southcote come after and they got 'er back upstairs, but while they was strugglin' to get 'er back in bed Miss Southcote fell an' banged 'er head and twisted 'er leg bad.' She stopped abruptly. 'Thass it, missus. Thass all I knows.'

'Thank you, Liddy,' I said after a moment. Others? What others? And a madwoman – confused after a seizure, Mrs Lugg had said – who was not mad at all? 'You have done very well and I promise to keep secret all that you have told me. Now, I shall take you back to the kitchen. Mrs Dagget will have the food ready.'

'I'd sooner have a penny, missus.'

'What?'

'Ha'penny then.' Her eyes were narrowed and defiant. ''Tes a grand house, missus, that you live in. I reckon you won't miss a copper. So if you'm pleased wi' what I telled 'ee, 'tes worth a ha'penny for me – and,' she swallowed, nervous in spite of her forceful tone, 'an' the bread an' cheese as well – to take for young Sam. He didn't get no supper tonight 'cos he dropped a bucket an' spilled buttermilk meant for the pigs all over the yard. Master leathered him and locked him in the privy till dark an' Ma Lugg stood over the rest of us in the scullery while we ate our kettle broth to make sure we couldn't save 'im a scrapin'.'

I might have been amused at her impudence had it not been for the harrowing thought of the boy who had been punished and made to go hungry for so minor a crime as a dropped bucket. Liddy's protective concern for him set a different aspect altogether on her bargaining.

I reached for my reticule and found a coin. Then I stood up and took it to her. She stared down in disbelief as I pressed the coin into her hand.

'A sixpence,' she breathed. 'Never 'ad a sixpence to myself 'afore. Oh, missus . . .'

'When the packman next calls you may all have a treat with it.'

'Oh, no, missus. 'Tes not for spendin'.' Her face for the first time was unguarded in its delight. ''Tes to be hidden and saved against the time when I'm growed an' Ma Lugg don't have no more 'old on me.' She bit off the words and her greeny-grey eyes, beautiful eyes I saw now I was close to her, with dark long, curled lashes, lost their animation. Her head went down again. Her grubby hand clenched tightly over the coin.

'You must keep it safe. Have you anything in which to carry it back to Trebarth?' I asked.

She shook her head.

I went to my workbasket and rummaged until I found a calico pocket I had once used to carry such few valuable coins I had owned when I was Miss Beardmore, travelling alone. It was old but the stitching was still secure and the strings entire. 'Here,' I said. 'Put the sixpence inside this little bag, then tie the strings round your waist under your dress.'

She needed no second bidding. Without embarrassment she hitched up her skirt to reveal a threadbare flannel petticoat and tied on the pocket. 'Thanks, missus,' she said fervently, letting her skirt drop and examining it to make sure nothing of the pocket showed. Then she looked up at me, puzzled. 'You'm kind, missus,' she said. 'I thought you was more like to give me a whippin' for asking as I did. Ma Lugg would've.'

'The world is not composed of Mrs Luggs, Liddy,' I said. 'And it seems to me that if you expected a whipping it was brave of you to ask for that penny.'

She shrugged. 'Well, you spoke nice to that Kitty. P'raps I 'oped you'd not be 'ard on me.' She broke off in sudden agitation. 'Oh, missus, 'tes getting on. I'd best be quick an' go. 'Er said straight 'ere and back and talk to nobody. I'll have to run all the way.'

I gave her the letter and took her through to the kitchen then waited until she left, hugging to her thin chest the bulky package of food, wrapped in an old pudding cloth, that Mrs Dagget had put ready. It was quite dark now, but she refused the offer of a lantern. 'Moon's comin' up. An' I knows the road.' And she was gone with the stealthy swiftness of an alley cat into the darkness.

Mrs Dagget wafted her hand in front of her flaring nostrils.

'Smells like a polecat,' she said dourly. 'Can't abide bad smells in my kitchen. No, don't shut the door, Nan. Give the fresh air time to circulate. You can take the besom and sweep the step afore that muck that fell off her boots gets trailed in. And you, Kitty, what are you doing moping here? Shouldn't you be 'tending to Mrs Penhale's supper tray?'

'I shall want nothing more this evening, Mrs Dagget,' I said. I looked round at them. They were all flagging and yawning from the excitements of their long day out. 'I think it would be best if you all retired for an early night. I am sure there is nothing so urgent that it cannot wait until you are revived by a good night's sleep.'

'Thank you, ma'am,' Mrs Dagget said, relieved enough to favour me with a thin smile. 'I can't say as I'll be sorry to put my feet up. Fairs is fine and dandy but they're hard on a body that isn't used to them. You three, you heard Mrs Penhale. Take yourselves off. And what about Martha, ma'am? Where's she to?'

'She is sitting with Miss Kensa until she falls asleep. I will see to her before I retire myself. You go home now. I will lock the door after you and put out the candles.'

She lit a taper from the embers of the kitchen fire and put it to the candle in one of the lanterns that stood on a shelf by the back door. 'I'll say goodnight then, Mrs Penhale.'

'Mrs Dagget, before you go.' I followed her to the door. The night air wafted in, cool and earth-scented. 'Tell me, what is kettle broth?'

'Kettle broth? Why, 'tes what the poorest people make do with when they can't afford the luxury of decent food. 'Tes hot water poured over stale bread and sprinkled with salt to give it a morsel of taste.'

'Oh, I see. Well, good night, Mrs Dagget.'

I turned the big key in the lock and shot the heavy bolt. I took one candle in its tin holder from the dresser and blew out the rest. Darkness swooped down from the high corners of the kitchen to hover beyond the pale flicker of the solitary flame. The kitchen was cold and my footsteps were loud in the emptiness. I shivered and hastened my steps back to the parlour. But the fire there did nothing to warm me because the chill came from within, born of the desolate thought that young children who worked so hard and long in the fields could be fed such mean fare, while the people who used them worse than the animals they tended grew fat and prosperous on the proceeds of their labour.

I lay awake a long time that night and uppermost in my mind, now that I had time to reflect on it, was disappointment that Daniel would not be home tomorrow and it would be another long week before I should see him.

I was used to being alone in this vast, soft feather bed. Used to waking in the small hours, disturbed by the creak of old woodwork settling and shifting, the batter of wind and rain against the casement, the screech of some animal out in the gardens. Used to knowing that once awake, it would be hard to catch sleep again. Every noise, every whisper of draught seemed not so much muffled by the bed curtains as magnified by being drawn in and trapped between their indigo folds. But it was different when Daniel was beside me in the bed. Then, when I awoke in the darkness, the steady sound of his breathing was so comforting as to lull me back to sleep rather than to cause my nerve ends to tingle with alarm. Often, I would put out my hand to touch a crumpled fold of his nightshirt or, gently so as not to wake him, move closer to where I could feel the steady warmth emanating from his body. These small reassurances that I was not alone in this forbidding room were usually enough to ensure the dreamless relaxation of deep slumber. Occasionally I had woken curled tightly against him, or to find his arm thrown across me. Then I would lie very quiet until he stirred, when I would move myself to a less presumptuous position before he awoke, for there was a reserve in me that caused me to shrink back from such close, unconscious contacts. It was not exactly embarrassment, more an uneasiness that Daniel might be displeased at my indelicacy or think that I wished to trespass over the lines he had clearly drawn before we were married. I did not wish to do anything to jeopardise his friendly regard for me.

There was nothing to cheer me in the other news contained in Daniel's letter. Rather it left me more unsettled than before, because his enquiries about the Sinclair family had turned up information that gave a tantalising glimpse of Juliana and her adoptive parents yet withheld her present whereabouts. He had guessed aright that the landlord's wife at the Lamb knew of them. Mr Sinclair had been a hatter in a small way of business, having moved to Plympton from Totnes and staying but three or four years before moving on again. To, Stonehouse, she thought.

I also learned that Mr Sinclair gave good value with his hats and was thought of as a sober, upright man, if inclined to be somewhat stern in manner, but his wife seldom left the house, and my informant knew little of her. She did remember the daughter, though, as being a shy and pretty girl of about fifteen or sixteen. There was a son, too, a few years older, who worked with his father in the business. They moved rather suddenly, as she recalled, about the time when there was a serious outbreak of scarlet fever in the district. She seems to think that the daughter took the infection badly and was sent to the country to recuperate and Mr Sinclair decided to remove to where she might benefit from sea air on her return.

A shy and pretty girl. I saw the child in the miniature grown to girlhood. Could set her now in the context of her small, close family. Yet though I knew a little more of her past circumstances I was as far as ever from knowing how or where she lived now. Daniel had written that he would make further enquiries round about Stonehouse. Did I really wish him to continue? A vast yawn overtook me. I was too tired to think of it now. Tomorrow . . .

I was jolted awake from the very edge of sleep. A noise. Not the wind at the casement or wooden boards settling. A soft tapping and a breathy sob. Every muscle in my body tensed and though a part of my mind mocked such silliness, I had an instant's pure fright in case it really was Meraud Penhale dragging her weedy shroud towards me. But it was a noisy and importunate little ghost, for the tapping became an urgent rapping, the door burst open and footsteps pattered loudly across the bare boards.

I was out of the bed in time to catch her as she flung herself at me. Her hands knotted round my neck in a stranglehold. She burst into a torrent of sobbing.

'I w . . . woke up,' she hiccuped, 'and I sh . . . shouted for Jess and . . . and nobody came . . . and it . . . it was d . . . dark and I w . . . was frightened.'

'Hush now. Hush, lovey.' I helped her on to the bed and held her there, clutching her tightly, rocking her until the sobbing diminished. I silently cursed myself for not having realised that, used as Kensa was to having Jess sleeping close by, she might be distressed to wake and find herself entirely alone. But she had been so deeply asleep after the unusual exercise of the day that I had not expected her to stir before daylight. I had dismissed Martha without a second thought.

'I don't want to be on my own.' She snuffled her hot, wet face into my shoulder, still clinging to my neck. 'I want Jess. Where is she? I won't go back by myself.'

'Nor shall you.' I drew the covers up over us both and

smoothed back the tangled hair from her damp cheeks. 'You shall sleep here. I will plump this pillow up for you. There. Cuddle down and hold my hand and I will tell you of all the nice things we shall plan to do when Papa is home again.'

She was asleep in minutes. I disentangled my hand and, lulled by the soft, regular sound of her breathing, I followed quickly after.

I was up and dressed long before Kensa woke. I motioned Kitty to silence when she appeared with the water jugs but, heavy-eyed and drooping, she was disinclined to sing or chatter this morning, merely restricting herself to a great deal of mournful sighing.

When Kensa eventually stirred, I took her back to the nursery. She quickly pretended complete forgetfulness about her fright and reverted to her usual imperious, complaining self. In the long battle I had to get her washed and dressed, I had frequently to grit my teeth and remind myself of the scared little girl who had run to me in the night. It was not easy when I was constantly compared unfavourably to Jess.

'You can't do *anything* as well as Jess,' she finally said, wincing as though I was putting her to torture when I gently ran the brush through her tangled hair. 'You're cruel. Jess is very kind and loves me. You must be sure to tell her to come back today.'

'Jess cannot be expected to rise from her sickbed just to attend to one spoiled girl who is perfectly able to manage without her for a day or two.'

'She must come back before dark,' she said, scowling. '*She* never leaves me on my own at night.'

I did not answer directly. I looked round the room and said thoughtfully, 'This room is quite pretty, but it is not very big, is it? Quite cramped, in fact.'

'I like it,' she said instantly.

'I was wondering . . . but perhaps, no, it is too soon. After all, you are still very young and not ready for anything more grown-up.'

'What do you mean?'

'No. It was a foolish idea. I will say no more. You are perfectly happy to be treated as the baby you still are.'

'I'm *not* a baby. I shall be ten next month.'

'Ten, indeed.' I raised my eyebrows. 'That is a very great age. I would have thought a proper grown-up bedchamber quite appropriate for one so advanced in years. Still, if you do not wish for something any elegant young lady might think most desirable, then of course I shall not press you. It is such a shame, though. Had you been interested, the empty room next to Papa's dressing room would have been ideal. It has a wonderful view over the front gardens and would look perfectly charming with new furniture. Something light and dainty in walnut would have been just the thing. But there it is. You are perfectly content to be confined, as you have been since you were a babe in arms, in this nursery wing.' I gave her silky pale hair a final stroke of the silver-backed brush and replaced it on the dressing table. 'There. Now, if you wish to do something kind for your beloved Jess, you may help me to choose one or two things from her room that she might wish to have with her while she is forced to rest.'

'I won't have Jess staying away! You must send Dagget in the carriage to fetch her!'

'Kensa, if Jess was capable of it,' I said, trying for patience, 'she would already have returned. You know she would never stay apart from you willingly. She has had a nasty accident. You must accept that and be patient until she is well enough to come back.'

She dragged her feet after me through the door that linked her bedchamber to Jess's.

'It's not the same here without Jess,' she said, staring round miserably.

'Of course it isn't,' I agreed. 'Which is why I think you might be more comfortable sleeping in my dressing room while she is away rather than having Martha to sleep here in Jess's bed.' I paused to allow her to consider this, then said casually, 'The dressing room has a view over the front gardens. If you were considering eventually moving into a grown-up bedchamber at the front – and I am sure Papa would be delighted to furnish it as you wished in time for your tenth birthday – it might be pleasant to try sleeping at that side of the house for a night or two, just by way of an experiment, as it were.'

After a moment, she said grudgingly, 'What kind of a bed would I sleep on?'

'In my dressing room? Your own if you prefer it.'

'I insist I shall have my own bed,' she said imperiously.

'Very well. We could have it set up under the window, so that you could sit up and look out at the garden before you sleep and when you wake in the morning.'

'I'm not in the least interested in the view,' she said, heaving a martyred sigh. 'But if it pleases you, *step*mama, then I suppose I'd better do as you wish.'

I smothered a smile, feeling pleased that I had sowed a few thoughts that might eventually lead to a flowering of independence and less reliance on Jess Southcote's smothering attentions. 'Perhaps you can tell me where Jess keeps her nightgowns, Kensa,' I said briskly. 'And I think she would like her own comb and brush, would she not? And a handkerchief or two, and perhaps her best shawl. Do you know, I think I shall take these things along to her

289

myself. Should you like to come with me, then you may see for yourself how Jess is? I do not know how far it is to Trebarth but if it is any distance we may ask Dagget to take us in the carriage.'

She brightened considerably at this and though it soon became clear that she had little idea of where Jess kept her things, she at least attempted to be helpful.

I had a strong sense of intrusion on a private space as I opened drawers and cupboards in search of these few items. The room was bigger than Kensa's bedchamber but seemed a great deal smaller because of the quantity of furniture of all kinds crammed round the walls. Most of it was of a better quality than I might have expected from a servant's room. A fine gilt-framed mirror, a bow-fronted mahogany tallboy and a tapestry-covered armchair were among the pieces that would not have looked out of place in a guest bedroom. Jess had made herself very comfortable here and I wondered if, squirrel-like, she had acquired things that took her fancy over the years from other parts of the house. A brass spirit stove occupied a small rosewood table beside the armchair, a pretty china teapot with a matching cup and saucer and plate arranged beside it. Not for Jess the sturdy earthenware that the other servants used. A set of small pans stood in the hearth. This was doubtless where she made the toffees and sweetmeats that Kensa so loved, and the herbal teas that seemed so effective when Kensa was ailing. The air was scented strongly with bunches of dried leaves and flowers that hung in bunches to dry on a string above the mantelshelf.

'I expect Jess would soon make herself better if she had the right herbs,' Kensa said. She frowned at them doubtfully. 'But I don't know which she would need. I think that one is sage. I gargle with sage tea when my throat is sore. And that is pennyroyal, for earache. I don't know any of the others.'

I pinched a leaf of marjoram and inhaled its spicy fragrance. 'I dare say Mrs Lugg has her own herbs,' I assured her. 'I hear she is skilled at looking after sick people. Now, do you suppose there is anything else we should take for Jess? No? Then I think we must go down to breakfast before Mrs Dagget gets too cross, and afterwards I thought we might look through your wardrobe, Kensa. You have so much in there that you never wear or have outgrown. We will see what might be altered and brought into use or passed on to Mrs Miles for distribution among the poorer villagers.'

I was glad to remove myself from Jess's cosy little nest. It was too full of her heavy, covetous presence. I did not want to glimpse her frilled and be-ribboned undergarments bursting up from an opened drawer, or touch the cheap, dark, musky-smelling satins and silks of her best dresses which her white fingers had smoothed and stroked. I felt a curious distaste at having to handle the things we were to take to her today, especially her hairbrush, which held a few strands of coarse black hair in its meshes. I was thankful when Kitty brought me a basket to put everything in. I washed my hands well before we went down for breakfast as though I was fearful that some contamination might still cling to them, and when Dagget brought the carriage round later, I was almost beginning to regret that I had not sent one of the maids on the errand, for I really had no great wish to play the Lady Bountiful with Jess. But there were others on the farm whose plight touched me far more and I had the vague, perhaps vain, idea that I might in some way be able to help Liddy and the other children once I had made myself familiar with the situation there. A courtesy visit would surely do no harm and might possibly do some positive good. There was also, shamed as I was to admit it, a far less laudable reason why I felt moved to make a personal call at the farm: pure curiosity as to the events of yesterday and a desire to know the reasons for Mrs Lugg's excessive discretion regarding the true facts.

Dagget could only take us a mile or so up the lane in the carriage before we had to descend and take the last stretch on foot up a narrow track full of deep dry ruts that could take nothing less sturdy than a farm cart. The fields we had passed bore all the evidence of good husbandry – hedging and walls in good repair, neatly tilled fields springing with corn and barley and potatoes, glossy red-brown cows hock deep in lush grass – and now we walked between apple orchards heavy with tiny hard green pellets that would grow to a rich harvest by September. The farm itself, a low granite building under a deep thatch, its barns and stables and outbuildings all set snugly against the hillside, made a tranquil and idyllic picture in the sunshine. Except for a few bent figures working in the fields we had seen no one and the yard itself was empty save for a few speckled hens pecking among the cobbles and a scrawny, rawboned dog chained to a barrel, which set up a hysterical barking as I opened the gate. Farmer Lugg, his squat, rotund figure clad in a working smock, leather breeches and gaiters, came out cursing from one of the stables and aimed a kick at the dog, which yelped to silence and cowered back, chain clanking, into the barrel. Then Farmer Lugg stopped, realising that the dog had had a reason for its barking, to shade his eyes against the dazzle of sun. His scowl swiftly changed to an ingratiating smile as he hurried forward.

'Mrs Penhale, this is an honour. And Miss Penhale.'

'Good morning, Mr Lugg,' I said, inclining my head coolly and feeling offended on the dog's behalf. Poor thing, to be punished for doing its duty in warning of the arrival of strangers.

'And a fine one, too. My good wife'll be fair set up to have you visit.' He waddled ahead of us to the front door, to thump with his meaty fist on its stout panels, open it, then put his head inside to shout, ''Tes Mrs Penhale come to visit.' But he still held the door half-closed for several minutes more while he spoke of the prospect of rain that would be bad for the harvesting of the potato crop, and enquired about Daniel's health. Inside a deal of whispering and scurrying seemed to be going on behind the door and Farmer Lugg's red face was deepening to purple with effort of making conversation by the time the door was tugged from his hand and Mrs Lugg appeared. Her hands fussed at her person, smoothing her skirt as though an apron had just been hastily removed, touching her hair to adjust an elaborate lace cap that had perhaps replaced something more everyday. Behind her one of the Lugg girls was disappearing speedily up the stairs in a satin wrapper, her hair gorgon-like with curling rags.

Mrs Lugg's broad smile made her cheeks into two fat, rosy apples. Fulsome words of welcome poured from her lips as she ushered us from the small dark hall into her stiffly furnished front parlour that smelled mustily damp from lack of use. Her black eyes did not smile though, or offer a welcome. They remained hard and calculating, even as she cried, 'Sit you down, Mrs Penhale – that's the most comfortable chair – and allow me to offer 'ee tea. Or would a glass of elderberry wine be more restorin' after your walk? Yes, I'm sure 'twould be. And a nice drop o' ginger beer for Miss Kensa.' As she spoke she bustled about reaching glasses and stone bottles out of a cupboard. 'My elderberry's the finest of my wines, I always reckons. I'd be obliged for your opinion, ma'am, you being well travelled and more experienced in these matters than ever I'll be.'

'It is quite excellent,' I said, sipping politely, then discovering to my surprise that it really was light and delicious. I took a deeper draught, then set down my glass and said, 'I have brought a few things I thought Jess might like with her. I was sorry to hear that she had had an accident. How is she this morning?'

'Oh, middlin', Mrs Penhale. Only middlin'.' She shook her head so that the frills of lace shook about her plump jowls. ''Twas a nasty shock to her whole system to go tumbling downstairs like she did.'

'She fell downstairs? How very distressing.'

'Caught her heel in the hem of her skirt, she reckons, and down she went. 'Tes a wonder she didn't break every bone in her body 'stead of just twisting her knee, which has swelled up shocking, and givin' herself a mort of bruises and a proper 'ard knock on the head.'

'And scarcely less of a shock for you, Mrs Lugg, to find not one but two invalids on your hands when you returned home. Did you find her lying where she had fallen?'

''Twas lucky that our old, faithful servant Annie – we keep her on out of sentiment though her's well past useful work – was also in the house. Though proper knotted with rheumatics, poor soul, her was able to help Jess to a sofa and look after her until we returned not long after. I did see right away that poor Jess'd not be fit to go back to Kildower, so I took the liberty of puttin' her to bed here and sending you a note accordin'.'

'I am very grateful to you for your kindness to Jess,' I said, adding innocently, 'especially when you are already burdened with one invalid. I trust that your other relative did not suffer any neglect through Jess's being unable to attend her.'

'Not in the slightest, thank the good Lord. Her slept

peaceful as a babe all through. And 'er woke such a deal
better, and so much her old self, that I think her'll be fit for
travelling home soon.'

'That is good news,' I said.

Kensa had been growing more and more fidgetty during
these exchanges. Now she whined, 'Where is Jess? When
are we going to see her?'

'Well, m'dear, I don't know as that's wise just now,'
Mrs Lugg began smoothly, but for an instant, and quickly
masked, there was a flash of alarm in her eyes. 'When I last
looked in her was deep asleep.'

'Kensa, Kensa,' I cut in reprovingly, 'I know you are
anxious to visit Jess, but you must not be impolite. Contain
yourself for a moment or two longer.' I smiled at Mrs Lugg.
'Please do forgive Miss Kensa. I am sure you will understand
that it is her attachment to your cousin that makes her
somewhat fretful and impatient to see her.'

'Oh, surely, surely. But as I was sayin', Jess is sound . . .'

'Of course, we should not dream of waking her if she is
sleeping. But just to satisfy Kensa, we will look in on her
for a moment and leave the basket so she may find her things
when she wakes. Or perhaps you think it best that we return
later in the day when she has woken up?'

'Oh, no, ma'am,' she said hurriedly. 'Such inconvenience.
I – Jess – wouldn't want you to be troubled to make a second
journey.'

'It would be no trouble at all, Mrs Lugg,' I said blithely.
'Why, Mr Penhale would expect nothing less of me with
regard to a servant who has given such long and devoted
service to his daughter. In fact, thinking of it, perhaps it
might be best to return this afternoon when Jess is awake,
then I could stay with her for longer.'

'On second thoughts, Mrs Penhale, p'raps 'twould be best

for you to peep in at her now.' Mrs Lugg's smile had become a little fixed.

'You think? Well,' I pretended to consider, then nodded briskly. 'I confess I do have a great deal planned for today that I should not wish to set aside. Now Kensa, you must be very, very quiet. Do you understand?' She nodded. 'Good. Now finish your ginger beer and I shall finish my glass of this most excellent elderberry wine and then perhaps, Mrs Lugg, you will be kind enough to show us to Jess.'

Mrs Lugg rose hurriedly from her chair. 'Do help yourself to another glass of wine, Mrs Penhale. I'll be back in a moment. I just remembered, I left the pot with a fine meat pudding bubbling hard on the fire.' She gave a trill of false laughter. ''T'will be boiled quite dry, for Annie'll not think to look at it, and what'll Mr Lugg have to say if his dinner's all spoilt?'

She closed the door firmly behind her, but it did not quite muffle the sound of whispered voices and a creaking of footsteps up the stairs. I wondered what other little deceit was being prepared, for so far Mrs Lugg had managed a very fair web of lies. It galled me to think that I would have been thoroughly convinced had I not already heard a very different tale from Liddy, and I grew more and more intrigued to know the reasons for such a deception.

It was a long few moments before she returned, her smile as broad as ever. 'Sorry to have kept you, Mrs Penhale. 'Twas as I thought, I was just in time to save the puddin'. Now if you'll follow me.'

She heaved her bulk up the narrow stair which gave on to a small, dark, windowless landing. The bedchamber we entered seemed scarcely lighter, for the blinds were pulled down and the massive half-tester bed hung with flowery red and brown curtains blocked off what light was left for it occupied most of the floor space.

Mrs Lugg signalled us to wait and tiptoed ostentatiously across to peer at the figure in the bed.

'Is that you, Nella?' Jess's voice was no more than a whisper.

'Oh, we've disturbed 'ee! There! I said to Mrs Penhale we should let 'ee sleep. Her's here, see, with Miss Kensa.'

'No matter.' A white hand raised itself and fluttered back to the counterpane like an exhausted dove. 'It's time I roused myself. It's just that I can't seem to keep my eyes open.'

'Then you mustn't try, m'dear. Sleep is the best doctorin' you can 'ave. Anyways, they just want a peep to see you'm comfy and cosy.'

'Miss Kensa, too, the little pet. But I'm so tired, Nella.'

There was the sound of a yawn. Like the stilted conversation it rang somewhat forced.

Mrs Lugg beckoned us over.

'Oh, Jess, are you very ill?' Kensa's voice wobbled as she stared wide-eyed at her nurse.

'Just bruised, Miss Kensa. Nothing that won't heal given time. So your poor old Jess won't be able to be with you for a few days yet.'

There was actually very little to see of the invalid. The parts of her above the covers were enveloped in the massive folds of what I presumed to be a nightgown of Mrs Lugg's. She lay very still and stiff amid mounded pillows. A white shawl was closely wrapped about her head. One eye, her nose and mouth were all that were visible. The eye was half-closed as though the lid was, or pretended to be, too heavy to open properly.

'We brought you some things,' Kensa said miserably. 'Your best shawl, and your hairbrush. And I want you to be better soon and come home to be with me.'

'We are all keen to see you better, Jess,' I said, trying to inject some warmth into my voice. 'Though of course you must take all the time you need to make a full recovery before you return. The maids offer their good wishes and Mrs Dagget has sent some of her calves' foot jelly. She says a spoonful twice a day is very strengthening.'

'Do thank her. Thank them all for me.'

Mrs Lugg cleared her throat. 'Don't want to fatigue Jess, now, Mrs Penhale, do we?'

'Of course not. Goodbye, Jess. Mr Penhale will be glad to know you are in good hands. And if there is anything at all you need to aid your recovery, pray do not hesitate to send word to Kildower. Come now, Kensa.'

I put my hand on Kensa's shoulder to guide her away, but she shook off my grasp and pressed closer to the bed. Then, with a choked sob, she said, 'Oh, Jess, can't you come back with us?' and reached out to touch Jess's hand as it lay limp on the counterpane.

Jess's movement was involuntary. A turn of her head within the folds of the white shawl. Her hand, those white grasping fingers, moving to clasp Kensa's. 'Soon, Miss Kensa, soon as maybe,' she said, genuine emotion sounding for the first time in her voice.

And then it was that I glimpsed what they were trying to hide from me, before Mrs Lugg in a smooth, fast movement for such a fat woman rearranged the shawl round Jess's head and shooed Kensa away from the bed.

I made no indication that I had seen anything untoward. But I was no longer surprised that Jess wished to remain hidden until her face had returned to normal. For apart from a shiny black eye which might, possibly, have been passed off as an accidental trip on the stairs, down from that eye to her heavy jaw and continuing on her neck into the collar of her nightgown ran four deep, livid, parallel scratches. Far less easy to explain those away as caused by a fall. If I was any judge they had been made by nails which had raked the length of her face. Her assailant's struggles, mad or not, must have been violent indeed. She had left her mark well and truly on Jess. So at least one little mystery was solved, though some – the reason for secrecy, the mysterious 'others' – still remained to tantalise.

Every door on that dark landing remained tightly closed. If the madwoman was concealed close by there was no sign or sound of her. We returned downstairs to find both the Lugg daughters simpering and preening in the hall, the curling rags having done splendid work in the matter of profuse ringlets. They were clad in frilled and sprigged muslin which sat a little uneasily on such robust, strong-armed girls. At the sight of them, Mrs Lugg's hard eyes for the first time softened sentimentally and she was immediately eager to sweep us back into the parlour for further refreshment.

'Phyllis and Dora do both pine for good company, Mrs Penhale. They learned such good parlour manners when they was to Saltash. Everyone do remark upon it. A whole year they spent learnin' to be ladies there at a fine school, Mr Lugg being willin' to spare no expense where his children are concerned. Why, he'm thinking of putting our boy Luke to the Grammar School in Plymouth shortly.'

'Very laudable,' I murmured, remembering, chillingly, other children about the farm who warranted no expenditure at all.

'Phyllis do sing most sweetly in consequence o' the way 'er was learned,' Mrs Lugg pressed on. 'As for Dora, their teacher said 'er'd never seen a girl so young as did such fine drawn-thread work. Dora, fetch the cloth you'm working on to show Mrs Penhale. And Phyllis, your music's in the parlour, you could perhaps . . .'

'We must be on our way, Mrs Lugg,' I interrupted hastily. 'I really have a great deal to do today.'

'Oh, 'tes a great shame, the girls will be proper disappointed. Perhaps another day, then. When you'm not so pressed.'

'Indeed.'

'Or, p'raps . . .' She eyed me with a thoughtful and predatory look I had noticed before in the faces of ambitious mamas intent on leaving no alleyway unexplored in the interests of their marriageable daughters. 'P'raps . . . well, 'twould be no trouble for them to call at Kildower sometime when they'm passing. I do assure you, Mrs Penhale, that my girls have more refined natures than any hereabouts that I can think of. They know how to behave themselves like the proper young ladies they've been brought up to be. And on social occasions, the art of conversation, the latest dances, 'tes all theirs to command. 'Course breedin' makes such a difference. Trebarth has been *owned* by Mr Lugg's family this last sixty year. It makes for stability, if you take my meaning. 'Tes different with *tenant* farmers, now, always being beholden.'

She rattled on in this vein for some moments. I understood her drift perfectly. She had plans for Phyllis and Dora. The farm prospered, her girls were being groomed for the kind of good marriages that would raise the standing, not to mention the fortunes, of the whole family. To this end, *entrée* to Kildower and the patronage of the Penhales would be, she believed, a considerable social advantage to her daughters.

I had no intention of offering any such thing, but I saw that it could be to the benefit of Liddy and the other apprentices to let her believe that I might.

'Your daughters are a credit to you, Mrs Lugg,' I said. 'I quite agree that they would add grace to any social gathering. If a suitable occasion arises . . . Well, we presently live a quiet life at Kildower, but who knows what the future holds?'

She drew my words in like a fish swallowing down a worm that is dangled temptingly before its eyes.

''Tes 'andsome of you, Mrs Penhale,' she said. 'Proper handsome. You'd not regret it, I promise you.'

'I'm sure I should not,' I said crisply. I opened my reticule and took out five shillings. 'Now, Mrs Lugg, I would wish you to take this to buy Jess anything she needs.' I pressed the coins into her not-unwilling palm.

'Most generous,' she breathed.

'Oh, and one more thing. It comes to me that you are the very person I should consult about a certain difficulty that has arisen at St Bride's. I should like to enlist your help, if you are willing.'

'Anything, Mrs Penhale,' she said, greedy now to curry favour. 'Anything at all, if 'tes in my power.'

'Mrs Miles, the vicar's wife, is having considerable difficulty in persuading the villagers that it is in their best interests to allow their children to attend Sunday school. What they need is a good example set before them by a forward-thinking person such as yourself.'

'Me, Mrs Penhale?'

'I should regard it as an act of great kindness if you would allow your apprentices to attend regularly each Sunday.'

Too late she saw the hook. Her eyes narrowed.

'It would merely mean sending them to church an hour early. A minor inconvenience, I think you will agree, that will be more than offset by the prestige of being seen as a person of the greatest charity and foresight.'

She looked slowly from me to her daughters and back again.

'Charity and foresight, Mrs Penhale?' she said. 'That's all well and good, but I 'as to tell you that Mr Lugg is very fierce in his objectin' to any sort of book-learnin' for those that 'ave no real need of it. Says it encourages a needless amount of thinkin' which only leads to mischief.'

'Then I trust you to persuade him,' I said, holding her glance steadily. 'May I rely on your support, Mrs Lugg?'

After a moment's contemplation she nodded, the sourness that had been hovering in her expression dissipating as her cheeks puffed out into a smile. The bait was swallowed hook, line and sinker.

'I'll do my best.'

'Good. I look forward to seeing the children there tomorrow. And you, of course, at church, Mrs Lugg.'

And breathing a prayer that my stratagem might work, I made my farewells, took Kensa by the hand and thankfully escaped.

I woke early on Monday morning with a fluttering sense of nervous excitement. I tried to make myself lie still, but it was impossible. Today Rhoda was coming for her first lessons in drawing and painting. Today, for the first time since I had laid them down more than six years previously, I would take up pencils and brushes again. It was something that I had resolved to do for the sake of a talented child. It was also something that I had stringently avoided in the years that I had been a governess. And though in my heart I knew that any course other than helping Rhoda would have pressed heavily on my conscience, I was in no doubt as to the risks.

I slipped from bed and went to the window, hugging my

arms against the morning chill. I leaned my forehead against the cold glass and stared out. Risk. A word one might use more readily in connection with explorations to darkest Africa or a journey across the Alps in winter or chancy investments in flashy money-making schemes. A word likely to cause eyebrows to be raised in amusement when used to describe the taking up of an artistic pursuit. But in my case the risk was all too real.

A thin haze of milky-pearl cloud covered the sky but already it was burning off as the sun gained strength. It would be a fine day and I should be able to take Rhoda outdoors for our first lesson together. I should set Chloe and Kensa some easy work and when that was done, for this first morning, they could amuse themselves playing where they would in the garden. I would devote myself entirely to Rhoda, as I planned to do on the three mornings, Monday, Wednesday and Friday, she would come to Kildower. Mostly today we would spend the time in walking and observing and discussing what we observed. I would attach labels to those attributes she already knew by instinct – form and texture and tone and perspective. Then, sometime during our walk, we should settle to sketch some subject which particularly caught our interest, a gnarled tree, a clump of budding flowers, a piece of lichened stone. And when we had finished we should set the sketches side by side and examine them. Not in order to compare her work unfavourably with mine, but so that we might judge if one or the other had achieved some extra quality that gave it freshness and life; or where attention to some small detail might have improved the composition. So had I first been taught on those rare and precious occasions when Mama was prepared to devote time to me. They were the only times when she had been scrupulously honest and fair and prepared to listen to my views and criticisms without laughing them aside or flying into a temper. They were lessons I had never forgotten. They had been the foundations upon which I had been able to build and develop my own style, and from those lessons I had developed the ability to look objectively at my own work and other people's. To view what was lauded by others with a cool eye. And always to appreciate worth, however unfashionable or outrageous it might be considered by those who presumed to dictate taste. All this I hoped to pass on to Rhoda.

I had new pencils and sketchbooks ready which I had taken from the generous provision in Kensa's schoolroom. One set for Rhoda. One for me. When I had carefully sharpened the pencils and drawn the sketchbooks from the shelf – ordinary books containing cheap paper suitable for a child's scribblings but which would do until I could order better from Plymouth – I had handled them with a sensuous pleasure that had jolted me. As though the years had swung away to the time before I had made a bonfire of every picture I had ever painted, to a time when to take up a pencil or pen or brush and make the first mark on a pristine sheet of paper was the most particular pleasure. When I dreamed of painting. When I lost myself in painting and hours, whole days sometimes, disappeared, dissolved into brush strokes of swirling, merging colour. When I saw nothing and needed nothing else. Remembered, too, the emptiness after the intensity, the all-consuming concentration of painting died away and the real world crowded back. Then the vacuum would refill with less pleasant emotions: a sense of loss, of anticlimax and, all too often, dejection and disappointment that I had not achieved what I intended. It was then that the need for distraction, the need to bury failure under layers of frenetic, unthinking activity became paramount.

And in those sobering moments came a glimpse into understanding of Mama, of a life driven and fractured by the demands of the demon that was her talent, that promised so much, yet held perfection tantalisingly beyond her grasp. There lay the danger. To follow slavishly where the demon led, sacrificing everything else in order to submit to its stern demands.

That day in the olive grove, when I painted the best picture I had ever done, was the day when I knew myself to be most in peril of being tempted. Resistance had not been easy. I had understood too well that having made the choice to live an ordinary, safe life I must not compromise or look backwards with misguided thoughts of what might have been.

Yet now I was to break the promise I had made when I tore myself away from my mother's world.

What that would bring, I did not dare to think.

I was too keyed up with nervous energy to stay still. Kensa was sound asleep in my dressing room, her favourite dolls ranged at the foot of the bed. She did not stir as I crept about quietly getting washed and dressed. She lay on her back, her silky-pale hair spread over the pillow, and I smiled to see how angelic she looked in sleep as she never was awake. Without her scowls and glares she was a different child, the child her father saw, that Jess saw. She had kicked the covers down and I gently pulled them back around her shoulders. I brushed my hand against her cheek. How vulnerable she looked in sleep. Fine, translucent skin stretching pale across the delicate bones of cheek and jaw, gold-tipped lashes casting frail half moons of bluish shadow under her closed eyes. Easy at a moment such as this to understand why she was so protected and indulged, and I felt a stab of regret that I must be the one to appear hard and unkind in her eyes. I tried to explain to her that it was for her own future good that she walk in the fresh air instead of coddling herself by the fire, that she display better manners, that she attend to her school work. But I could not expect so spoiled a child to readily accept radical notions that went against her experience and inclination. All I could hope for was that time and familiarity might soften her feelings towards me.

I could safely leave her now it was daylight. If she woke she would not be frightened, but I guessed she would probably sleep on until I returned. Yesterday it had taken me all my time to get her to stir from her bed in time for church. She had certainly slept long and deeply these last two nights, as though the unusual amount of exercise had exhausted her.

I found a shawl and slipped from the room. I ran lightly down the stairs. The maids were astir. I could hear the familiar slipshod clatter of Kitty's footsteps somewhere near the hall and Nan's sleepy voice, both cut off sharply as a door closed. I drew the bolts on the front door and went outside, still worrying that I might have encouraged Kensa to do too much and that she might succumb to one or other of her ailments. Without Jess's jealous guardianship of Kensa's routine, her afternoon rest had quite gone by the board. Indeed I had done my best to keep Kensa busy and active from the time she rose to the time she went to bed, though it was hard going. She did nothing willingly. She either flounced about in a temper or did what I asked in the slowest, sulkiest way possible, or affected an air of tragic languor. Though she exasperated me beyond reason, I did my best to remain calm by clinging to the hope that eventually she would tire of such petty displays and we might achieve a more reasonable relationship. And I did see a few glimmers of light in the gloom cast by her recalcitrant attitude. One was in the tentative beginnings of a friendship with Chloe Miles, which I felt would do much to draw her from the coddled isolation of her existence at Kildower. The other lay in her interest in the new bedchamber. That particular seed seemed to have rooted itself quite firmly.

I had taken care not to press her but she had raised the matter herself on the way to church yesterday. She threw in the query amid a welter of complaints. I was forcing her to walk when Papa would have insisted on taking the carriage on such a grey morning with rain threatening. It was stupid to go so early merely because of some silly Sunday school which was nothing to do with us. *She* did not wish to mix with flea-ridden children from the village. And no, she could not walk any quicker, because her legs were aching dreadfully. Then, in a particularly aggrieved voice, she flung at me, 'Where will Jess sleep if you make me move to a different bedchamber?'

'I shall not make you do anything, Kensa,' I said mildly. 'If you wish to remain in the nursery, then please do so. However, should you decide to remove to a better room, then I expect we might find a place for Jess not too far away. Perhaps this afternoon we could take a proper look.'

'I shall be far too tired to do any such thing this afternoon,' she said.

'Well, one day, when you are feeling up to it.'

She gave a contemptuous sniff. But after dinner, with only a token show of reluctance, she had accompanied me upstairs and we had settled on a room for Jess at the end of the corridor that *might* be suitable, *if* she chose to move.

The air still held the moist freshness of the rain that had drizzled down last evening. The hem of my old brown dress was soon soaked as I strode across the grass in my stout boots. I had my pen knife and a pair of scissors in my pocket with a view to culling a few sprays of greenery from the shrubbery and whatever flowers I could find growing about the gardens. Some sprays of the yellow rose, perhaps, that sprawled over the kitchen garden wall, and the newly opening ox-eye daisies that grew in vigorous clumps amid the long grass at its foot. I had resolved to try to brighten the atmosphere of the house, to bring lightness and colour to relieve the gloom of the shadowy corners. I was not sure that I could succeed – that anyone could succeed – but at least I would make an effort against the dismal weight of all those sombre shadows. What better way to start than with flowers and greenery? Armfuls of colour in the hall, the parlour, the dining chamber, standing the branches and blossoms in stone storage jars from the kitchen if necessary, for there was not a decent vase in the place to my knowledge. The whole house was starved of ornament. A house of masculine taste, masculine dark colours which did nothing to fight the gloom, but merely added to it. It was time I began to impose something different upon Kildower. Something more feminine. If Daniel was agreeable, I might even begin to make a few changes in the decor. Get rid of some of the heavy dark furniture, have chairs and sofas reupholstered in lighter colours . . . new curtains . . .

'Oh! Pirate! Down! Down, you rascal?' A tangle of hair and slobbering tongue and lolloping paws tore out from the kitchen garden as I gathered the daisies, and leaped up in ecstatic, panting greeting. At the same time Captain Penhale's voice bellowed his name from somewhere within the garden. I walked through the archway to find the Captain sitting on a rough bench in the shelter of the wall with Zack Bligh, both old men puffing at their church-warden pipes and silently contemplating the orderly rows of peas and beans and young cabbages.

'No, please do not get up,' I began. 'Please. I did not mean to disturb you.'

But Zack shuffled to his feet. 'Best be gettin' goin',' he grunted, tapping out his pipe. 'Was there somethin' you was wantin' particular,' missus?' He eyed the armful of greenery I was holding. 'Seems like you've been doin' a bit o' prunin'.'

'They're for the house, Zack. And while I'm here, I might as well ask about flowers. Could you bring up a regular supply to display indoors?'

'Never growed nothin' special in the way o' flowers,' he said. 'No call for 'em, see, and shrubs and trees not bein' as much trouble.' He jerked his head at the wall. 'They ole yeller roses and the white jasmine on yonder wall was 'ere 'afore I come so I let 'em be. Same with gilly flowers and marigolds and sweet lavender, which come up like weeds where they didn't oughter. P'raps I'll leave 'em be 'stead o' pluckin' 'em out in future. Not as I'd call 'em grand flowers. Mind, those you'm holding is no more'n weeds.'

'Weeds or not, they are beautiful,' I said stoutly.

He bared his few blackened stubs of teeth in an approving grin. 'Thass what I says, missus. Like they li'l daisies and piss-the-beds – beggin' your pardon – as come up on the lawns. They'm just as pretty, though the Cap'n here carries on shameful when I lets too many of 'em stay. 'E should 'ave the job o' rootin' they up, for 'tes painful slow work for a man o' my years.'

'Less of your lip!' the Captain growled. 'I pay village lads to do the real hard work. All you do is stand about gossiping with those as should know better than to give you encouragement.'

'Village lads is come today, gone tomorrow, as well you

knows, Cap'n,' Zack said amiably. 'Won't none of 'em put up wi' what I has to. As to flowers, missus, well, 'tes a bit late for seedin' they for this year, but I'll be happy to do what I can.' He touched the shapeless, earth-coated lump of felt that was his hat, 'I'll bid you good morning, then, missus . . . Cap'n.' He hobbled off towards the hothouse and sheds against the far wall.

'Damned peasant,' the Captain muttered. 'Don't know why I put up with him.' But there was a glint of affection in the rheumy old eyes as he watched Zack go.

I took Zack's place on the bench, Pirate instantly settling himself heavily on my feet, his head on my knee, his golden-brown eyes locked yearningly on my face.

'Well, madam?' the Captain demanded tetchily. 'Well? Was there something you wanted of me other than to turn my hound into more of a fool than he already is?'

'Do I need a reason?' I countered, turning my face to the sun, which was just beginning to emerge from the dissolving clouds. 'May I not enjoy a moment of your company without having to find an excuse?'

'Humph! Women, in my experience, do nothing without cause, being a breed given to sly manoeuvrings in order to get the better of honest menfolk.'

'Why should I have any need to do that?'

'You tell me, madam!'

I absently stroked Pirate's ears.

'What is there to tell, save that I woke early and came out into the garden to pick flowers for the house? Had Pirate not pounced on me I should not have known you were here at all.'

'Blasted dog,' he muttered, 'ruining a man's privacy. I've a mind to take my stick to the treacherous brute.'

Pirate reduced this remark to the empty threat it was by enthusiastically beating his tail on the gravel, wafting showers of stones over the Captain's old-fashioned buckled shoes.

We sat in silence for a moment, the Captain puffing a cloud of aromatic smoke into the mild air then, abruptly, he barked. 'So you lost interest in the Trewithens, then?'

'What? Oh, of course not. When you feel ready to tell me what you know of their history, I should be . . .'

'Deceitful, untrustworthy crew, every last one of them.'

'Surely not all. Are you not forgetting that Daniel was married to a Trewithen?'

He gave a short laugh. 'I forget very little, madam, even though I'm as old as Methuselah. No, 'tis a fine history of strife and treachery and backstabbing that has gone on from the time a Trewithen bought this tract of land in the days of good King Hal with the burnt-out ruins of the priory that stood upon it.'

I shuddered. 'I have heard the tale of the burning of the priory from Mrs Miles. Such a cruel act.'

'Hah! And who is rumoured to have plotted the despatch of the nuns and the woman he'd denounced as a witch? One Conan Trewithen.'

My hand froze on Pirate's head. The hound butted at it with his wet nose. Slowly my fingers began to move again.

'And why did he do it?' the Captain went on. 'Because he wanted rid of a wife he'd married for the money that allowed him to buy his own vessel and go trading along the coast. But she proved barren, and over-pious, to boot, so he was soon lusting after a farmer's beautiful young daughter who was kept too well guarded for him to have his way with her without benefit of marriage lines.'

'His *wife*? He burnt to death his own wife?' Any hoarseness in my voice could be attributed to nothing but shock at such a dreadful tale.

'Aye, or so the legend goes. Mayhap 'tis a barrel of nonsense, but the people of St Bridellan believe it well enough, curse and all.'

'Curse?'

He gave a great guffaw, startling a woodpigeon that had been eyeing the cabbages from the top of the wall into wildly flapping flight. 'Naturally there'd have to be a curse. Such a good tale wouldn't be near so satisfactory without one. Seemingly it was the wronged wife's revenge. She screamed it out over the roaring of the flames, that the Trewithens should never know a moment's peace or happiness in love or marriage. That brothers and sisters, fathers and sons, mothers and children would be constantly divided by hatred and deceit from generation to generation.' He swivelled his head to look at me. 'Reckon that was a satisfying sort of curse, d'you not say so, Mrs Penhale? Has a vengeful, Old Testament ring to it, such as the parson might read out on a Sunday. Generation to generation. Perhaps she really was a witch. She certainly had no intention of Christian forgiveness, for all her pious reputation. But that's women for you – say one thing, do the opposite.'

'Perhaps you would not have been too ready with forgiveness,' I said dryly, 'if you had the unfortunate prospect before you of being reduced to a crisp by your spouse.'

He guffawed again. 'I take your point, madam. But, damme, I still thank my stars that I never tied the knot with any of the wide-eyed beauties who fluttered their lashes at Saul Penhale in his prime. The sea was all the woman I ever trusted. And in the end she proved as fickle as the rest and scuppered me good and proper when she grew bored with the cut of my jib.' He spoke without rancour, as though time had long since taken the bitterness away. Then, his eyes still on his crippled leg stretched stiffly before him, he said slyly, 'So what do you think to the present bearer of the name Conan Trewithen, who has returned from the South Seas to plague the Penhales?'

The name instantly conjured the man into my mind. That lean dark face . . . the flinty eyes. And, treacherously, the skin of my wrist seemed to feel the touch of his thumb, warm and caressing, easing under the cuff of my glove to where the pulse beat. I took a breath before I spoke. 'It was unfortunate that I was with Kensa when he made himself known, which was a shock to her. It was in the village. Daniel will not be pleased. He warned me to be on my guard. But how did you know I had met him?'

'You'd be hard put to hide anything in a small place like St Bridellan.' He looked at me now, his gaze steady. But his pale blue eyes in their nest of wrinkles were not unkind. 'Which is something it is as well to bear in mind. Gossip here flies about like chaff in the wind and grows and alters in the telling and retelling.' For a moment I wondered if I had been seen with Conan Trewithen that first time in the saint's glade. Innocent though the meeting was – that I was – I felt a prickle of guilt. But it could not possibly be for he went on, speaking more generally. 'So remember that, Mrs Penhale, when some juicy village scandal comes to your ears. There might be no more than a grain of truth in it but the denizens of St Bridellan will probably have bedizened it in the same way a raddled old whore covers herself in layers of paint and rouge in the hope of making herself more attractive. But you did not answer my question. What did you think of him? What was your impression?'

'A hard man,' I said slowly. 'Bold . . . forward . . .'

The Captain nodded. 'Aye, he was always bold, and a spell at Botany Bay, if a man does not succumb to heat and flies and despair, is guaranteed to harden and embitter even

313

a weakly character. And Con Trewithen was never that. Rather, he was a young devil in his day, with a will and a temper to match. A charmer, too, and well favoured.'

'A charmer! But he was a thief, a robber.'

'How else should he have drawn men to his side, eager to follow blindly where he led? Or women who'd scratch each other's eyes out to gain his bed? He had a silver tongue, laughter in his eye, and the devil in his soul. A deadly combination.'

'He is not so well favoured now, and there is little laughter left in him, I think,' I said softly.

'Then the devil has claimed him for his own. From what you and others say, his punishment, or the Trewithen curse, take your pick, one or t'other, has finally removed his better qualities and left him with the worst.'

'You sound almost sorry, Captain.'

'Aye. I believe I almost liked the rogue once. When he was young and following his family trade of cards and dice and cribbage, which there's no denying he was good at. He'd hands so quick and a conversation so lively it was almost a pleasure to be gulled by him.'

'He was a card-sharp?'

'His father taught him all the tricks in the book, and he inherited the fine manners essential to the trade. A gentleman down on his luck will always command sympathy and lure the gullible into believing they might better such an easy-going fellow. But he had a brilliance at the trade his father or grandfather never had. His pa was too fond of his brandy ever to have a clear head and finally drank himself into his grave. His grandfather was too reckless by far. He was the one who lost the remnants of the Trewithen fortune, and Kildower itself, on the turn of a dice, so that he was forced to move to a cottage in the woods down by the creek.

But Kildower was soon abandoned by the new owner and eventually fell prey to wind and weather. It was in a parlous state when I clapped eyes on it and decided that if I was to be washed up on shore – beached like a lump of useless flotsam – then this was the place I should like to see out my last years, for I could see it had the promise of a fine place for a lad to grow and some day to inherit.'

'Daniel?'

'Daniel.' He frowned at his now-cold pipe, then turned it over slowly and tapped it so that the ash scattered down into the gravel like grey snow. 'Though there've been times when I've wished I'd satisfied myself with a new villa across the water in Plymouth instead of believing that I'd found a patch of heaven on earth here on the banks of the Lynher. Daniel would never then have entangled himself with the Trewithens and brought himself a deal of trouble.'

'He loved Meraud deeply, did he not? Such a tragedy that she died so young.'

He put the pipe into the deep pocket of his coat.

'You've kept me here jawing long enough, madam. My belly calls me to breakfast.' He got stiffly to his feet, steadying himself on his silver-handled stick, and looked down at me. 'They say the god of love fires his darts blind. It was Daniel's lot to be a hapless victim. The tragedy was not that she died, but that she ever married him at all.' He gave a curt nod and said brusquely, 'Now I'm to my breakfast. I'll say good day to you, Mrs Penhale.'

I was on my feet, setting Pirate bounding in excitement about the gravel, before he began to move. I caught his arm.

'Captain Penhale, please. There is no one else I should care to ask, no one in a better position to speak honestly. You see, I know so very little about Meraud, about Daniel's first marriage. Will you not tell me more? I should so much like to understand. And Daniel . . . He is very reserved in speaking of her.'

'So you think to worm confidences from me, eh?'

'Not confidences, of course not!'

He turned away and began to walk up the path with his awkward, hobbling gait. I sighed and followed him. If he would not speak, then I could not force him. But suddenly, at the arched entrance to the garden, he looked back and barked, 'Keep up! Keep up! Or you'll force me to raise my voice and tell the world things that ought to be kept decently private.'

So as we walked back to the house he gave me his account in gruff phrases of a marriage that was not at all as I had imagined it to be from the little that I had gleaned from Daniel.

'Meraud . . . I could not like her, there was a falseness, a pretence in her character that I couldn't abide. Daniel never saw it. He was besotted by her, as only a young man first in love can be. All too easy to see why. She was very different from the pretty, well-schooled misses he met in Plymouth. She'd run free like a wild, woodland creature all her life. Father too drunk to bother, her mother too sickly. And by the time they were both dead, her brother, the only one who had any real care for her, had taken up with a rabble of malcontents and was busy pursuing his own misguided destiny. So the girl was left to her own devices and her eyes lit on Daniel as a fine catch. And no red-blooded lad could have resisted her for long. She dazzled him with her fey looks, her way of talking and looking at a man with those strangely slanted eyes, so that his guts fair melted. Aye, I was no more immune to her charm than the next man, even though I misliked her and guessed that it wasn't Daniel she wanted so much as the house and the position of mistress of

Kildower that she coveted. So she trapped him, snared him in his innocence and desire, as she might have snared a rabbit in the woods, and with no more pity.'

We were almost at the house and he paused, panting a little from the effort of walking and talking. He waved his stick fiercely.

'Rattle me bones, you've gulled me into indiscretion, madam.' But his tone was more subdued than I might have expected, as though opening the gates of memory had allowed regret and sadness to creep through and soften him.

'Poor Daniel,' I said, my own heart, too, sad and soft.

'And poor Meraud.'

'You felt sympathy for her?' I said, surprised. 'But you said . . .'

'I misliked her, true, but I couldn't help but be sorry for her. As she had snared Daniel, so she herself was now trapped. She'd forced his hand by getting herself with his child. But she miscarried within two months of the hasty wedding. She had a bad time of it. And I reckon that the suffering wrested the change that I saw in her afterwards. As though the days she lay in bed recovering gave her time to think deep about the situation she had brought upon herself.' He swished his stick at the low, bushy lavender hedge alongside the path, setting a cascade of sharp fragrance into the air. 'I never reckoned much to the catching and caging of wild birds. A throstle or a robin beating its wings against the bars of its prison until it falls exhausted don't make a pretty sight. That was what Meraud reminded me of in the time she had left – a year and a half, no more – before the river took her. She couldn't learn, you see, to live like a lady, with servants to command and a fine house to order. She knew nothing of the things ladies keep themselves busy with, sewing and music and reading and tea parties. She wanted to be free to wander the woods and the river and the creek, lonely places, as she had always done. She only went with Daniel to Plymouth the once and she refused to go again. Everything frightened her, the crowds, the carriages, the noise, and most of all having to meet strangers – Daniel's friends – and entertain them to dinner, or go with them to assemblies and such.'

'She was very young.'

'No more than sixteen when they married. Daniel made that his excuse for her. He was patient. Patient and blinkered. Because he loved her he believed she would gradually learn in her own time. But I could see different. All she ever wanted was to run free. She was out in all weathers though she was thin as a lath and looked as frail. There was a hardness, a single-mindedness, that drove her into walking miles for hours on end or rowing herself about on the river. When Daniel was here he put a stop to that once she was breeding again. But the minute his back was turned, she'd be off. There was a terrible restlessness driving her. As though something out in the woods and the hills called to her, some peace she searched for but couldn't ever find, never would find.' He hesitated, then said quietly, 'Or perhaps she did, in the end, God rest her soul.'

I drew in my breath sharply. 'You mean . . .'

'I mean nothing. I know nothing. I didn't see what happened, no more did anyone else. All I'll say is that her drowning came as no surprise to me. And if I am right then some might believe her sinful, others brave. For my part I reckon 'twas the last selfish act of someone untroubled by conscience. And I hope her spirit has found the freedom it was so desperate for. Otherwise the pain she caused others was never worth it.' He broke off and glared at me with a return of his usual irascibility. 'So are you satisfied, Mrs

Penhale, that you kept me from my breakfast so that my belly thinks my throat's been cut? Have I gossiped to your satisfaction? Does it make you happier to know that your predecessor was so unsatisfactory? No, I can see from your face that it don't. For what I thought then, or think now after all these years, matters not a jot, is that not the case? 'Tis what Daniel thinks that matters. For Daniel was happy enough with what he had, what he *believed* he had – there's none so blind as those that will not see – for so short a space of time. Not time enough for him to grow impatient with her or discontented. Which was a great misfortune, for he has lived, and lives still, with the illusion that nothing in life will ever match that golden age of youthful passion. And his blindness may be permanent now, which is a sad condition to bedevil a man in his prime. 'Tis beyond my skill to know how to treat his infirmity, for I've tried. All I got for my pains was a flea in my ear.' He cast me one last challenging glance from under his bushy white eyebrows. 'It remains to be seen if you can restore his sight, Mrs Penhale. A daunting task, and whether you'll have the will or the inclination I can't yet be sure.'

With a curt nod he hobbled off down the side path that would take him to his own quarters, calling Pirate to heel, the hound looking mournfully back at me as though wondering why I did not follow.

I went back into the house and slowly climbed the stairs towards the room where Meraud's daughter, my charge, still slept. She stirred as I opened the door to the dressing room, stretching her arms wide and yawning.

'Come along, sleepyhead,' I said calmly. 'Time you were up and about or Chloe and Rhoda will be here before you are even dressed.'

And she could never have guessed, for it never would

have done for her to know, that whenever I looked at her through that whole day I was reminded of her mother, who had freed her own wild spirit and by so doing bound others to her memory with ties so strong that they might never be broken.

The week established itself to a calm and satisfying pattern. The two mornings I was able to spend with Rhoda were a delight in themselves. Her eagerness and breathless enthusiasm deepened my own excitement in taking up sketchbook and pencil again. We sat that first morning in a sheltered corner of the shrubbery with a mossy old sundial as Rhoda's chosen subject. We drew it from different angles as the sun rose in the sky to shorten and slowly turn the shadows. I believe we would happily have continued there all day had not Kensa and Chloe burst upon us, arms linked and suppressing giggles, sent by Martha to remind us of the time.

'And what have you two been up to?' I asked, closing my sketchbook with reluctance.

They exchanged mirthful looks and Kensa said airily, 'Oh, we played all about the garden.'

'And in the stream or the ponds by the looks of your stockings. Goodness me, your skirt hems are all wet too.'

'Oh, we're only a little bit damp, Mrs Penhale,' Chloe assured me earnestly. 'We were examining the flora and fauna, you see, making notes for our nature diaries.'

This set them off again into bursts of giggling. Which was explained later when a thunderous Mrs Dagget came to complain, just as the Miles girls were leaving, that fun and games was one thing but hundreds of baby frogs set loose on her clean kitchen floor quite another. And if any of they nasty slimy varmints got into her pantry before Nan could gather them into a bucket and put them back into the pond where they belonged, she'd a mind, begging my pardon, to take her besom and paddle the backsides of those responsible.

I made profuse apologies to Mrs Dagget and told the two culprits sternly that not only must they do the same but they must go to the kitchen to apologise to Nan for causing her extra work, and help her to find and catch every last frog before I should allow Chloe to leave.

There was a deal more hilarity as they chased the last hopping creatures under the tables and dressers. Rhoda added her own excited squeals as she joined in the fun, though Kensa was inclined to stand back and point out the frogs for the others to pick up and I saw her shudder and flinch as a froglet hopped too close to her foot. Her role in the escapade, apparently, had been not to catch the creatures but to hold the jars for Chloe to fill. But that in itself was an achievement for a child who usually shrank back from contact with any animal, be it dog, cat or innocent froglet, and despite the fact that I must appear to be stern with her, at heart I was thrilled that she had succumbed to normal childish mischief. Indeed, she looked far more muddied and grass-stained than Chloe, because she had insisted on dressing up to impress her visitor in a starched, white, lace-trimmed dress. Chloe's hand-me-down dark print had emerged from the frog hunt looking far more presentable.

Except for the one simple dress I had made for her, Kensa had nothing so practical in her elegant wardrobe, as I had reason to know. I had begun a rigorous turnout of her clothes, which was a far more arduous task than I had supposed because it seemed that everything she had ever owned had been hoarded away in cupboards and drawers by Jess, much of it evidently untouched for years by the look of the yellowing heaps of baby clothes lying in the dusty corners of drawers. Several bundles of outgrown woollen garments stored at the back of the highest shelf of the press were considerably holed with moth and there was nothing to be done but to burn them. But even as I regretted the waste, when such things might have found use among the poor of the village, I felt a certain satisfaction in having found this evidence of slovenliness on Jess's part, this flaw in her guardianship of the nursery. A satisfaction that increased when I suggested to Martha that, after I had finished my work of sorting out Kensa's clothes into what might be kept and what given away, the day and night nursery would benefit from a good spring clean so that all would be nice and tidy for Jess when she returned. And Martha, quick to agree, let slip that when Miss Kensa's bed had been moved there had been an unexpected amount of fluff accumulated under it. 'Oh, I didn't intend no criticism, ma'am, I dare say Jess was due to see to it herself, save that she had her nasty accident.' But there was a gleam in her eye that told me that Jess had fallen short of Martha's own high standards in the matter of domestic order and cleanliness and she was glad I had provided the opportunity for it to be tactfully mentioned.

During these few days it was easy to delude myself into believing that this satisfying routine would continue indefinitely. Even the house seemed marginally brighter when children's laughter rang through it. The shadows were certainly less noticeable with windows wide open to let in the warm, garden-scented air, flowers and foliage arranged in improvised containers in the gloomiest corners and Martha bustling the young maids hither and yon as she impressed upon them her own well-tried methods of tackling dust and disorder.

But on Thursday evening two visitors jolted me unpleasantly into realising that less comfortable matters lurked not far away.

Kensa, having yawned her way through supper, had not protested overmuch when I suggested an early night. Indeed, these last evenings she had taken little persuasion because I had offered to sit and read to her when she was tucked up in bed. Although Daniel had told me that she enjoyed reading, she was actually a poor, slow reader, which was hardly surprising considering her antipathy to schooling and governesses. I had discovered quite quickly that whenever she picked up a book it would be one of a few well-thumbed favourites, simple tales with short, easy words. She had stubbornly refused to move on to anything more suitable for her age until, out of desperation one day in the schoolroom when she was making an untidy attempt at hemming a handkerchief and the whining note in her voice as she complained that her back ached because she had sat still too long was driving me to distraction, I snatched a copy of *The Life and Adventures of Robinson Crusoe* down from the shelf, opened its pristine pages and began to read aloud.

'Chapter One. In which I do not heed my father's advice,' I said in a voice loud and firm enough to drown her complaints. 'I was born in the year 1632, in the city of York, my father being a foreigner of Bremen . . .'

Within a minute or two she had stopped talking. Within a very few more she had stopped her pretence at needlework and was listening with a concentration I had never observed in her before.

I had found a way to catch her attention, though I used it sparingly. It would not do to let her dream her way through the hours meant for school work. But I enjoyed reading aloud and this new innovation, the story at bedtime, was satisfying to us both.

But tonight the excitements of Man Friday's discovery had kept Kensa fighting sleep for longer than I expected.

The long June evening was darkening as I slipped quietly from the bedroom and went back down to the parlour where the candles were already lit. Regretfully I took up the sketch-book lying open on the chair which I had set at the window. Too late now to complete the drawing I had begun earlier of the mulberry tree. I settled myself on the sofa and riffled through the pages. Already many of them were filled, some with a series of quick drawings of the same subject from different angles, some with sketches of views about the garden or the house. In every spare minute I had picked up my pencil, eager to capture whatever I saw around me, with no thought to any future painting but merely to exercise my hand, my eye, my mind, as they had not been exercised these last years. I was turning to a fresh page and thinking I might draw the candelabra on the mantelshelf and the play of light and shade on the wall when I heard the clatter of the front door knocker.

For a brief, joyous second or two I thought it might be Daniel returned unexpectedly. Common sense immediately reasoned that he would scarcely knock, knowing that the door remained unlocked until we retired to bed. Then who could it be, so late?

I heard the rattle of the heavy latch, the murmur of Martha's voice and the deep masculine tone of a man – a voice I recognised with a start of panic.

Martha came into the parlour and said, 'A gentleman, ma'am. A Mr Trewithen. I told him it was inconvenient for him to call at this hour.'

'I am not at home to the gentleman, Martha.' I began, my hands tightening on the sketchbook, but he was already following Martha into the parlour, handing her his hat, gesturing aside her indignant, 'Sir, I asked you to wait.'

'So you did, but I preferred not to do so. Ah, Mrs Penhale,

good evening to you.' He flourished an exaggerated bow. 'I hope I find you in good health.'

'Shall I stay, ma'am?' Martha said, no whit abashed by this importunate intruder. She set her hands aggressively on her hips.

'Thank you, Martha, but I believe that will not be necessary.' I stared, cold and unflinching, at Con Trewithen. 'I shall allow the *gentleman* five minutes to explain the nature of his errand. You may return then to show him out.'

She left with some reluctance, no doubt to hover in the hall lest I should have need to call for her urgently.

'Well, sir,' I said sharply. 'Explain yourself.'

I sat very straight on the sofa, the sketchbook set aside, my hands clasped in my lap, praying that no trace of the commotion of my thoughts showed in any aspect of my bearing.

'Explain? What is there to explain? I merely felt the urge to make a call upon my brother-in-law, but finding him from home, I thought to pay my respects to his wife.' He raised a sardonic eyebrow. 'Do I see disbelief written on your face, Mrs Penhale? Well, I confess, you are right to disbelieve. To be frank, I knew very well Mr Daniel Penhale was not here. He seldom is, and I find myself so engaged with important matters that I have yet to find time to visit him on the rare occasions when he is at home.'

'Kindly state your business and go, Mr Trewithen,' I said. 'You are not welcome here.'

'My business? Should I have need of a reason to call upon my relatives by marriage? But perhaps it is that I am not suitably dressed for such a visit.'

He was prowling about the room as he spoke, alert and predatory, a hunter surveying unknown territory. He whipped round suddenly, holding his arms wide. 'Do I somehow fall

325

short of your exacting standards? Pray do tell me, madam, if this is the case. I am willing to make any change you think would improve my appearance.'

He was immaculately dressed and groomed, as well he knew. Neither in the rags of our first encounter, nor in the sensible clothes of the working man, as I had seen him on the day of the fair, but wearing a cutaway coat of dark blue over a silk waistcoat in tones of paler blue, cream and burgundy. A cravat crisply white under his chin, long legs encased in trousers of white nankeen, white hair oiled and tied back. Every inch the gentleman. Other things to notice too. His flinty eyes had an unusual brilliance, his sallow cheeks were flushed. I caught a rich waft of brandy fumes as he sauntered across the room and leaned perilously close, to say softly, 'You do not answer, Mrs Penhale. May I then take it that you approve of how I look?'

'I neither approve nor disapprove. I merely wish you to take your leave.'

'But I am not ready to go.' Thankfully he stepped back, to stare once more round the room. 'The family homestead is admirably restored. I never had occasion to enter it before, you see. Though as a boy I remember forcing a broken door with friends and rampaging through the decaying rooms. We thought ourselves very brave though we saw none of the ghosts reputed to haunt the place.' His glance mocked me. 'You know, of course, about the ghostly nuns, Mrs Penhale. I have in recent years experienced too many horrors wreaked by living fiends to be scared now of mere phantoms, but there are few in St Bridellan who would choose to spend a night under Kildower's roof for fear of catching the sound of ancient plainsong. It is said – you have doubtless heard the tale – that this heralds certain misfortune for the hapless eavesdropper.' His laugh rang out, short and humourless.

'Dear, dear, you have turned a little pale. I trust I have not frightened you. But I am sure I have not. You are not the sort to be alarmed by silly superstition. You are made of sterner stuff.' He paused, then continued, insolence lacing every word. 'Indeed, you must be, to suffer such cruel neglect from a husband who chooses to absent himself for most of the time.'

'That is enough, Mr Trewithen.' I rose to my feet, wishing I were taller so that he need not tower over me, wishing there was an army of manservants beyond the parlour door that I could call upon to throw him out. 'You are drunk and I wish you to leave this instant.'

'Drunk? Never! I merely shared a bottle of excellent brandy with friends in a Saltash tavern to celebrate a profitable afternoon and the winning of a fine horse off a braggart naval lieutenant.'

I should not have bandied words with him. I should have stayed cold and silent until he tired of baiting me. But I did not because I could not. I wanted to hit back, punish him for the way he had forced his way in, for his undisguised insolence.

'So you are back to your old cheating ways,' I said through gritted teeth. 'Well, your ruffianly friends and your greed for other people's property brought you to ruin once. The next time you are caught it will be the hangman's rope. I cannot say I shall feel in the least surprised . . . or sorry.'

He was across to me in two strides, standing so close I could feel the flushed heat of his body. His voice was low and hard. 'These so-called ruffians I once ran with were desperate men, for sure, but I will tell you why they were desperate, Mrs Penhale. Because there was no other course open for them but to beg or starve or steal. Because they were the poorest of the poor. Some turned off from their work, with families and sick children or wives to care for, and refused parish relief. Others the flotsam of the war with the French, crippled men left too damaged to be of use to the army or the navy, their bravery and patriotism conveniently forgotten by smug generals and admirals grown fat on the adulation of the populace.'

'So they turned highwaymen and ended swinging from a rope or exiled to Botany Bay. That must have been a source of great rejoicing among their poor widows and wives and sick children.'

His mouth twisted to a grimace. 'I make no excuses for myself. I was young and headstrong, and saw it as an adventure – to take from those who had too much and distribute it among those who had nothing.'

'A veritable Robin Hood,' I said with heavy sarcasm.

'But those others,' he went on, as though I had not spoken, 'The innocent . . . I shall grieve for them, feel their pain, for the rest of my days.' He took a slow breath, the anger draining from his voice, the brandy-induced flush paling in his cheeks. 'As I shall grieve for the sister I neglected while I took myself on those foolish adventures . . . Meraud.' His flinty eyes narrowed. He said softly, 'Do you see her sad little spirit wandering this unhappy house, Mrs Penhale? When you lie in your soft bed awaiting your husband's embrace and your husband turns to you, do you hear her voice whispering that dear Daniel is not the paragon you would believe?'

'Stop this!'

'Do you hear her telling of how he lusted after her, seduced her, got her with child, and forced her to agree to a marriage she never wanted?'

'Lies! All lies!'

'Oh, you may have heard a different tale, but I have the

story from Meraud's own lips, the last time I saw her. My last day of freedom. When I found her vomiting from some evil brew she had taken to rid herself of the child. She was sobbing, terrified at what was happening to her, and I was beside myself with anger when I discovered the reason. I told her not to think that she must marry. Bastard child or no, I should take care of them both. I remember her gratitude, her relief, and I silently vowed that Daniel Penhale should answer for what he had done. But that night, our little band of desperadoes fell into an ambush. I could do nothing, then, to save her. The rest you know.'

'You are wrong. Wrong! It was not like that. Daniel would not . . . Could never be as you say.'

'Poor Sophy,' he said, his voice changing, a note threading through it that I had not heard before. Something almost rueful, tender, underlining the words. 'Such a sensible, loyal little thing. So straightbacked and straitlaced and honest. All the ardour in your tight little soul kept well hidden in case, once released, it refuses ever to retreat to that cold cave where you keep it locked away.' His grey eyes seemed to have a less flinty gleam. In that instant they seemed almost . . . No! No! I would not look into them. I would wrench myself away from the hand that came up to touch my temple to smooth back a wisp of hair. The fingers, so light a caress, that traced the line of my cheek, the curve of my lips, rested there. 'Such a waste. To be fastened in a marriage as arid as the desert sands.'

A tap on the door and Martha entered, disapproval written in every line of her sturdy body. And saw?

Nothing untoward. He was too quick of hearing, too lithe, too careful, for that. So she was merely relieved that the importunate Mr Trewithen appeared to be taking his leave without any fuss and that Mrs Penhale stood dignified and stern without a word, as was only proper in the circumstances. Such effrontery to push his way in like that! Gentleman or no gentleman, that wasn't proper behaviour. She gave him his hat in silence and closed the door after him with a decided bang.

And I was left with his touch burning on my lips and the shaming knowledge that far from shrinking back from him, as I intended, I had not moved an inch from that caressing, so-gentle hand.

The reverberations of that encounter had scarcely died away before Kitty was pushing Liddy through the parlour door.

'Another letter from Trebarth for 'ee, ma'am. I brung Liddy straight in, like you asked me to if 'er come again. An' Mrs Dagget wants to know if 'er's to put bread 'n' cheese ready for the maid to take, like 'er did last time.'

My hands were still shaking as I took the note.

'Please, Kitty. Thank you.'

Kitty clip-clopped away and I gathered my wits and unfolded the paper.

It was penned by Jess herself, telling me that she was much improved and expected to return to her duties on Sunday.

'*My legg is panefull yet but I cn get abowt and I now dear Miss Kensa will be missing her Jess so I shud not wish to prolong her distres . . .*'

I stood in the parlour looking at the heavy, careful writing and felt my spirits sink even lower.

'So, Liddy,' I said slowly, 'Miss Southcote is on the mend.'

She lifted her thin shoulders.

'Dunno. Keeps to the parlour, missus, So Annie says.' She frowned in an effort to be helpful. 'Madwoman's gone,

330

though. 'Er was fetched away two days since. 'Id behind the hedge when I seed the carriage as come for her waiting down the bottom o' the lane. Master and the gen'leman as come for 'er carried 'er down from the house. Annie said missus been giving 'er a draught to keep 'er quiet.'

'A gentleman came for her?' I said. 'What kind of a gentleman?'

She shuffled her dirty bare toes on the carpet.

''Twas nearly dark so I couldn't see so much. 'Ad a tall black 'at an' a black coat. But a gen'leman, from his voice. Spoke proper, like the vicar an' Mr Penhale.'

'Could you hear what he said?'

'Only a bit.' She frowned. 'He spoke to the lady waitin' in the carriage. 'Eard her clear enough. Sorta' cryin', 'er was, as they got the madwoman inside. 'Er said, "What 'ave we done to 'er, my poor darlin'" An' 'e said, the gen'leman, "'Tis for the best," an' 'er answered – I think 'twas – "'Er looks like to die. If I'd known 'twould end so, I'd never 'ave agreed to any of this." Then the carriage door shuts and they was off.'

I was only half-listening. The troubles of the poor, demented woman seemed remote against the dangerous reality of Con Trewithen and the gloomy prospect of Jess's return.

Liddy, completely unabashed at this second visit to a grand parlour, chattered on in excitement about going to Sunday school and Mrs Lugg saying they could go each week if they got their duties done early as I penned the briefest of acknowledgements to Jess. I did not write off the plan that was building minute by minute in my mind, as I might have done had I felt more kindly disposed towards the woman. She could find out for herself when she returned, else she might take it into her head to cut short her convalescence and attempt to thwart me.

'An' Mrs Miles says she'll give a penny to the first one as gets to Sunday school,' Liddy was saying. She giggled. 'Me an' Sammy says we'll get stuck in the door, 'cos we'll both be wantin' to be first in. An' Mrs Miles give us a currant bun each. D'you think 'er'll do the same on Sunday, missus?'

'I dare say she will,' I said, beginning to recover a little now that there was the clear possibility of some positive action. Edith Miles and I had both decided that a little bribery in this deserving cause, including a supply of Mrs Dagget's freshly baked buns, would not be unpleasing in the sight of God. When word got round of such munificence we were confident that the Trebarth children would be joined by others.

When Kitty fetched Liddy away I took up my pen again, more briskly this time, and wrote a second note to Edith in which I apologised for having to halt Rhoda's lessons temporarily as I had decided to take Kensa on an overdue visit to Plymouth. I did not know how long I should be staying but, among other articles on a growing shopping list, I wished to make a selection of good-quality art materials for future lessons, which would resume as soon as I returned.

It was as good an excuse as any. The truth – wishing to put a good distance between myself and the two people who for different reasons disturbed my peace of mind – I kept to myself.

I was taking a chance, I knew. But I pushed caution to the back of my mind. Daniel might be upset that I had not consulted him over the visit. And if Kensa should take ill, as she had done before, then I should certainly be held responsible.

But I wanted him. I needed him. I needed his strong, quiet reassuring presence to calm the turbulence of my mind. I needed to get right away from this house with its unquiet spirits. I needed to be in a place that held no reminders of Meraud's pale ghost.

I rang for Martha and gave her the note to be taken to the vicarage. Then I went quietly upstairs to pack my bags.

Chapter Seven

I roused Kensa early the next morning and let her dress and eat her breakfast before I told her of our change of plan.

'We are going to see Papa?' Excitement flooded her face and was almost instantly erased by a wash of fright. 'But going to Plymouth gave me a horrid rash – it itched and burned and the doctor said it was the sea air and nerves. And Jess will not be there to put the ointment and the bandages on.'

'In the first place, you are older now and much stronger,' I said confidently, having decided that calm reassurance was the best antidote to nerves, for myself as much as for Kensa. 'In the second we have managed perfectly without Jess this last week. I see no reason why we cannot carry on a little longer.' I smiled and straightened the draggle-tailed bow in her hair. Martha's touch, I had to admit, was less painstaking than Jess's in decorative matters. 'We shall not go too much in the sea breeze if we find it has an unfavourable effect, but there are plenty of other things we can amuse ourselves with. I am not sure how long we shall stay, but I hope to persuade Papa to allow us a week at least. Now, I do not enjoy travelling with a weight of luggage, and we already have a box of garden produce and cream and butter to take for Mrs Venables, so I have packed one bag for you, but you may tell Martha if there is anything else you wish to take – a doll – a book or two.'

So *Robinson Crusoe* was packed together with the borrowed copy of Mrs Phipps' new volume and she held tight to her favourite doll as the carriage bore us off.

Everything conspired to give us a pleasant journey. Even the Captain's words to me provided a warm inner glow. 'You are going to Plymouth unannounced?' His whiskers had jutted threateningly towards me. 'Hah! I might have known you'd turn out a managing, presumptuous woman. You've got that look about you.' Then his unexpected bark of laughter rang out. 'Damme, if it weren't that my travelling days are done, I might have gone along just to see the expression on Daniel's face when he finds you on his doorstep. Well, good luck, Mrs Penhale. I reckon something to jolt him from his expectations might serve him very well. And mayhap will benefit your interfering self.'

My spirits bolstered with what passed as the Captain's approval, I stared about with lively interest at a green and flowing landscape with the distant glitter of sea and river, very different from the mist-shrouded views of my journey from Plymouth to Kildower with Daniel. The morning was blue and calm, the horse sprightly – for Dagget cared for it like a child and, apart from riding it on errands or to the blacksmith, kept it cossetted – and there was an impromptu entertainment on hand while we waited for the ferry at Torpoint.

A band of tumblers and jugglers had gathered a small crowd. Even their tawdry finery took on a noble aspect under the strong sun as, to the beating of a drum and the clash of cymbals held by two barefoot children, several youths and girls performed remarkable somersaults and feats of balance and others tossed burning torches about as carelessly as if they were harmless sticks. Kensa was enchanted by a bold-eyed, laughing man wearing a baggy frilled shirt and scarlet breeches. He was a conjuror *par excellence*. He miraculously turned scarves into bunches of flowers, made doves and rabbits disappear into thin air, and when he brought round the hat he drew two eggs and a silk hand-kerchief from under the rim of Kensa's bonnet – to her round-eyed wonder – when she tossed him the coppers I had given her. Then, with a flourish, he presented her with a rosebud that appeared to leap into his hand from her ear. 'A gift to a generous lady,' he cried, shaking back his mane of vigorous black hair and moving on with his hat, 'and who else will throw a coin and earn a rose from Rob the Magician?'

'This must be a magic rose,' she breathed. 'It'll probably never die. I'll keep it safe to show to Chloe. *She* could never have been given such a thing. Oh, and how wonderful to be able to walk on your hands, and to throw those fiery torches without getting burnt. They must all be very clever, and they look so happy and cheerful. It must be such fun!'

'So it must,' I agreed, not wishing to spoil her enjoyment by telling her that the rose was probably filched from someone's garden and the wide smiles, the magician's patter, the scanty, eye-catching costumes, were all tricks intended to part a bemused crowd from its money. Nor did I draw her attention to the little group that crouched well beyond the crowd by the troupe's battered wagon. A couple of bent old crones, a few ragged, bare-bottomed infants playing in the dust. One young woman, well advanced in pregnancy, shuffled to get comfortable against the wagon wheel, another huddled under a thick black shawl as though it were a winter's day instead of a fine June morning, her shoulders heaving as a hard, painful cough racked through her. Not so much fun on the road for those who were old or ill or breeding or even for the young and healthy when rain and storms made travelling hard and kept customers away. But let Kensa keep her illusions. Let the magic stay with her for a while longer. There was time enough for grown-up cynicism to wipe the romance from her eyes.

'Are they gypsies, Mama? Jess says gypsies are nasty thieving creatures who steal babies if they can, but these do not look nasty at all.'

'Not true Romany gypsies, I think,' I said, 'who are no better or worse than the rest of us, whatever people say. But travelling people nevertheless. I dare say they make their living going to fairs and wrestling matches and other outdoor spectacles where people gather. But come, here is the ferry. Where is the boy who will see to our baggage?'

The river sparkled blue-green and silver under a cat's-paw of wind and the air held the salty tang of the sea. We had the excitement of a man-o'-war moving down river as we crossed to the Devonshire bank, with its great gun decks, its looming masts and spars and the spread canvas of its sails towering over us as the ferry manoeuvred round its stern.

'I think those sailors are nearly as clever as the acrobats,' Kensa decided, staring up in awe at the men running like monkeys about the rigging.

'Very nearly,' I agreed solemnly. 'And just imagine how it must be to work up there when the ship is rolling in heavy seas.'

'They'd have to be as brave as Robinson Crusoe then. Do you suppose any of them will ever be shipwrecked on a desert island?'

And such interesting speculations carried us on to land where, as we made the last stage of our journey by hired cab, I endeavoured to distract Kensa from any apprehensive thoughts of ill health by asking her what she knew of

338

Plymouth and where she had been on her rare visits. Apart
from the few well-known tales of the great sea dogs like Sir
Walter Raleigh and Sir Frances Drake, she knew very little
and she was quite ignorant of the town's geography. Her
visits seemed always to have been circumscribed by illness
or too much rain or sun or wind. It seemed there had hardly
been a climactic condition that had suited her here, and with
so many days having to be spent in bed or confined indoors
it was no wonder the child and her nurse had been glad to
leave and Daniel himself anxious to see Kensa safely back
to her comfortable routine at Kildower.

Looking at her pale, fine-boned face, her nose wrinkled
in distaste at the smell of horse and straw and battered old
leather, I prayed that she would take no harm from my hasty
decision to leave Kildower, and in particular from the badly
sprung discomfort of this final ride, though she was more
put out than poorly at the moment.

'Papa would never let me ride in such a poor equipage,'
she sniffed. 'He always hired a proper carriage to meet us
when I came with him before. A very *smart* carriage.'

'Well, Papa does not know we are coming, does he?' I
said cheerfully. 'So we must make our own way as best and
as quickly as we can. Regard it as an adventure to tell Chloe
when you return. Oh, and look Kensa! Look! There is one
of Papa's brewery drays! See how splendidly bold the name
Penhale is drawn on the side. And now we are on the long
straight road that runs up to the town. I remember that fine
new building which your papa told me was the Royal Union
Baths. It cannot be far to Nutmeg Street now.'

Mrs Venables threw up her hands in shock when she
opened the door to us, but in an instant she was all beams
and welcome. 'Why, I might have known you was coming,
Mrs Penhale, for I've had as fine a rack of lamb as ever you

did see delivered this morning, and I was only thinking 'twas a pity there was only one gentleman to eat it, but now you'll be able to enjoy it together. Now come you in and I shall fetch you some of my elderflower cordial, which is very refreshing this hot weather. And you looking so bonny, Miss Kensa. Oh, I am so pleased you'm come.'

Daniel returned for his dinner at two o'clock. Kensa and I were washed and rested and sitting, for my part with some nervousness, in the parlour by the time his footsteps sounded in the passage. But whatever restraint or disapproval he might have felt were quite overcome as Kensa flung herself on him with a cry of, 'Papa! Papa! A surprise.'

When at last we were sitting at ease over the remains of the truly excellent lamb and a fine gooseberry tart he was still looking at Kensa as though he could not believe she was here. He had demanded to know every detail of our journey, shaking his head in disbelief that we had managed all so smoothly and had apparently suffered no ill effects. I was thankful that Kensa looked no more fatigued than she had when we set out. Indeed, her appetite seemed to have been improved rather than diminished by the rigours of the morning. But perhaps it was that she was so busy telling him of the acrobats and jugglers and the wondrous magician, whose prowess grew ever more splendid in the recounting, that she absently ate more than she usually did.

I watched him as Kensa talked, noting the weary shadows under his eyes and a lack of colour in his face, as though he had been driving himself hard, without much relaxation or rest. In the few moments we had alone, before he took up his hat to walk back to the brewery and Kensa came rushing up to bid him goodbye, I said, 'Have all the problems at the brewery been resolved?'

He frowned. 'Apparently so. But troubles never come

singly. As is usually the way when one thing goes wrong, another follows. I have never known a time when so many things have pressed for my attention at once, particularly in the malt house – disputes, broken machinery, spoiled malt. But I must not bore you with my troubles when you have had problems enough at Kildower. Poor Jess. Such a thing to happen when she was kind enough to help out her cousin, and how very distressing for you to have to cope without her. She is such a pillar of strength – and Kensa must have been beside herself with grief. She is so deeply attached to Jess.' He nodded slowly. 'I can see the wisdom in distracting the child with a visit to Plymouth, but I do beg you to watch her for any signs of indisposition. I intend no criticism, my dear Sophy, for I can see that Kensa is looking well at the moment, but to chance a visit without Jess . . . She understands, you see, even the most subtle indications that Kensa is sickening, and the Plymouth air, as you know, is not favourable to . . .'

'It was not a case of distracting Kensa,' I said, sharply, riled, hurt even, perhaps childishly, not only by his lauding of a woman I disliked and distrusted, but by his assumption that my visit to Plymouth was purely in Kensa's interests. As though nothing else counted. 'There were several reasons why I decided to come to Plymouth, and should it seem so strange a thing that one of them should be that I wished to see something of my husband and understand a little more of how he spends his time here?' Almost as the words were out I regretted them, and there was no time to say more before Kensa was pushing between us. Daniel seemed, for once, scarcely to notice her. His glance met mine above her head. It was a strange look. Puzzlement was there, and surprise, and something far more intense that seemed to deepen the colour of those startling sea-blue eyes, as though for the first time he had really looked at me and appreciated my presence since I had arrived.

'Papa!' Kensa tugged at his sleeve. 'Papa, when will you be home again?'

Now he dragged his gaze away, picked up his hat from the table by the door, and said, rather gruffly, 'I shall be back as soon as maybe. I intend to make the most of every moment you are . . . both of you . . . here.' And with one last, unreadable glance at me he was striding out with his long easy lope down the steep street.

The thought that I had overstepped the mark with Daniel worried at me all afternoon. I should have known better than to have spoken so impulsively. Possibly I was a little more overwrought from the journey than I had thought, though it had all seemed very straightforward. But when Daniel returned, he was, to my relief, in a lighthearted mood and whisked from under his coat two slim parcels.

'They caught my eye as I passed the shop on my way home. It was impossible to resist the lure of something so indispensable for this hot weather.'

'Oh, thank you, Papa!' Kensa cried, tearing off the paper. 'Oh, it's so pretty.'

They were Chinese paper fans, identically patterned save that mine was in shades of cream and yellow and brown, Kensa's pink and white.

'How charming!' I exclaimed, unfolding mine to examine the flowing lines of birds and flowers. 'So delicate. And exactly the right colours to match my summer gowns.'

He smiled, and as Kensa stepped round the parlour, fanning herself vigorously in parody of a lady of fashion, he took me aback by saying softly, 'Am I forgiven for my ungracious behaviour earlier?'

I felt myself colour. 'Daniel . . . Surely it is I who should
. . . I did not mean to snap.'

'No, do not be embarrassed. The fault is entirely mine.
You were right to speak out. I must have seemed bearish
and ungrateful, and this to the one person I should not wish
to offend.' He touched my wrist. And I wanted, suddenly,
to catch hold of his hand, hold it tight, feel his fingers warm
and strong grasping mine, wiping away the memory of a
different – unwanted – touch. But his gesture was light,
fleeting, gone before I could believe I might have the power
to alter it. Gone before I could submit myself to another
foolish impulse which might have spoiled the moment, when
Daniel was doing his best to restore the accustomed tranquillity and respect of our relationship.

'Shall we start over again and pretend you have just
arrived?' he said.

I smiled. 'We may, indeed.'

'Then I shall ask you properly how you are, and how you
have spent your afternoon and what you would like to see
and do during your stay in Plymouth, which I do most
sincerely hope will be a long and pleasant one.'

So the tone was set and we were at ease again with each
other. Mrs Venables bustled in with the tea tray and over
finely cut sandwiches and the lightest of sponge cakes we
cheerfully planned how we would make the most of the days
ahead.

It was only after Kensa had gone to bed that night that I
could properly discuss with Daniel all that had happened at
Kildower in the two weeks when he had been in Plymouth.
The subject of Conan Trewithen had already been raised by
Kensa when we were taking a gentle stroll on the Hoe in the
balmy evening air. With one hand in Daniel's and a parasol

in the other as protection against the low rays of the sun, she had been giving him a giggly account of the frogs in the kitchen to which I was only half-listening. My eyes were on the Sound and the snail trails of small boats drifting across water as flat and smooth as tightly stretched blue-green silk in the evening calm, my mind distracted by dreamy thoughts of how I should depict the scene on paper and whether I should be able to purchase a supply of my favourite textured De Wint.

'Papa, this strange man, Mr Trewithen, spoke to us and said he was my uncle. Mama said he was telling the truth, but that you would tell me more of him.'

I jolted out of my dream.

'Mama wrote and told me of the encounter,' Daniel said carefully.

'But if he really is my uncle, why haven't I seen him before?'

'Because that happens sometimes in families. People fall out . . . become estranged.'

'Did you fall out with him then? Why did you, Papa?'

'It was a long time ago, sweetheart.'

'But you must remember.'

'Yes, I remember, but it is something I do not wish to speak about. All I shall say is this. He is a bad man who was cruel to his sister, your real mama. He was also a thief who was punished by being sent abroad for many years. That is why you have not seen him before and why I have told you nothing about him. I did not expect ever to see him again in St Bridellan and I hope he will not stay long. But while he is here it seems quite likely he will try to strike up an acquaintance with you again. If you do chance upon him when you are out with Mama, you must not speak to him or listen to him. Do you understand?'

'But, Papa . . .'

'Do you understand, Kensa?'

'But why?'

'Kensa! I am waiting!'

His severe tone brought her up short. She blinked up at him in surprise. I saw her mouth open as though to argue, then hurriedly close again as he continued to frown at her, waiting for her answer.

'Yes, Papa,' she said meekly.

'Good. Now I shall not refer to the matter again and I do not expect you do so either. Is that clear?'

'Yes, Papa.' This time she did not hesitate. But I could see she was still puzzled at his unaccustomed harshness and, as any child would be, made even more curious by the subject being forbidden. It was still in her mind when she was on the verge of sleep that night.

I laid down *Robinson Crusoe* when her eyelids began to droop and as I leaned across to straighten the sheet and kiss her goodnight she muttered crossly, 'Chloe has lots of aunts and uncles and cousins. I haven't got any at all. It's not fair. I think Papa is unkind not to let me have just one uncle.'

I smothered a smile. 'We cannot have everything we want in this life, my love,' I said gently. 'And you are blessed in so many other ways, with a loving Papa and a fine house to live in.'

'How can *you* understand!'

'Very well, as it happens. You see, my papa died when I was a baby and my mother became estranged from both her family and my father's. She ran away from her home to London, then to the Continent, taking me with her. I was just a babe in arms, so I never had the good fortune to know any of my relations.'

She stared at me in surprise. Her tone was still cross.

'Why did your mama fall out with her family?'

'Oh, there were many problems, I think. But mostly it was because she wanted to be an artist. She felt she needed to go away in order to study and work and travel.' I drew the sheets around her shoulders. 'Grown-ups always have their reasons, Kensa. Perhaps they are not always good reasons, but when you are a child there is no other course but to accept them. You must accept your papa's decision and not question it, as I had to accept my mama's. When you are older and have more understanding, then will be the time to make your own judgement.'

She pondered this for a moment, then said, 'That man – my uncle Trewithen – what did Papa mean about him being cruel to my mama? What did he do?'

My hands hesitated on the sheets. That had struck me, too, as an odd word for Daniel to choose. Con Trewithen had run with a disreputable, thieving band and in doing so had been negligent and uncaring for his young sister's welfare. But cruel?

'I expect he meant that your uncle upset your mama when he got himself into trouble,' I said, tucking in the sheet and kissing her cheek. 'Now, settle down and do not worry your head about things that cannot be altered. You have had a long, busy day and you need your sleep.'

'Night,' she muttered. Then, her voice a little lost, a little plaintive, trailed after me in the dark. 'I think if my real mama was alive she would have liked me to be friends with my Uncle Trewithen.'

'Good night, Kensa,' I said firmly and closed the door.

When I returned to Daniel in the parlour I braced myself to tell him of Con Trewithen's visit to Kildower. I made as little of it as I could, but Daniel said grimly, when I had finished, 'I feared this. The man has no shame. We must warn Zack and Dagget to keep a sharp eye out for him in future. He must be turned away the moment he sets foot in the grounds.' He had been sitting comfortably at ease, but now he rose to his feet and paced angrily about the room. 'To harass you in this manner. It is insupportable. I will not have it. A cruel, evil man such as he.'

That word again. Cruel. But Daniel seemed to collect himself and with a murmured apology – 'Forgive me, Sophy, but the man has always had a dire effect on my temper' – he sat down again, frowning at his hands clenched in his lap. 'We shall speak no more of him.'

'But I should like to,' I said quietly. His head came up. I met his eyes without flinching. 'I realise the subject disquiets you, but I am not your daughter, Daniel, to be silenced with a command. I am your wife.'

'There is nothing more to be said.'

'I believe that there is.'

His glance hardened.

'The matter is closed.'

'I think it cannot be closed because this hatred you have for Meraud's brother goes far deeper than condemnation for his reckless way of living. Whatever it is that happened in the past affects you deeply now. I hate to see you upset, and if to speak of it would help ease your mind . . .'

He gave a short, bitter laugh.

'My dear Sophy, your sympathy does you credit, but there is nothing you or anyone else can do to right a terrible wrong.'

'Then something did happen.'

'Of course! But why should you think that to speak of it could possibly help destroy a memory?' He flung himself from the chair and began his pacing again, sending the candle flames fluttering so that his shadow leaped and twisted against the wall. His voice was strained with the effort to control his anger. 'It is best you remain innocent of such depravity.'

'Daniel, you forget,' I said softly. 'You forget that my upbringing was scarcely conventional. Life was cheap and the living hard in the back streets of Rome and Florence and Paris. My playmates were often gutter brats, the children of petty thieves, beggars, pimps, prostitutes. My own mother's lifestyle – her radical free-talking friends, her lovers – set no example of conformity. I heard things, and saw things of which a gently reared woman might remain ignorant all her life.' He stood half-turned from me, staring down into the empty grate, one hand on the mantelshelf, every line of his body declaring the tension in his mind that I longed to ease. I stood up and went to him. I rested my hand lightly on his sleeve, feeling the tightly clenched muscle beneath the cloth. 'I am not a daintily raised parlour miss. I do not need to be sheltered from disagreeable facts lest I fall into a swoon. I am your partner, your friend, Daniel. Will you not let me share your trouble and perhaps help to bring you some comfort?'

A jangling of harness and the thud of hooves as a horse passed by in the dark street outside. Then silence. Daniel turned his head slowly to look at me. His eyes looked more green than blue in the candlelight, darkly brilliant against the shadows that carved his face into the sculptured frozen beauty of a Greek statue.

We stood motionless. And as we stood there the thought came to me with perfect clarity, and completely without volition, that I should always remember this moment. When I was an old, old woman I should remember standing here in this plain little parlour with my hand on my husband's sleeve, looking into his eyes. Drowning in their sea-coloured depths. I should hear the tired horse passing the window, the whisper of our breathing, the steady thump of blood coursing strongly through my veins. And though I wore the toothless, bent and withered frame of great age, I should once more feel myself young and vigorous and vibrant with life and hope.

'Sophy,' he said on a sigh. 'Sophy, I . . .' He shook his head, as though to clear it and, wordlessly, like a man who gives in to a compulsion that overrides his reason, he drew me into his arms and held me close. So we stood, I scarcely daring to breath for fear of breaking the fragility of this different, unexpected mood that suddenly enwrapped us. Then, before he released me with a sigh, he rested his cheek on my hair while he told me, without anger but in so desolate and bewildered a voice that it near broke my heart, that the child that Meraud had been carrying when she married him, the child she had lost soon after the wedding, had been that of her brother, Conan.

I was alone. The wood was very dark and I could hear Kensa and Daniel calling my name, but their voices were fading and I could not raise my own voice above a whisper. Then I was standing by St Bride's Well in the moonlight and Rob the Magician threw a rose into the water and said, 'The goddess is there, in the pool. Can you see her?' And her face looked up at me through the water, beautiful and ageless, her hair flowing like green weed in the current. Then she was gone and the glade was dark and I heard the drag of sodden skirts, the squelch of watersoaked flesh over the grass and a bubbling choking voice began to laugh . . .

Oh, God. I shot up in bed, my hands over my ears to cut out the sound of Meraud's drowned laughter. I opened my eyes to the faint glimmer of moonlight through the curtains.

The black wisps of nightmare slid away and I let myself sink back to the pillow.

But my mind still churned. Daniel's revelations had only served to tangle the web of contradictions. And in the middle of this web, like a pale, ghostly spider, was Meraud Penhale. The only one who could have known the truth. But that truth had been swept into the Lynher and drowned, as she had drowned.

Conan Trewithen's face swam into my consciousness. In a way, I could have wished that I was the swooning sort who shocked easily and who had no opinions beyond those of the male who dominated her existence, be it father or husband. I should then have been able to accept Conan Trewithen's guilt without question. But I could have sworn that he was sincere in his belief that Meraud was carrying Daniel's child, though I had not been able to bring myself to say this to Daniel, for fear of distressing him even further. For Daniel was completely convinced, unshakeably so, that the child was the result of incest. And if neither of them was lying, that pointed to Meraud as the culprit. But why?

I tried to find a cooler place on the pillow. The only thing that Daniel and his erstwhile brother-in-law agreed on was in seeing Meraud as frail and helpless, in need of protection. And themselves as protectors. Only the Captain, who stood apart and regarded her with clearer eyes than those blinded with love, saw an inner strength and determination underlying her apparent frailty, and was wary of the duplicity he sensed colouring her actions and motives.

The more I tried to see the sense in all this the less sense it made. I gave up in the end. There was only one certain fact in the whole business: Daniel and Con Trewithen were sworn enemies because of what had happened and emnity between two such strong and determined characters, both believing themselves in the right, was a recipe for trouble. Which thought did nothing whatsoever to restore me to the arms of Somnus.

After the restless, broken night I was glad to see the dawn. By the time Daniel stirred, I was up, dressed and sitting by the window writing long-overdue letters to Mama and Sir Richard with the curtain drawn back an inch to let in a crack of that particularly pellucid light which seems peculiar to places by the sea.

'How industrious you look,' he said sleepily.

'It is the most beautiful morning. It is a pity you must spend it fastened away in the brewery.'

'Then perhaps I shall not incarcerate myself for the whole day!' He threw back the sheets and stretched vigorously. 'I will go in merely to hand the reins over to my chief clerk and then I am yours to command. Tell me what you would like to do and if it is in my power to grant it, I shall.'

'A trip to Timbuktu? Or the East Indies? Or shall we just explore Plymouth town?'

'I think Plymouth might well be far enough for one day,' he said solemnly.

We smiled at each other and I felt my spirits lighten. It was evident that he had put aside the sombre mood that had encompassed him last evening. Indeed, when he fetched in the brass can of hot water that Mrs Venables had left outside the door, he said, quietly, 'That unpleasant business I spoke of yesterday ... I shall not refer to it again.' He poured water into the bowl, then picked up his razor and stropped it vigorously. 'I would not wish anything to mar your visit.' He set the razor down on the washstand, picked up his shaving brush and mug and worked up a head of lather, all the time concentrating rather more than was warranted on these routine tasks. 'You see, it means a great deal to me to

351

have you and Kensa here. I had not quite realised how much I had come to value ... rely on ... the intervals I spend with you at Kildower for refreshment until I was forced by circumstance to forgo my last visit. To have you both here now is an unexpected blessing. And if there is anything at all that I may do to make your stay more comfortable or more interesting, then pray let me know at once.' He cleared his throat, a touch of hoarseness having come into his voice, seemed about to speak again but thought better of it and began instead briskly to brush lather on to his chin.

My hand had stilled above the paper as he spoke, his hesitant manner affecting me strongly because I knew all too well how difficult it was to express feelings which one experienced deeply. Too late I saw the blob of ink slide from the pen and form a large blot that threatened to drop from the paper on to my skirt. I hastily mopped at it, my, 'That is kind, Daniel. Thank you,' sounding distracted in consequence rather than full of the warmth and appreciation that I had intended. When all was in order again I glanced up, thinking to make amends, but immediately, as though embarrassed by speaking so emotionally or perhaps believing he had embarrassed me, he took the conversation off on a different tack and, by the time we had planned a rough itinerary for the day's sightseeing, the moment was lost.

But the pleasant feeling of contentment which his words had engendered added an even happier bloom to my day at least and promised well for the rest of our visit.

Both of us were a little cautious about proposing too vigorous a schedule for fear of overtiring Kensa and that first day I found myself watching her closely for signs of the dreaded rash or the unnatural pallor that would herald a bout of sickness or lassitude. But thankfully she survived without ill effect a drive to various vantage points about the town so that we might gain an overall view of Plymouth and in the afternoon a walk around the more fashionable thoroughfares. She was beginning to drag her feet a little by the time we took what promised to be our regular evening stroll over the rough ground of the Hoe, but it was merely healthy exhaustion after a full day. She was asleep before I had finished reading to her that night, a sound and solid sleep untroubled by the nightmares or restlessness that broke her rest so often at Kildower, and awoke lively on Sunday morning so we all three went to the morning service at St Andrew's Church instead of leaving her to rest in the care of Mrs Venables.

'It is a great contrast to St Bride's,' I murmured as the organ thundered out the final voluntary and we gathered ourselves to make our exit with the crowd milling past the impressive three-decker pulpit that dominated the centre aisle. 'How modern it all is, and such a large congregation.'

'Foulston's renovations have certainly brought a new airiness and order that were lacking before,' Daniel said. 'And the old pew rental system was a thorough disgrace. But I must confess that I had a fondness for the overcrowded clutter of the old interior, neglected though it was. I was particularly sad when the ancient screen was pulled down and sold, though it is true a great many more people can now be accommodated with the extra gallery space. Ah, good morning, to you, Roderick. You have not met my wife and daughter.'

The differences between St Andrew's and St Bride's went far deeper than mere architecture. No suspicious looks and guarded greetings here. People went out of their way to acknowledge Daniel with pleased surprise and warmth. It was clear that he had a wide circle of acquaintances. I was introduced to several members of the Scientific & Literary

Dining Club to which Daniel belonged, including the chief clerk of the brewery, a Mr Rudge, and his wife. He a tall, thin, cadaverous man, she a wiry, chatty little person, who walked with us through the churchyard before we parted to go our different ways.

'The ladies in church wore lovely dresses and bonnets,' Kensa breathed reverently as we strolled homewards through the Sunday-quiet streets. She seemed a little over-awed at being part of so fashionable a throng.

'Ah, but I was proud to be with the two most charming and beautifully dressed ladies among the congregation,' Daniel said gallantly.

'Did you think so, Papa?' Kensa turned her head to catch her reflection in a haberdasher's window. 'You don't find this style a little *passé*?'

Daniel smothered a chuckle with difficulty. Kensa had learned the word only yesterday and it looked well to becoming a popular fixture in her repertoire.

'Not at all,' he managed. 'Very up to the minute, I would say.'

'*A la mode*, Papa,' Kensa corrected him, twirling her pink-frilled parasol airily.

'Of course,' he said. 'Why, I believe the two of you will set the Plymouth fashion scene by the ears.'

I smiled at his nonsense, but I was glad I had given my wedding gown its first airing since our wedding day. I had been doubtful about packing it but had decided that dress would be a good deal more formal in the town than in the country and I had wished, for Daniel's sake, to make a good impression. It had certainly compared well to the other gowns at church and since I had removed a few of the more excessive frills, I felt it suited me a great deal better than previously. The pearl necklace Daniel had given me complemented the excellent quality of the rich cream silk Mama had insisted upon and I had noticed Daniel's proud and approving glance upon me several times during the morning.

I had worn my pearls and my silver brooch often, but I had not yet had the occasion to wear my beautiful topaz necklace, nor could I foresee any occasion when I might wear it at Kildower. Which was a shame. Perhaps thinking of it lying unused in its velvet box prompted me into mentioning the possibility to Daniel of entertaining some of his friends and their wives to supper one evening.

'But that is a wonderful idea!' He halted so suddenly that I almost lost my balance. 'Sophy, I should like that above anything! I have been kindly invited to the homes of my friends on many occasions, but in my bachelor state I have shied away from returning their hospitality other than taking the gentlemen to some chophouse or inn for dinner, but Nutmeg Street . . .' He frowned, his enthusiasm fading. 'Do you suppose we could manage there? It is not very grand. If it were Kildower, now . . .'

I laughed. 'I was not planning a rout with a hundred guests, Daniel, which I am sure Kildower could encompass with no trouble at all. No, it would not be in the least formal – a buffet supper, cards, music, perhaps.'

'Music? But we have no instrument.'

'A harp or some such might be hired, I am sure. Do any of your friends have musical talents? If not we might engage a musician. We should need more china, of course, and table linen. I have told you before the linen is a disgrace, and I have not yet completed embroidering the new napkins. Perhaps a few more chairs . . . a card table or two. How many should you like to invite?'

We decided after a great deal of discussion during the

rest of the day that six couples, including Mr and Mrs Rudge, should be invited for next Saturday evening. This was a convenient number to be accommodated at once in the parlour without too much crushing. It would be a sit-down supper at nine o'clock, which might just be managed if the dining table was extended, that to be cleared and set aside and a pair of card tables set up for those who preferred whist or cribbage to music and conversation when the eating was done.

We were so carried away by our plans that I had finished writing out the invitations and was carefully folding them before Daniel looked up from his newspaper and said doubtfully. 'Of course, Sophy, it might be that we should have to change the arrangements, if Kensa became ill.'

'Kensa?' That brought me up short. 'To be honest, Daniel, the thought had not occurred to me.' I held a lighted spill to the finger of wax, dropped a blob on to the last invitation and sealed down the fold. 'I suppose we must bear the possibility in mind, though so far she has shown no ill effects from the removal to Plymouth.'

He nodded thoughtfully, then said, 'It may be fancy on my part, but there seems to be a difference about her. She has more energy, a liveliness . . .'

'Certainly her appetite is improving. Did you notice how she tucked into Mrs Venables' excellent squab pie at dinner? It may be that she is beginning to grow out of all these troublesome complaints. Children often do.'

'I should dearly like to think so, though it would not do to be over-optimistic and thereby allow her to overstretch herself.'

'My opinion is that with delicate children such as Kensa it is important not to allow them to brood upon their illnesses but to keep their minds occupied with other interests. When

Kensa is absorbed in something – playing with her friends or listening to a story or even trying to remember a list of French words – she has no time to worry about the minor aches and pains to which she seems distressingly prone. I cannot help but believe that keeping her mind occupied with pleasant diversions is bound to have a beneficial effect on her whole system.'

'And you think mixing with the Miles children may help this process?'

'I do.' I paused, then said carefully, feeling that the subject might be usefully broached, 'Jess does not approve, of course. Her devotion to Kensa is laudable, but I feel her protectiveness is a trifle restricting, especially now that Kensa is no longer an infant but a growing girl who needs encouragement to spread her wings a little.'

Daniel shook his head, smiling. 'My dear, if you had nursed Kensa devotedly through years of illness – everything from the croup which nearly took her from us when she was no more than eighteen months of age, through every childhood ailment and all the distressing bouts that you have already seen a little of – you would not be so quick to reproach Jess for her careful guardianship.' He shook out his newspaper. 'Have patience, Sophy. I am sure, if and when your theories are proved, she will be the first to offer her support.'

'I hope so,' I said.

But I was not in the slightest convinced.

It was a busy week that followed. Now that I was to entertain for the first time as a married woman, I determined to do my very best to make it as lively and interesting an evening as I could. Mrs Venables was in her element, brushing aside any hint that it might be too much work. 'Oh, Mrs Penhale, 'twill be a tonic to look out all my old receipts. If 'tis to be a cold supper, I always think you can't go wrong with a nice boiled tongue and maybe two or three roast spring chickens and the same of dressed lobsters. And for puddings – well, perhaps you'd like to think about a strawberry cream and a charlotte. And if I find I need an extra pair of hands on the night, if 'tis agreeable, I can always call on one of my sister's girls.'

'Will I be able to stay up for this supper?' Kensa demanded to know and looked ready to fall into a sulk when I said that it would be much too late for her.

'But you shall have a taste of everything beforehand to make sure it is all perfect – even a glass of wine if Papa allows it. And you may certainly wear your best dress and stay up to greet the guests,' I said cheerfully. 'In fact I should like that very much, because I shall be very nervous and it will be a great reassurance to me to have you there looking so pretty that all eyes will be upon you and nobody will notice that I am quivering like one of Mrs Venables' blancmanges would do if it was left out in a gale.'

So I coaxed a reluctant giggle out of her instead of a pout and made a point of drawing her into the discussions when Daniel took us to the warehouses to choose the extra furniture and the china, glass and table linen we should need. I was expecting her to lose interest quickly in such a mundane domestic activity, but she proved surprisingly keen to investigate everything and air her very decided opinions. Daniel only laughed when she unerringly chose the most expensive items.

'She has her father's eye for quality,' he said approvingly when I, still nervous of reckless expense, might have made a more modest selection. 'Now, is there anything here you think suitable for Kildower? Please do say, Sophy, while we are here.'

'Then those Chinese vases. A pair of them,' I said, recklessly entering into the spirit of the game. 'The largest size. Anything less would be lost in the hall. And I noticed some rather elegant lidded Worcester vases earlier – white with a delicate decoration of flowers and birds. Ah, there they are. I am sure those would brighten up the parlour.'

There was a guilty thrill to all this expenditure. And a thrill of a different sort when I found a shop that sold the art materials. It was a joy to be able to order exactly what I pleased, from an easel down to sticks of charcoal, and I took extra pleasure in seeing the light in the shopman's eye when I told him where the goods might be delivered and the account sent.

'Mr Penhale? Mr Penhale the brewer? Oh, of course, madam. It will be attended to straight away, and pray be assured of my instant attention to any further orders you may care to make.'

Daniel's stock ran high in Plymouth. I found that very pleasing. And perhaps it was that knowledge that caused me to think that there was a more relaxed air to him here than in Kildower. He might work long and often irregular hours and be tired in consequence, but he was a man absorbed with a business he enjoyed and was respected by his peers and those he employed. That was clearly evident when Kensa and I paid a visit to the brewery. He had been surprised and hesitant when I made the suggestion.

'Are you sure, Sophy? You will not be bored? Well, perhaps a peep into the brewery before we drive out to Stonehouse.'

'Goodness me, Daniel, I do not wish merely to peep! I am interested in understanding the whole process. And I believe it would do Kensa no harm at all to know the nature of the trade that keeps her in pretty frocks and dolls and the many other luxuries you shower upon her.'

There was one other visit I had determined to make before the week was out, but one that I viewed with a great deal more trepidation. Daniel had discovered the whereabouts of Sinclair & Son, Hatters, in Stonehouse.

'It seems that the family settled there from Plympton,' Daniel told me. 'It is in a respectable street near the Marine Barracks. All I have been able to discover is that the business is now run by the son, assisted by his mother, Mr Sinclair senior having died some three years since. Unfortunately my enquiries have revealed that nothing is known of any daughter, Sophy. No young girl removed with them to Stonehouse and there is no knowledge of any married daughter living elsewhere. So I fear we must conclude that if she was sent away hurriedly to the country during an outbreak of scarlet fever . . . well, perhaps she did not escape the contagion.' His voice died away on a note of regret.

'Yes. I see.' I felt an unexpected wash of sadness. Although I had thought myself distanced from this unknown sister and had never quite been able to decide whether I should take the last fateful step to approaching her adoptive family, the moment I suspected that it might be too late and my sister long in her grave I knew that I was deeply disappointed. 'Poor Juliana.'

'Of course, we could not know for certain unless we speak directly to those most involved.'

'Then I believe that is what I shall try to do, Daniel, though I hesitate to write. A letter seems so formal and stark.'

'Then I shall accompany you to Stonehouse at the first opportunity. Would it help if we made the purchase of a new hat for me the pretext of our visit?'

'Oh, Daniel, it would indeed.' I was grateful for his understanding. 'If I am to acquaint Mrs Sinclair with my relationship to Juliana, I should prefer it to be face to face and as diplomatically as possible in order not to distress her too much. But if the moment is not opportune then we may take our leave and return at a more suitable time.'

In the event Daniel decided both visits might be made on the same day, so early on the appointed morning Kensa and I made the short walk to the brewery. The day was overcast, the air sticky and close and the hot breeze provided no refreshment. Straw and dust whirled about us in wild eddies as we crossed the busy loading yard led by a young lad who had been posted at the gate to watch for us. It was a relief when we entered the brewery building, made cool by the thickness of its stone walls.

'Master's to the malting floor,' the boy said, leading us nimbly up a flight of stairs and along a dark passageway and opening a door to a wide, dim floor spread with a deep gold carpet of barley grains. A line of men wielding shovels paused in their work of turning the grains to touch their foreheads respectfully. The moist, sharp aroma made Kensa wrinkle her nose. 'What a horrid smell, Papa,' she complained as Daniel came hurrying towards us. 'I hope we shan't have to stay in here long.'

'But it is not so unpleasant,' I said. 'In fact I find it quite agreeable.'

'It is the smell of barley that has been steeped and now begins to grow,' Daniel explained with a smile, scooping up a handful of grain to show us. 'See the little rootlets, Kensa. This grain has lain in here for three days and must stay one or two days more while the starch within the grain turns to sugar. When it is pronounced ready, it is dried in the kiln, which transforms it to the sweet crunchy malt from which we will brew our finest light ale.'

'And there is a stray cat got in!' she squealed. 'Behind you, Papa.'

He laughed. 'That is no stray cat, Kensa, but one of our most respected employees.' The lean black cat twined sinuously round Daniel's legs. He bent to tickle its ears. 'Smoky is the finest mouser in the business. He and his two friends fight a perpetual battle against the mousey hordes who see our good barley as so many dinners and suppers. Now, shall we go through to the kilns? Then I will take you over the brewery proper.'

It was a fascinating tour of Daniel's little empire, made the more so by his knowledge and expertise. 'From the first I intended we should aim for quality instead of the cheap and indifferent brew that had previously only been sold to lesser households and ale houses.' He smiled. 'The Captain prophesied doom when I sold other investments in order to extend the original building by the addition of the maltings and install the most up-to-date machinery. But I knew if I was to succeed in my aim I needed control of the barley from its moment of harvesting and every modern aid to improve the process.'

'It must be exceedingly satisfying to know that you have succeeded so well.'

'Beyond my expectations, if I am honest.' We had finally arrived at the counting house and stood at the window looking down at the bustle in the yard below. Kensa was perched on a tall stool, nibbling the peppermint toffee Mr Rudge had offered her, while the two junior clerks scratched away at their ledgers. 'Year by year Penhale's Light gains ground. We sell now to some of the finest families in Devonshire as well as many of the best run hostelries where it daily gains in popularity, even in places where cider has formerly held sway. Sales to the Baltic are growing apace and as profits increase so I intend to buy more inns to provide further outlets for our various brews. Not that I intend to overstretch myself. Steady progress has always been my motto. I do not have only myself to consider, but the livelihood of my workers. Though we do take on extra men in July and August when the barley harvest comes in, most are regular hands and several of the older men were with the brewery long before even the Captain took over. I relied on their experience to guide me when I was green to the trade. Now their sons and in a few cases their grandsons follow on. That loyalty and continuity is not something I take lightly.'

'It is noticeable, even to a visitor such as myself, that a pleasant atmosphere prevails here.'

'You think so?' He turned to me, pleased, then said as though he might be accused of immodesty, 'Well, brewing is a good steady trade that attracts a reliable, hardworking sort.'

'But it is more than that, is it not, Daniel? A fair master will always command respect. And on all sides I see evidence of your generosity, from the tailoring shop where the men's working clothes are made, to the provision of free schooling for the younger apprentices.'

He shrugged, a little embarrassed. 'If they are prepared to work long hours, and often at hard physical work, to increase my profits, then surely it is the least I can do.' He was quick to change the subject. 'Was that a rumble of thunder I heard? I fear we might be in for rain. I think we had better make haste if we are to get back to Nutmeg Street in the dry. I have ordered a carriage for eleven o'clock.'

I realised why he had not suggested we drive straight on to Stonehouse. Our clothes had inevitably acquired a considerable amount of dust and clinging barley barbs as we passed through the room where the grain was being riddled to remove impurities. And to compound my untidy appearance I had a black smear of coal dust along my sleeve, acquired when we had been passing down the stairs to view the stokehole of the kiln. A workman had been coming up the stairs and, instead of waiting on the small landing to allow us passage, had thrust roughly past us.

'Take care, man!' Daniel had cried, too late. The workman's sleeve caught mine and he immediately burst into a profusion of apologies when he saw the effect of his grimy elbow catching my sleeve, though I could not rid myself of the thought that his action had been deliberate, intended to annoy. But perhaps it was the effect of the sprinkling of coal dust on his face that caused the whites of his eyes to glitter strangely or the ugly scar running the length of his cheek that gave him a bad-tempered, crafty look.

'Clumsy oaf,' Daniel muttered when the man had sped on up the stairs. 'I think I made a mistake listening to his tale of woe when he came begging for work a few months since. A dying wife, he said, a sick child ... I am not so sure now that either exists. Oh, he labours well enough at a dirty job, but he has an unfortunate tendency to set himself at odds with his fellows, and I believe him to be a little careless with the truth at times. Well, he'd better watch his step, or I shall have to put him off. I'll not stand for my other men being put out by his mischievous tongue, nor my wife being jostled in an unmannerly fashion.'

'Oh, pray do nothing hasty on my account,' I said. 'It was probably an accident.'

It was the only sour note in the whole of the visit and I quite forgot it until I saw that I should now have to change my gown instead of merely brushing and freshening the one I was wearing.

The thunder, thankfully, seemed to have moved away and I thought the sky had lightened somewhat as we walked back to Nutmeg Street, where a surprise waited for Kensa. A large box stood in the middle of the parlour floor, and when she opened it her face went pink with delight.

'Oh, Papa,' she breathed. 'Oh, it is beautiful. Oh, thank you Papa!'

She flew across the floor and hugged him.

'It is your mama you must thank,' he said, laughing. 'She seemed to believe you might find some amusement in it.'

'Oh, yes! Oh, Mama. Thank you too.' The breathless kiss and hug she bestowed on me were completely artless and unaffected, if brief. She instantly ran back to examine the toy theatre. 'Oh, look, such lovely scenery. Much nicer than anything Chloe has, and the little figures are so real! Oh, Papa, do I have to go out with you now? I'd much rather stay here and play.'

'Of course,' he said. 'I do not think we shall be long in any case.'

I exchanged a warm glance with Daniel. I had not wished to involve Kensa in my visit to the Sinclairs but I had not thought she would be willing to be left behind. How tactfully he had managed it.

The carriage was at the door by the time I was hastily changed, my hands trembling a little as I pinned my silver brooch on to the collar of my coolest gown, a fine cream cotton sprigged with tiny gold and green flowers, and replaced my straw bonnet with its simple decoration of a knot of green ribbons. The looking glass told me I looked well enough. Not for the first time I was thankful that waists were once more where nature intended them to be. I had not the height nor the slenderness to carry off the high-waisted Empire style that had so suited Mama. I was much more comfortable, and indeed felt surprisingly graceful, in the new fashions, which suited my rounded bosom and hips and narrow waist, though I dare say the skill of Mama's dressmaker had much to do with it. Her clever seaming and darting probably contributed much to the overall pleasing effect, which was fashionable without being intimidatingly so. I felt I should make a good impression on the Sinclairs. It was a thought that boosted my confidence.

We alighted from the carriage in a street of pleasantly genteel houses many of which, Daniel told me, were occupied by sea captains both active and retired, and though normally I should have looked about with interest, I could not set my mind to anything but finding Sinclair & Son, Hatters.

It turned out to be a modest establishment set in a small cul-de-sac. A jangling bell announced our entry to the shop and a short, florid-faced man, presumably young Mr Sinclair, bustled forward, washing his hands with invisible soap and water at the prospect of a customer.

But it was a woman working at the high desk in the far corner who took my eye. A slight woman of perhaps five-and-fifty dressed in black with a widow's cap set on her wispy grey hair. As people so often do when they feel themselves to be watched, she looked up, her busy pen halting over the ledger, and smiled at me. She was not a pretty woman, nor possibly ever had been, but her smile was kind though it restored little vitality to a face that was careworn and faded in repose. It was her smile that impelled me forward and encouraged me into hurried speech before I lost my nerve entirely. 'Are you Mrs Sinclair? The senior Mrs Sinclair? Then may I have a word? My name is Sophy Penhale, Mrs Penhale. You will not know me but . . .' I glanced to where Daniel was trying on a silk hat with Mr

Sinclair hovering at his elbow and said, very quietly, 'It is a personal matter. May we speak in private?'

She looked puzzled, casting a hesitant look at her son's back, but moved from the desk and indicated that I should follow her through a curtained doorway into a dark passage and thence into a small parlour.

'And what is this personal matter?' she asked, turning to me as she closed the door.

Now that the moment was here, I groped to find the right words.

'It is difficult for me to speak on such a personal subject,' I began. 'It is about your daughter, Juliana.'

The effect on her was precisely what I had dreaded. Her hand flew to her throat and her face went a deathly ashen shade as though she might faint.

'Oh, Mrs Sinclair. The last thing I wished to do was distress you. Let me help you to a chair.' I sat beside her and chafed her icy hand. 'Where might I find smelling salts? Or a glass of water?'

'That will not be necessary,' she managed after a moment in a strained whisper. 'It was the shock. I have not heard her name spoken for so many years.' She took a deep, shuddering breath, the colour coming back into her face. 'What have you to do with Juliana?' The name came from her lips on a sigh. 'It has been so long. Why do you come to trouble me now?'

I swallowed. There seemed no way to soften what I must say. 'It is my understanding that you adopted Juliana when she was a baby.'

She drew in her breath sharply. 'How did you know that? It was never common knowledge outside the family.'

I reached into my reticule, carefully unwrapped the miniature and put it into her hand. She stared at it for a long, long moment then she raised her eyes and looked into mine.

'Who are you?' she asked in a whisper.

'I am told – my mother told me – that Juliana is my half-sister. Juliana was her first child, born out of wedlock.'

Mrs Sinclair closed her eyes. Tears seeped from under her lids and ran in helpless streaks down her cheeks. She lifted the miniature to her breast and held it there, rocking back and forth, as though it were the child itself she sought to soothe. 'All gone ... all gone. So many pictures.' Her voice was scarcely audible, the phrases broken, disjointed. 'She was so pretty. It was my pleasure to sketch and paint her, my dear daughter. *He* said it would make her vain, but that was not her nature. And afterwards ... afterwards ... he destroyed them all, everything that I had to remind me. Such innocence and beauty ... lost, betrayed.' Her eyes flicked suddenly wide and fearful. 'You must say nothing to my son. Nothing!'

I heard then what she had heard: the sound of footsteps approaching.

In a trice she had the miniature in her pocket, was brushing away the tears. 'Allow me to keep this, just for a short while. I beg you with all my heart, Mrs Penhale. Please. Oh, please. I will return it to you. I give you my most solemn promise.'

'But it belongs to my mama. It is all that we have.'

'Your address?'

'Nutmeg Street, number fifteen,' I said, torn between sympathy for her evident anguish and bewilderment at the turn of events. 'But ...'

'Trust me, Mrs Penhale. I will not betray your generosity.'

'Mother? What is this?' Mr Sinclair's florid face seemed even redder as he strutted belligerently into the parlour. 'Mr Penhale tells me his wife had some private business with you.'

'Ah, Tom.' She rose nervously to her feet. 'Mrs Penhale was just leaving.'

'What private business?' he demanded suspiciously. 'I cannot think of anything that might not be spoken of freely in my presence.'

'Of course not, Tom. Mrs Penhale took a momentary giddy turn due to the heat and I brought her into the cool of the parlour to recover.' She spoke in the meek, apologetic tone of a woman who has long since learned to bend humbly to male authority. 'It was just that Mrs Penhale recognised our name. She wondered if we were the same hatters who had an establishment in Totnes and when I said that we were she enquired about Juliana. Mrs Penhale was at school with her for a short time, you see.'

Mr Sinclair was equally set back by the mention of Juliana's name, but it was anger rather than anguish that darkened his face before he swiftly assumed an ingratiatingly bland expression. 'Ah, poor Juliana,' he said, his voice oily with what I was sure was false regret. 'It was tragic that she died so young.'

'I was just about to explain to Mrs Penhale that it was the fever that carried our dear girl off before her sixteenth birthday.'

'Yes, yes. It was all very dreadful,' he said. 'A great loss, of course, but I have cautioned you before about wallowing in these morbid thoughts, Mother. You know it will only lead to one of your hysterical turns, and I'm sure Mrs Penhale does not wish to be delayed any further when her husband is waiting to leave.'

I was ushered firmly out of the parlour and into the shop with no more chance to speak to Mrs Sinclair save than to bid her goodbye. Daniel, who appeared not to have found anything to suit him, took one look at my face then reached for my hand and drew it comfortingly into the crook of his arm. Mr Sinclair bowed us out and begged us to favour his establishment with a further visit. But his ingratiating smile was missing and the door seemed to close behind us with a bad-tempered crash.

I told Daniel what had happened as we walked to the street corner. He paused there, frowning. 'How very odd. Do you trust Mrs Sinclair to return the miniature? If not, I will go back and demand that she return it now.'

'No,' I said quickly. 'No. I hope – I believe – she is trustworthy. Besides, there is something else here, some family conflict. She is a sad woman, and I did not at all like her son. I am sure he would be the sort to make her life a misery if she gave him the least excuse.' I sighed. 'At least I know now that Juliana is dead. Now, I suppose, I must write and tell Mama.'

And Daniel gently closed his free hand over mine in silent sympathy as we walked towards the waiting carriage.

The storm broke in the night accompanied by rain so heavy that I feared for safety of the roof slates. I seemed to be the only one disturbed. I wakened at the first crack of thunder and rose to shut the window. Daniel merely turned restlessly as the noise invaded his dreams and when I hastened into Kensa's room I found her deep asleep. I sat by her bed until the storm rumbled away into the distance in case she woke frightened then crept back yawning to my own bed. But tired as I was sleep did not come instantly. Mrs Sinclair's anguished face haunted my mind, then I worried that I had allowed the miniature to leave my possession, for even if Mrs Sinclair was to be trusted, what about her son? Suppose the miniature fell into his hands? From what Mrs Sinclair had told me, all other likenesses of Juliana had been deliberately destroyed. It would be appalling if this last memento was lost too. But there again, had Mrs Sinclair told me the truth? My instinct had been to believe her, but how glibly she had invented the tale that I was a schoolfriend of Juliana's. Eventually I slept, though I was scarcely refreshed when I rose the following morning. And so much to do, for Daniel and I would tonight entertain our first guests. But at least the rush of activity left little time for brooding on anything else.

'I'm proper grateful the storm freshened the air,' Mrs Venables declared, her face flushed from her toils in the kitchen. 'That heat fair wears a body out, and 'tes a mortal trial to keep the milk from turnin' and the butter from running to grease in such sultry weather. Now, ma'am, if you'll steady that end of the table, I'll fit in the extra leaf. Then perhaps you'd give me your opinion on the arrangement of the furniture in the parlour.'

At six o'clock, when Daniel returned from the brewery, he looked about in amazement at the transformation that had taken place in his absence.

'Have I come to the right house?' he enquired, peering into the parlour, where the comfortable new chairs and sofa upholstered in a dusky rose cut-velvet were set in twos and threes about small tables bearing bowls of flowers.

'Of course you have, Papa,' Kensa said, giggling. She took his hand and tugged him across to the dining parlour. 'You must shut your eyes, because this is the biggest surprise.'

'Good heavens!' Daniel exclaimed when Kensa told him he could look. 'Such splendour! Why, we could ask the royal family to take supper here and feel no shame.'

The extended table near filled the room, and Kensa and I had spent an age arranging the white napery, sparkling crystal and silver, and setting a trail of ferns down the centre of the table interspersed with posies of yellow rosebuds. The effect was, as I had hoped, light and summery.

'I set out all those ferns, and made up the little posies,' Kensa said. 'It had to be done very carefully. See how they make a pretty waving pattern against the white cloth. It is exceedingly *à la mode*.'

'Oh, most certainly,' Daniel agreed gravely.

'Kensa has been exceptionally helpful,' I said. 'I should not have done nearly so well had she not been here.'

She had, at first, been very disdainful. 'Mrs Venables should do that,' she had said, turning away when I asked her to fetch out the silver from the sideboard.

'Mrs Venables has more than enough to do in the kitchen today.'

'If Papa were here he'd be very cross if he thought I was doing servant's work.'

'On the contrary,' I said carelessly as I counted out table napkins, 'I believe he would be delighted that you wished to learn how a table should be prepared when company is expected. It is an accomplishment that every genteel lady of taste acquires to her advantage. After all, how could she possibly hope to supervise her servants if she herself has not the first idea of etiquette and procedures?' I sighed and shook my head regretfully. 'But there . . . I was forgetting how young you are. It was perhaps unwise of me to broach the subject when such an *advanced* and *fashionable* accomplishment would be best left until you are older and more able to understand all the niceties.'

'I'm nearly ten!' She swung round, scowling. 'I'm perfectly old enough.'

'Well, if you really feel you might cope . . .'

She marched to the sideboard.

'Of course I shall. Show me!'

Which I was only too happy to do.

All that remained now was to put ourselves ready before our guests arrived. I helped Kensa to dress in her best white muslin before I attended to my own toilette. It was a very pretty dress, deeply frilled and scattered with pink satin bows and with a wide pink satin sash. But I had a struggle to fasten the twenty tiny buttons down the back of the bodice, and when I had finished weaving the matching pink ribbons into her pale, smooth hair I regarded her thoughtfully.

She had put on a little weight. I had not particularly noticed it before, but now it was plain to see that her more active life and consequently improved appetite were beginning to have an effect. She had not worn this dress since her father was last home at Kildower. Then, the bodice had hung a little loose on her; now it fitted snugly. And I could see a difference in her face. The delicate bone structure seemed less in evidence, as though a fine and subtle rounding had softened its fragile contours. There were other changes, too – the hint of colour in her cheeks, the slanting eyes bright with excitement, with health. I caught my breath, realising that though I had watched her carefully at first, these last few days I had quite begun to forget that this was a child liable to fall ill at the merest hint of stress. And I did not think it my imagination that she had also been less inclined to whine about her aches and pains.

I left her fluttering her fan and prinking at her reflection in the glass and went to make my own toilette, feeling decidedly cheered by the thought that perhaps she might, at last, be throwing off the tendency to succumb to the many troublesome ailments that had dogged her since childhood.

These happy thoughts seemed to set the tone for the whole evening. Everything went as smoothly as I could have wished, from the smiling arrival of our guests through to the last farewells long after midnight. Kensa was at her enchanting best, Mrs Venables' fine spread was consumed with gusto, the fiddler I had engaged turned up at exactly the moment when the guests rose from the table and were ready to be entertained for an hour and join in a chorus or two while their digestion recovered, the card players remained good humoured in defeat and conversation flowed with interesting diversity on topics ranging from the prospect of a steam omnibus being built in Plymouth, the forthcoming regatta and the regatta ball – both of which we were pressed most warmly to attend – to the failing health of the king.

When the door was finally closed on our last departing guest we sent a yawning Mrs Venables to her room and Daniel and I wandered back into the parlour. Some of the candles had already gone out and two more were guttering in their holders on the chiffonier in the far corner. Daniel went to pinch out the flames and I, feeling a weight of weariness beginning to replace the excited tension of the evening, gathered up the one candle remaining on the mantelshelf to light us to bed.

'Tired, my dear?' Daniel said.

'A contented tiredness.' I turned to smile at him. 'It went well, I think.'

He did not answer straight away. He merely looked at me as I stood in the little puddle of light cast by the solitary candle. My eyes were stinging with weariness and because he hesitated still in the shadowy far corner it was impossible to see his expression clearly. For a moment I thought he did not answer because he was in some way dissatisfied.

My smile faded. 'Daniel? Did something displease you?'

'Displease me?' His voice was husky. 'The devil it did, Sophy! Good grief, I am filled with admiration. It was splendid. No, it was just that I wished to say,' – he cleared his throat – 'wished to compliment you on your appearance. You look – looked – very well, this evening. Very well, indeed.'

'Thank you, Daniel,' I said a little shyly. I touched the topaz lying warm and heavy in the hollow of my throat. 'It is the necklace and earrings that you gave me that lift this yellow gown out of the ordinary.'

He moved his hand in an abrupt, dismissive gesture. 'The jewellery counts as nothing, Sophy. If it did, Mrs Roderick would have outsparkled you with her plethora of brooches and rings, which she certainly failed to do. No, you . . . well, let us say that I was proud, very proud of you tonight.' He began to move towards me, moved from shadow into the shimmering edge of the candlelight, only to stop again, frowning, as if there was some unwillingness, some odd reluctance cautioning him to keep a space between us. The wavering light flickered across his high cheekbones, the angle of his clenched jaw, the fall of his flax-pale hair against the gold of his skin.

And, looking at him I felt that I looked at a stranger, a man that I did not know as my husband, but someone I had just met and saw clearly for the very first time. Someone who would draw my fascinated eyes in any crowd, who would make other men look insignificant.

He raised his hand. 'Sophy . . . I . . .' I thought he meant to reach across the space that divided us and touch my face . . . my hair . . . and a sudden heat, like the burning heart of the candle flame itself, seemed to blaze right through me, taking my breath, taking every logical thought from my head. My whole being shuddered with the weakening intensity of an excitement so strong, so that I almost lost my grip on the candlestick as I swayed towards him, as though I were helpless as a blade of grass that leans to the powerful tug of the breeze.

'*Sophy?*'

Did he really breathe my name as though it came to his lips for the first time? Did he actually touch my cheek? No, it could not be, because even as I closed my eyes and thought it . . . imagined it . . . hoped for it . . . he was carefully taking the candle from me, saying in his usual kind and respectful tone, 'I am an inconsiderate oaf, keeping you here when you are half-asleep on your feet. Come, my dear, let us to bed.'

And when we were undressed and in bed, as I knew he would, out of that same respect and consideration for the lateness of the hour and my supposed exhaustion, he merely kissed my cheek before turning away to sleep, for which I suppose I should have been grateful.

But for the first time in my married life I understood that gratitude was a cold and lonely bedfellow. And with all my heart, with all the intensity of the newly awakened fires that scoured my body in the dark reaches of the night, I wished it could be different.

I awoke the next morning to the bewildering knowledge that everything was different, yet nothing was altered.

A Sunday in Plymouth. Not so much different from last Sunday, save that the day was cool and overcast, with a freshening breeze. We attended church and returned to a fine roast beef dinner. We spent the afternoon in our parlour, Daniel reading a newly purchased copy of Mr Southey's *Life of Nelson* while I wrote letters to Captain Penhale and Edith Miles, and Kensa played with her toy theatre, oblivious in her absorption to the amused smiles Daniel and I exchanged as we listened to her manipulating the tiny actors and speaking out their parts. Later we took our usual walk over the Hoe, returning windblown. Kensa went to bed, then Daniel read aloud to me the more interesting snippets from his book as he came to them and I sat at the window making a quick sketch of the view down the street until it grew too dark to see and Mrs Venables called us to supper.

An agreeable day, both of us a little subdued, perhaps, but nothing that might not be excused by the excitements of last evening and tiredness from the late night. And when the time came to retire, Daniel, being greatly fascinated by the great hero's history, said that he thought he might stay up a little longer to finish the chapter he had just begun over a second glass of brandy. He kissed my forehead before I went up. The lightest of touches, his lips cool and firm against my skin. A dutiful husband's kiss, no different from any other he had bestowed upon me. I then went quietly upstairs, glanced in to see that all was well with Kensa, and prepared myself for bed.

So the day ended much as every other day had since I had rejoined Daniel in Plymouth save that tonight, in my nightgown, with my bare feet chilling on the polished boards, I stood in front of the glass and gazed for a long time at my reflection, not out of vanity but out of despair. The same young woman that Daniel had taken to be his partner and friend, the mother to his child, the mistress of his house, looked back at me. Daniel had seen me from the first as someone admirably suited to that position. Someone quiet, competent, sensible. Someone so ordinary, so *dull*, with her undistinguished features and unfashionable rosy-cheeked colouring and straight brown hair, that there could be no possibility of any unfortunate emotional entanglement to complicate a perfectly straightforward agreement. *I do not ask or expect that we should fall in love with each other,*

Miss Beardmore. I have known the agony and the rapture of that relentless passion. I would not wish to know it again. His words came back to haunt me now. And Mama's, weaving a mocking counterpoint in my mind. *You are a fool not to comprehend the trap that opens up before you.* But the trap was perhaps not quite the one that Mama had envisaged. Nor I.

I shivered. Love was the trap. Love for a man, who could never love me because his passion, his desire, was for another woman, someone I could not challenge or think to outwit even if I had the means ... someone made more perfect, more desirable because she lived now only in his mind, haunting his memory. A frail, beautiful, unassailable ghost. And the love that burned within me, that yearned for recognition, for expression, must forever be contained, withheld. For I knew that to give Daniel the slightest hint that my feelings towards him were changed would expose me to the full weight of his disapproval and disappointment, would cause him to turn from me with disgust. He wanted nothing more from me than quiet affection and by giving him that I earned his respect.

Respect! God in heaven, it was not respect or affection I wanted now. I crossed my arms and hugged them tight to my ribs where a great hollow of longing and pain was formed. It was ... It was ... Oh, God, I could not bear to think of it.

I ran across the room and flung myself into bed. Cowering down beneath the sheets, shuddering as though an ague had taken me. It could not be. It could not be. I must not torture myself. I did not want to love him like this, in this uncontrollable, weakening way. I would not give in to it! I must fight against it. I had so much to be thankful for, too much to lose by silly, histrionic behaviour. Oh, but my blood, my bones, ached and yearned for that which I could not have, and the only pitiful release was in the tears that soaked my pillow before, at last, I slept.

It seemed that I had not been asleep five minutes when I was brought rudely awake by a hammering on the front door. Daniel was already out of bed, pulling on his dressing gown. He tore from the room to answer the summons, returning almost immediately to fling on his clothes.

'The brewery,' he snapped out grimly. 'Fire has broken out. It was discovered early, thank God, and we have our own water engine, but anything might happen. It is something I have always dreaded.'

He did not need to tell me of the hazards. I had seen them for myself. Despite constant sweeping, dust and debris from the dried barley seeped everywhere in the maltings, clinging to walls and wooden beams, collecting in drifts in dark corners. It needed but one careless spark from a lamp . . . a candle.

'And this wind . . .'

'It has begun to rain,' he said. 'At least that is in our favour.'

'Take care, Daniel,' I called, shivering behind him in the hall as he threw the front door open and a blast of wind-driven drizzle flapped at my nightgown. I do not think he heard me. He ran out, pulling on his coat, and I closed the door.

I had half a mind to get dressed and follow him rather than wait helplessly here for news, but turned to see Kensa halfway down the stairs and Mrs Venables on the landing above her, a shawl over her nightgown, her iron grey hair hanging in two thin braids around her alarmed face.

'What was that noise? Where is Papa gone?' Kensa wailed.

379

I swallowed down my own fear and managed what I hoped was a reassuring smile.

'There is a little trouble at the brewery. A small fire, nothing for you to worry about. It will soon be put out.' I walked up to her and put my arm around her shoulders. 'Come back to bed, my love. You will catch cold, else. There is nothing we can do.'

Mrs Venables, hastening down, said, 'I always thinks a nice glass of warm milk is powerful soothing at troubling times. Shall I heat some for Miss Kensa? 'Twon't take but a minute to stir up the kitchen fire.' Her tone was blessedly matter of fact but I saw how the candle trembled in her hand and the distress in her eyes. She was as aware as I of the implications of a fire at the brewery.

'I think a glass for each of us, Mrs Venables,' I said. 'And fetch up Master's brandy bottle, if you please.'

So the three of us sat in Kensa's room, sipping hot milk laced with Daniel's brandy until Kensa snuggled back into bed and quickly fell asleep. Then Mrs Venables and I sat quietly talking until, with the first glimmer of dawn, Daniel returned.

He was grey with fatigue and covered with grime and soot, but grimly triumphant.

'We confined it to the malt store where the fire started. We lost every bushel – if it was not burnt, it was ruined by the water – but that is nothing compared to what might have been.' He winced as he tried to remove his coat.

'You are hurt,' I said quietly. 'Here, let me help you.'

His shirtsleeves were scorched ribbons and his hands and forearms were patched with livid wheals and blisters. Mrs Venables fetched a bowl of freshly drawn water and some clean cloths and I gently bathed his burns and bound them up while he told me how all the brewery men living round about had rushed in to help. 'It was quickly out, thank heavens, due to the alertness of the men who had come in at midnight to turn the barley on the malting floor. They spied the culprit and raised the alarm.'

'Culprit?'

'Aye. That bastard Wilks, the fellow who nearly knocked you down on the stairs. He was seen sneaking out of the store. But he was too quick for them – he was gone before they realised what was happening.'

'But why?'

'God knows. Some grudge, I suppose. Against me, though I cannot think what, or someone who works at the brewery. All I know is that if I could lay my hands on him I would gladly wring his evil neck. And it strikes me to wonder if he was responsible for some of the other mysterious troubles we have suffered lately. They have only begun recently, since he was taken on, in point of fact. Well, we shall see if he can be tracked down in the morning and brought to justice, though I have the feeling he will have some well-hidden rat hole to lurk in until he feels safely forgotten about.'

Daniel was too restless to sleep for long, in too much pain from his burnt hands, I think, though he would not admit it. He was up and about again in a couple of hours, cursing as his bandages made him clumsy with buttons, and was off to the brewery again, anxious to assess the damage by daylight.

The clearing up and restoration of the malt store and the problems inherent upon the loss of the malt consumed all his time and energy in the next few days and the drizzly weather added to a sense of anticlimax after the sunshine and pleasant days we had enjoyed the previous week. Kensa and I were kept much indoors. I set her to writing a story that we might act out in her theatre and though the spelling and handwriting were atrocious, her imagination was untrammelled and the result – a tale of good fairies and wicked elves and a princess who got lost in a wild wood and was rescued by a brave little girl – was far better than I might have expected.

'Well done,' I said warmly when I had deciphered the ungainly scribbles. 'This will make a fine play. And do you know, I think it deserves a wider audience. If you like, we could put on a special performance for Papa, and I dare say Mrs Venables would enjoy it too.'

'Oh, yes.' She clapped her hands in excitement. 'I shall be the princess . . . and the brave little girl who rescues her . . . and the good fairy. I can do all those voices. You can be the wicked elf who casts a spell on the princess to make her lose her way, and you can make the sounds of the wild animals and the howling wind that makes the princess afraid.'

'You will have to make another copy of the story for me, then,' I said, suppressing a smile at being relegated to these minor and unattractive roles, 'I will write out the words you have spelt wrongly, and we shall need some new characters, shall we not? I could cut those out for you and you could colour them.'

I enjoyed myself in seeing Kensa absorbed and excited. The inward struggle to subdue the unwanted emotion I felt for Daniel might leave me confused and enervated and take some of the savour from the ordinary tasks which I had previously so much enjoyed, but at least I could take satisfaction from leading Kensa gently into ways in which learning did not seem too much of a chore.

The little performance went down very well. Our audience of two clapped vigorously when all was done and Daniel announced that as a reward he was proposing to take his talented family to the Theatre Royal the following evening.

'The real theatre, Papa?' Kensa gasped.

'Oh, I realise that it will compare unfavourably with the performance I have witnessed tonight,' he said solemnly, 'but I hope you will manage to tolerate its shortcomings.'

As we sat in our box the following night I think both Daniel and I were more taken with watching Kensa than in the melodrama unfolding on the stage. *The Brigand* was a lively piece, set on a mountain near Rome, abounding with action and colour enough wholly to enchant a child witnessing her first theatrical performance. She gasped and laughed and sighed with every twist of the improbable tale, completely lost in it, and clapped loud and long at the end. The theatre itself was magical to her. She stared around wonderingly at everything, from the domed ceiling painted with a fresco of zodiac emblems to the noisy, boisterous crowd in the pit below. And if the theatre seemed a little shabby and neglected to the adults and somewhat lacking in patrons in the expensive seats, to Kensa it was nothing short of fairyland.

'Do you think that Papa will allow us to go to the theatre again before we go back to Kildower?' she asked at breakfast the next morning as she spread strawberry preserve lavishly over her second slice of toast.

'We shall have to ask him when he returns,' I said, adding carefully, 'But that may be a treat that will have to be left to our next visit, so do not be disappointed if he cannot oblige us this time.'

As I spoke, I glanced warily at the letters which I had placed by Daniel's plate. He had gone into the brewery early and would be returning at any moment to take his breakfast and open his post. I had already opened the one letter addressed to me, a cheerful, newsy missive from Edith, enclosing a note from Chloe to Kensa. In the margins Rhoda had made tiny pen and ink drawings of flowers and a line to say that she was working hard every day and would have much to show me on my return. There was also a letter from Kildower for Daniel and I could not suppose that the message it contained would be anything to bring me joy. Even the sight of Jess's carefully formed hand, the black ink stark against the white paper, filled me with distrust and misgiving. I had thrust it to the bottom of the pile, feeling repulsed at the touch of it as though the paper itself harboured some evil essence that Jess had smoothed into its creamy folds.

Foolishness! Foolishness! Yet when Daniel came to open the letter, his face told me that I had not been so far wrong in believing it to contain unpleasant news.

'The Captain is not well,' he said in a troubled voice. 'Jess says it is a recurrence of his old gouty condition. He is confined to bed with a great deal of pain and fever.'

'Then I must return at once,' I said.

He frowned. 'Jess says there is no need to be alarmed, the Captain is in no danger, but naturally she feels we would wish to be told. Having seen him in these attacks before I think there would be no harm in delaying your departure until tomorrow. That will give me time to make arrangements for my absence at the brewery then I may accompany you and Kensa to Kildower. I can also send word for Dagget to meet us at Torpoint at noon.'

I felt a leap of irrepressible relief that we were not to be parted too abruptly. 'Perhaps you could plan to stay at Kildower for a few days,' I said. I kept my eyes on the coffee I was pouring and my voice cool and level. 'You are in need of a rest, Daniel. It has been an exceedingly tiring week for you, and do not deny that your hands are still painful, for I bandage them every morning and see they are still much inflamed.'

He hesitated, then said, 'There is still much to do. But I will see how things go today.'

And with that hope to cling to I set about the packing with rather more enthusiasm than I could have raised if Kensa and I were to have returned hastily and alone. My spirits still sank though whenever I thought of going back to the cold and gloomy embrace of that shadowy house with Jess Southcote waiting to spill her pernicious, restricting influence on Kensa. But at least Kensa had taken one step towards removing herself from babyish dependence on her nurse. '*If* I move out of the nursery,' had lately become, '*When* I move to my new bedchamber.' Her papa, needing little excuse for generosity, had enthusiastically taken up the idea. No half measures with Daniel. An elegant new cherrywood bed with a matching dressing table and washstand that Kensa had admired in one of the warehouses would be delivered well before her birthday, then an upholsterer would be engaged to advise on the rest of the furnishings. No doubt it would end up the prettiest child's bedchamber in the county, but I could have wished it was in a different house. An airy villa on, say, Townsend Hill where John Foulston, the architect, had built his own fine house and where we had driven one day with Daniel. Or any of the other breezy heights above Plymouth. But Kildower it was and Kildower it would have to be and it was no use pretending, or wishing, any other.

I was occupied with Kensa's packing when Mrs Venables came up to tell me that a Mrs Sinclair had called to see me.

I ran downstairs with some relief for I had quite made my mind up that, whether it was convenient or not, I must call upon her today to demand back my miniature. Knowing that Kensa was playing with her toy theatre in the parlour, I ushered Mrs Sinclair quickly into the dining parlour.

'Please do sit down,' I said, indicating one of the chairs placed against the wall and seating myself beside her.

She perched nervously on the very edge of the chair. Her appearance seemed even more colourless and drab than it had in the shop, the careworn lines in her face more deeply etched.

'Please do forgive me for not coming sooner, Mrs Penhale,' she whispered, as though she feared to be overheard. 'This is the first chance I have had. And I cannot stay more than a few moments or my son will wonder why my shopping has taken so long.' She indicated her laden basket. 'Even taking a cab I shall still be longer than usual. He does not care for me to linger away from the shop.' She delved into the pocket of her rusty black skirts, reverently drew out the miniature and unwrapped it from the scrap of felt with which she had protected it. 'See, it is quite unharmed.' She held it out to me. Her voice trembled with emotion. 'I thank you from the bottom of my heart, Mrs Penhale, that you allowed me this time of remembrance. It has been very precious to me. I feel . . . I feel, you see, that it has at last enabled me to mourn Juliana properly, when before even her name could not be mentioned from the shame, and all traces of her were destroyed as though she had never been our child.' Her voice trembled away, then burst out strongly. 'But I was not ashamed, not of Juliana. It was shame for my own cowardice. And for shame of him and what he did.' She suddenly grasped my hand, closing it tightly over the miniature. 'I know now that for Juliana's sake I must speak. You share her blood, Mrs Penhale. You have a right to the truth.'

'You said that she died of the fever . . .'

'That is the lie *he* decided upon when he sent her away. My worthy husband, who valued his trade and his respectability above everything else and was terrified of the scandal that might ensue if the truth came out. But now he has been cold in his grave these last three years and my conscience will not be denied any longer. No, Mrs Penhale, it was not the scarlet fever that Juliana died of. She was murdered by my husband's lusts, as surely as if he had put his hands around her throat and strangled her.' Her tight grip over my hands caused the frame of the miniature to dig into my fingers, the sharp discomfort serving to intensify my awareness of the almost mad glitter in her eyes. 'Juliana died among strangers, three days short of her sixteenth birthday after giving birth to my husband's child.'

I stared at her, bereft of words. Her grip slackened on my hands and the glitter in her eyes seemed less intense, as if she had already found some release in speaking of that which had been forbidden for so long. Then she began to talk again, softly, laying out Juliana's short life before me, laying out her own, in a sad quiet requiem for her daughter's soul.

'I understand now that my husband, Thomas, married me because I was my father's only child, though I believed it then to be out of love for me. My father was a hatter in Moretonhampstead, and Thomas began as an apprentice who, once out of his apprenticeship, sought to improve his station by marrying me with an eye to inheriting my father's business. He was very personable and I was swept away by his flattery and my father, who loved me dearly and wished for nothing more than to make me happy, had no qualms about giving his consent. So Thomas achieved his avaricious ends, and he moved into my father's house as his son-in-law.'

She let go of my hands and clasped her own loosely in her lap. Her eyes, unfocussed, stared into the past.

'The year after my son was born, I gave birth to a sickly daughter who lived for only a few days. I was so damaged by the difficult and prolonged birth that the doctor said I should never again be able to conceive and I was so inconsolable at the loss of my child that there was a danger that I might fall into a decline. It was the doctor who mentioned to my father about a Mrs Warrener who lived out on the moor who helped girls from good families who had got themselves into trouble. There was every likelihood, he said, that a healthy replacement for my lost daughter might be found which would restore my spirits if I could be persuaded to accept the child of another. So, within a week of losing my own daughter, I held Juliana in my arms and loved her from that moment. Indeed I never considered her anything other than my own flesh and blood, for I was able to feed her at my breast as I should have done the daughter I had lost. I sometimes had the fancy that the spirit of my dead child, who could never have been strong, had found its way into Juliana's body and that she looked at me through Juliana's laughing green eyes.'

'My mother's eyes,' I whispered.

Mrs Sinclair's face twisted with pain. 'I always felt such gratitude to the woman who had borne Juliana. That is why, when the good doctor asked on Mrs Warrener's behalf for some token of Juliana's well-being that could be passed to her mother, I gave him the portrait. That was much later. When she was growing bold and bonny and carefree, the apple of her grandfather's eye and much loved by everyone who knew her. But when she was eleven years old, everything changed.'

She rose to her feet, to pace restlessly back and forth. 'That was the year my father died. Believing, in his innocence, that my husband would continue to be affectionate, kind and generous, wanting to shelter me as he had always done, he left everything to my husband's control

. . . the house, its contents, the business, the money. There was not even an annuity or some other provision which might have given me a modicum of independence.' She gave a short bitter laugh. 'But even if there had been, I was probably too meek, too much the coward to have contemplated escape. I endured. As so many women have to endure. My husband reverted to his true nature from the moment he knew of his inheritance. He had no need, then, to pretend to be affectionate. He let free in private the ruthless, sneering bully that he had always kept under control, while cleverly maintaining an air of respectability to the outside world. And to make sure that his dominance was absolute he removed us from the place where I had friends, to live among strangers. First he set up business in the market town of Newton Abbot, where we lived in some style until he over-stretched himself and was forced to leave hurriedly, and then to Totnes and finally Plympton. And all the while Juliana was growing up, becoming a lovely girl. And then . . . and then . . .' She bowed her head, struggling for control, her shoulders shaking.

'Please, Mrs Sinclair,' I said gently, 'there is no need to distress yourself with these terrible details. It is enough that I know . . .'

'Is it? Is it?' She swung round, fierce and glittery-eyed once more. 'Do you not understand? I need to speak. I need to tell you that by my cowardly silence I allowed to continue that . . . that violation which ended with her disgrace and death. And make no mistake, I knew well enough what was happening. What wife could not? Night after night he left my bed and went to her. And I did nothing . . . nothing . . . save pull the covers round my ears so I could not hear her sobs, and pretend to be asleep. And I watched my lively, gentle daughter change to a cowed, unsmiling shadow and could do nothing to comfort her because that would have been an admission of . . . compliance. And how could I have explained that to Juliana without trying to protect her from my husband, whom I feared?'

She stood very still, challenging me with her eyes. Then that short, bitter laugh rang out again. 'Not a pretty confession, is it, Mrs Penhale? No wonder you are struck dumb. But I assure you there is nothing you could say that would in any way assuage my guilt, even if I wished it, which I do not. I welcome the suffering, you see. It is my penance. It makes me feel alive as I have not felt alive these many years.'

She began her restless pacing again.

'There is not much more to this sorry tale. The inevitable happened, though Juliana was too innocent to understand the reason for the absence of her courses. But Thomas knew well enough and taunted me with the evidence of her fertility while I was barren. She was some months gone before Thomas decided her pregnancy could no longer be hidden. So early one morning he told her to pack a bag and he took her away. He would not tell me where. I never saw her again. He informed me of her death and that was all. It was only after his death that I discovered the papers relating to Juliana and her daughter.'

'Her daughter!'

'He had taken Juliana into Cornwall and placed her in the care of a woman who I suppose was accustomed, like Mrs Warrener, to look after young women in Juliana's predicament. I do not know how they communicated. Perhaps through some third party, as had happened with our old doctor. There was a letter telling him of her death and a paper showing that my husband had deposited a large sum of money with this woman to pay for the upkeep of the child until she was old enough to be apprenticed to some suitable trade. The woman signed a paper to the effect that she would make no further claim on "Mr George Smith, gentleman, of Newton Abbot, for the maintenance of Adelaide Smith". So he covered his tracks and conveniently washed his hands of his own child.'

'But Adelaide . . . Where is she now?'

She shrugged. 'I only know where she was.' From her pocket she drew a crushed piece of paper. 'I am still a coward, you see, too much under the thumb of my son, who takes after his father in many ways, who was always jealous of Juliana and my love for her. Nor do I have anything to offer a child. I shall never go in search of Adelaide now.' She pressed the paper into my hand. 'I think you are a good woman, Mrs Penhale. You will know what to do if ever you should find her. And now I must take my leave.'

I closed the door after her and went slowly upstairs. In the silence of Kensa's room I looked at the paper in disbelief.

The name on it was Mrs Lugg. The address, Trebarth Farm, St Bridellan.

Chapter Eight

'Welcome back, sir, ma'am!' Martha's smile warmed the chill of Kildower's hall.

'Thank you, Martha,' I said, and looked beyond her to where Jess Southcote was gliding down the stairs holding her white hands out in welcome to Kensa.

'Jess!' Kensa danced past me and flung herself at her nurse. 'Oh, Jess. I've been to the theatre, the real, grown-up theatre, and to Papa's brewery ... and I've so many new things to show you.'

'Steady now, Miss Kensa!' Jess said in a low, laughing voice. 'You'll knock me off my feet. You forget, I've been a sad invalid these last weeks. But, then, perhaps you have had no thoughts to spare for your poor old nurse while you have been so busy enjoying yourself in Plymouth.'

'Of course I have, Jess!' Kensa cried. 'I thought of you every day and wished you were with me. But next time you'll be able to come. When we go to Plymouth for the regatta.'

'Hush, my pet. There's no need to over-excite yourself. You know it does you no good.'

'But I haven't been poorly once while I've been in Plymouth. And Jess, you should have seen the people there. The ladies *très, très à la mode* and so many fine soldiers in uniform.'

'How untidy your hair is! And what have you been doing

393

to get the hem of your dress so soiled? But never mind, your faithful Jess will soon have you looking spick-and-span. And what sort of funny talk is this you have brought back? Tray . . . what was it?'

'*A la mode*. It's French, Jess,' Kensa said proudly. 'I've learned a lot of words from Mama.'

'Oh, *French*. Well, if you ask me, those who feel the need to speak the language of Old Boney have poor memories. It makes me shudder just to think of all those hundreds of innocents who've had their head chopped off by our old enemies, not to mention our brave soldiers massacred at the great Battle of Waterloo. Now, come along, Miss Kensa. There's time for a nice lie-down before you come down to dinner.'

I listened to this exchange while Martha took Daniel's hat and Kitty rushed forward, beaming, to greet us and to help Dagget unload the baggage into the hall. I watched Jess's white hand fold securely over Kensa's. Watched her lead Kensa away. And it seemed that I could sense Kensa's eagerness diminishing, taking with it some of her energy, so that she already looked frailer, lighter as she walked upstairs beside the statuesque figure of her nurse.

Daniel and I hastened to see Captain Penhale before we did anything else. I fully expected to find him lying weak and feverish in bed, but he was sitting at his chart table, his bandaged foot on a stool. The gout had done nothing for his temper but he was scarcely the invalid I had envisaged. Pirate flung himself at us in an ecstasy of whining and leaping. The Captain cursed him loudly and, to our anxious enquiries, favoured us with an evil glare.

'There's naught which won't be cured by a few days on

spring water, hard tack and a good dose of black draught to clear out the bowels.'

'I am relieved to see you have made such a swift recovery,' I said.

'Recovery? I was never ill. Merely discommoded by the devil jabbing his pitchfork into my great toe, which made walking a torture.' His eyes narrowed in suspicion. 'Don't tell me you felt obliged to return on my behalf! Who's been blabbing, eh? Rattle me bones, I can guess. That damn-fool interfering Southcote woman! Forever creeping around where she's no business to be wanting to plague a man with her potions and ointments. Told her straight, as a loblolly boy I'd sooner have the stable-lad than an upstart female who fancies herself the be-all and end-all on the subject.'

'Then you are a disagreeable, ungrateful old man. Jess was only trying to help you,' Daniel said. 'And she was perfectly in order to let us know you were not well.'

'Pah! Too fond of the sound of her own voice, that one.' His tone softened a little. 'In any case, you look more of a subject for her attentions. What's amiss with your hands, then?'

Daniel explained to him about the fire and I scratched Pirate's ears and thought of Jess's message. One might be charitable and grant that she had written out of altruism. Or one could make a more cynical assessment. Jess had wanted Kensa back here, back where she belonged, with her nurse, not miles away in Plymouth with her interfering nuisance of a stepmother who might be filling her head with all sorts of unsuitable ideas. The Captain's attack of gout, mild though it was, had given her a convenient excuse to make sure that we made a swift return to Kildower.

'Seeing that you are back,' the Captain was saying, 'if you want to make yourselves useful you can take that excuse for a dog for his walks until I've a dependable foot again. He needs the rumbustiousness exercised out of him.' His bellow of a guffaw rang out. 'I made the same offer to my lady Southcote. That got rid of her faster than a dose of rotten pork through a tender belly, for she's as little love for Pirate as he has for her. Now take yourselves off, I've my log to attend to. And I shall expect you well before the end of the afternoon watch else the beast will drive me mad with mithering to go out.'

So after dinner, wrapping ourselves up against the damp wind, Daniel, Kensa and I walked down to the creek and back with Pirate. I had insisted that Kensa should accompany us, though she wailed that she hated Pirate, who was too rough and would knock her over.

'You said you hated cats because they scratched you, yet you got on well enough with Mrs Venables' Ginger,' I reminded her. The big cat, a sleepy, lazy creature, had often wandered in to be stroked and petted. There was not a malicious bone in its over-fed body and Kensa, after an initial fright when it wove itself, purring, round her legs in greeting one evening after we returned from our walk on the Hoe, had grown accustomed to it by the end of our stay. Enough to allow it to curl up on one occasion on her lap. 'Pirate only means to be friendly when he bounces round like that and if you keep between me and Papa we shall be able to protect you if he gets excessively eager. But I dare say once we are on our walk he will be more interested in searching out rabbits than bothering you.'

I accompanied Kensa to the nursery to get her outdoor things in order to forestall the inevitable objections Jess would make.

'If I may make so bold, Mrs Penhale,' she began, 'Miss Kensa has had a long, tiring day of travel. Would it be wise for her to go for an exhausting walk?'

I looked at her as though taken by surprise. 'You are not very observant are you, Jess?'

'I'm sorry, ma'am, I don't . . .'

'Had you not noticed how well Miss Kensa is looking? She has gained a little weight and she has colour in her cheeks. It is my opinion that this is entirely due to regular exercise in the fresh air which in turn has helped considerably with her appetite. A walk will do her no harm at all, I assure you.'

'Ah, yes, ma'am, I can see you might be deceived into thinking so,' Jess's smile was regretful. 'But I should warn you that Miss Kensa's looks can sometimes be deceptive. She has had good spells like this before, but so often they prove the herald of a sudden decline into ill health.'

'I shall take the responsibility for that,' I said sharply. 'Kensa, put on your strong boots, for the walk may be muddy after the rain, and you will need your cape, for the wind is chilly.'

Jess made to follow Kensa into the night nursery, but I called her back.

'Miss Kensa is perfectly capable of putting on her own coat and boots,' I said. 'You must realise, Jess, that you do her no favours by babying her. It is important that she learns to be more independent. I must insist that in future you encourage her to wash and dress herself. Your role should only be to supervise and encourage her, as I have been doing, not to set her back into lazy ways by well-meant but quite unnecessary cosseting.'

Jess's mouth tightened. She lowered her lids over her dark eyes and bowed her head stiffly.

'As you wish, Mrs Penhale,' she said after a pause that managed to be narrowly short of impertinent. 'If you think that is best.'

Then she raised her lids and looked at me and there was, for an instant, something in her expression so dreadful that it stiffened the hair at the back of my neck and set goose bumps cowering up my arms. It was something beyond mere hatred and resentment, and far more to be feared. For there was a terrible knowingness about it, a taunting, mocking triumph, as though she knew herself to be invincible and whatever I might say and do was of so little consequence that she could afford for the moment to pretend to submit herself to my puny authority.

I had never liked the woman, but I had never before been aware of the evil in her. Now it seemed to radiate from her in thick, rank waves. It took all my willpower not to step back from her. Then Kensa idled back into the room with her bonnet askew and her cape unfastened and Jess was Jess again, fussing over her charge, straightening and tugging and patting until Kensa's clothes were in order, bidding her to take care, and all the while smiling as though her only aim was to please.

That evil look haunted me for the rest of the day, but Jess was not yet finished with her unpleasant surprises. That night, as I walked upstairs to bed, leaving Daniel to finish his brandy and set the bolt on the front door, I heard a soft, silky rustle in the hall below. I glanced down. The shadows were deep and dark and the light from the few candles lighting the stairs did not reach into them. There was nothing to see. But someone was there, watching, waiting. Every nerve in my body signalled it. I continued up to the landing and turned into the corridor. Then I stood quietly until I heard soft footsteps cross the hall. When I stepped back to the landing, Jess was at the parlour door, tapping on it, opening it so that a shaft of light from within illuminated her hair lying loose at her back, the rich colour of the silky red dress. Then she went inside and the door closed behind her. She was alone with Daniel, exactly as she had been the first night I had come to Kildower, but this time I was not prepared to creep to bed and try to put it from my mind.

I ran swiftly down the stairs then, steeling myself for whatever I might witness, I opened the door and walked in.

My first thought was relief at the innocence of the scene that met my eyes. My second was blood-chilling anger that Jess Southcote should be here at all at this time of night, flaunting herself before my husband in her sluttish finery.

Daniel sat in his chair by the empty hearth, long legs crossed, brandy glass in his hand, just as I had left him a few moments since. Jess stood in the middle of the carpet, her fingers splayed in a dramatic gesture against her heavy bosom, obscene white against shiny dark crimson. She had been speaking in a low, urgent voice. She stopped abruptly the moment she heard the door open. Her head whipped round, her eyes narrowed with surprise and annoyance. Then her hands slid down to link themselves demurely at her waist.

'Why, Jess,' I said. 'I should have thought you in bed long since. Is there some problem? Is it Kensa?'

'No, Mrs Penhale, Kensa is peacefully asleep,' she said with a little flickering glance towards Daniel. 'No, it's . . . a small private matter I wished to speak to Mr Penhale about.'

'And are there not enough hours during the day when you might have sought a private interview with Mr Penhale?' I asked coolly.

Daniel sighed and put down his glass.

'Jess did not wish to cause you any alarm, Sophy. She thought it best to ask my opinion first before she brought a certain matter to your attention.' To my chagrin he favoured Jess with a tolerant smile. 'For so many years, you see, I have relied on Jess to report to me on domestic affairs, good

and bad, whenever I have returned to Kildower, so that I
might give her advice or deal personally with any problems
that have arisen in my absence.'

'I see,' I said. I closed the door, swept past Jess without
a glance and settled myself on the sofa. 'So it is a case of
old habits dying hard, is it, Jess? Well, that is understandable,
I suppose. It must be a little difficult for you to adjust yourself
to a new order when you have been set in your ways for so
long. Yet forgive me for saying so, but I cannot think it the
act of a thoughtful servant to disturb either mistress or master
at this time of night with what you have declared to be a
small matter.' Now I looked at her directly, allowing my
glance to range disapprovingly over her loose hair, her shiny
gown. 'So, Jess. What is this urgent business that will not
wait until morning?'

She hesitated, then said, 'Mrs Penhale, I was worried to
speak earlier for fear I might be overheard. The servants are
all now in bed. You see, I do not wish to cause unnecessary
trouble or gossip.' As an excuse it seemed highly dubious,
but I could not fault her manner, which had become
submissive and humble, her shoulders bowed as with a
weight of worry, her voice edged with exactly the right
amount of pained regret that I should think ill of her. As a
performance it ranked on a par with any we had seen at the
Theatre Royal. 'It is a difficult thing to speak of. I have too
trusting a nature I know, and I don't wish to point a finger
at any particular person, but I'm deeply upset at the loss of
something very dear to me.' She broke off, evidently too
moved to go on, raising one hand to cover her eyes so that
we could not see that they were perfectly dry.

'Jess, Jess, you must not upset yourself,' Daniel said
gently. 'Perhaps you have just mislaid it.'

'I have looked everywhere, sir,' Jess said on a strangled

sob. 'Besides, I know where I left it and now it has gone.'

I could not for a moment distinguish with whom I was more angry, Jess for her dramatics or Daniel for being fooled by them.

'What is it that is lost?' I asked coldly. 'And where did you come to lose it?'

Jess has lost a brooch,' Daniel said, frowning at me as though in rebuke for my sharpness.

'A jet brooch,' Jess managed to say tremulously. 'Containing a lock of my dear dead mother's hair. It has disappeared from the place where I keep it in my room. I know it was there when I left for my cousin's where I had my accident because I saw it – I thought to wear it then changed my mind. When I returned it was gone.'

'It could not have gone unless someone took it. Let us not mince words. Do you mean you believe it to have been stolen?'

She lifted her shoulders in a helpless shrug. 'What else am I to think? There would have been the opportunity, with so much upheaval and disturbance in the nursery in my absence.'

'In the night nursery and day nursery only, which I may say were badly in need of a thorough turn out and spring clean. Your room was not touched, Jess, save by Miss Kensa and myself when we looked out one or two of your things to take to you at Trebarth. Do you perhaps believe we might have taken your brooch?'

'Of course not, ma'am! But if the maids were un-supervised . . . Then there were several days when you were unfortunately absent before my return. Well, the door was not locked – any one of them might have been tempted.'

'The maids go about the house unsupervised for a great deal of the time. Nothing has gone missing before.'

Too late I recognised the trap. She raised her head to look not at me but at Daniel.

'But there was that little incident of the food taken from the pantry, was there not, sir?' she said in tones of sweet reasonableness. 'The culprit was never discovered.'

Daniel's frown deepened.

'It was a minor matter, Daniel,' I said quickly.

'Nevertheless . . .'

'Thank you, Jess,' I said. 'You have stated your case clearly. You may go to bed now and I shall take the matter in hand tomorrow.'

Short of downright refusal, which would have thrown her into a bad light, there was nothing left to her but to retire from the arena gracefully. She made a slow, majestic curtsey. 'Thank you, Mrs Penhale . . . Mr Penhale.' Then she raised herself up and, with one final triumphant glance at me and a very different, lingering glance at Daniel she left the room.

'What is this about stolen food, Sophy?' Daniel asked when the door had closed behind Jess.

I motioned him to silence and moved quietly to the door. I flung it open. Quick as I was, Jess was swifter. If she had been leaning against the door panel, listening, as I suspected, she was too clever to be caught. She was a mere whisk of dark silk and soft heavy footsteps walking swiftly up the stairs, melting into the shadows on the landing.

'For God's sake, Sophy, what are you about?' Daniel slammed his glass on to the table at his side and sprang to his feet. 'The poor woman was distraught. What need was there to speak to her in that manner?'

I whipped round.

'Because she means mischief.'

'Balderdash!'

'Then why else should she come creeping to you at this hour with some trumped up tale of a missing brooch? – Just as she did the very first night I came here when she thought I was safely in bed. What was her excuse then?'

He stared at me blankly. 'She wanted to let me know that Con Trewithen was returned to Bridellan.' His face darkened with anger. 'And what is this about "trumped up tales"? You are accusing Jess of lying? Of listening at keyholes? That is ridiculous. I have never had any cause to doubt her word. She is the soul of honesty. And you have not answered my question. What stolen food? And why had you not told me of it?'

'Should I have written to you in hysterics because a custard tart was missing from the pantry?'

'You did not even mention it when I was home.'

'Because it was too unimportant! The work of a thieving stable cat! I had forgotten all about it until Jess spoke of it.'

Jess.

I went cold. She was sole instigator of this ugly squall of a quarrel. Daniel and I had played straight into her hands. Daniel because he could see no further than the image of devotion, of willingness, of kindness she had always taken care to present to him. Myself because I had looked too deeply into her nature and distrusted everything I saw there. And, who knows, perhaps it was Jess herself who fostered those two differing impressions, seeing advantage in it, seeing a way to drive a chasm between husband and wife, a way to retain the power over Kensa that she had begun to feel slipping from her grasp. Power over Kensa meant power over Kensa's father. And there, I was sure or it, lay the heart of the matter. The object of her desires. Daniel. The way she had boldly looked at him tonight only confirmed what instinct had warned me of the other time I had spied her, in her silky dress and with her hair tumbling down her back, gliding from the shadows to accost him like a whore flaunting her wares to a likely customer.

And he defended her! A spasm of jealousy seared me. I fought it down. That was not the way. I must stay cool, alert, wary. Besides, I had no way of knowing if Daniel had ever sought ease in her body. Probably not. There was a curious, blinkered innocence in his regard for her as though he was scarcely aware that she had dressed to tempt him. But what had happened in the past was of no importance. It was the here and now that mattered. The future. And what was to be done to guard against the wiles of a manipulative woman in whom my husband could see no wrong.

We were silent now, Daniel and I. His anger seemed to have leeched away, as mine had. There was nothing left but a cold emptiness that seemed to ring still with the echoes of our arguing voices. The stretch of carpet between us yawned like a void.

I took a deep, calming breath. 'We are both tired, Daniel. I think we should retire now and speak of this tomorrow, when we are more composed.'

'Indeed,' he said. And turned to snuff the candles.

Daniel's burned hands had provided him with a reason to avoid making love to me. But never, if I was awake, had he failed, burnt hands or not, to give me an affectionate kiss before he slept. Not tonight, though. Tonight he turned away from me without a word. But then, wary of rebuff, I made no move, spoke no word of reconciliation either. So there we lay, the two of us separated by pride and indignation as much as the width of the bed. And I believe it was a good while before either of us relaxed enough to sleep.

* * *

We did speak, politely but with a certain careful stiffness, about the missing brooch over breakfast the following morning. As though we both feared to speak a wrong word for fear of rousing wrath in the other. It felt very strange. I had thought that we neither of us were people who would squabble in such a way. Yet we had, and it frightened me to think how fragile the links that bound us together, how easily they might be shattered beyond repair.

So it was decided what must be done. We both agreed that the matter, of course, must be looked into. He said that he thought it proper that I, as mistress of the house, should interview the female servants once it had been established that the brooch was missing and not merely mislaid. It was unlikely that the outside staff could be involved but after he had visited the Captain to see what sort of a night he had passed he would have a quiet word with Zack, to gain his opinion. So we went our separate ways, and a thoroughly unpleasant morning it was.

I went up to the nursery first where I was not best pleased to find Kensa, still in her nightgown, sprawled on the floor with her toy theatre and the breakfast dishes littering the table. The evidence of Martha's and Nan's hours of scrubbing and polishing had vanished. The room was more cluttered and untidy than it had ever been, as if Jess had deliberately set out to flaunt the fact that this was her territory. A huge fire, totally unnecessary on a day when the midsummer sun was strong outside, cascaded new white ash to join the scattering of the previous days' ashes in the hearth and puffed heat into the cloying atmosphere.

I made no comment. Time enough later. The pressing matter was this wretched brooch. Jess was all meek smiles and willingness, as false a facade as my own pretence of cool attentiveness. She showed me her room, every drawer pulled out, all cupboard doors open, so that I might see how thorough she had been in her search. She showed me the space where the box containing the brooch had lain in a drawer stuffed with darned cotton gloves and handkerchiefs.

'It's the thought of the thief rummaging about among my things that's so nasty,' she said. She shook her head, the picture of offended virtue. 'And to think she may be living off the fat of the land under Kildower's roof. Such ingratitude! Such wickedness! I hope when you find out who it is that you'll not turn soft on her, Mrs Penhale. A good spell in gaol or transportation is too good a punishment for such a one.'

'You seem very certain that it is a woman.'

'What else should I think, Mrs Penhale?'

'That such speculation is best left until we have some proof.'

She favoured me with a pitying smile, then leaned towards me, lowering her voice confidentially. I caught the musky waft of her, a smell of some aromatic scent overlying the faint stale odour of her body, and I could see the white trace of the scars on her cheek.

'Would you grant me leave to speak plainly, Mrs Penhale? What I have to say may be helpful to you.'

'Very well,' I said, curious despite myself to gauge what mischief she was about now. I had no illusions that she meant any kindness.

'Out of a long experience of being responsible for the running of Kildower in the master's absence I have found that there are few from the poorest classes to be wholly trusted. Look at these young maids that Mr Penhale took in out of the kindness of his heart. All three rubbish from the gutters, and likely to slip back into bad ways given half a chance.'

'Really? I have found them perfectly biddable, and they have considerably improved in their work since Martha took them in hand.'

'Oh, I agree Martha seems a decent enough person, though I'd beg you to be watchful for a while longer yet. Sometimes maids will put on a good show until they feel themselves settled, then become . . . well, too free in their manners or dishonest or liable to make unsuitable friendships with men, if you take my meaning, ma'am.'

I did indeed. Her words were little drops of poison dripping in my ear. Under the pretence of being helpful she meant thoroughly to undermine my confidence in those around me.

'Good heavens, Jess,' I said lightly, 'I had not realised you were such a Job's comforter. You will have me believing next that old Zack is running a bordello in the stables and Mrs Dagget has stolen the silver spoons and plans to melt them down over the kitchen fire.'

Her expression darkened fractionally at my mocking tone, but quickly her rueful smile was back. 'Well, Mrs Penhale, you may laugh, but if I'm proved right don't say I didn't warn you.'

'I appreciate your concern, Jess,' I said, still keeping that light, amused note in my voice, 'but I have always preferred to base my judgement of other people on observation and experience rather than on hearsay.'

She bowed her head gracefully, but not before I had seen the flash of temper in her eyes.

'Of course, Mrs Penhale,' she said with studied meekness.

'Now, please see that Miss Kensa gets dressed. She may wear one of the new prints we bought in Plymouth. We shall be going out later this morning. And in future, Jess, Miss Kensa will come down to breakfast with her papa and me as

407

she has been doing in Plymouth. We shall expect her downstairs by eight o'clock each morning.'

I did not look to see how she took that change to her cosy routine, but I could not imagine it was anything but badly.

I had already told Mrs Dagget of the missing brooch when she came to see me on her regular morning visit to discuss the day's menus. She had been at first indignant, then worried.

''Tis not a nice thing to think that one of they might be light-fingered. Yet I can't bring myself to believe they'd touch anything so valuable.'

'There was the matter of the missing food from the pantry.'

'Oh, that.' She shook her head. 'No. I favoured in the end that 'twas one of they cheeky gardening boys, egging each other on for a wager. Besides, nothing's gone missing since and there's been opportunity enough. But I'll not say a word, Mrs Penhale, and when you put it to them, you'll judge the better who's telling the truth and who not.'

I hated to do it. They filed in and ranged themselves in front of me. Martha first, then Kitty, whose clumping footsteps had been considerably modified by the acquisition of brand new shoes, of which she was so proud that I believe she had shortened her skirts by an inch to show them off the better. The shoes were Martha's doing. 'I was driven to distraction, ma'am, by the girl's clatter, so I despatched her to the shoemaker to have a decent pair made.' Then came the two sisters, looking over-awed at being summoned so formally to the parlour.

'I have not sent for you because of any dissatisfaction with your work,' I began without preamble. 'Quite the contrary. You have wrought wonders, Martha, since you arrived, and I am greatly pleased by the progress shown by you younger maids. I shall hope this excellent work will continue. However, a somewhat distressing matter has come to my attention.'

I watched them carefully as I explained. Nan and Joan seemed to shrink together for support. A frown replaced the first start of shock on Martha's face. Kitty looked blank, her slow mind taking a moment to absorb the import of my announcement, then she burst out, 'Oh, poor Jess. 'Er'll be proper upset,' before Martha hushed her and said evenly, 'This means that we'm all under suspicion. Well, I for one am willing to swear my innocence on the Good Book, though I don't suppose for a minute that'll be enough to satisfy her that's made the complaint.' I noticed the touch of contempt in her voice. I was heartened by the knowledge that I was not the only one in Kildower with an antipathy towards Jess Southcote. 'I've nothing to hide, Mrs Penhale, nor can I think that Kitty or Nan or Joan would stoop so low. They'm honest, in my opinion, and I'd suggest you come upstairs this very minute and go through our rooms in order to make sure we're none of us hiding nothing. If you find aught there as shouldn't be, I reckon I've gone more'n fifty years without learning much of human nature.'

We trooped up to the attics and I reluctantly began the unhappy task. Joan and Nan shared one room, while Martha and Kitty had a small, narrow room each. All were plainly furnished with a bed, a washstand and a chest of drawers, the contents of which were quickly examined, and the hard flock mattresses on the bed lifted, at Martha's insistence, to ensure nothing had been hidden beneath. Out of courtesy and a reluctance to pry I allowed each of the maids to open the drawers to display their contents within while the others waited in the corridor outside. Martha's room was first, then that of the two sisters. By the time I reached Kitty's bedchamber I knew, with relief, that the task would be quick and easy, because none of the maids had much in the way of personal possessions. Kitty flung open the drawers with enthusiasm. 'Keeps my spare petticoat and drawers in 'ere, see, ma'am . . . an' this deep one at the bottom's for my bonnet and gloves an' the new ribbon I bought at the fair . . .' She broke off with a gasp as, tugging the drawer out to its full extent, she saw what had tumbled from the back to lie exposed among the pathetically sparse contents. 'Oh, ma'am . . . thass not mine!'

Had the situation not been so serious I should have laughed at the look of comical surprise on her round face. But I did not feel at all like laughing as I stared at the velvet-covered box, flown open from the sudden movement to reveal the dark gleam of jet, the coarse dullness of a strand of brown hair.

'The missing brooch.' I said softly.

'But it can't be!' she wailed. 'I never put it there! Honest to God, ma'am, I never.'

We reached for it at the same time, my hand closing tightly over Kitty's rough red one with its broken nails and chapped skin. A hand that was not cossetted and beautiful but showed the evidence of hard physical – willing – work. Unlike that other one, that supple, grasping, deceiving hand, the one that I could not have borne to touch me for all its smooth gracefulness.

In that moment I knew what I must do. It was wholly illogical when the evidence lay before me, the evidence that I was meant to believe, the evidence that would have driven Kitty from Kildower. Whether it was a case of my heart ruling my head or whether it was pure animal instinct, I could not tell. But I think I could not have made any other decision and remained comfortable with my conscience.

410

'Kitty, do you swear you did not take this from Jess's room?' I said in an urgent whisper.

'Oh, no, ma'am! No!' She could scarcely get the words out as the full horror of her predicament began to dawn on her. 'Oh, God. Oh, dear God,' she whimpered. 'What shall I do? I'm not a thief. I'm not!'

'Do nothing.' I smoothly slipped the box into my pocket, then took her by the shoulders and gave her a little shake. 'Kitty, look at me.' Her frightened eyes looked up piteously into mine. I could feel the shudders of distress running through her heavy frame. 'I believe you. But you must say nothing about this. This must remain a secret between you and me. Do you understand? Do you?'

Her round eyes were full of bewilderment. She managed to nod.

'I shall try to find out who put the brooch there, but if I am to do that I must have your word that you will say nothing to anyone. Not even to Mr Penhale or Mrs Dagget or Jess Southcote – *particularly* Jess Southcote. Nobody! Do you promise me that?'

'Yes, ma'am,' she whispered.

'This is our secret. Yours and mine. It will go badly for me as well as you if we are found out. Remember that if you are tempted to speak. Now I shall dismiss the others and you take a moment to tidy your things and compose yourself. When you have recovered from this shock, go back to your duties as if nothing has happened. You are innocent. I found nothing here. Keep saying that to yourself and put anything else from your mind.'

So I had the brooch, but how I should proceed from then on, I had no idea at all. In the end, I thought it might be best to leave the brooch temporarily 'lost'. I took it down to my peaceful little private room and locked it for the time being in the chest with my grandmother's letter and the mementoes of Juliana and left the smiling Mistress Hilary to guard over my guilty secret.

I told myself over and over again in the next few days that the means justified the ends. But it made having to lie to Daniel no easier and I was forced to remind myself that it was for a good reason. My inner conviction that Jess was responsible for putting the brooch in Kitty's room was strengthened when I told her that my search had revealed nothing. She was too clever, of course, to give herself away, but her mouth compressed to a tight line and she said, just a little too quickly, 'But did you search thoroughly, Mrs Penhale? All the little hidey-holes, the corners, the backs of the drawers?'

'There are few hiding places in those tiny rooms,' I said, 'and all were most properly investigated, which was very distressing for the maids. It is unpleasant to be made to feel guilty when you are innocent.'

'Innocent? I trust none of them! Especially that stupid girl, Kitty . . .' She broke off, making a visible effort to control her urgency. She even managed a pale, tight smile. 'This is a large house. It may be that the thief hid her booty somewhere else.'

'Or perhaps this thief is a figment of your imagination, Jess,' I said, frowning. 'After all, you did fall down the stairs and a blow to the head can have unfortunate effects. Lapses of memory are not unheard of in such cases.'

'There's nothing wrong with my memory,' she said through gritted teeth.

'You can hardly be the best judge of that,' I said with an air of surprise. 'I understand that persons so afflicted do not always realise that they have become forgetful! But you must not worry too much about it. We shall all try to keep a careful eye on you to make sure you do not overstretch yourself until we are quite sure you are properly recovered. And consider yourself fortunate, Jess,' I added tartly, 'that you have an indulgent master and mistress prepared to overlook the trouble you have put them to. It was very foolish to make wild accusations without being certain of your facts. Remember that in future if you are ever tempted to put a melodramatic interpretation on a perfectly innocent situation. Next time you may not be so lucky.'

'But I . . .' Her mouth hung open for a moment, then shut like a trap over what she had been about to say. Only the vicious expression smouldering in her eyes remained to reveal the frustration of one whose expectations had gone seriously awry.

Daniel and I continued to edge carefully around each other with excessive politeness whenever we were together, but it was frighteningly easy in a house the size of Kildower to find occupations that kept us apart. Sometimes I wondered if, had we still been in Nutmeg Street instead of Kildower with all its gloomy associations, its echoing spaces, we should quickly have become reconciled. But here the shadows seemed to foster brooding thoughts, jealous thoughts which constantly tormented me. It was unfair of Daniel to take Jess's part. Why was he so blind to her true nature? How could he not see that she was hateful?

My thoughts had drifted along these lines – it seemed to be inevitable whenever I was alone – before Mrs Dagget came into the parlour on Saturday morning to discuss the menu for the following day when the Miles family were to return with us after morning service and stay for dinner. It was a struggle for a moment to give her my full attention. I told myself, severely, that I must not give in to such futile brooding. It served no purpose. After all, I dare say Daniel entertained equally unhappy thoughts about my distrust of the woman who had been the one indoor servant to remain loyal all these years. The one he could always depend on when others came and went. Who, with her capacity for deception, had *ensured* that she became the only dependable one.

'Mrs Penhale? You have doubts about the sirloin of beef? Well, if you don't think . . .'

'No, no, Mrs Dagget, that sounds admirable. Forgive me, I was a little distracted. Now, what would you suggest for puddings, remembering that there will be five children of assorted ages as well as four adults.'

Exactly! I would wager a pound to a penny that Kitty was not the first maid to find herself the object of Jess Southcote's wicked attentions. Oh, there must have been servants who had left of their own accord, but how many had been helped on their way when they looked likely to prove too efficient or too settled or too worthy of Daniel's commendation?

I heard what Mrs Dagget said and I murmured agreement or shook my head at what I hoped were appropriate moments, but when she finally left I was still unaware of what the final choice had been. I paced to the window and stared out unseeingly over the rain-drenched gardens.

No wonder servants never stayed long at Kildower. Any that showed promise must have been as ruthlessly treated as Kitty, manipulated into some situation where Daniel could see how lazy this housemaid was or untrustworthy that cook. How she would have enjoyed pouring her false regrets, her hateful insinuations into his ear then standing back to watch the satisfactory results.

But why Kitty? Poor ungainly Kitty, who tried so hard to please, yet in no way could be termed efficient or influential. Why her? The answer came on the slow trickle of rain down the glass. Because she was the easiest target and because she was my personal maid and likely to stay faithful now her matrimonial hopes had been dashed. Through Kitty Jess could attack me, for I was the one who threatened Jess now. She had watched and waited to see how best to unsettle me and now she had made her first move. But that there would be others, I had no doubt.

It was only a matter of time.

The visit of the Miles family acted upon the house and upon those within it like a great healthy draught of fresh air. The giggles and chatter of five excited little girls were enough in themselves to set the adults at ease and Mr Miles waxed ecstatic over the carving on the mantelpiece in my private room.

'Most certainly Druidic in origin,' he declared as we sat at dinner. He helped himself absently to a further slice of roast beef. 'And like enough to the carving at the well for me to speculate on a definite connection. I dare say that the hare was the representation by the Druids of the original deity of the spring as worshipped by the local tribes. The Druids, you understand, were the priestly sect of the Celtae. The pagan legends speak constantly of their gods and goddesses taking the shape of animals and birds at will.'

'What sort of god d'you suppose Pirate would change into, Papa?' Chloe asked innocently.

'A very clumsy one,' Daniel said in an undertone, setting the girls off into further giggles. Pirate, who had been banished completely from the Captain's quarters, having trodden once too often on the gouty toe in an excess of high spirits, raised his head on hearing his name and flopped his tail enthusiastically against the floorboards. I had sternly ordered him to lie outside the open door and somewhat to my surprise he had so far made no attempt to creep into the dining chamber, but dutifully lay watching the maids come and go with the dishes. Perhaps there was something in him that might yet respond to training in obedience.

'Ah, but how I should like to have the power to look into the past to see what manner of temple stood here,' Mr Miles went on, too lost in contemplation even to notice the interruption. 'To be a witness of the ceremonies that were performed in the sacred oak groves, the awe-inspiring gloom which Tacitus describes as inspiring reverence and never to be approached but with the eye of contemplation. Of course, one gets a glimpse of the might of these ancient Druids in the great circles and lines of stone still left about the country. Dartmoor is particularly rich in these artifacts. I took a walking tour over those desolate heights in my youth and wherever I looked there was some object to study and record, from sacrificial altars to pillars that seemed to mark long-lost roads or ceremonial pathways across the trackless wastes of heather. Mrs Bray sadly tells me that a great deal has been lost in recent years through the people of the moor removing stone for their enclosures, or due to downright acts of barbarism by gangs of drunken youths deliberately smashing and ravaging these ancient monuments.' He shook his head sadly. 'This urge to destroy and despoil that which is irreplaceable seems to me almost as great an evil as the human sacrifice which the Druids practised.' He brightened. 'There is a very good account, which may interest you, of a sacrificial ceremony in . . .'

'Now, my dear,' Edith interrupted firmly, 'that is not at all a proper subject for the dinner table.'

'I do beg your pardon.' Mr Miles looked a little shame-faced. 'I'm afraid I have a tendency to be a little loquacious on the subject, but I find it so fascinating that history – our human history – lies all about us waiting for recognition by those with eyes to see. Why, we may be enjoying this excellent roast beef on the very spot where blood was spilt to placate the goddess of the spring.'

'Augustus!'

'Of course, of course.' He applied himself to mopping up his plate of rich gravy.

'Besides,' Edith went on firmly, glancing at the round-eyed children, 'Mrs Penhale and I have quite decided that the goddess of our spring is a very tranquil and peaceful deity. I am sure she would have abhorred any such nasty ceremony. Is that not so, Sophy?'

'Most certainly,' I said, and was glad – for the maids' sake as much as the children's – that Daniel then turned the conversation to more recent history by offering to lend Mr Miles his copy of Southey's *Life of Nelson*. Joan and Nan were both within earshot as they waited to clear the dirty dishes before bringing in the next course. Kildower was well enough set up with spectres without adding human sacrifices to the count of chanting nuns and a drowned wife. Nor was I, myself, too eager to dwell on Kildower's dark past. I had too many nights on my own in Daniel's absence when the settling creaks of old timbers could all too easily be interpreted as the slow drag of feet, and the howl of the wind seemed like the moan of unhappy voices. All the same, it was intriguing to think that the place in the house where I felt most comfortable and unthreatened was my little room, which held a dedication, if the vicar was correct, to the goddess of the spring. As though the carving – the stone itself – continued to exude the serene and peaceful atmosphere that characterised the little glade.

The puddings, I was relieved to see, were properly tempting, the lighter junkets and meringues balanced nicely with a substantial boiled gooseberry pudding and a currant tart. When we were replete, Edith and I left the men to their port and retired to the parlour to drink coffee and the children were given leave to amuse themselves as they would. They raced away up to the nursery, little Violet doing her best to keep up with the others on her chubby legs.

'I could swear Kensa has grown a full inch while you have been away,' Edith said, watching them go up the stairs. 'The stay in Plymouth seems to have suited her.'

'I believe it did.' I smiled. 'But I am afraid she is patronising Chloe most dreadfully with her tales of all that she has seen and done.'

'Chloe is well able to stand up for herself,' Edith said, laughing, as we went into the parlour, followed by Pirate, who flopped beside me and laid his head on my foot with a contented sigh. 'Did you hear her when Kensa told her about the magician? "Oh, we saw him too," she announced in the most blasé voice possible. "He came to the village and magicked an egg out of my ear as well as a marigold and took a real live dove out of Violet's pocket." Kensa was quite set down, poor child.'

'It will do her no harm,' I assured her. 'The rough and tumble of children's play is just what she needs.'

'I confess I was as bemused as the children by the man's sleight of hand.'

'Magic indeed!' I poured out the coffee, then said thoughtfully, 'But I am surprised the troupe bothered to make their way down to St Bridellan. There cannot have been much in the way of pickings for them here.'

'Oh, their performance was impromptu, a way of wresting

a few coppers out of the villagers while they waited for some of their womenfolk who were visiting St Bride's Well. There was sickness among them, you see – a woman, a weakly new-born infant . . . The troupe quickly moved on, but the woman is still here, poor wasted creature. She is encamped near the pool with her husband, the magician. I have asked them if I might help, but the magician guards his independence with fierce pride.'

'Do you suppose I could do anything for them?'

She shrugged. 'A little broth for the invalid was all that he would accept from me.'

'Then I shall take something of that nature and sound out the situation. Poor things. It is inclement weather to be living out of doors if one is healthy, but for a sick woman . . .'

'I suppose they are used to it, and they have a shelter of sorts, fashioned from leaves and branches. And at least they live where they wish to be, under the sun and the stars, not fastened in a poorhouse or some squalid corner of slum.' She gave a rueful sigh. 'So I tell myself to placate my conscience.' She brightened. 'But on a happier note, you will be pleased to hear that the attendance at Sunday school begins to improve. I should like to believe that it is the good example of the children from Trebarth that has wrought the change, but I fear it is the prospect of a penny for the first comer that has caused the increase in numbers. Nine this morning, no less. Though I was hard put to stop Liddy Binns pulling out the hair of a boy who claimed to be before her. I had to settle the matter by giving them a penny each. She is a fierce little thing, but bright. She can already write her name and is so eager to learn that she practises her letters by drawing them in the earth with a stick while she is about the farm, and she makes Sammy do the same.'

The picture of Liddy fighting for her penny made me

chuckle. But the mention of Trebarth brought to mind the private interview I must have with Mrs Lugg as soon as I could. I had looked at her in church this morning and wondered bitterly if she had acquired her fine satin dresses and nodding plumes from the profits of her lucrative trade in human misery. For I could not imagine that any poor girl forced by her condition to live out the time of her disgrace at Trebarth would be gently treated in Mrs Lugg's hard hands. Liddy's account of the 'madwoman' was still fresh in my mind, and the old servant's talk of 'others'. How easily, with a little knowledge, one might see the pattern. Girls brought out to the remote farm until their babies should be born . . . and God knows what agonies to be gone through at the parting with their infants. No wonder the 'madwoman' had flown at Jess, no wonder she had to be kept drugged and the woman – her mother? – in the coach had been so distressed to see her condition. I would wager that far from being mad she was no more than some poor girl driven to grief and violence by her pitiless treatment at Mrs Lugg's hands.

'So Mr Penhale is to return to Plymouth tomorrow?' Edith was saying.

I nodded and picked up the sketchbook Rhoda had brought to show me, saying extra brightly, for I hated the thought of Daniel leaving and must fill the aching void his absence would bring with sensible, absorbing activity. 'I shall expect Rhoda and Chloe at the usual time, if that is convenient to you.'

'If you are sure,' Edith said a little shyly. 'I feel it may be an imposition.'

'Nonsense! To teach – no, to *guide* someone so naturally talented as Rhoda is a joy.' I riffled through the pages of the sketchbook. 'I can already see how much she has taken to heart in so short a time. She will soon be outpacing her tutor. Besides,' I added softly, 'I have Rhoda to thank for giving me the occasion to take up drawing and painting again. I should not have had the courage otherwise.'

She looked at me in surprise. 'Courage? That is an odd word to choose. What was it you feared?'

I closed the sketchbook and smoothed my fingers over its board cover. 'I feared becoming obsessed,' I said slowly, 'becoming enslaved, as my mother has been, to a compulsion, to an ideal that can never be reached. I felt the pull of it once and I drew back – stopped painting altogether when I was eighteen – because I was afraid that once I surrendered I should be drawn into my mother's rootless, self-centred way of living.' I had already confided to Edith something of my upbringing. Now, aware of her sympathy and understanding, I ventured to say, 'But since I have started painting again after this long space, I feel the waste of the years when I did not so much as lift a paintbrush, and the urge to paint, to create, comes back as strong as ever now that I have begun. It is like being allowed to dip into a treasure chest that I had once thought locked and barred to me. Yet I worry still that it is not right for me to succumb to a temptation that might lead me into selfish ways. Oh dear, I am putting this badly and sounding foolish.'

'Not foolish at all,' Edith said with an odd, wry note in her voice. 'I understand you very well. It is the perpetual dilemma for a woman with an interest or a talent that pulls her strongly in one direction while the ties of love and duty tug her the opposite way. It takes strength of will to balance the two, but it can be done.'

'You think so?'

'I know so.' There was mischief in her smile. 'I will let you into a secret, if you promise me to let it go no further than Mr Penhale and beg him to be discreet. My husband is sensitive on the subject, believing it reflects badly on him and that we would be the subject of cruel gossip in the parish if it became generally known that I earn more than the living provides. Poor love. He cannot help it that he has no private income to sustain his family and that I did not bring even the merest smidgen of fortune to the marriage. No one would have raised an eyebrow had the vicar married an heiress and provided himself with comfortable independent means for the rest of his days.' She shook her head. 'I have never understood why inheriting a sum of money immediately grants a woman respectability while if she seeks to earn money from an occupation it is somehow deemed to be unseemly.'

'But what is it that you do?' I asked, intrigued.

Her brown eyes sparkled behind her owlish glasses. 'You may think that you are drinking coffee with the wife of the vicar of St Bride's, Sophy, but underneath this disguise lies my other persona. That of Mrs Eudora Phipps.'

'*The* Mrs Phipps? The author?'

'No less.' She put her finger to her lips. 'Bar Daisy, who is old enough to understand the need for discretion, the children do not know.'

'But how exciting!'

'More exciting than anyone would realise when my publisher is demanding another tale and the children have measles and there are parish duties to be undertaken and one is recovering from the last confinement or anticipating the next.' She laid her hand thoughtfully on her waist. 'Mind, the latter event can be a great spur. The prospect of another mouth to feed has a tendency to concentrate the mind powerfully on the creation of another story and causes one to make use of every moment that might be snatched from a busy day. As is the case at the moment.' Her mouth curved in a warm, secret smile. 'Come December there will be an addition to Mrs Eudora Phipps' published works as well as an increase in the Miles family, and this time I pray that it will be a boy, for though I am perfectly content with my dear girls and care only that the new baby will be healthy, Augustus feels sadly the lack of a son.'

From outside the door came the sound of male voices. She leaned forward and said quickly, 'So you see, Sophy, it might be managed. And what is more, I have the strong belief that these two aspects of my life complement each other in the most strengthening way. My children benefit from a mother whose mind is invigorated by excursions away from the routines of domesticity and my writing is certainly enriched by all that I observe daily in my children— their activities, their imaginings, their fears and hopes. After all,' she added in a laughing whisper as the door opened and our husbands strolled in, 'I write to entertain them as much as the wider audience and my stories grow up as they grow up. Who knows, perhaps one day I shall launch into the Gothic mysteries that are so popular among young women who love to have their blood chilled, or even some great work of adult literature that will make dear Augustus proud, at last, to be associated with the dreaded Mrs Phipps.'

Then she turned a smiling, innocent face to her husband, leaving me both astonished at her revelations and with a great deal to think about.

It was late afternoon when our visitors left. The house seemed very silent after they had gone but their visit had done a great deal to ease the tension between Daniel and myself. We were very much back on our old, easy footing and it was a cheerful threesome who took Pirate for a walk before supper. The drizzly rain had cleared though mist lay heavy over the hills and the sky was louring. We kept to the gravel paths, Kensa between us chattering so busily about the day's excitements that she quite forgot to squeal nervously whenever Pirate's lolloping bounds brought him perilously close. After Pirate had run off some of his energy, I coaxed him to walk sedately to heel for a spell.

'Do you know, I have never seen the beast so steady for so long,' Daniel said, watching him with amusement. 'He is evidently a dog who responds to a woman's touch.'

I laughed. 'A woman's wiles, more like.' I delved into my pocket and drew out a handful of Mrs Dagget's shortbread biscuits. 'He has a wonderful appetite for anything sweet, so when he is obedient I reward him with pieces of biscuit and praise him excessively. That way when I am forced to scold him it makes more impression on his doggy brain. I take no credit for the system. I saw its excellent results once when I was teaching the children of a contessa in Italy. The count had the most obedient, clever dogs I have ever come across, all trained by the same kind method. Animals, like children it would seem, respond the better when ruled by patience, kindness and firmness rather than by harsh attempts to beat them into submission. Oh, not that I was suggesting the Captain ... I mean, I never saw him lift a finger to Pirate even though he shouts ...'

'If patience is essential to training a dog, then I am the first to agree the Captain is lacking in that quality,' Daniel said amiably. 'His old dog was just as rumbustious even into ripe old age, though it was half the size of Pirate and therefore less likely to knock the legs from under you when it was in an enthusiastic mood.' He paused, narrowing his eyes. We had walked in a wide circle on the paths around the house and had fetched up near the main gates. A man was hurrying down the lane towards us from the direction of the village, waving his arms to catch our attention.

'Sir, sir,' he shouted. 'Vicar asked me to give you the news as I passed.'

'What news is this?'

'Just come from Plymouth, sir. 'Tes King George. He'm gone to his maker. Died in the early hours of yesterday, so 'tes said, and they ol' Duke of Clarence is king above us now.'

Daniel gave the man a shilling for his pains and he trotted off, bearing his doleful tidings in the direction of Trebarth.

'So that is the end of an era,' Daniel said as we walked back to the house. 'Four Georges in a row and no one alive to remember a king by any other name. It will be strange to have a William on the throne.'

'A more sober-living man than his late brother, I understand.'

'Aye, that is true. And he will be a popular king with the people of Plymouth. He has had a long association with the town, not least in recent years with his patronage of the regatta. Well, it seems to me that we cannot let the occasion go without some little ceremony to mark it. When we get in perhaps you would call all the servants into the parlour and I will go and persuade the Captain to join us.'

When everyone was assembled Daniel made his sombre announcement, followed by a kindly little speech in praise of the late king which caused Mrs Dagget to wipe her eyes on her apron, Nan and Joan to sniffle in sympathy and Jess Southcote to fix her damson-black eyes on Daniel's face with a look of reverent intensity. Then Daniel ceremoniously poured a tot of brandy for each of the men and a glass of Madeira for the women and gave Kensa the task of handing these round, which she did slowly and carefully, her face pink with the drama of it all. Then we raised our glasses to toast the health of our new king, William the Fourth, whose reign had now begun.

Our mood remained respectfully solemn that evening. As Daniel said, levity somehow did not seem proper and even Captain Penhale, who condescended to stay for supper, forebore to cast too many lurid oaths in the direction of his gouty foot and confined himself instead to accounts of deaths at sea, which he evidently felt more suited to the occasion. After one particularly gory tale of a cabin boy who had fallen overboard and been eaten one limb at a time by a shark in the South China Sea I was more than pleased to see Zack, who had come to help him back to his quarters.

The talk in the kitchen, I discovered later, had taken an equally morbid turn, Dagget and Zack joining the women round the table to add to the lugubrious tales. It was hardly surprising that all this melancholy conversation, the emotion roused by the unusual event, together with the effects of Madeira wine on systems unused to it combined to give the two young sisters nightmares. At least that was the excuse I made for them when Daniel, white-lipped with shock and anger, would have had them pack their bags and leave the house first thing in the morning.

Since Martha's arrival, she had seen to it in her motherly way that Joan and Nan retired to bed early. So at a little before nine, she sent them off. Shortly after that the Daggets left for their rooms by the stables and Zack went to attend the Captain. Kitty and Martha were last up, to clear the supper things and put all ready for morning, so the sisters had been in bed and fast asleep a good hour, by my reckoning, when Martha came into the parlour to see if there was anything else we needed before we retired.

All this I pieced together the following day, but then, as Martha began to snuff the candles and Daniel went to bolt the front door, there was no more thought in my head beyond relief that the memorable day had given Daniel and I the chance to become on comfortable terms once more. But a few moments later my complacency was shattered.

I had taken my candle and stood at the foot of the stairs, Pirate pressing hopefully against my skirts in case I relented and allowed him to go up with us instead of leaving him behind to sleep in the hall. Martha came out of the parlour, Daniel clanged home the bolt and I gave Pirate's ears a last scratch and was just about to order him to the old rug where he slept when I felt him tense under my hand, his floppy ears going forward, a soft warning growl rumbling in his throat.

'I'll bid you good night, sir, ma—' Martha began, then stopped as her candle flame like mine bent in a sudden draught of icy air and she was forced to shield it with her hand.

We all heard it then. The inky shadows reeled madly round us from the draught-blown candle flames as we stood, frozen out of all movement, listening to the faint, eldritch, unearthly shrieking far, far above us.

With a deep bark, Pirate flung himself from me and up the stairs, his claws scrabbling and scratching on the treads. Then we three were running after him, Daniel's long legs taking the stairs two at a time, Martha panting after us, crying, ''Tes up in the attics, whatever 'tes!' Pirate was a grey, flying streak along the gallery, then up the narrow stairs to the attic corridor where one dim candle burned in a sconce outside Martha's door and the shrieking resolved itself into two terrified voices wailing a duet of fear and distress.

427

I do not know quite what I expected – fire, flood, murder – when Pirate heaved himself against the door of the young maids' room and burst it wide with a crash as it hit the wall, but my candle lit only the sight of Joan and Nan clinging to each other in one of the beds, strands of straggly red hair plastered to their tear-streaked white faces.

'What on earth is the matter?' I cried, catching Pirate by the scruff of his neck before he could terrify the girls even further by leaping all over them, but they were too locked in hysteria to obey. It took Daniel's deep voice thundering sternly for them to stop and Martha rushing forward to shake sense into them before they hiccuped to silence.

'It was 'er!' Joan's voice was a hoarse thread of sound. 'We was fast asleep . . . An' I woke up and she was standin' over us . ... an' . . . an' 'er reached towards us . . . an' touched me . . .' She gave another hysterical shriek. ''Er touched me and 'er fingers was all bones and covered with seaweed. You could smell it, all wet and dripping . . . 'Twas 'er ghostie come out o' the river to haunt us.' Then on a great wail, ''Twas the one that drowned . . . Master's wife as drowned . . .'

Her voice died away and I heard Martha say briskly, 'Silly girls, 'tes naught but you were dreaming. Rousing the house like that! For shame! There's no such thing as ghosties and if you'd said your prayers like I learned you you'd not be dreaming of such nasty things.'

But it was at Daniel I looked, Daniel who stood, ashen-faced, carved from stone, staring blindly at the two girls shuddering in the bed. Daniel I ran after when he turned abruptly and brushed past me as though he did not know I was there, who thrust past Kitty standing gape-mouthed outside the door, past Jess Southcote, who came hastening up the corridor holding a silky grey robe tightly round her nightgown, crying. 'What's happened? Is someone hurt?', her hair loose about her shoulders, fluttering out one white hand as though to detain him but ignored as though he did not even hear or see her.

That same hand caught at my sleeve. 'Mrs Penhale? Has there been some accident?'

'No . . . no! Let me pass.'

And I fancy she might have clung to me a little longer, keeping me from following Daniel, save that Pirate growled, and I felt the hair on his neck stiffen under my hand as he pulled threateningly towards her. She moved back quickly then with a hissing intake of breath. 'That brute . . . take care, Mrs Penhale, he is dangerous.'

Pirate slipped my hold when we reached the stairs to pad on ahead as though to lead me, my candle somehow staying alight to guide my stumbling feet. When I reached our bedchamber the light flew before me to reveal Daniel standing at the window, the heavy curtains thrust back, the lattice flung wide, letting in the damp air and the faint luminescence of a moon struggling through thin layers of cloud.

I set down the candle and ran to him.

'Daniel. Daniel.' My voice was a whisper.

He did not turn and I spread my hands against his back, smoothing them against the fine grey broadcloth, feeling the hard outline of his shoulder blades, the tension of taut muscle overlaying his ribs. I laid my cheek against his coat, wanting to give comfort, wanting to be comforted.

'Daniel. It was nothing. The girl had a nightmare. She will be ashamed of herself in the morning. She did not know what she was saying.' My voice trailed away, daunted by the implacability of his silence.

I could not reach him.

My hands fell to my sides. I took a step away, the aching tenderness that yearned to share his pain consuming my heart like a hungry flame. But it meant nothing to him. Nothing. I could not console him. Only one person could do that and she could never be with him this side of the grave.

Far off in the darkness an owl's cry wavered. The sound seemed to rouse Daniel. With a sudden, violent movement he whipped round to face me. I looked into the face of a stranger. The flesh seemed to have tightened across his cheeks, leaving the broad, hard bones gleaming white against the black hollows beneath and the sunken eye sockets above. His eyes were the only colour, blazing blue-green, wild with anger, with agony, I could not tell which. 'Do you know what they say about me in the village?' The words ground out between his dry lips. 'Do you? Do you not hear the whispers, see the sly looks?'

'Daniel, please . . .'

'Do you ever wonder why no village woman will stay in this house, though I offer them fine wages and good living? It is because they believe in curses, in witchcraft, in ghosts and ghouls that will not rest until they are avenged.'

'They are superstitious peasants! It is the same the world over! Please, please do not torment yourself so.'

'Not one of them will step across my doorstep for fear the shade of Meraud Trewithen, who was one of them, remember, not a bastard incomer out of the stews of Plymouth, will cast her drowned shadow over them.'

'What does it matter what they think? I do not care.'

'Do you not?' His eyes burned like hot blue flames. 'Not even when they whisper that Meraud will never rest until I, Daniel Penhale, am brought to justice? For they believe – and this is what they whisper behind their hands – that I murdered my wife. That I tired of her and her restless, wandering ways so I killed her and threw her body into the swollen river and let the spate carry my guilt away.' His voice faded to a tired, breathy whisper. 'As God is my judge, Sophy, my only crime was to love her too well, yet I am forced to live with the knowledge that there are those who could believe me capable of such a terrible violation. And I will not have it. I will not have this . . . this ugliness, this sickness brought into my house.' He flung himself down into a chair, put his head in his hands. 'They must go. Both of them. Tomorrow.'

The voice in my head, the sensible voice of reason, said clearly, 'It is no use. It is not you he wants.' Repeated it over and over as I went to him, sank to my knees beside his chair and put my arms around him.

'Hush, hush, my dear,' I said softly, rocking his head to my breast, as I might a grieving child. 'Who cares what ignorant, cruel people say?'

'I thought that time would still their tongues. That time would allow me to forget, and that a new beginning might be allowed me, but just when I begin to hope . . .'

'It *is* a new beginning. I am here, Daniel, your wife, your friend. You are not alone any more.'

He sighed and straightened himself, gently breaking my embrace and taking my hands between his. They were newly released from their bandages so I could feel the patchy texture where the blisters had been. He kissed my forehead. So warm a touch against my skin, so cold a reverberation in my heart.

'You are good, Sophy. Good and kind and sensible. I do not deserve you.'

'Never say that!'

'But it is true. When you agreed to marry me I did not anticipate this sort of upset, this shadow from the past throwing its disrupting influence on the quiet, comfortable life I thought we might lead.' His mouth tightened. 'And all through the stupidity of two hysterical maids.'

'You cannot really mean to turn them out, Daniel,' I said softly.

'Can I not?' Abruptly he let go of my hands. 'It was on an impulse I brought them here at all. A foolish, ill-considered impulse. I should better have thrown them a sovereign when they came a-begging and turned my back.'

'But you did not. It was an act of charity, whether you like the sound of it or not, and that implies a certain responsibility towards them. They are only children, after all. Scarcely older than Kensa. Would you turn Kensa out of the house if she had a bad dream? And heaven knows she has enough of those according to Jess.'

'Dammit, Sophy! Do not be clever with me!'

'I merely plead for two orphan children who live here with people who are now their friends. Martha is becoming like a second mother to them.'

'I will find them another place.'

'Throw them among strangers? That is a cruel punishment for two children guilty only of having a nightmare!'

He had sprung to his feet. I scrambled up to face him. In an odd way I welcomed anger – in Daniel, in myself. There was release in it. It helped to overcome the despairing echoes of those dreary words . . . good . . . kind . . . sensible. I did not wish to be any of those things at that moment. I wanted to hit out. To hurt.

'Taking out your spleen on such helpless victims sets you scarcely above the superstitious villagers you so scorn! Those stupid people forced the crippled shoemaker to live outside the village because they believe his hunched back brings ill luck. Are you so different, to be frightened into a ridiculous course of action by a child with a head full of Madeira fumes? *She* may believe the shade of your dead wife returned from her watery grave to haunt the attics, *you* should know better. Meraud is gone for ever. She will not come back to haunt Joan or Nan or anyone else.'

I saw him flinch. And for an instant there was such raw pain in his eyes that if I could have taken back the words I would have done. But the pain was quickly masked. His expression was remote; his voice low and cold when he spoke.

'So be it, Sophy. You shall have your way. But warn them well. If there is another disgraceful scene such as occurred tonight, I shall have no alternative but to put them off.'

Then he went from the bedchamber and closed the door softly behind him.

And I do not know where he slept – or if he slept – that night, save that it was not in my bed.

I did not fall asleep until dawn. When I woke it was to the sound of the carriage moving on the gravel below the window and Dagget's voice soothing the horse. I pulled on my dressing gown and flew downstairs in time to see Martha waiting by the door with Daniel's hat, and Daniel himself bidding farewell to Kensa. Jess was hovering nearby holding a small package in her hands.

He looked up as I hastened to him. He gave me a brief, courteous nod, a faint, polite smile. And for the benefit of the maids – nothing more, for I believe he had not set foot in the bedchamber leave alone taken note of whether I slept or not – he said, 'You were sleeping so peacefully, I had not the heart to wake you,' and bent to brush a farewell kiss on my cheek.

'Oh, sir, you must not forget the ointment I made up for you.' Jess swayed forward to press the package on him. 'It contains an extract of marigold, excellent for burns and the healing of sore flesh. Be sure to use it freely and your hands will quickly improve.'

'That is most kind of you, Jess,' he said warmly.

He smiled at her and blew a last kiss to Kensa as he took up his hat but he did not look again at me. It was Kensa who ran to the door to wave him off, Jess who stood at her back while the carriage moved smartly up the drive. These were the two smiling faces he would remember. Not mine.

A bad, sad start to the week. Later I should look back and remember the day we learned of the king's death. It marked an end and a new beginning for the nation. And, had I but known it, the beginning of painful change, a time of turmoil for those under Kildower's roof. A strange time, a tragic time for us all. But I knew nothing of this as I went slowly back upstairs to prepare myself properly for the new day.

There was much to attend to in the following days, not least the two maids to be scolded and warned against future flights of fancy, though Joan remained surprisingly stubborn in defence of her story. I arranged as a temporary measure that Martha should move her bed in with them, which she was more than willing to do. 'They poor motherless toads do want for a guiding hand. Don't you fret, Mrs Penhale, no ghosties will dare bother their dreams with me and the word of the Lord to guard them.'

There was satisfaction and comfort to be got in the very ordinariness of routine; resuming lessons for Kensa, for Rhoda; visiting Captain Penhale, whose temper improved or worsened according to the state of his gouty toe; taking

Pirate for walks; and those blissful quiet times of escape when I could disappear to my room and lose myself in the sheer sensuous pleasure of setting up the easel, pinning a new sheet of paper to the board and flooding the paper with translucent colour. It pleased me to think of Edith perhaps snatching the same quiet moments to add a few lines to her latest story.

There were two other tasks I set myself that week. The first was to visit the magician and his sick wife, the second to take myself to Trebarth to question Mrs Lugg.

There was no question that I should not take Pirate up to the pool. He had become my devoted shadow and had a tendency to set up his mournful banshee howling if I was out of his sight for too long, which did nothing for anyone's nerves. I was glad to have him loping along beside me, his nose snuffling down among the leaf mould and tree roots, feathery tail up and swishing wildly for joy in the search for a rabbit or bird to chase. Although I had not seen sight nor sound of Con Trewithen since our return from Plymouth, I still had memories of that first unwanted encounter at the pool. I felt a little safer with Pirate to guard me.

There was no one at the well. The sound of trickling water was all that disturbed the tranquil silence, but I could smell burning wood and moved towards the faint thread of grey-blue smoke I glimpsed between the tree trunks.

The moment we entered the glade Pirate moved to press closely to my skirts, his head reaching forward, nose testing the air, as though he sensed something unusual here that he was not yet sure of. The presence of strangers no doubt, and as we neared the little encampment I heard the rumble of a growl in his throat.

The man came out of the trees silent as a wraith to bar our path. It took a moment before I recognised him as the merry-eyed charmer who had coaxed a rose from Kensa's ear. The gypsy-black curls hung greasy and lank about his grubby collar, there was a thick growth of black stubble on his chin and his bold, laughing eyes seemed to have shrunk to shards of hard brown marble in their shadowed sockets.

'You are the magician I saw performing at Torpoint,' I said without preamble.

'So? What is that to you?'

'Mrs Miles, the vicar's wife, tells me there is a sick woman here. I came to bring her some things and to see if there was anything else you needed.'

'We want nobody's charity. We manage well enough.'

I held out my basket. 'There are fresh eggs, a new loaf, a jar of good beef tea. Please take them for her, if not for yourself.' When he did not move or answer, I said, 'Then perhaps I may see her. Or will you tell me what ails her and I will bring her something to give her ease?'

'She wants no visitors. There is nothing anyone can do. She has mortification in her belly that nothing but a miracle will cure. The waters will do that if anything will. At least she believes so.'

His stubbornness and his pride were both touching and exasperating. But I had to respect them. I set the basket down.

'I will not take this back. Please take it if only as a small token of my thanks for the pleasure you brought to a small girl with your performance that morning in Torpoint. I hope the waters perform the miracle you hope for.'

I left him still standing there, unmoving, behind him the arch of branches and leaves that formed the little shelter, the twig fire smoking before it, the woman lying motionless on a mattress of piled bracken fronds by the smoky blaze covered with a dirty grey blanket. All that could be seen of the poor creature was one wasted hand curled on the blanket and a cascade of straight hair, black as a raven's wing, lying in touchingly youthful profusion over the folded shawl that served as pillow.

Before I left the glade I dipped my hand into the spring and breathed a prayer for her, then tied my handkerchief – all that I had on me to offer to the goddess, the saint – to a branch of the ash tree, where it fluttered gently in the soft breeze among the tattered remnants of so many other emblems of hope.

Hope. That was the emotion that was uppermost when I went to Trebarth the following morning. Hope that was soon dashed by Mrs Lugg once I had told her the nature of my errand.

She had welcomed me with beaming smiles and gushing words, bustling me into the parlour, begging me to take tea . . . a glass of damson wine . . . a piece of saffron cake fresh from the oven. But when I refused, when I told her the nature of my errand, her smile became fixed and her eyes narrowed to hard, piggy slits in the overblown flesh of her cheeks.

'Well, now, 'tes an odd sort of thing for you to be asking, if you don't mind my saying. This girl, this Juliana, what's she to you then?'

I had my story ready. 'I have recently discovered that Juliana Smith, as you knew her, was related to me. I know a little of her history, that she unfortunately bore a child out of wedlock and that you, Mrs Lugg, had the care of her during her confinement. Some ten years ago, that would be.'

She gave a false trill of laughter.

'Why, Mrs Penhale, I've been helping women in their hour of need since I was no more than a girl when my ma took me to learn 'er trade. There can't be many children hereabouts that I've not helped into the world. 'Twould be terrible hard to recall one in particular.'

'Juliana died shortly after the birth.'

'Ah, so many do,' she said dolefully. 'The Lord giveth and the Lord taketh away. 'Tes at birth we are closest to death, that's for sure.'

'But surely it would not be difficult to remember this particular one,' I said pleasantly. 'After all, she lived here at Trebarth for some months and you were paid a sum of money to ensure that her child was looked after and educated until she was of an age to be apprenticed to a suitable trade.' I did not take my eyes from her face, which had now lost all pretence of a smile. 'It might refresh your memory,' I went on in the same light tone, 'if I fetched the receipt I have in my possession, which you have signed. Then again, I could consult the lawyer who drew up the contract. He will have records of the occasion when the money changed hands.' I had no idea if this was the case, or even if a lawyer was involved, but the mention of it had the desired effect.

'No ... no,' she said hastily, her eyes glinting with calculation. 'It does now come to my mind.' Evidently reassured by my encouraging expression, she allowed her manner to grow confidential. 'I gets begged, you see, from time to time, to take in wayward girls that gets caught in the family way. Such shame and upset they bring to their families.' She tapped the side of her nose. 'Discretion, you see, is what's called for. Word gets round when a body's proved to be trustworthy. I tell you, Mrs Penhale, I've been called an Angel of Mercy for my charitable work. Grown men have shed tears when they've thanked me for the care I've taken of their daughters and for the burden I've lifted from their shoulders in the matter of the disposal of the unwanted article – if you take my meaning – so that the girl might return to the bosom of her family relieved of an encumbrance and untainted by scandal.'

'Disposal, Mrs Lugg?' I asked, softly.

Her smile was bland. 'New homes, new families for the little dears, o' course. Bastards they may be but no one shall say Prunella Lugg don't give them as good a start in life as any child born with the blessin' of the parson spoke over its parents.' Something too smooth, too self-satisfied in that fat, bland smile sent a chill down my back, but she went on quickly, 'Now this Juliana you speak of . . . I recollect it was the milk fever carried her off. Been sickly all along. Her strength all went to her womb, as so often happens in those of a melancholy temperament. Mind, 'er had a temper at times. I reckon that's what brought on the milk fever, 'er getting in a paddy when the wet nurse fetched the child away. As I told her at the time, 'twas too late for hollerin' and carrying on. She'd better have showed the same spirit nine months sooner, 'stead of moonin' an' swooning over some lovesick lad. That way her'd have kept her legs crossed, slapped her lover's face and not brought trouble on a decent family.'

I clenched my hands so tightly that my nails bit deep into the flesh. I had to bear with this until I had the facts. Not think about the man Juliana called Father creeping into her room night after night while her mother muffled her ears to her cries. Not think about her terror, the loneliness of her abandonment, her death among strangers.

'So Juliana died,' I said, keeping my voice steady. 'She is buried here, in St Bride's churchyard?'

'For the best, her pa thought. In the circumstances. He sent money for her to be laid to rest decent and private. Her lies by the wall on the creek side.'

Nobody to mourn. Nobody to care.

'And the child? Adelaide Smith?'

'Ah, yes. Adelaide.' A hesitation, so slight as to be almost unnoticeable. Then that fat, smooth, untrustworthy smile. 'Like my own daughter, 'er was. Once her was weaned I brought her back to the farm and cared for her just as 'er pa had wanted. Why, 'twas me learned her her letters and numbers afore a chance came when she was six or seven for her to be apprenticed to a nice refined sort of trade. A distant relative of Mr Lugg's living near Honiton came for a visit. Her was a lacemaker and took a real fancy to little Adelaide and offered to take the girl and train 'er in the lacemaking. So off Adelaide went, happy as the day, to a good home. And stayed happy. Which is a comfort for me to know for 'twas no more than two years later she was carried off by a morbid flux of the bowels.'

There was a smiling glibness, an all-too-convenient finality about the tale that struck a dissonant chord in my mind.

'How sad,' I said. 'Then perhaps you would furnish me with the address of this relative, so that I may write to her in order to learn a little of Adelaide's last years.'

'Oh, her was carried off just after Adelaide, of the very same thing, which struck down many people thereabouts at the time.'

'I see,' I said, unsurprised.

'I wish I could have been able to give you happier tidings, Mrs Penhale, I truly do. But there 'tis.'

'Thank you, Mrs Lugg.' I rose to go. 'You have been very helpful.'

She bustled to open the parlour door for me and Pirate rose to greet me from the mat where I had told him to stay. I bent to pick up the leash with which I thought it best to restrain him in case he decided to war with the yard dog or chase the Luggs' chickens. Then I turned back to Mrs Lugg and said, 'You mentioned a wet nurse. Would she be a local woman?'

Again that hesitation. Long enough for a crafty brain to consider the possibilities before speaking. 'Was once, but long gone.' She shook her head. 'Husband died, her remarried and went to live Helford way. Don't even remember her new name.'

She opened the front door and the yard dog set up a violent yapping, flinging himself frantically about at the end of his chain. I was glad Mr Lugg was not there to kick him to silence, busy as he was out in the fields with his haymakers. I bade Mrs Lugg good day and made my way back down the rutted farm track to the lane. But I did not go immediately back to Kildower. Instead I kept to the lane, walked past Kildower's gates and straight on to the village. There I went into the churchyard and walked slowly among the graves until I found the one I was looking for. It was almost hidden in a neglected corner where an old ash tree beyond the churchyard wall spread its green shade.

I stared at the mounded earth, the small tilted headstone just visible under the rank growth of dock and plantain and long grasses. I stood there for a long time until Pirate whined softly and nuzzled his wet nose comfortingly into my hand.

Then, my eyes dazzled with tears, I crouched down and brushed the long grasses aside and laid the wild flowers I had gathered on the way – purple vetch, sweet clover, wild rose – against the insignificant stone that read, 'Juliana Smith, aged sixteen years'.

Chapter Nine

The one all-pervading worry to me as the week progressed was that Kensa seemed to be losing some of her energy. On Friday she woke heavy-eyed and listless. Jess sent for me and wanted to keep her in bed. 'As I said, ma'am, if you recall, this was bound to happen,' she said with the complacency that made my nerves bristle. 'Her nature's too delicate to stand all the excitement she's endured lately. Especially the romping with Miss Chloe. I could see on her last visit that it was taking Miss Kensa all her time to keep up with Miss Chloe's wild games.'

I had no recollection of any such thing. Rhoda and I had stationed ourselves near the mulberry tree to attempt a landscape of the view across the grounds with the wooded hills and glimpses of the river winding up the deep green valley. Chloe and Kensa had been playing perfectly sedately, with the occasional outburst of giggles, in the nearby shrubbery, which they had decided was just the place a prince and princess might hold a ceremonial banquet.

But I let it go and said briskly, after feeling Kensa's forehead, that she had no fever and to be confined to bed on such a glorious summer's day would do more harm than good. For once Kensa herself was on my side. 'I want to play with Chloe,' she said, petulantly knocking away Jess's restraining hand and struggling from under the bedclothes.

'We're going to invent a new play for my theatre today.'

'If you overstretch yourself and make yourself worse your papa will not be pleased when he comes tomorrow, Miss Kensa,' Jess said reprovingly.

Kensa's lip trembled. 'But it's not fair. I want to get up. Why do I have to be like this again? I don't like feeling wobbly and tired all the time.'

'Because you don't listen to your old Jess, silly moppet. She's told you about running about and upsetting your system.'

'Nonsense,' I said brusquely. 'Healthy exercise and fresh air never did any child harm.'

Jess's look managed to convey both pity and condescension for my silly ideas, but before she could speak I said to Kensa, 'In any case Papa will not be home tomorrow so there is no question of his being displeased.'

'Not home?' The words jolted from Jess as though she could not hold them back, then she swallowed and said in a level voice, 'I mean, has Mr Penhale been detained in Plymouth? I hadn't been told.'

'No reason why you should be, Jess,' I said coolly. 'But yes, I have heard from him to that effect.'

I could see the question why burning on her tongue but she did not quite have the courage to ask it. Or perhaps she knew, in this moment when she was somewhat thrown off balance, that she might reveal more of herself than she intended. I did not choose to enlighten her. In any case Daniel's reason, a lecture and demonstration on mesmerism and animal magnetism that he wished to attend, was merely an excuse to keep apart from me. That was something I could scarcely bear to admit to myself leave alone a woman I did not like.

So I gave Kensa a hug and said I would help her this

once to get dressed and that she was sure to be better once she had eaten a little breakfast. Then when the Miles girls came we should all go and sit in the garden under a shady tree with lots of cushions and rugs to make us comfortable. While Rhoda and I painted, she and Chloe could think up ideas for the theatre which Chloe could write down, so that she, Kensa, need not lift a finger if she did not wish to.

So it turned out and it was true that she gradually perked up during the course of the morning so that she was able to eat a decent dinner after the girls had gone. But that night she suffered a bad bout of her old sickness and I had no recourse but to let Jess keep her in bed the following morning. And that was the morning, too, as though to pile trouble on to trouble, that when I returned from visiting Captain Penhale I found one of the pair of Worcester vases fallen from its place on the mantelpiece in the parlour and smashed to fragments on the hearth.

Martha was beside herself with anguish at the sight. 'Ma'am, I dusted the mantelshelf myself early on, for I won't let Nan touch nothing too precious, and I'm certain I put it back safe.' Her honest eyes were troubled. 'But if it was my fault, then I must pay.'

I sighed. 'It was an accident, I am sure, Martha. Perhaps a draught. Heaven knows there are enough of them in the house. Mr Penhale may be able to get a replacement in Plymouth. But please, I beg you, Martha, take care how you tell the other maids. I want no encouragement to tales of ghostly hands flinging ornaments about. That would greatly incense Mr Penhale. I had sooner say that I knocked it over myself.'

'But that wouldn't be the truth, ma'am,' Martha said sternly. 'And a lie's a lie however 'tes justified. No, I must shoulder the blame and there's an end to it, for even if there was a draught I must have left it too near the edge for it to be swept off like that. If you could take it out of my wages, a bit at a time, then I'd be beholden.'

I had no intention of doing any such thing, though I did not make an argument of it. I dare say I might find some sensible reason for the smashed vase before the next pay day so that her pride and her conscience might be salvaged with dignity.

When the girls had left the previous day I had given a note to Chloe to give to her mama as I thought she might be able to make a certain enquiry for me about the village when she went visiting the parishioners. I went early to church on Sunday morning, a warm, breezy day, and hurried round to the little room she used for her Sunday school. It was a poky little place that had previously been used as a store. Only two pupils sat at the rough board table this morning, scraping away at their slates.

'Getting the hay in while the weather holds comes before all else, I'm afraid,' Edith said. 'Even my star pupil – and the keenest for the penny – is absent.'

'Liddy?'

'The same. Oh, and I think I may have found out something useful for you.' She glanced at her pupils and drew me to a corner. 'This wet nurse you asked about – there was a woman who often took on the role. Her husband did die, as you believe to be the case, and she married a St Germans man, a waggoner, five or six years ago.'

'And moved to Helford?'

'To St Germans.'

'Ah, yes, that could be the case.' Enough truth to give the story credence, enough of a lie to discourage further investigation. 'Thank you, Edith.'

She gave me a curious glance but tactfully refrained from

asking why I should need this information. I smiled gratefully and whispered, 'I am trying to track down a child she may have nursed. It is a long and not very edifying story but I shall tell you the whole of it one day when we may be private. Do you have the woman's name?'

'Her new name is Pearce, Clara Pearce. She was a Binns before that.'

'Liddy's mother?'

'I'm not sure. There is a whole tribe of Binns scattered about the district, apparently. Anyway, she lives close by the church at St Germans. She should not be hard to find.' She glanced at the watch pinned to her waist, told the two children they might go and gathered up the slates to return them to the little pile on the end of the table. Before she put them down she selected a slate from the larger heap. 'See, this is Liddy's work from last week.'

Her name was spelled out in large ungainly letters at the top with the alphabet filling the rest of the slate.

I looked at her name and a curious excitement surged up in me. I picked up the slate. 'May I keep this for today?'

'Of course.' Her fair eyebrows rose to the untidy strands of fair hair falling onto her forehead. Then she shook her head and laughed. 'No, I shall not ask you why. You must have a reason. Now we had best be going or the service will be begun.'

Never had hymns and prayers seemed so slow or a sermon so long. I had even wished Pirate was with me to deliver a few pointed howls in order to encourage Mr Miles to hurry a little, but I had drawn the line at bringing him to church and had left him skulking dolefully in the house. I almost ran home, told Mrs Dagget I did not know what time I should be back for dinner and called Dagget to bring the carriage round. This time I did take Pirate. Whether for luck or with an idea of protecting me in case Mrs Pearce proved aggressive I do not know, but I was glad all the same of his faithful company as we rattled towards St Germans.

I found the place, almost in the shadow of the great ivy-smothered bulk of the church tower. While Dagget turned the coach, I knocked at the door of the small cottage a small boy had pointed out to us, but there was nothing small about the woman who opened it. She was taller than me by a head and twice as broad, with great beefy arms, a plump good-natured face, several chins that wobbled mightily with her booming laugh and a mop of greying hair crammed anyhow under her cap.

'Aye, 'tes true, I'm Clara Binns as was,' she cried to my query. 'Come you in, ma'am, if you can get in. Now scat, you young varmints, outside with 'ee. Sit there, ma'am on the settle.' With one swing of her arm she swept several young children out through the door and swept me and Pirate inside. 'There now, a bit o' peace at last. Now what can I do for 'ee, Mrs Penhale? Would 'ee be to do with the Mr Penhale of Kildower? I'd heard tell 'e married again.'

I explained that I was Mrs Daniel Penhale, fully expecting to see the familiar suspicious, dour look that characterised the St Bridellan women come into her face. But instead she beamed at me.

'Then I'm more than glad to meet 'ee, ma'am, for Mr Penhale was good to my first husband, Binns, when 'e was took with lung fever and couldn't work no longer and me with nine at home to feed and not knowin' which way to turn. Never a week passed but there'd be a shillin' and a loaf or a bag o' flour or some such left. Nor was I the only one.' She gave a scornful toss of her head. 'They said 'e only did it to put hisself in a good light, bein' possessed of a guilty conscience in other matters. But I saw they never

scorned what he give 'en and I dare say they take 'is charity
to this day and give him no credit for the kind man I knowed
'e to be. 'Course I was born and bred in Saltash. Never did
take to many in St Bridellan. Close, unfriendly lot, I always
found. Can't say I was sorry to leave after Binns died and
Will Pearce 'aving lost his missus thought we might set up
together.'

I had no notion of any of Daniel's charity among the
villagers, but I could see how like him that was and the
revelation warmed me to this large, garrulous woman.

I said carefully, 'I believe you once acted as wet nurse
for a child Mrs Lugg of Trebarth was looking after.'

Her great laugh boomed out. 'A good deal more'n once!
Borne seventeen I 'ave altogether. Most of 'em still livin'.
Fourteen by my first 'usband. Three by this 'en. Always 'ad
one at the pap, and milk overflowin' for those poor scraps
parted from their mams that ol' Ma Lugg sent me.'

'There is one child in particular I am anxious to trace,' I
said. 'Her name is – was – Adelaide. Adelaide Smith.'

The jolliness washed away from her face, leaving it
woebegone. 'Oh, my, I did grieve for that one. 'Ad her longer
than any of 'em. 'Till 'er was five or six it'd be, around the
time Binns died. 'Er'd got to the useful stage, see, and Ma
Lugg wanted her back. 'Twasn't just the coppers 'er paid
me for 'er keep that I missed, which I don't deny was
welcome, but I thought of 'er as one of my own. Her did cry
somethin' shocking when 'er 'ad to go, though I'd kept tellin'
'er some day her'd have to leave me. But I wept a bucketful
when her'd gone, I do tell 'ee.' She shook her head dolefully.
''Specially since I knew the place 'er was going to wouldn't
hold much joy for 'er.'

I took a deep breath. 'And where was that, Mrs Pearce?'

'Why, Trebarth, ma'am,' she said. Again that doleful

shake of the head. 'Hard folks, the Luggs. Her especially. At one time I wouldn't have dared say it, for I looked to 'er for the coppers the wet nursing brought in. But I can say it true now, for I'm not beholden to her and my man's bringing home good money, reg'lar.' She lowered her voice and said darkly, 'Never did like the thought o' the babes so many of those poor young girls bore that never survived. Too many, if you ask me. And a few I could name in the village as wasn't particular about another mouth to feed. Ma Lugg'd attend them then be off wi' another bundle to be buried in the back field at Trebarth, no questions asked and an extra shilling or two to weight her purse. Stillbirths, her always said, lying toad. No, my Liddy didn't fall on no bed o' roses there, mark my words.'

'Liddy?' I said faintly. 'Liddy Binns?'

'She still calls herself that?' She beamed. 'She wouldn't be named Smith. Wanted to be Binns like the rest. An' her was always Liddy. Adelaide was such a mouthful. That pleases me powerful, that do, that her's not forgot 'er ol' ma, for her'll be a big girl now, ten or eleven by my reckonin'.' She stared at me worriedly. 'Ma'am? You all right? You look a mite pale. Sit you still an' I'll fetch you a drop o' water.'

I sat for a while with Mrs Pearce as she rattled on about her children, her life, her good husband, and I thought of many things. The grave of my dead sister, Mrs Lugg's lies, of Mama who began it all, of Liddy Binns – Adelaide Binns as she had written clear across her slate – Adelaide Sinclair . . . Adelaide Smith . . . whatever the name, it could not alter the fact that she was my sister's child, who had been for so long under the cruel thumb of the woman who farmed babies and disposed of them as ruthlessly as her husband disposed of his stock.

Before I left I told Mrs Pearce the truth of my relationship to Liddy for there seemed little point in hiding the true facts now. I no longer cared if the whole world knew of it. I watched the great happy beam spread across her face.

'Oh, 'tes the best news I heard in many a year. But you'll fetch the dear maid to see me when you'm claimed 'er, won't 'ee?' Then she curled her meaty fist and shook it in the air. 'Iffen you 'as trouble with they Luggs then you remind 'en that I knowed more about 'en than they'd like made common knowledge. And tell 'en that I'm not afraid of they and I'll back 'ee up, Mrs Penhale, and willingly tell my tale to any magistrate should 'er prove awkward.'

I directed Dagget to go straight to Trebarth. There was no thought in my head save that I must snatch Liddy away from the Luggs before she had to spend another night in bondage to them. I felt sick with loathing for what they had done and the jogging journey back seemed painfully slow, for every minute, every hour that passed kept Liddy chained a little longer in servitude.

When we suddenly drew to a halt, I yanked open the window expecting to see a herd of cows or a string of pack mules blocking the road and intending to add my voice to Dagget's in order to help clear our way. But it was merely two horsemen who held their mounts across our path, making it impossible to pass.

Dagget let out a string of oaths. The men laughed.

'Take heart, old man,' one of them called. 'We do not mean any harm. I merely wanted a word with your mistress.'

While the other rider continued to block our way, he urged his mount alongside the coach window and doffed his hat.

'Good day to you, Sophy. I happened to be in St Germans and saw you there. It seems so long since last we met that I was overcome by a compulsion to wait here on the road in order to speak with you.'

My stomach had lurched the moment I saw who it was sitting so easily on the big, rawboned bay horse. *Stay calm,* I thought wildly. *Do not let him see how he disturbs you.* 'And now you have done so, Mr Trewithen,' I said through gritted teeth. 'Kindly remove yourself and let us pass.'

His flinty eyes, cold and mocking, denied his smile.

'But that is no way for a well-brought-up young woman to address a gentleman who wishes merely to make a civil enquiry as to her health and well-being.'

'That is no business of yours.'

'Come, come Sophy, of course it is. We are related through marriage. Why, I should be thought a mannerless brute if I did not take an interest in your welfare. And I do most sincerely feel it my duty to ensure that you are not finding that time hangs too heavily on your hands at Kildower in the absence of your neglectful husband.'

'Duty! I doubt you know the meaning of the word. And I gave you no leave to call me Sophy.'

He pressed his hat to his heart. 'Ah, but that is how I think of you. Our relationship is too tender to admit of any other form of address.'

'Balderdash! Kindly tell your friend to move. I am in a hurry.'

'When I am ready.'

'For pity's sake, Mr Trewithen!' Beside myself with fury at the delay, at his mocking voice ... at myself for the turbulent way my mind was distracted by a remembrance of his touch, I clenched my fist and banged my hand on the glass. 'It is a matter of urgency!'

'Whatever can be so urgent that has kept you gossiping in Clara Pearce's cottage and now sends you scurrying off with a face as pale and doleful as a wet Sunday?'

I felt, unexpectedly and infuriatingly, a great rush of tears welling up. I hated to cry, to show myself up in front of anyone else. If I ever wept it was always, always in private, so that no one could glimpse my weakness. Now all the recent frustrations and upsets seemed to surge upwards in a vast wave of emotion that I was hard put to control. I turned my head abruptly so that my tormentor should not glimpse my turmoil and managed to say quickly, before my voice cracked, 'If you do not move, I shall set my dog on you.'

He laughed. 'I have no fear of that brute.' And indeed, to my chagrin, Pirate, after raising his head to see if the disturbance was worth his attention, had flopped back to sleep. Then, though I kept my eyes on a crack in the leather of the seat opposite in order to concentrate my will on fighting this weak urge to cry, I knew his manner changed. I heard it in his voice. 'Sophy? What is it?'

'Nothing to interest you,' I managed after a moment. I took a deep, shaky breath, swallowed hard and turned back to him. 'It is not for myself that I beg you to let us go. It is for the sake of someone else. A child. A defenceless child.'

A deep frown drew his black brows down.

'Meraud's daughter . . . my niece?' he asked quickly.

I shook my head. 'It is nothing to do with Kildower.'

His frown deepened. 'Then who?'

I could look at him steadily now. 'It is a child who needs my protection. That is all you need to know and all I choose to tell you. Now will you let me go, or do I have to go on my knees and grovel for the privilege of being released from your tormenting?'

He had the grace to look not exactly ashamed – his face, his nature, was too hard to admit any such emotion, I was sure – but uncomfortable.

With a last frowning glance at me he wheeled away his horse and called to his companion. They stood to watch us go and it was only when we were well on our way once more that I realised that I had seen the other man before. Very differently dressed – no fine green jacket and white breeches then, nor was he set upon a dappled-grey horse – but roughly clothed and covered with grime as he thrust past me on a dimly lit stairway. But the scar on his face could not be altered, nor the surly cast of his countenance.

It was the man whom Daniel suspected of starting the fire in the brewery.

I had expected . . . What had I expected at Trebarth? My mind was so upset that I did not give much thought to it beyond knowing it would not be pleasant, so I kept Pirate by me on his leash as I hastened up the rough track to the farm. Drawn by shouts, I crossed the yard to the hysterical barking of the farm dog leaping on the end of its chain. I heard a door open behind me and Mrs Lugg's voice bellow a curse, but I did not pause to look. Beyond the barn lay a wide rickyard. A wagon loaded with hay drawn by a pair of oxen stood close to the half-built haystack at the far end. Both Sammy and Liddy stood on the wagon, pitching hay on to the stack, where two men spread it about evenly. Sweat ran down the children's pink, sunburned faces and arms, making clean trickles in the dusty grime of their skin. Even as I looked, Liddy paused to catch her breath, putting her hand to her side as though a stitch caught at her, and Farmer Lugg, standing below, called her to get on, and to my horror raised his pitchfork to jab at her thin, bare legs. She was obviously accustomed to such treatment and sidestepped nimbly. Farmer Lugg's son, lounging in the shadow of the barn slaking his thirst from a tankard, gave a loud guffaw.

'Go on, Pa. Make 'er dance again, idle bitch!'

I flew forward. 'How dare you!' I cried. 'How dare you treat a child so, you great bully!'

Farmer Lugg was so surprised that I tore the pitchfork off him and threw it to the ground before he realised what was happening. I heard one of the men on the rick laugh out, then swallow it back. I looked up at Liddy.

'Come down off there.'

She looked warily from me to Farmer Lugg.

'Can't, missus,' she mumbled. 'Hay's got to be stacked.'

At that moment I heard Mrs Lugg's voice. 'Mrs Penhale. Mrs Penhale,' she puffed, coming up behind me. 'I thought 'twas you. Did you knock? I'm sorry, I didn't hear 'ee.'

'No, I did not knock, Mrs Lugg,' I said coldly. 'It was not you I wanted, but my niece, Adelaide Smith.'

Her jaw dropped. 'Your niece? But you never said . . .' She began but something in my expression made her stop. Farmer Lugg had regained his pitchfork and his voice.

'What d'you mean, comin' here and orderin' me about?' he blustered. ''T'ent none of your business what I does.'

'It is very much my business, Mr Lugg,' I said, but I think it was Mrs Lugg's warning glance that silenced him.

She began again on a sweeter note. 'Now, Mrs Penhale, come inside and we'll talk this through quietly over a glass of wine, as ladies should.'

I ignored her. 'Come down, Liddy,' I said, looking up at her and holding out my hand. 'There is nothing to be frightened of. I have come to take you away from here.'

Sammy jabbed her with his elbow. ''Er means it,' he said in a loud whisper. 'Go on, Lid.' Still doubtful, she dropped to her knees and then slithered down the piled hay and landed at my feet.

It was then that Pirate growled, a low warning note deep

in his throat, and I saw that the Luggs did not mean to let me go easily. I stood with my back to the wagon and the three of them, the man and the boy with their pitchforks, Mrs Lugg arms akimbo, made a tight half-circle, trapping Liddy and me within.

'Liddy's got work to do, Mrs Penhale,' Mrs Lugg said softly. 'And you'm made a terrible mistake. This 'ent the one you was after. 'Er'll tell you herself. 'Er's Liddy Binns. Isn't that right, Liddy?'

Liddy looked fearfully at their faces and I felt her edge from me, as though the threat of the Luggs' displeasure was too much for her to ignore. But what she would have said was immaterial, for I saw someone else had come into the yard. A man on a rawboned bay horse who assessed the situation in one swift, wily glance and called out, 'Ah, there you are, Mrs Penhale. I was just coming to see what was keeping you. This is the child you were telling me of, is it?'

'It is,' I said clearly. 'And we are ready to leave now.'

The Luggs fell back. Con Trewithen smiled his flinty-eyed smile. 'Farmer Lugg . . . Mrs Lugg . . . It is a long time since I had the pleasure of meeting you, but you will doubtless remember me.'

'Aye, near 'anged for a thief, you was, Con Trewithen, as I remember,' Farmer Lugg bawled, but a well-dressed, hard-looking man on a fine horse was not to be trifled with in the same way as a mere woman, and he was careful to keep his distance. 'I'd heard you was back and looking for trouble.'

'And seem to have found it,' Con said softly, 'right here at Trebarth. Well, well, what have you been up to, Farmer Lugg, to cause Mrs Penhale to look so harassed?'

'Nothing! Nothing at all!'

'Oh, just a little misunderstanding,' Mrs Lugg said with

a false trill of laughter. 'A bit of a muddle over Liddy 'ere. Why, 'tes so long ago I took her in, out of the goodness of my heart, that I almost forgot where and how she came from. But it do seem I begins to remember.'

'Good,' I said, 'because had you not, Mrs Lugg, I have a witness prepared to speak up about it.' I paused to let that sink in, then said, emphasising each word, 'And about other things, if it should be necessary.'

'Other things?' she said warily. 'Oh, my, can't think what that might be,' but her piggy little eyes glinted with alarm and cunning.

'And the one thing that would make it necessary to speak out would be if I catch any inkling of further bad treatment of your apprentices,' I went on. 'For then I should have to make further enquiries into how they came to be at the farm and the nature and legality of their indentures. So take care, Mrs Lugg. I wish to see those children better clothed and fed in future, or I shall want to know the reason why.'

I snatched up Liddy's hand and walked over to where Con was waiting. Then without looking back I walked away, Liddy trotting bewilderedly on one side, Pirate the other and the man on the horse guarding our backs as we went.

I thanked Con Trewithen afterwards. I could do no other. I did not want to be beholden to such a man, but it was only fair to admit that I might not have removed Liddy so easily had he not turned up when he did.

'I need no thanks,' he said lazily. 'It was mere curiosity that drove me to see what you were up to. And I am still at a loss to know what you are about with this scarecrow child.'

He had dismounted from his horse when we reached the carriage and stood holding the reins loosely in his hands. I did not answer him directly. I looked into Liddy's wary, frightened face. 'Do you remember Mrs Binns, Liddy?'

Her eyes widened. ''Course. 'Tes a long time ago, though. I lived wi' her in a proper house down along the village. 'Twas lovely there. Never got hit once.'

'I have been to see her today, because I wanted to be sure you were the one I was looking for. And now I am.'

'Looking for me, missus? What for?'

'Because . . . because I know now that your real mother – not Mrs Binns who looked after you when you were a baby – your real mother was my sister.' I let this sink in for a moment. 'You are my niece. I am your aunt.'

'But . . . but . . . my real ma . . . where's her to then?'

'She died just after you were born, here at Trebarth where she was staying.' I smiled at her. 'And now I am taking you to live with me at Kildower, where you came to see me before. You will never come back to Trebarth again.'

I think it was too much for her to absorb. She still looked deeply bewildered. I glanced up at Con Trewithen. 'Does that answer your question?'

His thin, hard face was expressionless. He nodded.

'I am glad that I let my curiosity lead me to follow you,' he said curtly.

I sighed, smiled, feeling the luxury of relief now that it was over. 'I believe I am glad too, Mr Trewithen.'

He said no more but handed us into the carriage. Then he mounted his horse, touched his hat and cantered off down the lane, leaving me to regard Juliana's child with amazement and the beginnings of joy.

If I said that Liddy fell joyfully upon her new life, or that she was immediately welcomed by everyone, I would be wrong. The maids were shocked at her story, but there was a modicum of wariness in their attitude. After all, she was still scruffy Liddy Binns to them, and there must be some adjustment before they could start to regard her as Miss Adelaide. For a start, she was filthy and verminous. On close inspection her hair was crawling with lice and it seemed the best way to deal with that was to scrub her from top to toe, burn her clothes, crop her hair short and then rub turpentine into it. All this took place in my dressing room, Kitty lugging up buckets of hot water and vigorously aiding the scrubbing process, which Liddy bore with stoic silence, only the fearful expression in her eyes bearing testimony to her disbelief that this could possibly be anything to her advantage. She would not be detached from her pocket containing the precious hoard of fifteen pence, though, so that took a bath with her and she did not utter a word of complaint afterwards when it must have clung most uncomfortably to her waist under her dry clothes.

Kensa had recovered somewhat during the day and was now sitting up in bed looking washed out and frail when I went in search of something for Liddy to wear. When she heard about Liddy she turned round eyed, then tossed her head with a touch of the old hauteur which had not surfaced so much lately. 'I shan't want her in the nursery with me, a dirty creature like that, even if you are her aunt, Stepmama.'

'Indeed no, Mrs Penhale,' said Jess, looking shocked. 'She might have all sorts of infections. It wouldn't do to let Miss Kensa near her in her weakened state in case she picks up something nasty. Besides a rough girl like that . . . it is scarcely suitable.'

I said acidly, 'The reason she is in such a state, Jess, is that your Lugg cousins are cruel, heartless people. They thought the girl had not a relative in the world and so could be worked and half-starved and beaten, with no one to say nay to them. So I will not have you turn up your nose at her as not being good enough for this nursery. Think on, you will treat her well or I shall want to know the reason why.'

Jess at first recoiled at my tone, her eyelids flickering nervously at my attack on her cousins, but she recovered quickly, to say in an ingratiating manner, 'Oh, dear, ma'am, I'm sorry to hear your opinion of those at Trebarth, though I have to remind you that the relationship to me is very distant, and I do agree that Mrs Lugg has a somewhat rough and ready nature, whereas my branch of the family was brought up gentler. And of course I'll be pleased to welcome the poor little soul into the nursery. Should you like me to make up a lotion for the head lice, ma'am? I have a good receipt containing aniseed which is effective in keeping them at bay.'

I accepted this olive branch coolly. But on the matter of moving into the nursery the 'poor little soul' was not exactly amenable once she had got her bearings. 'Don't want to go with her,' she said stubbornly. 'Don't like 'er. Her'll tell on me to Ma Lugg and they'll get me back.'

'Mrs Lugg has no claim on you, Liddy,' I repeated, over and over. 'I am your aunt. I am here to protect you and care for you.' She took this very literally, which was hardly surprising bearing in mind the circumstances of her young life and the strange new environment in which she found herself, and determinedly clung to my side wherever I went. When I woke that first morning I even found she had moved from the bed I had had made up for her in my dressing room and had curled up on the floor beside my bed. Thankfully I persuaded her to stay in her own bed after that, for I feared what Daniel might say if the same thing happened while he was home. I did not even know if he would approve of her sleeping so close.

So I now had two shadows, the great shaggy grey dog

and the thin, silent child in Kensa's too-short, too-frilly
dresses and a pair of too-large slippers. They were old ones
of mine which would have to do until the shoemaker could
cobble up some new ones for her, which he promised to do
as quickly as he was able when I sent for him the following
day.

I wrote to Daniel straight away to tell him of my success
in tracking down my niece. At least this was good news to
relay to him, as well as the less pleasant tidings about Kensa.
She seemed again to have entered the seesaw of good days
and bad days, but the only hopeful difference was that now
she seemed determined to fight against the enervating effects
of her ailments and would drag herself away from Jess's
smothering attentions if she could, especially when it was a
day when Chloe would be here.

I wrote to Mama too, but my letter crossed with one from
Sir Richard, full of gossip about the king's death – how he
had been sitting in his night chair when he had cried, 'Oh,
dear, dear, this is death,' before he expired, and how his
gross body was so decayed it made the embalming difficult.
Then an account of the new king's day – he was a temperate
and regular man, it seemed, who ate plainly and drank only
sherry wine in moderation, never more than a pint a day –
and whom it was generally felt would make a worthy
monarch. But right at the end of the letter he turned to more
personal matters and I sensed the sad wistfulness behind his
words.

'*Your dear mama has become a little tired of Highgate
and fancies she will remove back to Italy. I have begged her
to stay a while longer in order to avoid the heat of a
Mediterranean summer and so far I have been successful.
You understand, my dear Sophy, that I would have her as
my wife and indulge her every whim in the matter of*

461

travelling, but she will not consent, being set against any permanent tie. Nor, for all my hopes, do I think I might change her mind now.'

I felt for kind, devoted Sir Richard, but I feared he was destined always to be denied his wish. But I wrote back in cheerful vein and renewed my invitation for him to visit us and if possible to persuade Mama to accompany him, though I doubted if she would. Knowing her as well as I did, I could not envisage her putting herself out to visit a part of the country she had always claimed to detest when more romantic places called to her restless nature. Especially since my investigations had not turned up the beautiful, talented, long-lost daughter of Mama's imagination, but scruffy, ill-used Liddy – who did not even have the advantage of being a helpless infant. Dear me, that would not suit Mama. Had she not always made every effort to deny her years? The sudden appearance of a near-adolescent grandchild would be a serious blow to Mama's vanity. No, she would not be in any haste to meet Liddy, but when Mama was gone abroad perhaps a visit here might help Sir Richard to overcome his disappointment and, in a small way, it would be some return for his many kindnesses to me and for his guardianship of Mama.

Captain Penhale gave one of his great guffaws of laughter when he saw the crop-haired waif who followed me closely into his quarters. ''Tis a strange creature you have there, Mrs Penhale. Did Zack dig it out of the cabbage patch?'

Liddy scowled at him, keeping at the same time a firm grip on my skirt for reassurance. 'Didn't come from no cabbage patch. An' I'm not a critter, I'm Liddy ... No, Adelaide. Thass my proper name. An' I can write it true. An' Missus ... Missus Aunt Sophy ... says I might be Adelaide Penhale if Master agrees to it. So there!'

The Captain scowled fearsomely back. 'Hah! Too free with your tongue by half. You'd best take care.' He jerked his head towards the window. 'The queen of the sea's out there listening to what you say. Don't know what she might do if you step too far out of line.'

Liddy's eyes widened as she stared at the figurehead out in the garden. 'Who's 'er?'

The old man got to his feet, wincing as his gouty foot touched the floor. 'Now, if you'll come along with me, I'll introduce you properly, as I must all young persons who hope to take the Penhale name. And if you show her the respect due to her station, she'll look on you kindly.' He held out his free hand. 'Will you walk that far with me? I need a bit of help as well as this old stick of mine.'

Liddy looked from me to the Captain's outstretched hand. I saw a tenderness in the old man's eyes that I had never remarked before and thought of a small, orphaned boy he had once looked upon in the same way. And in Liddy's face, as though she instinctively sensed she could trust him, a wavering in the wariness that always seemed to be uppermost. She let go my skirts and went to him without another word. She carefully led him to the window, where she knelt upon the seat. Then they both leaned out of the casement to view the figurehead closer and I felt as I watched them, the old man and the child, that Liddy had found her first friend in Kildower.

In view of Liddy's arrival and of Kensa's continuing indisposition, Daniel sent word he would be home on Friday afternoon. I was overjoyed, yet there was an underlying apprehension that I could not dispel. The lingering shadow of the arguments that had soured our last days together still hung frighteningly close. And, apart from the smashed vase I must tell him about, there was another dilemma. That scar-faced man I had seen with Con Trewithen. I knew I should tell Daniel about where and with whom I had seen him, but there was a strange reluctance on my part to speak, to expose Con to the inevitable accusation of collusion. It was all to do, I knew, with his rescue of me at Trebarth. I was deeply grateful to him for that and felt strongly that I did not wish to worsen the already bad feelings between the two men. But loyalty to Daniel tugged me the opposite way. It was only right that the culprit should be brought to justice.

The nightmare when it came was terrifying. A result, I suppose, of that burden of worry. At least that was what I told myself when I woke tangled in the sheets, sweating, terrified, in the small hours of Friday morning. Afterwards, after those terrible two days, I wondered if it was something more than that, if the dark, sad spirits of the house had invaded my dreams to warn me.

It began slowly. I was walking through the woods. I had been to St Bride's Well and was carrying a crystal bowl of spring water to take to Kensa. I knew she would only need one sip of it and she would be cured forever, but the wood was getting darker and the path turned to viscous mud into which my feet sank so deep that I could barely lift them. Then Jess was there, floating above the quagmire, the silky violet skirts of her dress blowing in the gale. 'Kensa is mine. Kildower is mine. Daniel is my lover,' she screeched. She hurled a rope at me and it turned into a livid green snake that wrapped itself tightly round my body so that I could not move. 'You'll die now,' Jess said. 'Meraud's ghost will get you.' I heard the sickening squelch of drowned footsteps and, though Con and Daniel were laughing somewhere nearby, I could not make them hear me because of the swell of the music, rising, chanting, the clear, sweet notes of women's voices weaving a harmony of such terrible beauty that the pain of it was too much to be borne. And the drowned woman laid her rotting hand on my shoulder, its white bones breaking through sodden, shredded flesh.

I awoke, my mouth wide on a silent, terrified scream. And in that instant of waking, the voices were still there, reverberating all around me through the molten darkness. Still there as my hands clawed for the candle. Stopping dead the moment the wick ignited to a growing blue and yellow flame, the sudden silence seeming as loud and painful in my ears as the music had been.

I had not heard them! Of course I had not. It was the dream, that was all. To hear them heralded misfortune. Nonsense, nonsense. I would not believe such silliness. Besides, the voices themselves had not seemed near as frightening as the rest of the dream . . .

In a little while I carefully straightened the bedclothes, breathed deeply of the moist, cool night air wafting in at the window and settled down again. But I left the candle to burn itself out, the brave little flame keeping the shadows, the voices, at bay until I sank at last to sleep.

Friday began with reassuring ordinariness. Kensa was well enough to get up and dressed and, the day being drizzly, when Chloe and Rhoda arrived, sheltering under a great umbrella of their papa's, I took all the girls down to my little room, which seemed considerably smaller with five of us and a great dog gathered inside, but infinitely more friendly than any other room in the house. I continued making a copy of the device engraved on the mantelshelf, which I thought I might present to Mr Miles, Rhoda was sketching Mistress Hilary, and Kensa and Chloe were absorbed in enacting their new drama in the toy theatre. This was clearly much influenced by *The Brigands*, with

Kensa crying importantly from time to time, 'No, no, Chloe, like *this*. I know exactly how things are done now that I've been to the *real* theatre.' I had hoped Liddy might relax a little in the company of other children, but she remained tense and wary and she was quite bewildered at the sudden freedom thrust upon her. She had asked more than once what work she was to do if she lived here and when I had told her she had looked at me in bewilderment. 'Book learning, Missus Aunt Sophy? But isn't there no proper work to be done first off? I could muck out the stable,' she said helpfully. 'Or dig 'taters.'

'That is already taken care of,' I assured her. 'You do not have to earn your keep any more, Liddy. You will be occupied enough with schooling when you get into the way of it.'

'So I can learn readin' and writin' an' such all day?'

I smiled. 'If you wish to. But I hope you will find time to play as well.'

It would take a while, I thought, to acquire that last art, but she was ferociously keen to begin her schooling. Now she sat hunched over a copy book, carefully writing the list of three-letter words I had pointed out to her, her lips moving as she worked out what they spelled. Though I sat up late last night finishing a print dress for her out of some breadths I had bought in Plymouth intended for Kensa, she still managed to look like a scraggy feral cat among three domesticated ones, with her spiky cropped hair and the alert, distrustful look in her sharp eyes.

We were all busy and absorbed when Nan tapped on the door.

'Martha do say if you can come, ma'am,' she said in a scared little voice. 'Her's in the hall.'

With a sigh I put down my pen, told the girls I should be

back in a few moments, and followed Nan back through the house. The hall was always extra dark on wet days, when scarcely a glimmer of light seemed to penetrate the small high windows set in the thickness of the outer wall. The two Chinese vases we had bought in Plymouth had brought a touch of much-needed colour into the gloom. I had augmented the vibrant red and gold of the peony pattern with sprays of fresh leaves and flowers – clear green of beech leaves and the pale yellow of a few irises I had found growing near the water gardens. One of the vases still stood. The other, I saw with dismay, was overturned, broke into two pieces, water and crushed leaves spilt out over the flags.

Kitty was hurrying down the stairs, duster in hand, as I came into the hall, Joan was already there with Nan, as was Jess.

'How did this happen?' I asked sharply.

'I don't know, Mrs Penhale.' Martha's lips were drawn into a tight line. 'I came into the hall and there it was.'

'Someone must be responsible.' I stared round sternly. 'And it is best that they own up now. Upset as I am at the loss of the vase, I understand that accidents happen and am prepared to be lenient. What I will not tolerate is for the culprit to hide behind a lie. Do you understand?'

Nods . . . and silence.

Kitty said, after a moment, 'I been upstairs all morning, ma'am, airin' and cleanin' the bedchamber. Didn't have no call to come down since I took the slops out first thing.'

'Joan?' I said. 'Nan?'

Hurried denials.

'No ma'am, not been near.'

'Been helping Mrs Dagget.'

'I gave the dining parlour a good turnout,' Martha said. 'Then I took the rugs out to the back to give them a good

467

beating in the fresh air. It was when I come back I found this mess.' She frowned at Jess. 'It must have gone with a fair old crash.'

'Indeed it did,' Jess said, shaking her head. 'I heard it from the nursery corridor. I came running to look over the gallery and there it was. That beautiful vase in pieces. And so strange,' she said absently, 'because there was no one around at all. It just seemed to have fallen for no reason that I could see.'

Joan gave a little wail, every freckle standing clear in her white face. '’Tes ’er . . . ’tes ’er who ’aunted me. ’Er's done it . . . ’er's come back.'

'We’ll have none of that silly talk,' I said severely. 'Jess, you should know better than to frighten the young maids.'

'Frighten them, ma’am?' Her face expressed righteous indignation, her damson-black eyes glinted with malicious satisfaction. 'I have said nothing to frighten anybody! I spoke only the truth. I heard a crash and there was no one here when I looked.'

'You implied . . . Oh, never mind!' I was seething too much to argue with her. Besides, it had been her tone of voice rather than what she had said that had set Joan off, and she had managed oh-so-subtly to foster exactly the kind of speculation that I wished most heartily to suppress and which would be sure to infuriate Daniel if it came to his ears. 'Now, Joan, listen to me. If I hear another word about hauntings I shall be very cross indeed. And so will Mr Penhale. I have told you what will happen if you carry on with this nonsense. You and Nan have a comfortable place here. I would not like to see you removed from it, but make no mistake, if Mr Penhale learns that you are persisting in this foolish behaviour, then I am afraid he will put you off. Now run along the pair of you and let me hear no more.

Kitty, I would be grateful it you would clear up the mess and save the pieces. It seems to me that the vase broke cleanly. Perhaps it may be repaired. Jess, I am sure you have work to do. Martha, might I have a word?'

I drew Martha to one side and waited until Jess was well out of earshot.

'What do you think to this?' I asked her. 'It is too much of a coincidence for the same thing to happen twice.'

Her face was set grimly. 'I might have believed I'd been careless that first time. But I've certainly nothing to reproach myself with here.'

'No. And it was no draught that toppled this heavy vase.'

'Nor no wandering spirit. And the dog was with you, ma'am.'

'Then who?'

'Couldn't say, ma'am. Didn't see anything that gives me leave to point a finger at anyone.'

But before she lowered her troubled eyes her glance flickered briefly in the same direction as mine did – at Jess Southcote crossing the gallery with her stately, gliding walk, returning to the little domain that she had ruled so securely for so many years.

By the time Daniel arrived, just before dinner, the wind was beginning to get up.

'The barometer is falling quickly, I'm told,' he said, taking off his rain-soaked hat and handing it to Martha. 'We shall be in for a blow later. As it is, we had quite a dusting crossing the river. I'm glad to be safe home before it worsens.' A pause as he shrugged himself out of his caped greatcoat. Then, free of it, tugging his coat straight, smoothing the folds of his cravat, turning slowly, almost reluctantly, to look straight at me for the first time. 'And how are you, Sophy?'

And as his glance met mine for one brief, unguarded instant his eyes blazed with a very different emotion to that expressed in the careful politeness of his tone. That burning sea-blue seemed to flash a response through my blood, forcing my heartbeat to race. But it was imagination . . . wishful thinking. Of course it was. He bent to brush my cheek in the coolest of kisses before Kensa claimed him. When he glanced at me again that strange intensity was quite gone. If it had ever been there. And his warm, kind smile was not directed at me, but at Liddy.

'So, Liddy, you are come to us. Who would have thought it? It is a strange tale indeed, but I for one am delighted that your aunt found out your true history. I hope you will be very happy living here at Kildower with us.'

She managed a hasty curtsey before she blurted out what had evidently been tormenting her mind, 'Shall you let me be a proper Penhale, sir, like Missus Aunt Sophy says?'

'Hush, Liddy, this is not the time,' I began, but Daniel, after a moment to clear his throat and make his expression properly solemn, crouched down to her height, took her rough paw between his own large hands and said, 'Is that what you wish, Liddy?'

She nodded fiercely. 'Binns is all right but I'd sooner have a grander name. Farmer Lugg wouldn't have no call on me then, would he?'

'He has no call on you now, Liddy, I promise you,' Daniel said very softly. 'You belong here now. And you shall be Liddy Penhale from now on.'

Her eyes searched his face for a moment with frowning concentration. 'And will I get a piece of paper with words that say I'm not Liddy Binns any more, so's everyone will know?'

'To be sure. I shall get it signed and sealed by a very important gentleman in Plymouth who knows about these things. Will that do?'

She nodded fiercely. 'An' it must say Adelaide. Thass grander than Liddy.'

'Of course.'

'Though I don't mind if 'ee calls me Liddy,' she added thoughtfully, 'for I'm none too sure I'd remember to be Adelaide all the time.'

'It shall be exactly as you wish.'

'Then thass all right then,' she said with a relieved sigh that seemed to come up from her boots.

And for the first time since she had come to Kildower her face broke into a grin of such pure delight that it wrenched my heart.

The wind rose steadily through the afternoon until by teatime it was like a wild creature hurtling itself at the windows, and it was so desolate with rain and sweeping cloud that it felt more like a winter's evening than the height of summer.

I stood at the parlour window watching the branches of the old mulberry tree bowing and tossing before the storm's frenzy as Martha and Nan brought in the tea things.

'A gale like this always makes me feel restless,' Daniel said, coming to stand beside me.

'You, too?' I smiled. 'I feel I must keep looking out to see what damage is being done.'

'Or perhaps it is something deeper in our nature that responds to the elements – like horses who become frisky in the wind.'

'Or bees. They grow bad-tempered, I understand, in windy weather.' A scatter of petals and leaves flew at the window to plaster themselves soddenly against the glass. I pulled my shawl a little tighter about my shoulders. 'I am glad we do not have to be out in it. I keep thinking about that poor woman in the woods with such inadequate shelter.'

'What woman is this?'

I told him of Rob the magician and his sick wife.

'I have been up once or twice with food though it is as much as he can do to accept it. They are proud people and I suppose they are used to the outdoor life.'

'But in a storm like this . . .' He shook his head.

'I will find time to visit them tomorrow and see how they have fared.' I glanced back at Liddy struggling to subdue needle and cotton as she made her first attempt at tacking stitches on a piece of spare material, and said softly, 'At least we have one poor outcast warm and dry and safe.'

'I am glad you found your sister's child, Sophy.'

'I would like to thank you, Daniel, for welcoming her so kindly.'

'Did you think I would not?'

'It would have been understandable. You could not have expected when you married me to find yourself burdened with my niece.'

'It is no burden. An obligation, perhaps. But even so, one which I have no hesitation in undertaking. Heaven knows, the house is big enough and the nursery could accommodate six Liddys without being overcrowded.'

'She has rather taken against the nursery,' I said. 'She associates Jess with the Luggs, you see, and it will be a long time before she loses her fear of them. She is sleeping in my dressing room as a temporary measure.'

Daniel frowned and I felt a tremble of apprehension that he might disapprove, but to my relief he nodded and said, 'Very sensible. But it comes to my mind that the furniture we have ordered for Kensa's new bedchamber might be replicated in a room for Liddy when she feels ready to move. I shall see about it when I return to Plymouth.

'Daniel, you are more than kind!'

He shrugged off my remarks. 'I shall always hope to treat Liddy with fairness.' Then he sobered and said anxiously. 'Kensa's latest bout of illness – it has taken her down, has it not?'

'She was quite poorly with nausea and purging earlier in the week,' I said. 'But today she is very much herself again.'

'She is very pale.'

'Perhaps another good night's sleep will put her right,' I said, hoping my optimism was not misplaced. Kensa's ailments were never that predictable. 'Now, shall we take tea? Mrs Dagget has made a wondrous saffron cake in your honour, and a dough cake and goodness knows how many kinds of sandwiches.'

But when Jess came to fetch Kensa, we were all engaged in a noisy game of spillikins and Kensa was greatly reluctant to go to bed.

To this day I wonder what Jess's thoughts were when she walked into the parlour and saw us. The shutters and curtains had been drawn early and Daniel had ordered the fire to be lit against the damp chill. So there we were, warm and snug, seemingly ensconced in a magically cosy circle around the card table. Excluding her, the loyal servant. Did she, at that moment, feel the blackness of despair? Glimpse the abyss that yawned between the fantasy of her hopes and the cold, plain fact of reality? I shall never know now. But perhaps some element of what she felt was in her voice, knifing across our laughter, for I remember how sharply I turned when she said, 'Come, Miss Kensa, it's past your bedtime.'

'I did not hear you knock, Jess,' I said.

'I knocked, ma'am,' she said in an oddly flat voice. 'Yes,

I knocked. But you did not hear.'

'Oh, Jess, no,' Kensa cried. 'I'm not ready for bed yet. I don't feel a bit sleepy.'

Nor did she look it. In fact, she seemed to have improved a great deal during the day and had become quite lively during the game.

'Mama, Papa, may I stay up? Just another game. I'm sure to win next time. Please!'

'Now, now, Miss Kensa, you know you must not overtire yourself,' Jess answered quickly in that same curious, strained voice before Daniel or I could speak. 'You will be the worse for it in the morning if you do.'

I was already out of temper with her. It seemed, since Daniel had come home, that she had set herself to be deliberately annoying. All afternoon she had been down from the nursery on some pretext or other, fetching a shawl for Kensa, wanting to bear her off to change her dress because of some imagined mark, bringing down a tray of still warm toffee that she had made, and always managing to throw in some sly, discomfiting little remark, exclusively directed at Daniel, always with her eyes fixed reverently on his face.

'It was sad, wasn't it, sir, about the loss of the vases . . . ?'

'Mrs Penhale did tell you, sir, how poorly Miss Kensa was on Tuesday? Of course, she was occupied with her niece, so she didn't see poor Miss Kensa at her worst.'

'I know Mrs Penhale doesn't approve of me making sweets, but Miss Kensa does so miss these little treats as much as I do the making of them. Perhaps this once, sir, you'd all share these and allow Miss Kensa a taste . . .'

And had I not already discussed the broken vases with Daniel – which he had been displeased about, naturally enough, but which he had dismissed eventually in his generous way as unfortunate but nothing for anyone to get too distressed over – had I not given him exact details in my letter of Kensa's progress, or my reasons long ago for not allowing her to fill herself with sweets, all this might well have provoked the discord she intended. That it had not must have riled her.

'Please, please, Mama,' Kensa begged now. 'I'm sure to win next time.'

'You'll not win,' Liddy said proudly. 'I'm better'n you.' Which she undoubtedly had proved to be. She had strong fingers from the hard labour about the farm and her grip was sure and steady.

'You mustn't tease Miss Kensa,' Jess said with a quelling look at Liddy. 'Not before she goes to bed. She'll get herself all upset and have bad dreams.'

'Then we'll play card dominoes,' Kensa said, ignoring Jess. 'I nearly always beat Mama when we play.'

Jess's low laugh rang out. 'Of course you do, my pet. But that can wait until tomorrow. Your old Jess will have a game with you first thing in the morning when you're properly rested and . . .'

'Thank you, Jess,' I said coolly, 'but I believe another half an hour will do no harm, do you not think so, Daniel?'

He smiled affectionately at Kensa. 'I believe it might be allowed, this once, if you are quite sure you are not too tired, sweetheart.'

'Not at all, Papa!'

She scrambled up to reach the cards from the secretaire. Jess continued to stand there, her white fingers fretting at her apron, her glance going from Kensa to me to Daniel. Settling on Daniel.

'Was there something else, Jess?' I asked a touch impatiently.

There was fury in her, I could see it in the flare of her

nostrils, the quiver of her lips over her large teeth. I thought for a moment she was going to burst out with some protest because we had gone against her wishes. Then she seemed to collect herself. She lowered her eyes.

'No, Mrs Penhale. Nothing more.'

She moved away with her smooth, stately walk, closed the door softly and was gone . . . and I felt as though I could breathe again, as though with her had gone some heavy, suffocating presence that had drained the parlour of its air.

But a feeling of unease remained with me. It made me restless, unable to concentrate, nagging at me like an aching tooth. I had grown accustomed to the atmosphere of the house, its unexplained cold draughts, its hovering shadows. Understood them now, perhaps. Accepted them for what they were. Echoes – sad and pitiful – caught in some eddy of time itself, to reverberate down the years, the centuries. Harmless, unless one's mind was such that it was easily persuaded to imagine otherwise. But this was different, sharper, and Pirate was no help to nerves suddenly on edge. Most of the evening he had spread himself like a grey and hairy rug before the fire. Only when Jess entered had he opened his eyes, not to greet her but to watch her, and when she had gone he also seemed to be overcome with restlessness. He could not seem to settle and I saw how his head, his floppy ears, kept pricking at distant sounds. A door banging distantly, the noise of footsteps on the floor above – Kitty probably, going to turn down the bed and rub the warming pan over the chilly sheets.

By the time Jess returned, Kensa was beginning to yawn.

'Run along, sleepyhead,' I said and without too much protest she came round the table to bestow her goodnight kisses.

'Sleep well, sweetheart,' Daniel said, and perhaps what

he said next added one more seething drop of acid into Jess's bitter frustration. 'If you feel well enough tomorrow, and this rain has blown away, I have a mind we shall drive to the coast, to Rame Head perhaps. There should be some fine seas driving in after this gale. Suppose we ask Chloe and Rhoda to join us? Should you like that?'

'Oh, yes, Papa!'

'If it is fine enough to sit out of doors, we could ask Mrs Dagget to make us up a picnic basket,' I said, delighted at the prospect.

'Excellent!' Daniel said. He ruffled Kensa's hair. 'So that is something pleasant to think about and give you sweet dreams. No bad dreams tonight, Jess, for your charge, eh?'

A small, breathy pause before Jess answered, 'I hope not, sir,' she said softly. She held out her hand, her white, grasping hand. Folded it over Kensa's. 'Come along then, my pet. Come with Jess.'

Only then was I aware of Pirate pressing against me, felt, rather than heard, the reverberations of the faint warning growl that rumbled deep in his throat. Daniel had turned his attention to Liddy, helping her to gather the cards and stack them away, but my glance followed the direction of Pirate's fixed stare. I looked at Jess, heard the rustle of her starched lavender skirts brushing against the doorway, the fading sound of her low voice against Kensa's light tones. Cut off abruptly as the door closed.

'Now it is this young lady's turn for bed. Sophy?'

I started. 'I am sorry. What did you say, Daniel? Oh, Liddy, yes . . . yes, I will take her up.' I managed a smile. 'I believe I have grown quite sleepy myself. The noise of the gale is very wearying.'

But it was not the gale. Nor was my inattention caused by the onset of tiredness. Quite the opposite. I had become preternaturally alert, as though every nerve in my body was over-tight. It was all I could do not to race up the stairs instead of taking them decorously and talking to Liddy – I do not know what I said, it could have been complete nonsense – then seeing her to bed. Everything she did seemed infinitely slow. I wanted to scream at her to hurry, hurry . . . and when she was at last tucked in I had to force myself not to run from the room, so as not to alarm her. Only when I was out in the corridor did I run, my soft kid slippers making but the softest patter on the boards.

The gale still battered about the house. Faintly I heard Pirate whining down in the hall. But clearest, loudest in my head was the noise that had begun as I watched Jess take Kensa out of the parlour. It filled my ears, filled my mind, seemed to float and twine about me. That unearthly, painfully beautiful chanting. Women's voices weaving a harmony of sound so clear that it held the crystal purity of water bubbling from an icy spring . . . warning me . . . warning me . . . of what?

I did not know, save that in some deep instinctive way it did not threaten me. All I understood was that it drew me to Kensa, that it was more compelling, more urgent with every moment that passed.

The day nursery was in darkness. I slipped through it to the crack of light coming from the inner room where Kensa slept. The door stood slightly ajar. Through the gap I saw Kensa sitting up in bed cuddling her favourite doll, then Jess came into view, walking from her own room into Kensa's, carrying a cup.

'Drink this up, my pet,' she said.

'Oh, Jess, must I?' Kensa said petulantly. 'I'd much sooner have hot milk.'

'You shall have that afterwards,' Jess said.

'But I don't like it.'

'Now I've told you, my pet, that if you are poorly tomorrow you will be much, much worse if you don't take this. It is what the doctor recommended, you know that. It is only a nice drop of peppermint tea.'

Kensa took the cup.

And it was then that I understood. And the instant I did, the voices cut off so abruptly in my head that I almost staggered.

I was through the door so fast that it smashed back against the washstand and sent some china object crashing to the floor. Kensa jumped and squeaked with shock. Jess's gasp turned instantly to a scowl when she saw me, her eyes liquid with hate, then she lunged for the cup.

But I had it first, snatching it so quickly that some of it spilled over my hand.

'What in God's name is this?' I gasped.

'Peppermint tea! Give it back to me at once!' Her voice was a screech.

'And what else besides peppermint? Tell me, you evil creature! Something to give a child bad dreams? Something to make her sick? Something to make her so languid she can hardly hold her head up?'

'It is harmless, I tell you! Peppermint to soothe a tender stomach.'

'Then if it is so harmless, I shall drink it myself – no, better still, I shall ask my husband to sample it.'

I whipped round and ran from the room, through the darkened nursery, along the corridor to the gallery and all the time I shouted for Daniel . . . calling him, calling him . . . with Jess panting after me, screaming imprecations. And I was nearly at the top of the stairs when she caught up with me, grabbing my hair, viciously twisting it, and just as suddenly letting go of it with a shriek.

Daniel was barely out of the parlour, but Pirate had flown up the stairs like a great grey shadow, and now he had pinned her to the bannisters, his teeth bared in a snarl.

'For God's sake, Sophy!' Daniel had taken the stairs two at a time, and now I fell into his arms, incoherent with shock and fright, my scalp burning where the hair had been torn from it. But I still held the cup. There was still half the liquid left in it.

'She was giving Kensa this . . .' I managed. 'Something to make her ill, not to make her better. Don't you see, Daniel? Sne's evil . . . evil . . .'

'No! No! Don't believe her!'

'The vases, too . . . She broke them! She was the so-called ghost who haunted Joan and Nan.'

'She's a liar! A lying bitch! She should never have come here! Spoiling everything . . .' Jess broke off, struggling for composure, desperate to restore the control she could feel sliding from her grasp. 'Sir, you know how faithfully I've served you, all these long years. I am innocent.'

'Daniel, taste this!' I thrust the cup into his hand. 'Drink it down. Please. This is the brew she was urging Kensa to drink.'

He frowned down at the murky liquid, raised it to his lips.

No!' The scream rang out. 'No!'

Daniel slowly lowered the cup, staring at it white-faced.

'Dear God,' he said in a stark whisper.

Then, as all the implications surged into his mind, I saw anger replace shock. He clenched his fist tightly round the cup, then hurled it down the stairwell, where it splintered to fragments on the flags, sending the fearful maids who had gathered in the hall scattering backwards to huddle together by the parlour door.

Jess was whimpering, a tearing animal sound that chilled the blood. She began to move slowly towards us as we stood at the top of the stairs, dragging herself along the balcony rail, hand over hand, as though the use had gone from her legs. Her eyes were fixed rigidly on Daniel. I think she saw only him, wanted to get to him, and even the threat of the dog who paced stiffly with her, his muscles tensed ready to spring, lips drawn back over his teeth, meant nothing to her now.

'I did it for the best. I did it for you, Daniel, my love, my darling.' She laughed wildly. 'I knew you wanted me. It was only a matter of time and patience. When you saw my devotion to dear Kensa, you would understand that I was the best one, the only one to be your wife.'

'And you poisoned an innocent child for this?' Daniel's voice was deadly cold. His grip around me was so tight I could scarcely breath.

'No, no, not poisoned, my darling. My little herbs only made her sickly, or sleepy. I just wanted you to open your eyes to see how devoted I was, how much love I had for you. Then you would realise our different stations in life didn't matter at all.'

She had reached the top of the stairs. She still held on to the balcony rail with one hand. With the other she reached out to Daniel.

'Come, my love. Come to me. We don't want her. Send her back where she came from.' Her mad gaze transferred itself to me. All the hoarded malevolence of her warped nature was in it, all the frustration and spite and cunning, spat out of her in a snarl. 'Let him go, you bitch! He doesn't want you – he never wanted you. You spoiled everything.' The outstretched hand curled and suddenly she launched herself towards me, both hands clawing for my eyes.

Afterwards it was impossible to say with certainty exactly how it happened. Did her foot turn on the top step? Did her heel catch in her skirt? Did she start falling before Pirate leapt at her in his anxiety to defend me? All we knew was that she was tumbling, bouncing from stair to stair, her arms and legs flailing. She screamed once, twice, in terror then, near the bottom of the flight, she somersaulted and the scream was cut off.

Then there was nothing but silence and a great broken doll in a lavender dress lying with its head at an impossible angle at the foot of the stairs.

I cannot now remember clearly what happened after that. I know that I was possessed of a great weariness and wanted nothing more than to lie down and rest until my limbs had stopped shaking and some warmth had come back into my blood, but that was an indulgence that I could not allow myself. There were two children whose needs were far greater than mine, two silent witnesses who had crept from their beds to watch. Kensa was still clutching her doll, her face ashen, her eyes huge with shock. Liddy was more bewildered than shocked. I cuddled them both to me, glad to feel the warmth of their two thin bodies against me, and I suppose I must have answered their questions properly, said the right comforting words, for presently Kensa lost that frozen, wide-eyed look and began to cry against my shoulder and Liddy said, with a disparaging sniff, 'Never did like 'er. 'Er always looked at me funny. Can we go back to bed now?'

'Not back in there,' Kensa wailed. 'I don't want to be on my own. Why did Jess have to be like that? I thought she loved me.'

'I think she did, in her way, my love,' I said, smoothing back her hair from her damp face. 'She just became a little strange. And of course you needn't go back into the nursery.'

'You can sleep with me, if 'ee likes,' Liddy offered generously. ''Tes a feather bed with proper sheets and pillows.'

I saw a flash of the old Kensa as she looked down her nose and said disparagingly, 'I always sleep in a feather bed. I suppose you're used to something much rougher.'

Liddy scowled. 'Never 'ad a bed at all. Slept in the barn wi' naught but a few rags for coverin'. Anyways,' she said truculently, 'if you don't want to share with me, that's all right. I'm 'appy on my own.'

'Well, I suppose for this once,' Kensa said hastily, the thought of a comforting companion to share the dark hours outweighing everything else.

So the problem was solved and when Daniel and I eventually came wearily to bed, we peeped in on them to find that they were curled up together like two young puppies, in deep, restorative slumber.

I thought I should instantly fall asleep when I got into bed, but the moment I shut my eyes I could see Jess tumbling, tumbling to lie broken at the bottom of the stairs. Daniel was in no better case. He had had the more stressful task of seeing to the removal of Jess's body to an unoccupied room downstairs where Martha, who had stayed calm and practical throughout and kept the young maids from flying into hysterics as they watched the dreadful drama being enacted on the gallery, had attended to her laying out.

'Why could I not see what she was about?' he said, in a tormented voice, as we lay staring into the darkness.

'Because she did not wish you to. Because she was sly and cunning.'

'But I should have realised.'

'Why should you? She even deceived the doctor, did she not?'

'That old fool! I hear he has retired now and gone to live in Bristol. Good riddance, I say.'

'And the Plymouth doctor, too, don't forget.'

'You think that rash was to do with her?'

'Possibly. I suppose there are herbs that would have such effects.'

'And to think she might have gone on,' he groaned, 'if you had not found her out. Can you ever forgive me, Sophy, for not believing you when you warned me?'

'There is nothing to forgive, Daniel. In your place, I should probably have done the same.'

He turned, reaching out to touch my cheek, but I moved at the same time and his fingers brushed my lips.

I could not help myself. I caught his hand gently and pressed a kiss against his fingers.

'Dear Sophy,' he said. 'I owe you so much.'

'Please, please, do not talk like that, Daniel' I said, hearing an uncontrollable edge of anguish in my tone. 'It is not a matter of owing me anything.'

'But it is,' he said softly. He moved his hand from mine and slid it under my hair, drawing my head to his shoulder. 'More than you could know.'

We lay there in silence for a while, and it seemed that the silence intensified and I became aware of his heartbeat pounding beneath my cheek, the gentle movement of his fingers twining in my hair. Which became, imperceptibly, something different . . . more languid, more searching – more exciting. And, suddenly, as if all the horrific events of the evening had somehow swept away the barrier of respect, of politeness, of courtesy that we normally showed to each other, now there was a searing urgency about our lovemaking. He did not take me gently, but with abandon, with lust, even, born of a need to dispel the dreadful images that haunted him. And I answered him in kind, not bearing to think how he might reflect on my lascivious behaviour in the morning but uncaring for anything but slaking the wild, wicked, delicious appetites that his hands, his body, his urgent kisses aroused.

Even when it was over and we lay panting, sweating, still clinging together like half-drowned victims of a shipwreck, I could not bring my wayward thoughts to order and rebuke myself for letting him see a side of me I had not even known myself was there. And when I fell to sleep, I believe I was still smiling.

The storm blew itself out in the night.

It was still early when I crept across the room, drew back the curtains and let the clear morning light flood into the bedchamber. Save for the evidence of the leaves and twigs littering the grass below, the violence of wind and rain might never have been. The merest zephyr of a breeze stirred against my cheek as I opened the window and the sky was once again the limpid blue of an English high summer.

I stood there for a long time, very still, drinking in the fragrance of the morning air, entranced by the play of glittering light and long green shadows across the lawns. Earlier, propping myself on my elbow, I had gazed in much the same way at Daniel's sleeping face and felt a similar inrush of delight.

We had survived the storm, Daniel and I. The tempest within the house as much as without. We had washed up on a calmer shore in a landscape scoured clean and safe and free from Jess's corrupting influence.

Jess. I shuddered as the ugly images I should always associate with her flickered in my mind. Yet even they seemed now to be diminished in strength, overpowered by the sunlight and overlaid with newer, more urgent memories of a very different kind of passion.

I heard the rustle of bedclothes, then the pad of bare feet across the floor. I did not turn, but when I felt Daniel's hands rest lightly on my shoulders it was all I could do not to lean back against him as I felt again that languorous rush of wanting that weakened my limbs and set painfully pleasurable sensations coursing through the most secret depths of my body.

'It is very early,' he murmured. 'Could you not sleep? Have you been disturbed by bad dreams?'

'I did not dream at all,' I whispered, surprised to find that this was so.

'And . . . and if I woke early, then I believe it was . . .' I hesitated, suddenly shy, then gathered my courage and rushed on, 'it was out of happiness.' I turned to face him, said urgently, for if ever there was a moment to speak what was in my heart it was now. 'Oh, please Daniel, do not take it ill that I should feel happy after all that happened yesterday, which was dreadful in the extreme . . . but . . . but *afterwards* . . . that is, last night after we talked and we . . . But before that . . .' I stopped, knowing I was making no sense and not helped at all by the set and serious look on his face. How could I say it? But I must. I must! 'Daniel . . . I want to be honest with you. We must be honest with each other – I cannot live a lie as I have been doing.'

His eyes, so warm a blue but a moment since, seemed to have turned cold, as though to warn me to guard my words. But I must risk his anger, risk that he would turn against me.

'I have failed to honour our marriage agreement,' I said, taking a deep, calming breath. 'I did not mean to fall in love with you, I did not want to fall in love with you, but it seems that I have done so. I . . . I am sorry, Daniel.'

'Sorry?' There was a curious, strangled note in his voice. 'Good God almighty, Sophy!'

'Believe me, I would not have had it happen for the world . . .'

His eyes were blazing at me now. Cold no longer, but full of an emotion it took a full five seconds for me to recognise.

'Dammit, Daniel, you are laughing!' I cried, aghast – affronted – at his indifference to my confession.

'Oh, my dearest Sophy, I am laughing at myself! Did you not realise . . . ? I thought I had given my feelings away more than once.'

'Then you . . . ?'

He sobered, fastened his arms tightly about me, held me to his heart. 'Are we not two foolish people?' he whispered. 'I have fought against loving you and failed most dreadfully.'

'But Meraud . . .'

'Meraud . . . Ah, Meraud.' He sighed and stroked my hair with gentle, comforting fingers. 'I suppose it was love I felt for her once. I thought so for many years. Now it seems so far off, as though it had all happened to a different person. I *was* a different person then, I suppose. A boy. A young man. Locked in a young man's infatuation . . . obsession. I clung to the memory of that obsession for far too long. I chose not to look for love again for fear of the pain it brought. I thought I could live more comfortably without its entanglements. Which made it difficult for me to recognise the stirrings of that subtle emotion when it reappeared. And to deny it when I did.'

'And when . . . when did you understand that you loved me, Daniel?'

There was a long, thoughtful silence. 'If I said it was that very first time I saw you at the Vaiseys' house . . . well, it would be a lie to say that it was love exactly . . . but there was something that made me look at you a second time. You seemed so small and demure, yet so very much in charge – of yourself as much as those hoydenish girls. I know that my sympathy was engaged. You were too young and beautiful to be incarcerated in a dreary schoolroom.'

'*Beautiful?*' I almost choked on the word. Then it was my turn to laugh. 'Never! My mother is beautiful. Meraud, I understand, was beautiful, as Kensa will grow to be . . .'

His hand slid under my chin. He turned my face so that I looked up at him.

'Beautiful,' he repeated and his voice grew husky. 'Oh, not in that sharp, obvious, fashionable way that turns all heads . . . but the beauty of intelligence, of quiet dignity, of a warm, generous nature that shines through your smile, your eyes . . .'

He fell to silence. Words, in that moment, seemed inadequate. We did not move, we did not laugh or even smile, but wordlessly we stared at each other with an intensity, a hunger that was almost too much to endure.

Until, very slowly, and with infinite tenderness, he lifted me up and carried me back to the bed. Where presently there was no need at all for questions, yet both of us found the answers that we were seeking.

Captain Penhale hobbled in as we were finishing breakfast to shake his head over the woeful details of Jess's treachery.

'I never cared for the woman, but I had never suspected she was as crazed as that.' He cast a sly, knowing look at

Daniel, then at me. 'I had a feeling when you came, Mrs Penhale, you'd be shaking us all up whether we liked it or not. But from the way you're both eyeing each other this morning 'tis more than one upheaval you've caused, if I'm not mistaken.' He gave a loud, ribald guffaw and I felt my cheeks burn.

It was strange, but I felt as shy with Daniel this morning as though I were a bride newly introduced to the intimacies of the marriage bed. And when the Captain had hobbled off again, we sat foolishly smiling at each other until we recollected ourselves and began to talk sensibly about what was to be done today.

There were unpleasant tasks awaiting us both. Daniel would attend to the formalities, inform the Luggs, being Jess's only known relatives, and the vicar, to arrange for her funeral. And I must supervise the clearing of her room and the packing up of her worldly goods until they could be disposed of as the Luggs' wished. I took Kitty to help me and I was glad I was not alone. The close, crowded room seemed full of Jess's dark presence, the musky smell that always seemed about her. Even Kitty wrinkled her nose in distaste when she looked around.

'I suppose that funny stink's those herbs she was always boiling,' she said. There was still a pan set on the dead fire, with the congealed remnants of her last, fatal brewing lying on the bottom, and the drying bunches of leaves hanging above the fireplace. And when I opened a cupboard nearby, there were stacked jars and bottles in profusion, containing ointments and salves and lotions and dried herbs. I closed it again quickly. That could wait. Heaven knows what was in her pharmacopia, but I had no wish to investigate at this particular moment.

But it was Kitty who came across real treasure.

She had just removed an armful of petticoats from a drawer when something fell out from among them. I caught the glitter of it as it fell to the carpet. In disbelief I stared at it.

'Oh, ma'am,' Kitty cried. ''Tes your fine necklace! How did it come there?'

Topaz and gold, it lay like a splatter of sunlight against the dark carpet. I picked it up slowly, remembering the footsteps I had heard hurrying over the upper floor last evening.

'She stole it,' I said softly. 'She stole it, intending to hide it where it would incriminate someone – you, probably, or Martha. Just as she did with her own jet brooch.'

It took a moment for my words to register on Kitty's slow and honest mind. Then she clapped her hand over her mouth. 'Do 'ee mean it was 'er – Jess – as put that brooch in my drawer to make it seem like I'd stolen it?' she gasped. 'Oh, ma'am, 'er was truly, truly wicked.'

'Indeed she was,' I said. 'She meant you to be sent from Kildower in disgrace. And you were not the first to be despatched by one means or another, if I am any judge. No house servants have ever lasted long here. Jess meant to reign supreme, the one maid who could always be trusted when others were proved feckless or deceitful or lazy.'

I shivered a little because I was reminded that I still held the jet brooch hidden in my chest. I could never return it to Jess. It could be sent to the Luggs' with the rest of her things and no one any the wiser. But I could tell Daniel about it now, without fear or favour. And that pleased me very much.

It was not long after that that Nan came hurrying upstairs to say that a man was at the back door, insisting on seeing me.

'He calls himself Rob, ma'am, an' he won't come in and

he won't go away, but he says he'll not go until you comes down, though Mrs Dagget told 'im to be off 'cause you was busy.'

'The magician? Oh, dear, I have not given his poor wife a thought today. Tell him I'll be down directly.'

He had hunkered down in the yard outside the back door. My first thought was how much older he now looked than the merry-eyed, laughing conjuror we had seen at Torpoint. All that roguish vitality was quite gone. He was shabby, drained, grey-faced with exhaustion, though he got to his feet lithely enough. Only when he got to his feet was there a hint of that other Rob who had charmed the crowd out of their pennies.

'Is it your wife?' I asked. 'Is she worse?'

'She's no worse, no better,' he said curtly. 'Which is why I came for you. Will you come? I will take you to her.'

'But where is she?'

'Not far.'

'You must give me time to change into stronger shoes.'

But such niceties had no place in Rob's world. He was already going from me, crossing the yard with his springy stride. He did not look back and, calling to Mr Dagget that I would not be long, I hastened after him.

We rounded the house and crossed the lawns at the front heading for the woods. And as we did so, I caught the sound of hooves thudding on gravel. I recognised the big rawboned horse cantering down the drive and stopped, my hand going to my throat. Conan Trewithen. I stood there in a lather of uncertainty. Should I run back and warn Daniel? Was there time? But I saw that Con would be at the house long before I could reach it in my soft slippers, now wet and slippery from the sodden grass.

There was nothing I could do. The meeting had to happen.

It was inevitable. But on such a day, when there was death in the house . . .

'Come.' Rob's voice was impatient. He stood at the edge of the wood, where he waited until I caught him up. Then he pointed.

She was crouched on a fallen log. She wore a faded blue dress and a ragged grey shawl. Her black hair streamed loose about her shoulders in a rich abundance that denied the gauntness of her face, a face once pretty and delicate, but now reduced to yellow skin drawn over fine bone.

'Will you see to her?' Rob asked.

'See to her?' I stared at him.

There was pain and sadness in his face, but a remoteness, a detachment too, as if a decision had been made and must now be seen through.

'I cannot stay. I have stayed too long already. She cannot travel any longer.'

'Rob, no!' The woman's cry was a howl of deep distress.

'It has to be. You know that. You've always known it. I have to move on. What is gone is gone forever. Let it go. Let me go. You will be better off here than on the road.'

He picked up a bundle that was lying beside her and hefted it over his shoulder. Then he leaned towards her. They did not kiss. He looked down at her. She looked up at him. Whatever they had to say to each other had already been said. Then, slowly, she lowered her head in fatalistic acceptance.

He did not look back. He went through the long grass to the thread of path and followed it into the wood. Presently, like the faint calling of a bird, I heard the sound of his whistling fading into the distance.

'Are you able to walk?' I said after a moment. For all the

distress I felt for the poor, abandoned woman, I was anxious to be back at Kildower.

'If you will help me,' she said in a thready little voice. Even to speak seemed to exhaust her, and her weight upon me was no more than a child's.

So carefully, infinitely slowly, we made our way from the wood's edge and took the long journey across the grass. I could have wished for a gardener's boy, or the stable-lad to come running to our aid, but no one was about. As we neared the house, I saw why. There was a knot of people near the mulberry tree. One held the head of Con Trewithen's horse, the others – I could see Martha there, and Kitty as we came closer, clustered in a close circle. It was Kitty who looked round and saw me, who ran across the grass, crying, 'Oh, Mrs Penhale! Come quick! Someone'll get killed.' And helped support the woman so that we could hurry.

Then I saw properly what was happening. And I let go the woman and ran, slithering and sliding, a slipper flying from my foot – feeling the sharp gravel slice into my stocking, my toes, hearing my voice screaming for them to stop, flinging myself between two men with wild, bloodied faces – Daniel and Con – pummelling each other to pulp.

A blow from one of them caught my temple. I staggered, and the world suddenly reeled frantically, and I thought there were two fearsome dragons panting, dripping blood over me, wanting to tear me to shreds.

Then a woman's voice cut across the dragons' growls and I blinked and was myself again, being held upright. By Daniel or by Con or both, both still snarling oaths at each other. The woman's voice came again.

Rob's wife. Staggering forward on Kitty's arm. Calling to them. Calling their names. Calling as though she knew them. And both men slowly turning at the sound of her voice.

I think they spoke her name together, or perhaps their voices fused into one wondering, disbelieving sigh as the faintness took me. I took the name they spoke into my dream. And when I woke I knew it was not a dream and Meraud Trewithen, who had become Meraud Penhale and had fallen in love with a travelling man and faked her own death all those years ago, had returned to Kildower.

Chapter Ten

In October of that year, Mama and Sir Richard paid a visit to Kildower. They had taken the steam packet to Plymouth and proposed to stay for a week before they left for Naples. Ostensibly – and to my great surprise – we were honoured with this visit in order that her grandchild, Adelaide, might be introduced to Mama. In fact, I believe it was her curiosity regarding the irregularity of my situation that had finally won her round.

'Well, well, so my straitlaced daughter is become a kept woman,' she said the first time we were alone. 'And under the same roof as the legal wife. How very droll.' And with a sideways glance at me out of her black-lashed green eyes, a small, knowing smile, 'I did warn you that marriage would not necessarily turn out as you expected.'

'Ah, yes. A trap, you said.' I smiled back at her. 'But then, you told me many things. Not all of them necessarily true.'

We were strolling down the grassy slope towards the woods in the mild sunshine. The rest of the party was walking ahead. Kensa and Liddy running in some game of their own, with Pirate lolloping about them. The three men, Daniel, Con, Sir Richard, deep in conversation.

The trees along the river valley were taking on the fiery reds and golds and yellows of autumn under a sky of faded blue. There was in the air the serene acceptance of the season. The time when the land slipped steadily towards the little death of winter, that deep reviving rest before the urgent business of another spring. That same serenity, that same acceptance, which seemed, at last, to have lodged itself in my own blood after the rigours and upsets of the summer.

'I suppose by that,' She said, a little tartly, 'you mean that you found your Beardmore relatives to your liking.'

'They are good, kind people,' I said. 'Your description of them was wholly inaccurate. And my father has left a fine legacy of generosity in the town . . . but then,' I added gently, 'the circumstances of my visit were very different. I was not a young girl, married off against her will to a middle-aged man.'

I had fled to Bovey Tracey two weeks after Meraud had arrived. It did not seem she would survive that long but she had, under the care of the new doctor, who was possessed of sound common sense as well as the most modern ideas. He had diagnosed ovarian dropsy and though he had shaken his head gravely over the outcome he had at least been able to direct us in the best way to encourage her appetite and relieve the distressing symptoms.

'Though she is not in any great pain, the discomfort and enervating effects are extreme. She is already severely wasted, save for the swelling in her abdomen, and the most we can hope for is to make her comfortable until such time as the disorder completely debilitates her system. She will need very careful nursing though to see her through.'

So for two weeks I had devoted myself to my husband's first wife who by her reappearance had, in one stroke, snatched away my respectability. And when she began to make a faltering recovery, I had taken Liddy and gone to Bovey Tracey where I found a half-brother still living, his wife, the widow of another, and a brood of children and grandchildren. A whole raft of relatives I had never known and who had taken me and Liddy to their kindly country hearts and helped soothe a spirit severely tested on the rack of love.

But I had not stayed. I could not stay. I had known that before I left Kildower. How could I? There was poor, bewildered Kensa of whom, despite all her trying ways, I had grown very fond. Her safe little world had been turned upside down, not least by the sudden reappearance of the stranger who was her real mother. Kensa needed every scrap of love and support I could give her. There was a house to run. There was a dying woman to nurse. And above all, there was Daniel, who had let me go with fear and pain in his eyes in case I should change my mind and decide, after all, to leave him.

'I have no right to ask it of you, Sophy. With Meraud here . . . and I cannot, for all she has done, turn her out . . . a dying woman . . .'

'Hush, my love,' I had said. 'We both, perhaps, need this little time apart. When I return we must talk of what shall be done.'

He had held me close against his heart. 'Remember that I love you. I cannot bear to think that you might not come back to me.'

And when I returned to Kildower, when I saw him again, it did not seem at all important that I should be returning to an arrangement at best irregular, at worst shocking. I did not care.

And perhaps, in that, some element of my mother's nature had surfaced in me, never to be denied again.

I told her that now. There seemed no need to be less than open with her. She threw back her head and laughed.

'Perhaps I always suspected it. But you had it well-hidden under that prim, missish mask you always wore. But since we are being honest, I will tell you that the life of a kept woman suits you well. You have blossomed. Why, even Meraud's brother seems to find you . . . agreeable. If I did not think you had eyes only for your beloved Daniel, I would say that he might have proved a worthy conquest. In fact, I find the prospect of staying a week under the same roof as Mr Trewithen is quite enticing.'

'Mama! You wouldn't . . . Not with dear Sir Richard here . . .'

She twirled her parasol. 'Oh, the lightest of flirtations, my dear. It will help to pass the time. He is a lively rogue, I think.'

Indeed he was. And a dangerous one. Since Meraud's return his behaviour had been impeccable, towards Daniel – who, ever generous and reasonable, had been the first to offer the hand of friendship when it was clear that Meraud and Meraud alone was the one guilty of the lies and deceit that had set the two men at loggerheads – and to me. Only once had there been a moment when I felt the soft, hot lure of temptation . . . of danger . . .

It was the evening after Meraud had made her shocking confession. We had all three stood about her bed in the quiet dusk listening in stunned silence to her thready voice pouring it out . . . how she had fallen in love with the travelling man and found herself carrying his child. But by then Rob, in the way of his kind, had disappeared one morning without trace from his encampment in the woods. How, in her desperation, she had played Conan and Daniel one against the other. Telling Conan the child was Daniel's then, when Conan was banished to transportation – lost to her for ever, she thought – and fearing that Daniel might reject her if he knew the truth, inventing the story of her brother's assault on her, to gain Daniel's sympathy.

Then after her marriage, the loss of Rob's child and the birth of Daniel's, she had found out the magician was again in the neighbourhood. She had faked her drowning and walked through the stormy night to the coast near Downderry where Rob Wood was with his troupe. And stayed with him through all these years.

'I did it for you, Daniel,' she whispered. 'For you. And for Kensa. I owed you your freedom and it was no life for a child with the travellers. I thought that if I was believed dead you would be able to marry again . . . a good woman who would love Kensa as her own.'

But however she justified her motives, all the sympathy I had felt for a poor, drowned, unhappy young girl was demolished at that moment. I was blazing with anger and indignation. How could she have been so selfish? All that cruel deceit. The distress she had caused, to Daniel, to Kensa . . . to Con.

I was still turning it over and over in my mind, desperately trying – and failing – to find some sort of forgiveness for her as I stood at the parlour window later. Con joined me and for a long while we stood in silence watching the sun slide down behind the distant hills. Then he said softly, 'If there is one benefit from this sorry mess, it is that you are free now, Sophy.'

'Free?' I was too angry, too upset, to guard my words. 'I do not want freedom, Con Trewithen. Not like this. Not in this sordid, messy way.'

'Nevertheless, you are released from this marriage.' His voice was quiet, insistent. 'Which gives me some hope . . .'

He broke off and I looked at him sharply. Looked into

grey and flinty eyes that held now some deeper, warmer quality.

'I had some idea of taking you from Daniel,' he said. 'It was part of my plan of revenge.'

'Like getting one of your cronies to fire the brewery?'

'Ah. I feared you might make the connection. Do not worry, Sophy. This is a time of confession. I shall be honest with Daniel, and while I am being honest, I would wish you to know that even though I meant to seduce you out of revenge, I find myself taken with the idea that we might fare very well together, you and I. There is something about you . . . some mysterious alchemy that draws my thoughts, my feelings . . . Do you not feel something of it, too?'

His touch on my neck was soft as down. My skin shivered in response. I closed my eyes. It would be so easy . . . so easy . . . Turn my back on Kildower and all its troubles . . .

'I am not quite the feckless gambler that I once was. I used my bondage in Australia well for it was possible even for one whose sojourn there was involuntary to make money. I put all that I had earned there into a good piece of land. It is a new country and full of promise. I shall stay here as long as my sister lives, of course, then I shall take passage to Botany Bay. As a free man I shall make a new beginning. You could be part of that, Sophy. And the child, Liddy. Will you consider it?'

It was so plausible . . . the three of us, kicking the dust of gloomy Kildower off our heels, building a new life in a land of new hope . . . and with Con, who with a touch could rouse my blood . . .

I took a deep breath.

'I think not,' I said steadily. 'Though I thank you for the offer.'

Con wanted me and I acknowledged that there was an

element in my nature that responded. But Daniel needed me, as I needed him. That was the difference. I had had the merest glimpse of the passion Daniel and I could share, but there was so much else we shared, too. So much to learn about each other that would give us deeper, more lasting joy.

The men had stopped just before they took the path through the woods down to the creek. They looked back, smiling, waiting for us. Mama walked on to join them but I held back a moment, turning to gaze at the house. I wondered if Meraud was watching us from her chair in the window of her bedchamber.

She was very frail now and I could no longer be angry with her. She had been foolish once and she had loved deeply – still did – a man who had, finally, deserted her. That was her punishment, I saw it in her eyes, heard it in her voice, that faded a little more each day.

And what should Daniel and I do when she was gone? Should we remarry? I did not care so long as we could be together, even if it was still to be at Kildower.

I remembered how I had felt when I first arrived. How I thought the house rejected me. How I had shivered in its gloomy shadows. Now in the peaceful autumn sunshine it looked neither sinister nor sad, but gravely handsome. A stern house, perhaps, but no longer unfriendly. Perhaps it had been Jess's dark, harmful presence I had sensed tainting the atmosphere, for even before I had arrived she had tried to poison the servants' minds against me.

'Told me she'd heard you was a hard woman, ma'am,' Mrs Dagget had said indignantly. 'And would put us out as soon as look. And Nan and Joan have told me since that 'er put terrible thoughts in their heads about ghosts and that you'd be ordering them regular beatings.'

No wonder they had responded with suspicion and fear.

'She'd a vicious tongue and a nature to match, that one,' Mrs Dagget continued. 'No wonder no maids ever stayed long. Still, there's no problem with gettin' maids in from the village now. Come begging for work, all sweet and smilin', since all their nasty tales about Master's proved to be rubbish.' She sniffed disparagingly. 'Ghosts indeed! And thinking a good, kind man like Mr Penhale capable of . . . of well, it's best not spoken of. I tell you, ma'am, I don't mind 'em scrubbing floors or washing dishes, but if any of they superstitious lot starts poking their noses in about Kildower's business, I packs 'em off with a flea in their ear.' Which was as close as she ever got to mentioning the irregular affairs of her employers.

That the servants had remained loyal and seemed content was a special pleasure. One of the many small pleasures that seemed to dispel Kildower's shadows. Like the sound of children's laughing voices. Like the hours spent painting. Like the long sweet nights I spent in Daniel's arms.

But perhaps, most of all, it was the gentler, kinder spirits in the house who had, at last, triumphed over the darker elements that had always haunted Kildower. The calm, devoted aura of the women who had once dedicated themselves to prayer and healing in the name of St Bride now seemed free to bring light and happiness to those who lived within Kildower's walls.

However wild the legends that had arisen, I knew with deep certainty that Kildower's ghosts meant no harm. How could they when, in life, the women had been the repository of goodness? I found it comforting to believe that their gentle presence still watched over us. Especially now.

I smiled to myself. It would be better, of course, for the sake of the coming child if Daniel and I married. I would have to tell him soon. Then we should decide.

'What are you smiling at?' Mama demanded, with a hint of her usual asperity, as I caught up with her.

I shook my head, still smiling. Then, impulsively, I tucked my hand in her arm and kissed her cheek, before we followed the menfolk down the path into the wood.

MASK OF THE NIGHT

MARY RYAN

Jenny knows her mother's face only through a portrait. She is a child when her beloved father is killed in a freak accident, leaving her alone with her grandfather to face the new century. But Jenny has her friends for company and, since her discovery of an old mask in the attic, a sinister stranger who comes to her bedside at night whispering dreams of the impossible . . .

On her visits home to Kilashane from her city life in the sixties, Dee is still fascinated by the big ruin of a house down the boreen and by the mysterious madman who haunts its grounds. And by treasures she finds amongst its shattered columns, a carnival mask, a gold signet ring and a faded leather diary telling of long-dead lives.

But these relics are only part of Kilashane's legacy; the passion and danger that come with them are more than Dee could ever have imagined. She and Jenny are linked by Kilashane's past – a history which casts shadows across generations, and across the seas and time from Venice to London to County Cork.

FICTION / GENERAL 0 7472 4521 5

More Enchanting Fiction from Headline

WENDY ROBERTSON

UNDER A BRIGHTER SKY

An impassioned story of love, repression and
freedom from the author of RICHES OF THE EARTH

When Greg McNaughton first meets the lively Shona Farrell,
lovely in spite of her dusty pit clothes, he knows he should forget
her. For she belongs to the staunchly Irish Catholic community
regarded with fear and suspicion by his own outwardly severe
Protestant family. And her fiery-tempered brother Tommo makes it
plain that Greg is not welcome in their home, throwing him out
into the cold, County Durham night in a fit of temper.

But Greg can't get Shona out of his mind. And Shona is fascinated
by the stranger and his perplexing family; in particular she wants
to find out what happened to his wife, the shadowy mother of his
little daughter Lauretta. When Greg suddenly leaves for
Manchester after the brutal murder of the good-hearted local
prostitute, Shona won't believe he's the killer. And so she follows
him to the teeming city, determined to unravel the mysteries of the
past and live under brighter skies...

'Good story, good background, good characters, another winner
from Wendy' *Northern Echo*

'Carefully crafted novel...spirited, widely different and colourful
characters' *Sunderland Echo*

Praise for Wendy Robertson's previous novel, RICHES OF THE
EARTH, also from Headline: 'Vivid characterisation, a compelling story
and a finely observed setting combine to produce an original and
memorable novel' Pat Barker

FICTION/SAGA   0 7472 4410 3

A selection of bestsellers
from Headline

THE CHANGING ROOM	Margaret Bard	£5.99	☐
BACKSTREET CHILD	Harry Bowling	£5.99	☐
A HIDDEN BEAUTY	Tessa Barclay	£5.99	☐
A HANDFUL OF HAPPINESS	Evelyn Hood	£5.99	☐
THE SCENT OF MAY	Sue Sully	£5.99	☐
HEARTSEASE	T R Wilson	£5.99	☐
NOBODY'S DARLING	Josephine Cox	£5.99	☐
A CHILD OF SECRETS	Mary Mackie	£5.99	☐
WHITECHAPEL GIRL	Gilda O'Neill	£5.99	☐
BID TIME RETURN	Donna Baker	£5.99	☐
THE LADIES OF BEVERLEY HILLS	Sharleen Cooper Cohen	£5.99	☐
THE OLD GIRL NETWORK	Catherine Alliott	£4.99	☐

All Headline books are available at your local bookshop or newsagent, or can be ordered direct from the publisher. Just tick the titles you want and fill in the form below. Prices and availability subject to change without notice.

Headline Book Publishing, Cash Sales Department, Bookpoint, 39 Milton Park, Abingdon, OXON, OX14 4TD, UK. If you have a credit card you may order by telephone – 0235 400400.

Please enclose a cheque or postal order made payable to Bookpoint Ltd to the value of the cover price and allow the following for postage and packing:
UK & BFPO: £1.00 for the first book, 50p for the second book and 30p for each additional book ordered up to a maximum charge of £3.00.
OVERSEAS & EIRE: £2.00 for the first book, £1.00 for the second book and 50p for each additional book.

Name ....

Address ....

....

....

If you would prefer to pay by credit card, please complete:
Please debit my Visa/Access/Diner's Card/American Express (delete as applicable) card no:

Signature .... Expiry Date ....